"PROVE TO ME YOU ARE INDIFFERENT AND I'LL LET YOU GO," HAWKE DARED.

"And you will honor your promise when I do?" Alexandra demanded.

"*If* you do," Hawke corrected her. "Yes, in that case I give my word I will release you. Now you must give yours—if you fail, you will cease this pretense and come to me willingly, as my woman."

"I give it. Now begin, that we may sooner be finished with this farce."

Slowly Hawke smiled, his hands gently grazing the upper swell of her breast. "What's the hurry, my dear? Unless you fear to lose?"

"Bastard," she flung out through gritted teeth. "I have nothing to fear from you!"

His smile grew wider and his hands dropped, tracing her breast to find the impudent bud at its center. To her fury, the crest immediately grew taut beneath his fingers.

"You will lose, my little hellcat. And the loss will give both of us infinite pleasure."

QUANTITY SALES

INDIVIDUAL SALES

DEFIANT CAPTIVE

Christina Skye

A DELL BOOK

Published by
Dell Publishing
a division of
Bantam Doubleday Dell Publishing Group, Inc.
666 Fifth Avenue
New York, New York 10103

ISBN: 0-440-20626-X
Printed in the United States of America
Published simultaneously in Canada
June 1990

10 9 8 7 6 5 4 3 2 1

RAD

. . . a Phantom of delight
When first she gleamed upon my sight;
A lovely Apparition, sent
To be a moment's ornament;
Her eyes as stars of Twilight fair;
Like Twilight's too, her dusky hair;
But all things else about her drawn
From May-time and the cheerful Dawn;
A dancing Shape, an Image gay,
To haunt, to startle, and way-lay.

—William Wordsworth

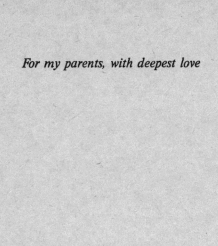

For my parents, with deepest love

Prologue

London, England
April 1816

The fog had risen throughout the afternoon, creeping along London's narrow alleys and broader avenues to veil the city in unnatural darkness. Those of the city's residents who were superstitious muttered anxiously as they looked skyward, and even the most practical of men hurried to finish their errands so they might turn homeward.

From the haven of a dark doorway a thin boy in baggy, tattered trousers looked out upon the drifting fingers of fog, anxiously studying their movement and density.

"This be yer last chance, ye caw-handed monkey!" his squat companion snarled. "Bring me the dibbs with no more argle-bargle, else the morning sun find ye floatin' under Blackfriar's Bridge." With a scowl, the man seized the boy's ear and yanked it sharply. "Buffed it fer ye too long already, I 'ave."

The boy did not shrink from his captor, and his young face showed no fear. The burly man hiccupped, a faint gleam of respect rising into his cold eyes. "Aye, a fast bunch o' fives ye 'ave, little man. Not a bit afraid, neither. My main bagger ye could be, right enough." Suddenly his face tightened, and he jerked the boy's ear cruelly, dragging him close enough to smell the stink of sweat, gin, and a recent meal of beef and cabbage. "Bedford, Alvanley, or 'awkesworth—take yer pick, boy. All the coves'll be 'ere tonight, I reckon. Quick dip in the pocket, then yer gone, like as 'ow I showed ye. An' don't try no tricks, fer I'll be watchin' yer like a bleedin' 'awk!"

With that, the squat man known on the streets only as Digger spun his captive about and launched him forward with a savage kick in the small of the back.

Pence—for so the boy had been nicknamed by his comrades of the street—twisted to avoid falling flat on the filthy cobblestones, showing the swift agility that had convinced Digger he would be a useful recruit. In an instant he darted off toward the crossing, where a line of coaches inched toward a wide marble townhouse ablaze with light.

The boy frowned, studying the restless fog. It would have to be tonight, for Digger gave no second chances. Tonight it must be then, while the fog offered him a sporting chance of escape.

It would be his only chance, the boy knew. If Digger found him first, Pence would be dead before the sun rose.

Chapter One

The fog drifted slowly, a thin yellow creature trailing sooty tendrils around Alexandra Maitland as she picked her way across the uneven London cobblestones. Her footsteps slowed, and she searched the deserted street uncertainly.

Blaze and bother! She hadn't the slightest idea how to get to the busy coaching inn where she had lodged since her arrival one week before.

The muscles of her back tightened painfully and her ankle began to throb, the old wound irritated by London's cold damp air. Every step she took over the slippery irregular cobblestones sent pain flashing up from her ankle.

Alexandra sighed and stepped carefully around a knee-deep rut in the road. London was nothing like she had expected. Growing up in India, where her father had been governor-general of Madras, she had often heard about the glory and elegance of the capital.

No one had mentioned the filth or the desperate poverty. Or the fog.

Alexandra shivered in the sharp spring wind, unaccustomed to the cold. She pulled her cloak tighter about her shoulders and watched the yellow fingers of fog inch before her face. Suddenly, memories of India swept over her, as hot and bright as this place was cold and gray. For a moment she once again felt the fierce light flooding the bazaars and the blast of hot wind, hot colors, hot sun. She saw her ayah haggling over cardamom and ginger with a swarthy old Parsee.

Unmoving, Alexandra stood in the cold London street, haunted by memories of warmth and laughter and a world that would never be hers again.

For that life was gone now, vanished like the drifting fog. The native uprising at Vellore had brought Alexandra's world crashing down around her. And then had come her father's unjust recall to London in disgrace. . . .

Her fingers tightened painfully on her dark pelisse, useless against the penetrating London cold. She shuddered, remembering her father as she had last seen him, his blood splashed across the white room.

She bit back a sob as a wave of bitterness swept over her. They should have known a man like Lord Maitland would never submit to disgrace. He would die first.

Shaking her head against the agony of those memories, Alexandra stumbled forward until she felt the black railing of a marble townhouse brush cold against her ankle. The fog had driven everyone from the streets, and even the hackney coaches had given up the day's business. Not that she could afford to hire a coach anyway, Alexandra thought bitterly.

Suddenly, a figure slid from the fog, a thin little man with his hat rammed down on his head as he scurried along. "Please, sir, can you direct me to—" Alexandra began, but the man had vanished into the fog before she completed her question.

The unnatural gloom of the afternoon had gathered into early darkness, and Alexandra realized night was upon her. From the mist ahead of her came tinkling laughter and the drifting notes of a waltz.

There was nothing to be accomplished by waiting here. With a sigh, Alexandra started off in search of someone who could direct her to Conduit Street.

At the next corner the fog thinned for a moment, disclosing a brilliantly lit square. Before the mist closed up again, she caught a glimpse of coaches making halting progress to the steps of a grand townhouse ablaze with light.

A *ton* ball, Alexandra thought, fighting down a wave of bitterness.

Laughter, music, jewels against flashing silk.

All of that should have been her world, but now it never could. Her father's death had closed that door forever, leaving Alexandra with bleak prospects. Who else, she wondered angrily, could claim the dubious distinction of having been rejected by four agencies within the same afternoon, and with such marked discourtesy?

Suddenly, Alexandra felt the skin along her spine quiver as if someone were watching her. Across the street a small figure slipped through the fog, darting furtively toward the square. Whoever it was disappeared down the narrow steps that led to the servants' entrance of a darkened townhouse.

Moving into the shadows, Alexandra slid the hood of her cloak up over her flaming red-gold hair, hair that seemed to attract entirely too much attention. Several times during the last week, complete strangers had stared at her quite rudely, while several men had gone well beyond impertinence and accosted her upon the street.

Her fingers tightened upon the small mahogany cane hidden within the folds of her cloak. She might need it tonight, for one look at the boisterous bucks crossing the square suggested this was no place for an unescorted lady to linger. Still, she told herself, someone there could surely direct her to Conduit Street.

The best route is always forward, her father had often announced in times of duress. For a second Alexandra's hand brushed against her eye, and then she moved forward toward the crowded square.

Not even such a fog as this could check London's restless gaiety for long. Despite the unnatural gloom the streets began to fill with the strange mixture of arrogant peers, country squires, and sharp-eyed harlots so peculiar to the capital. Prince and pickpocket, beggar and nabob rubbed elbows casually in this glittering night world, where social positions might be overlooked for a little while.

But even in this netherworld of garish extremes one man stood out, immediately recognizable. His broad shoulders and the fluid muscular grace of his walk set him apart, like a panther among chattering monkeys.

And this night, immaculate as usual, the Duke of Hawkesworth was startling in severe black evening dress, a gray-eyed panther sprung from the fog in search of prey. He gave the impression of energy barely contained, making men take an unconscious step back when he passed, and making women shiver delicately and peer up from beneath their lashes.

Unaware of the attention he drew, the Duke of Hawkesworth stifled a yawn as he sauntered toward Bedford Square. Another boring evening of fatuous conversation, arch innuendo, and insipid debutantes, he mused. Why did he continue to put in appearances at these functions? he wondered.

The answer came to him almost immediately: Because it was expected of the heir to one of the greatest fortunes in England. Because it was necessary for fostering his many political interests. Because it passed the time.

No, he had lied to himself for too long, the duke thought. Just once, he had to face the truth. The real reason he came was to find *her.*

Yes, my beautiful, faithless wife, I can feel you somewhere out there in the fog. You won't be strong enough to stay away much longer. Greed and boredom will drive you back, and this time I'll be waiting.

As he sauntered through the fog, none of these thoughts could be read on the duke's angular tanned face. Only a few of his closest friends could have detected the unusual tenseness about his jaw or the glitter of his silver-gray eyes beneath lazy lids. Near the square a few acquaintances greeted him. He nodded a cool acknowledgment but did not slow his steps.

He was a large man, yet he walked gracefully. The broad muscular shoulders that stretched the fabric of his immaculate black evening coat were mute testimony to his pugilistic skills, skills that had saved his life more than once as an officer on the Peninsula. His tanned face was set off by the snowy linen at his neck, where one simple diamond gleamed from the exquisite folds of his cravat. His clothes were excellent yet understated, in the style favored by Brummell, but they could not conceal his hard muscular body nor the raw power held barely in check.

And on this night all that caged energy was on edge, crying out for release. All through the day Hawkesworth had felt the old restlessness, the coiling urgency. She was somewhere nearby—he knew it, as certainly as he felt the surge of his own pulse. He could feel her presence seeping into his consciousness like the cold fingers of this damnable fog that coiled about him. Just as he had expected, greed had brought his wife back. And this time, he was ready for her.

She would not escape from him again, by God!

The fog toyed with all of London this night, veiling slum and elegant townhouse alike in its clinging gray misery. But the drifting tendrils did not particularly bother the small boy who skirted the well-lit squares. If he thought about the fog at all, it was with thanks for the refuge it offered.

For Pence had more tangible things to worry about. He was cold. Worse yet, he was starving, and his stomach tightened painfully at the memory of his last meal of cabbage topped with a meager bit of potatoes. When he saw the broad square before him, the boy paused only a moment, then darted silently down the narrow stairs in front of an unlit townhouse.

From his hiding place beneath the darkened doorway Pence watched a large gentleman stroll casually up the street. He looked as good a target as any—alone and not overly concerned with his surroundings.

Noting the solid breadth of the man's shoulders, Pence felt a moment of misgiving. What if he were caught? Newgate, for sure, he thought, his thin body trembling. Maybe transportation. What would his brother say if he knew of this desperate plan?

But Tom was gone, and Pence was alone tonight on the cold London streets with few choices open to him. Besides, the large gentleman looked flush enough. He could afford to spare a bit of blunt for his less fortunate fellows. They always conceal a nice, fat purse somewhere about their person, Digger had said. The problem was distracting them so they wouldn't notice when you pinched it.

Pence frowned, realizing he'd begun to slip into the peculiar argot of the streets. It was just as well he was leaving before he grew more familiar with this kind of life. Yes, tonight he would make his first pinch, and then he'd be gone before Digger could find him. The money would carry him to Yorkshire to look for Tom.

A slim figure obscured Pence's view of his target for a moment. The boy frowned, pressing closer to the edge of the stairs. Now this one was a beauty, and no mistake! She walked slowly, giving Pence time to see the way her flaming hair shone with tiny lights. As if aware of his scrutiny, the woman slipped back into the shadows, drawing her hood about her hair and face. Only then did Pence notice the small cane she carried.

Ah well, the limp was a pity, but her cane might have other uses this night, he thought.

Then the woman with hair like flame, too, was forgotten, for Pence had too many problems of his own to consider.

Chapter Two

The fog was thickening at an alarming rate. Anxiously, Alexandra tightened her hands about her carved mahogany cane, needing the reassurance of its solid bulk. There were too many people in the square now. Too many wild young men, too many polished coaches, too much careless laughter. The fog crawled across her skin, suffocating her, and she pushed unsteadily toward the opposite side of the square. Always she kept to the shadows, scattering the dank fog in trails as she ran.

A tattoo of flying feet made her lean harder upon her cane. All at once she stumbled upon a loose cobble and pitched to the side. Only the comforting support of her cane kept her from falling to the ground.

The support of her cane, that is, followed by a pair of large, powerful hands. Hands that gripped her elbows and tightened harshly. In a wild panic Alexandra began to thrash helplessly, only to be thrust against the solid wall of a man's body. Effortlessly, her assailant pressed her closer, quelled her struggles, then reached up to drag the hood of her cloak away from her face.

His eyes were glittering like silver stars in a freezing night sky as he looked down at Alexandra. In another time, in another place, this might have been a handsome face, she thought. But now, trapped as she was in the darkness of the London streets, the face brought her only terror.

"By God," the man rasped, "it really is you! At first I thought I must be dreaming, like every other time. But your greed brought you back." A muscle flashed in his jaw, and his eyes narrowed. "I've had men searching for you since the day you left—they almost caught you last year in Vienna, in fact. This time you'll not find escape so easy, my love!" At the final endearment his voice flattened into a harsh laugh.

Alexandra struggled to steady her throbbing pulse. The man was very handsome—or would have been, if bitterness and hate had not carved deep lines into his face. His brow was wide, over-hung with a thick lock of black hair. He did not appear to be a lunatic, she told herself hopefully, trying to quiet her pounding heart. "You mistake me, sir. I am newly arrived from India and do not number you among my few acquaintances in London. Now release me immediately and let me pass, for I have a great distance yet before me."

The man's mouth twisted into a thin approximation of a smile. "Not so far to go, my love. Or have you been away so long that you've forgotten our elegant townhouse in Bedford Square? Curi-ous—at one time you could talk of little else." His hands tight-ened, large hands, whose fingers bit into the soft skin above her elbows.

"Release me this minute, I say! It is clear you have mistaken me for another. No gentleman would hold a lady thus, against her will."

The man's eyes burned down into her face, his smile mocking. "Come, my dear, surely you can do better than that. I expected tears, perhaps, or sweet pleas for forgiveness." His eyes lingered upon Alexandra's lips. "A more intimate appeal to the memory of the pleasures we have shared—yes, that would be much more in your usual style."

Perhaps he is mad, Alexandra thought shakily. Reasoning with him seemed hopeless. Her trembling fingers met her cane, and she drew a quick breath. Without warning she swung the length of wood hard against her captor's shin—the only part of him she could reach, held captive as she was.

Solid mahogany met rock-hard muscle, and a raw curse split the air. With punishing fingers the man wrenched the weapon from Alexandra's hand and tossed the cane to the cobbles at her feet without taking his eyes from her pale face. "Ever one with a trick, aren't you, my little love?"

His eyes were cold and clear as the Himalayan snows by moonlight, Alexandra thought in growing panic. His angular face burned with implacable hatred, along with some other emotion she could not immediately recognize.

"Come, Isobel, you commence to bore me. Or have you forgotten your skill at more effective forms of persuasion?" His voice thickened as his hand slid beneath Alexandra's hair, tightened against her neck, and forced her head closer. She fancied she saw her own frightened image reflected within his silver eyes as his face approached relentlessly.

"Let us see what else may have changed between us, my faithless wanton wife!"

Alexandra's protest was ruthlessly cut off as the tall man trapped her lips beneath his. Nothing in her life had prepared her for the unyielding mastery of his touch when his mouth claimed her. He took without asking, forcing and shaping her lips with demanding strokes. Alexandra caught a little cry in her throat as his teeth crushed down against her mouth, bruising her lips. Almost immediately, her captor relaxed his assault, gentling his touch and opening her lips with his tongue.

In a daze Alexandra felt him invade her mouth, taking undreamed-of liberties. Exhausted and disoriented, she felt the ground begin to spin beneath her, and she swayed against him. Had he not anchored her waist with his strong arms, she would have fallen.

"I see your memory is as acute as mine, my dear." A low mocking laugh thundered along the broad wall of his chest. "I assure you, *I* have not forgotten anything about you, though I've fought the memories these two years."

His hands slid lower, kneading her hips as he molded her intimately against the length of his taut body. With an angry cry Alexandra tightened her fists against his chest and fought to push him away, but she was no match for his muscled breadth.

His smile as he looked down at her was mocking. "But you were ever a reckless lover and knew precisely how to inflame me. How unfortunate that you were unable to confine your charms to your husband! It dampens a man's ardor when he knows how many other fellows have shared the same space, you know."

"How dare you!" Alexandra gasped. She lashed out furiously at his face, but he merely captured her small fists within his hard grip. Her sense of helplessness fueled her anger. "Unhand me, I say! You compound your error, sir, and offend all propriety in this assault!"

Her captor merely laughed hollowly. "A stirring performance, my dear! I applaud you. But it strains logic to hear you, of all people, speak of propriety. I would have accepted a great deal, you know," he added slowly. "But your last escapade at Vauxhall was beyond swallowing, even by me. It was quite a sight, I may tell you—dampened silk over rouged nipples. You nearly caused a riot. If you meant to provoke me by flaunting yourself as a Cyprian, you were certainly successful, although perhaps not precisely as you had planned." His voice hardened. "I think I would have beaten you that night—yes, beaten you and enjoyed every second of it. You were clever to run off with Granville when you did."

Caught against his chest, Alexandra felt him shudder suddenly —whether at his memories or at the admission he had just made, she could not say. She only knew that his hands tightened brutally around her fists until she was fighting waves of pain. How could she make him see reason?

Her captor seemed to slip into a haze of painful memories. "How long did it take for him to tire of your tricks? How many other 'protectors' have you known since he cast you off? Perhaps it would have been better if you *had* died, after all."

The man's voice broke slightly, and Alexandra saw him struggle for control. Drawing a jerky breath, she sought words to convince him of the terrible error he made. When finally she found her voice, her words were slow and clear, as if she were speaking to a small child. "You must believe me, sir, when I tell you that I am not who you take me to be. I am newly arrived in London. I have *never* laid eyes on you until this moment. I am *not* your wife, though from what you describe, I can only think—"

He cut her off impatiently. "You persist in this weak story then? Really, my dear, you disappoint me! How could there be two such as you on this earth? Two women with hair like a flame of red and gold, eyes such an odd shade of aquamarine. And skin"—his thumb stroked the inside of her wrist, where her pulse throbbed wildly—"skin that flows like silk beneath a man's hungry fingers. . . ." His words trailed off into a harsh laugh. "You may preen yourself, my dear. Your hair is even more beautiful than I remembered. You have heightened its color, I daresay. Your skill is consummate. I think your charms would test the resolution of a saint. But I must not let myself off so easily, for I chose to override my own scruples and reason to have you." Implacably, he drew her wrists behind her, his voice hardening. "That is why I mean to break your hold upon me once and for all. You were the poison, by God, and now you shall be the cure! I'll have my fill of you this night, and then I'll be free of you forever!"

Alexandra studied the frozen determination in the man's eyes, the implacable set to his jaw. She felt the blood drain from her face then, for she saw there would be no reasoning with such a madman.

"Quite," he announced with a low jeering laugh.

Her mind reeling, she looked about for some avenue of escape. They were almost within the shadows at the corner of the square now, before an unlit townhouse. From the corner of her eyes she saw a shadow separate itself from the blackness beneath the steps and creep toward her. After an infinitesimal hesitation the figure drew closer and reached out stealthily in search of the gentleman's purse.

Alexandra saw no more, for her strong captor pulled her against his hard body to claim her swollen lips once again. She knew she must act quickly or all would be lost. With a little sob she caught his bottom lip between her teeth and bit down hard.

Sparks of fury shot through his eyes as pain had its immediate effect. She released his lip, and he jerked away, cursing as he probed gingerly at his mouth. The next instant, he whirled about with a surprised look on his face.

But he was too late. The young thief had already found the man's gold and was melting back into the fog.

Quickly, Alexandra bent to retrieve her cane. She breathed a silent prayer and swung with all her might behind the man's knees as he looked after the retreating figure.

Her aim was true. As she had hoped, her captor's legs buckled, allowing her to rip free of his grasp.

"You little bitch!"

She did not stop to wonder at the silence that followed his snarling epithet. Her heart pounding, she plunged across the square; only at the last moment did she see a team of prancing restless bays take the corner at a reckless pace.

As she ran in stark panic across the team's path, the cries of the horses and the coachman's fluent curses rang in her ears. On past a noisy band of exquisites she ran, closing her mind to their lewd suggestions for a more intimate form of exercise. When they saw her limping gait, however, their calls died on their lips and they drew back in distaste.

Alexandra did not notice that, for suddenly all her attention was centered on the darkness ahead where several small lanes led from the square.

She caught a ragged breath and plunged toward the comforting darkness, fully expecting her pursuer to overtake her at any moment. Behind her, a man's voice cracked out a command, and the horses quieted. In the sudden stillness she heard the lilt of a woman's voice, followed by a muffled moan.

And then she cast herself headlong into the welcome silence of the closest lane and let the darkness swallow her.

Chapter Three

Beneath his breath, Hawkesworth cursed long and fluently. First the guttersnipe had made off with his purse, and now Isobel was about to escape too. Hawkesworth watched in horror as her slim, cloaked figure darted unsteadily in front of a line of carriages rounding the square, setting the spirited cattle plunging in her wake.

By God, she'd nearly been killed! She must be desperate. Hawkesworth's eyes narrowed upon his wife's retreating form, noting her uneven gait and the way she leaned against the cane clutched to her side.

What new trick was this?

"Your Grace, be careful!"

The pale anxious face of Miss Felicity Wallingford, a Sussex acquaintance, appeared at the window of the coach beside him. Darting a last glance at the limping figure nearing the opposite end of the square, Hawkesworth called out a command to the harried coachman: "Take up the slack to the wheelers, man! I'll handle the leaders!"

With low coaxing endearments Hawkesworth approached the nervous bays at the head of the team. His movements were slow and fluid, his voice rhythmic as he drew along the inside bay.

Slowly, he raised his arm, grasped the harness, and slid a hand gently along the horse's sweating flanks. "Ho, my beauty. Steady on."

As he crooned, the beast settled down to a skittish dance, and the coachman soon had the other animals in hand. Just then, Hawkesworth heard a moan from within the carriage, followed by a muffled thump.

"Your Grace, I beg you—"

A footman was already lowering the carriage steps when the duke was hailed by Lady Wallingford. Reluctantly Hawke drew closer, for to turn away now would have given grave insult. His lips curled when he saw Miss Wallingford lying prone against the seat, her plump mama fanning her anxiously with an ostrich plume. Although keenly conscious that he was losing precious minutes, Hawke had no choice but to climb inside.

"You've no idea how glad we were to see you, Your Grace!" the old lady gushed, setting the remaining ostrich plumes twitching upon her head. One feather detached itself and drifted down toward the duke's nose, and he wondered if he might sneeze.

A quick glance at the polished lacquer walls and the etched glass panes showed the duke that Wallingford spared no expense for his family's comfort. Better for him to tend to the safety of his wife and daughter, Hawkesworth thought sourly, than to trade stale stories with his cronies at White's.

Hearing Miss Wallingford stir gently against the morocco seat, Hawkesworth set his face in a polite mask that revealed no sign of his impatience. "I am pleased to assist you, of course. But as your cattle are now quieted and Miss Wallingford appears to be coming around, I shall take myself off. You'll be wanting privacy to compose yourself, I should imagine."

Just as he turned to beat a retreat, another feeble moan issued from the prone figure on the seat. Lady Wallingford cast him an anxious look, and Hawkesworth sighed and turned back. He was immediately rewarded with a gentle cry and a stirring of Miss Wallingford's limp figure.

Anyone who had been privy to Miss Wallingford's alertness and keen scrutiny of the square only moments before would have been surprised by her present torpor. She was careful to conceal her sharp temper from any but the closest of family, however, so that the Duke of Hawkesworth found nothing odd in her behavior. And where the Duke of Hawkesworth was concerned, Miss Felicity Wallingford was never careless.

"I beg your pardon, Your Grace," she murmured, struggling gracefully to sit up. "You must be thinking me a poor creature indeed. It was simply the sight of the horses plunging about you. I was certain you would be t-trampled as you tried to still them. And you so brave, I'm certain you had not a thought for your own s-safety." Felicity subsided weakly against the seat, as if the exertion had outdone her.

After a quick, sidelong glance into the square, Hawkesworth leaned forward and assisted her upright. "I'm afraid you exaggerate my bravery, Miss Wallingford."

"I vow I do not, nor do I know how we can thank you, Your Grace. But it is clear you are wishing to be off, so we must not detain you further. I fear I've lost my taste for company anyway, and Mama will probably wish to return home as well."

Lady Wallingford studied her daughter blankly for a second, then broke into an energetic assent, her ostrich feathers fluttering dangerously.

"There is no need to thank me, Miss Wallingford. I am merely happy that I was on hand to assist you. I beg you not to cry off Lady Sherringham's fête, however, for I am sure you'll soon feel more the thing. In my experience there is nothing like a ball to restore a lady's spirits."

The merest hint of mockery in his drawl was enough to make Miss Wallingford blink suddenly. She fluttered her lashes again to reveal pale eyes glittering with unshed tears. "No, I have never been inordinately fond of balls and fêtes. I confess that I find most social occasions deadly dull—with far too much simpering and empty gossip."

The Duke of Hawkesworth's eyebrows rose in an ironic slant while his full lips curved into the ghost of a smile. "Your opinion makes you something of an original then, Miss Wallingford." He studied her pale face a moment, then glanced to the far end of the square, where he saw a slim shadow melt into the darkness of the nearest lane. "And now I must take my leave. Your coachman has matters well in hand." Almost as an afterthought he added, "My regards to Lady Sherringham."

Without looking back Hawkesworth made for the carriage door and jumped smoothly to the street. Miss Wallingford bit back a sharp retort, her keen eyes following the duke until he was out of sight.

"Mama, how *can* you contrive to be so utterly useless?" she snapped as soon as the Duke of Hawkesworth was out of hearing. Abruptly her gaze narrowed on his broad back. "Who could she be?"

Hawkesworth moved briskly but with apparent casualness toward the far end of the square. His silent approach went unnoticed by the laughing group of bucks with whom he had a scant acquaintance.

As a boy, his strength and courage had earned him the nickname Hawke. As a man, he still moved silently, and he made a bad enemy. Perhaps that was why the boyhood name had stuck.

On the Peninsula he'd taken down more than one man with his bare hands, sweeping out of the darkness in total silence. But after Isobel left him, he earned a new name—the Black Duke. His reckless indulgence in wine, women, and dueling soon became legendary.

God help the man who mentioned his wife's name within his hearing!

"Delightful bit of fluff, except for the limp, eh, Torrington?" he heard a pale young man titter to his stout companion.

The other fellow, his ample girth encased in a waistcoat rife with puce flowers, shook his head and laughed coarsely. "Taste don't run to cripples, Applegate. Fellow has to draw the line somewhere, don't you know?"

Hawke frowned. To a woman of his wife's vanity, a limp would be exquisite torture. If it were real, that is—not that Hawke believed it was for a moment. Too well, he knew Isobel was capable of anything—even of feigning a disfigurement—to get what she wanted.

Whatever that might be.

The lane where she had disappeared was before him now, its

black mouth beckoning silently. Cold damp trails of fog slid past Hawkesworth's face. Damned hard to see anything, but that would work against her as well. So close—he couldn't lose her now.

Suddenly, he wondered if it wouldn't be better to let her go, to put the whole affair behind him and arrange a divorce, as his friends counseled. God knew he had ample evidence for initiating a bill of divorcement in Parliament. The prime minister, Lord Liverpool, had even suggested it to him once—quite delicately, of course.

He could begin anew and find a decent woman who would bear the large family he meant to have. Robbie was almost five now, and he needed siblings to bring warmth back into his life. A divorce would mean a scandal, of course, but Hawke would count a scandal a very small price to pay to be rid of Isobel.

But the real obstacle was Robbie. The brave little fellow hid his pain well, but Hawke knew he missed his mother desperately.

Isobel had always been clever about the boy, buying his affection with trifling favors and trinkets from her frequent trips to London. Even now, Robbie remembered only her ethereal beauty but was too young to understand her cruelty in leaving two years ago. Hawkesworth hadn't had the heart to tell the boy the truth but said only that his mother had left to visit a sick relative and could not take him along.

Hawke's heart twisted as he remembered his son's tear-stained face when he discovered his mother had gone away without saying good-bye. Every morning for months he had asked if his mama would return that day. Gradually, the questions had grown less frequent, but Hawkesworth knew well that his son had not forgotten. Rather, with the sensitivity of youth, the boy had noticed how his questions hurt his father, so he had stopped asking.

After three months he had given up waiting for his mother's light step upon the stair. After six months he had retreated deep inside himself, leaving only a dim shadow of the gay child he once had been.

Hawkesworth tensed, hearing a muffled noise in the darkness. Slowly the fog drifted past him, curling through the cold iron rails bordering the lane. Motionless, the duke waited, but no sound came from the corridor of blackness around him.

A moment later, he began to inch forward, tracing his way along the metal bars. He cursed when his feet met a sprawling pile of vegetable peelings and garbage, and he narrowly avoided falling; a moment later he was assaulted by the stench of an open sewer.

So much for the glamour of the great metropolis, Hawkesworth thought cynically, trailing his fingers along the cold iron rails at his side.

Damn her for a conniving heartless bitch! he thought. And yet, when he had first seen Isobel, she had been exquisite, her hair aflame around a face dominated by strange compelling aquamarine eyes. She had spun a potent sensual web, and he—fool that he was—had allowed himself to believe in the magic. He had heard rumors of her irregular past, but he had persuaded himself they were merely the work of spiteful rivals.

Marriage had dispelled the magic soon enough. Within weeks, Hawkesworth had seen ample evidence of Isobel's ruthlessness and venality. Soon she gave up even hiding her indiscretions.

For three years Hawke had born the snickers of his contemporaries, even then holding on to hope, captive in the web of sensuality she wove. She had goaded him and betrayed him. And then, after pushing him to the very brink of madness, she'd abandoned him and their son.

But now the reckoning was come. His wife had mocked his trust and killed his hope, threatening to destroy his very soul. She had left him only ashes and an obsession that threatened his sanity.

But no longer, Hawke swore. Tonight he would find his scheming wife and destroy her hold over him once and for all.

No matter what the cost.

To either of them.

Chapter Four

Wherever Alexandra went, fear was her companion, driving her heedless through the darkness. Fear clawed at her heart and sent her blood pounding in her head. With every step her weak ankle cried out for rest, but she pushed on, fighting back the stabbing pain.

She dared not stop. He was too close. She could sense it even now.

Only a few feet away from the elegant square, the alley had narrowed almost to an arm span, rimmed on one side by an iron grill and on the other by a brick wall. The air was fetid with rotting garbage and open sewers. Suddenly, Alexandra's ankle gave way, and she nearly fell, then staggered to brace herself with a hand to the ground. When she lifted her palm, it was covered with filth.

She shuddered and halted briefly to draw a ragged breath. Squinting, she tried to penetrate the darkness before her, but the moving trails of fog were deceptive. Slowly now, she moved forward, more careful after her mishap. The muscles around her ankle tightened in wrenching spasms, pushed beyond endurance.

A muffled thump echoed down the narrow alley. She pressed back against the wall of brick, wincing as the sharp ridges bit into her spine. Breathlessly, she waited for the large figure to loom from the shifting fog, but no one came.

Feeling a draft at her feet, she looked down to see a black shape glide past. She nearly laughed out loud when she saw her pursuer was only a cat. She scolded herself silently and put fear behind her, waiting for her pulse to slow down.

Then she saw him, near enough to touch. He moved quietly, carving the gray fog into pale streams as he passed. Mutely, Alexandra flattened herself against the sharp bricks at her back, vainly willing herself to become invisible. He nearly fell once, stumbling over the same mound of filth that had caught her, and she heard him curse deep in his throat. He laughed silently as the black cat purred companionably at his feet.

"Are you bad luck, my friend? Then Isobel must be close at hand." The man's broad back blocked the alley as he studied the sooty air.

If he turned now, he could not fail to see her, Alexandra knew.

But he did not turn, and a moment later he pressed silently on, slipping back into the fog.

Only after long seconds did Alexandra dare to breathe, and then her indrawn breath gave way in an explosive burst. Maybe the cat had brought her *good* luck.

Heaven knew she could use some.

"Aye, a close call an' no mistake."

Alexandra started and dropped her cane as a small figure unbent from the gloom.

"Don't seem to favor ye overmuch, miss, if ye'll not mind me sayin' so. Took his attention off me right well, though, for which I'll be thankin' ye." The grimy little fellow grinned irrepressibly, holding out Alexandra's fallen cane, and she saw it was the urchin who had filched her captor's purse.

His brash smile warmed her as no fire could. "Did you really take his purse?"

"No business of yers if I did," he said tightly.

"Indeed it is not," Alexandra agreed, "and I've a great deal to thank you for. I only hope the lunatic does not return."

"Aye, the nob looks like he'd square up to advantage, an' no mistake." The boy's humor faded suddenly. "But I'd best be off.

Wouldn't half fancy runnin' into Digger right now. Reck'n he wouldn't stop at a fanning this time neither."

"Who is Digger?" Alexandra asked, struck by the urgency in his young voice.

"Reck'n yer right enough, miss, but ye'll forgive me if I'll not be answerin' that. Less known, less to answer for, ye understand. Now, if yer lookin' fer a way out o' this alley, why then, just follow me. Know it like my own home, I do." Without waiting for her answer, the boy padded off.

Alexandra struggled to keep to the pace he set. True to his word, the boy passed unerringly through the bewildering maze of alleys, each more squalid than the one before. Soon she lost track of time, fighting weariness and the throbbing pain in her ankle. At least her pursuer would never find her here, she thought grimly.

When at last the boy slowed his dogged pace, Alexandra saw lights haloed in the heavy fog. Her small guide turned abruptly. "Lookin' fer a place to hide then, are ye? Happen I can help. Ye'll be lookin' fer somethin' respectable, I'm thinkin', an' the Ten Bells be just the place. Landlord's a right 'un."

"I don't have a great deal of money," Alexandra said uncertainly. "Is it very expensive?"

"Cheap as ye'll find in London, miss—for decent lodgin's, that is. Hard times fer ye too then?" He cocked his head up at her, and for a moment she feared she might disgrace herself by crying.

"I shall manage, my friend. I daresay we both shall. Tomorrow I mean to find a position as a governess or a lady's maid."

The lad looked at her skeptically and shook his head. "No mistress in her right mind'd take ye on, beggin' yer pardon, miss. Not with that hair, nor that skin." Her companion reddened abruptly and dug his hands deep within his pockets. "Bit o' walnut rinse'll cover the gold like," he added in a muffled tone. "Need a character, too, I expect. Digger's wife used to fix 'em up proper fer servants what was sacked—after they paid her a tidy fee, o' course."

Oh yes, she had learned about character references. Her inquiries earlier that day had met only with derision when the agencies discovered she had none.

Had it been only several hours ago? It seemed like a lifetime to her now.

"Right then. Proper sharp set, I am, so let's eat before we consider the matter," her small protector said thoughtfully. "Happen we could help each other."

"You must let me stand the cost of the meal then. Though my funds are low, I can at least afford that."

"Ye'll get no argument from me, miss," the boy replied with a cheeky smile, thrusting out a grimy hand. "Name's Pence, or leastways that's what I been called here in town. Stroke o' luck that our paths crossed, an' no mistake."

Alexandra shook the urchin's hand warmly. "And I am Alexandra Maitland, just back from Madras. That's in India, you know, so I'm still very green about London ways."

"India, is it now?" Pence repeated with keen interest. "What I wouldn't give to see the East! Now, who would be the chief in Madras? Governor o' some sort?" He winked and added by way of explanation, "Maggie was forever sayin' a grand lie works better than a puny one."

Alexandra stiffened. For a moment she did not speak. "His Excellency the Governor-General is the highest representative of the Crown in Madras," she replied woodenly.

Caught up in his scheming, Pence did not notice. "Right then. We'll fix ye up with a character from the governor-general himself. Not many like to know any different. What's the nob's name then?"

"Lord Percival Maitland."

The boy looked up, his attention caught by her tone and the name. His eyes widened. "Yer brother, miss?"

"My father, actually. I'm afraid it's a very long story." The humor had drained from her voice. Suddenly, she was cold and tired and frightened again.

Pence whistled soundlessly. "Well I'll be d—" he began, but caught himself up hastily. He reached for Alexandra's hand and pulled her toward the lights at the alley's end. "Come on then, miss. This is one tale I'll not be missin'. And seein' as how yer foot must be painin' ye somethin' terrible, why feel free to lean on me."

Alexandra sighed and braced her arm against the boy's shoulder, allowing him to tug her forward. He was painfully thin, and the ridge of his shoulder was sharp against her. She wondered how he came to be prowling the London streets, for he certainly did not appear to be a hardened thief.

Perhaps it would be good to talk with the boy. He was an odd mixture of youthful spirits and practical wisdom. Perhaps he would be the very thing to pluck up her spirits.

They made an odd pair as they moved through the fog—the tall, slim woman half pulled by and half leaning on her thin, ragged companion. Caught up in their own thoughts, neither noticed the dark figure who watched motionless from a narrow recess in the wall behind them.

Chapter Five

"An' they wouldn't hear his side o' things?" Pence demanded angrily as they settled companionably into their meal sometime later. "Saved the whole region, he did! Kept the bloodshed from spreadin' farther—did that count fer naught?"

"I expect they needed to lay the blame somewhere," Alexandra said quietly. "My father seemed the best choice. You see, he'd made many enemies over the years for refusing to overlook certain"—she smiled thinly, and her voice trailed off as she shifted a piece of overcooked mutton about on her plate—"certain irregularities that had been accepted by his predecessors. They were glad to be rid of him, I think."

Pence shook his head sympathetically, studying her pale face. "Bad bit o' luck, that. What'd he do then?"

"He tried to appeal their decision, of course, but his dispatches were returned unopened. So he followed the only course open to a gentleman and a soldier. He made answer with his life."

The boy looked at her blankly.

"He shot himself."

"Saved his honor an' left ye to stand the racket?" her young companion snorted. "Proper beef-witted, if ye ask me."

"Perhaps it was," Alexandra said slowly, "but he was a man of strict honor. In the end it meant more to him than his life."

A firm tapping interrupted them, and a moment later the door opened on the florid, smiling countenance of the Ten Bells' proprietor. Mr. Samuelson had treated them well since their arrival, despite Alexandra's nondescript attire. Samuelson knew Quality when he saw it, although the Ten Bells wasn't often frequented by her likes. If the proprietor had reservations about her young companion, he kept them to himself.

"Sorry to disturb ye, miss, but yer trunks 'ave arrived. Shall I put 'em in yer room then?"

"Yes, please—all but the small wicker hamper, which you might be kind enough to bring to me here."

The landlord fairly beamed as Alexandra awarded him a glowing smile. Moments later, he returned with a woven hamper. " 'Ere's yer 'amper, miss." Suddenly the case began to pitch up and down, startling the landlord so that he nearly dropped it.

"It's quite all right, really. It's only my cat."

All smiles, Samuelson deposited the wicker box upon the table. "Let me know if ye'll be needin' anythin' else, miss." After a sympathetic glance at the cane propped beside her chair, Samuelson shook his head and left, drawing the door shut behind him.

When he was gone, Alexandra shot Pence a conspiratorial smile and raised the lid of the hamper. Immediately, a series of high-pitched squeaks pierced the air. "Don't fret, Rajah," she crooned as she reached into the basket and produced a sleek brown creature, which immediately sprang up to perch on her shoulder. "Pence, meet Rajah, my mongoose and most steadfast friend."

With a cry of delight the boy drew close and reached up to stroke the animal's velvety fur. "Grand, he is!" The mongoose sniffed the boy's hand curiously, then accepted his caresses with regal disdain.

"As proud as any of his namesakes, I can assure you. I think he's taken a liking to you. Would you like to hold him?"

Pence's eyes widened with excitement as Alexandra carefully placed Rajah in his open hands. After a questioning glance at Alexandra the mongoose settled himself gracefully upon Pence's arm, arching his long tail elegantly and turning to examine his new surroundings with bright pink eyes.

The proprietor of the Ten Bells had every reason to be happy that night. At precisely the same moment another traveler, also unmistakably Quality, sat drinking in a private room. Although the gentleman had just broached his third bottle, he betrayed no sign of its influence beyond a certain glitter in his lazy silver eyes.

Only the gentleman's close friends, of whom there were very few, could have told Samuelson that the glitter came from keen anticipation and not from the alcohol the gentleman had consumed.

With a low chuckle the Duke of Hawkesworth eased his long frame back into the comfortable, if shabby, armchair before the fire. Isobel would be in his keeping before the evening was out, he thought, well satisfied with the night's work.

His eyes were hard as he raised his glass and offered a silent toast to the flickering flames.

Alexandra mounted the stairs to her room an hour later, her spirits much restored. With Pence's assistance, she had penned a most impressive letter of reference from the Governor-General of Madras. As the boy had pointed out, no agency or employer would be likely to question a letter of reference from India very closely. The boy had also wisely advised her to seek a position in the country, where she would run less risk of encountering her pursuer.

Alexandra shuddered as she recalled the ruthless bite of her captor's fingers against her skin. He must be demented—nothing else could explain his actions.

She smiled bitterly. Anyone could see she was no seducer. Only a man possessed could take her for a practiced temptress—she who right now was no more than a penniless colonial with an ugly limp.

Alexandra shrugged and pushed the man from her mind, for she had plans to make. As soon as she secured a position, she would look into the case against her father and the disposition of his estate. After the uprising her father's detractors had raised charges of corruption against him and had begun a long and tedious inquiry into his private affairs while serving as governor-general.

They had found nothing, of course, for the charges were a pack of lies. But weak men always look to profit from a strong man's death, particularly when the man is unbending and has made many enemies. For five more years her father had waited for the Board of Control of the East India Company to vindicate him. Five agonizing years, during which she watched the torment of his dishonor slowly eat away at him.

When the board ruled against him, the last of Lord Maitland's hope had been shattered. In one stroke he had lost his back pay and a generous pension from the Crown for his long years of service.

But that was the least of what he had lost by the board's decision, Alexandra knew, for it was the dishonor that had cost him most dearly. Nor had his pain ended there.

Her aquamarine eyes hardened as she thought of the formal letter from London that had conveyed the news of the board's decision. All arrogant formality and rectitude, the missive had announced Lord Maitland's immediate recall to London to answer charges of bribery, corruption, and irresponsibility.

Her father had put a hole through his temple that very night.

The stairs swam before Alexandra for a moment. *Was your pride worth such a price, Father?*

She could still see the casual arrogant scrawls of the three men who had signed the recall notice. Their image was burned into her memory for all time. Anger blinded her for a moment so that she nearly fell.

Three signatures—three names she would never forget. Yes, Alexandra would make them pay dearly for what they had done. She had made a promise to her father.

It was that promise that had kept her going in the grim months following her father's suicide. Her affairs had been thrown into chaos after her father's death, and then, to make matters worse, his man of business had disappeared, leaving Alexandra with little more than the clothes she stood in.

Such problems might have made another woman despair, but

Alexandra was made of sterner stuff. Even now she felt no regret for those dusty rootless years growing up in India. They had been rich and exciting times and had taught her to know her own strength—something she had sorely needed when a riding accident left her with a shattered ankle.

Badly set, the sour-faced regimental physician had pronounced. The ankle would never mend. The more the girl used it, the worse it would get.

But Alexandra had had no intention of dwindling into an invalid. In secret she had had her ayah bring a native healer to the house so that she could hear his opinion. Oh yes, the wiry brown man had agreed, the ankle would never be as new, but there were ways to make it stronger. Oh, yes, very many ways.

And so had begun the long regimen of exercises and massage that had restored partial use of her ankle. Soon Alexandra had walked with only a trace of a limp, except on occasions when she overtaxed the weak joint. And by the age of seventeen, she had grown into a beautiful willful woman, confident of her own strength.

Except for the Devil's fire, Alexandra thought, feeling a faint tremor run up her spine. Except for the heat flashes that race across the blazing plain before the onset of the cooling monsoon.

"The Devil's fire" was what Ayah called the storms that terrified her young charge. And Alexandra had been able to find comfort in her servant's capable arms. Until Vellore.

Until the Terror.

Suffocating heat. The sickly sweet stench of blood.

Angrily, Alexandra shook her head, fighting the fragmented images, the only things that remained when she woke from the hellish nightmares. But she could never win the battle with her dreams because she could not face her enemy; in the morning she never remembered any more than fragments.

Her hand swept across her eyes for an instant. Pull yourself together, she told herself roughly. There were no monsoon winds in England. No relentless thunder to threaten her. She would be safe here.

Near the top of the stairs she raised her candle higher, for the passage narrowed, making the last feet especially difficult. *Better get used to negotiating stairs, my girl, for you'll be doing a lot of it in your new position,* she reminded herself grimly.

If she could find a position.

The room the landlord had given her was small but cozy, furnished with a narrow bed, two straight-backed chairs, and a chipped dresser. One small closet adjoined a narrow window that looked out onto a bank of fog.

After four months at sea this was unparalleled luxury to Alexandra, who had shared a tiny compartment with three other women on the way out from Calcutta.

With a little sigh she set the candle upon the dresser, tossed down her cane, and sank onto the bed. It seemed forever since she had rested. Wearily, she reached down to remove her half boot and massage her throbbing ankle.

Blaze and bother! She needed to wash and remove her dusty gray kerseymere gown, but right now she was too weak to think of anything but sleep.

On the dresser the lone candle began to gutter. She shivered as a cool current crossed her skin. With dreamlike immobility she watched the door to her closet quietly swing open.

What she saw then swept all other worries from her mind. Her throbbing ankle, her father, and her financial woes—all were forgotten in an instant.

"Really, Isobel," murmured the tall man who emerged from the closet, "did you think you could elude me so easily?"

He was immaculate in black evening dress crowned with snowy linen. In the light of the candle Alexandra saw that his hair was thick and dark, the color of mahogany dried and seasoned after days in the harsh tropical sun. His silver-gray eyes were wintrycold and glittering as he crossed toward the bed where she lay. He towered over her, filling the room with his broad shoulders, claiming all within it by the force of his presence.

"No—it can't be!" Alexandra whispered. "How did you find me?"

"It wasn't so difficult, for all the young guttersnipe knew his way about. The limp slowed you down." The man's eyes fell to the tangle of skirts where her ankle lay exposed. "How it must torture you to know your beauty is marred! Or is this simply another of your tricks? No, I see the scars are extensive. A hunting accident?" His tone was deliberate, taunting. "Strange—you were always a bruising rider."

Fear washed over her. She was being stalked by a madman! How could she make him see reason? "You mean to persist in this villainy? I shall call the landlord then and have the magistrate sent for. This is not the Middle Ages, sir. Such wickedness will not go unnoticed!"

"Tonight no one will notice anything I choose to do." A cold triumphant smile snaked across his mouth.

Alexandra's fingers dug into the thin coverlet on the bed. "Stand away from me, blackguard! Have you no shred of honor or decency?"

The man studied her dispassionately for a moment. "None at all. You have taken them from me too."

"I'll scream," she said breathlessly. "I'll scream until the whole neighborhood is roused!"

"Don't waste your breath, Isobel. Samuelson has been handsomely paid to ignore whatever he might see—or hear—this night."

"I don't believe it!" Alexandra was crushed beneath a suffocating wave of fear. This could not be happening. It must be a nightmare! This was England, after all—not untamed India!

"Go ahead and scream then," the man taunted. "You'll soon see the truth of what I say."

The certainty of his eyes hit her like a blow. She would find no one to help her. He had seen to that, too.

"Cur! Nay, hound of hell itself! Leave me alone, I tell you! I'll go nowhere with you—now or ever!"

The man stood looking down at her, his strange hooded eyes unreadable against the candlelight from his back. "Quite affecting. You almost persuade me to reconsider, Isobel," he said meditatively. Then his voice hardened. "Almost—but not quite." He reached into the pocket of his waistcoat and drew out a small brown bottle. "And now you will be so good as to drink this rather nasty concoction. I assure you, it will make what follows a great deal easier."

Alexandra's eyes snapped as she looked at the vial, and she

crossed her arms mutinously over her chest. "Drink it yourself and be damned!"

Her captor smiled thinly. "As I appear to be damned already, and have been since the day we met, I shall leave the drinking to you. But I warn you, I'll force you to drink if I have to, and you would find that extremely unpleasant."

"You wouldn't. . . ." Alexandra blinked at the merciless determination in his eyes, and her voice trailed off.

"I see you begin to understand me, madam. That is good. Now, drink," he ordered implacably, holding out the vial.

"I'll see you in hell first!"

"That, my dear, is entirely likely. You will still do as I say, however!"

Alexandra lashed out with her hand to dash the bottle to the floor, but her captor was quicker. He seized her wrist in midair and jerked her to her knees on the bed, wrenching her arm behind her and forcing her hard against his chest.

"Drink it, damn you! No more tricks!" There was raw anger in his eyes now, and Alexandra tasted the sour bite of fear in her mouth. "Or would you like me to turn that young guttersnipe over to a magistrate? I could have him hung for stealing no more than sixpence, you know," the stranger added jeeringly. "Though it baffles me that you interest yourself in the boy's affairs. Hardly your style, Isobel."

His fingers tightened suddenly, and Alexandra bit back a moan of pain. The ruthless set to his mouth told her she was cornered. She could not bear to think of what he might do to the boy.

Cold glass touched her mouth. "No!" she cried angrily, but the man saw his chance and shoved the bottle between her lips and forced her to drain the bitter contents. The spirits burned a fiery path down Alexandra's throat, spurring a spasm of coughing. Finally, the bottle fell away from her lips.

"Swallow it, my love," he said icily. "There's a good girl."

"I shall never forgive you for this!"

The man's eyes did not waver upon hers as the seconds ticked away between them. "In that we are even, my wife."

"You—you'll pay for this! I promise you that."

"I've paid already, Jezebel. More than you'll ever know."

"We shall see about that!" Alexandra cried in a raw voice, struggling against his unyielding grip, but her efforts only brought her closer against the muscled breadth of his chest.

With the hint of a smile, the stranger brought one knee to the bed and pulled her roughly between his thighs. "This time I *will* have you, Isobel—not once, but a hundred times. I'll teach you how it feels to crave something without pride or reason. I'll tame you, by God, and when I'm finished, you'll beg me to take you one more time!"

In growing horror Alexandra heard his savage promise, but somehow his voice was hollow now, drifting to her as if from a great distance.

Outside the window she noticed dim faces floating in the fog. First her smiling old ayah, then her sober father.

Last was her pale mother, dead these fifteen years.

Suddenly Alexandra remembered the little mongoose hidden in her wicker hamper, and she struggled to stand.

"Rajah!" she called out in a desperate plea. "Please! Rajah—" But the words caught in her throat, and the room began to swirl about her in long, fading shades of gray and black.

She was dimly aware of a lean face and strong arms gripping her waist. For an eternity she gazed into glittering silver eyes that froze her very soul.

Then the darkness took her.

With a savage curse the Duke of Hawkesworth whipped his straining horses. The team was just about shot, but he meant to make Seaford by daybreak. Before him stretched the Coulsdon downlands, bleached and silent in the light of the full moon. With wild, reckless energy Hawkesworth shot the horses beneath a dense canopy of beech trees that lined the road, their smooth trunks gleaming silver in the moonlight.

Rajah, she had called him before succumbing to the drug. Hawke cursed again. It had been a joke between them once, when she'd teased him for looking as aloof and ruthless as an Indian despot. Simply one more proof that her story was a lie.

As if he needed another.

And yet perhaps where this woman was concerned, he would

always be vulnerable. The thought struck a chill into Hawkesworth, and he lashed his team once again.

Behind the duke the groom grimaced and tightened his precarious hold upon the strap at the boot. His Grace was in a rare
taking tonight and no mistake—not that Jeffers could blame him.
She was a devil from hell, that one, and she would drive any man
to recklessness.

Still, it was not like the duke to take his anger out on his cattle.
Nor on his servants, for that matter, which was one of the reasons
Jeffers liked him so well, for all he could be a stern taskmaster.

The road veered sharply east then, and Jeffers gasped as the
well-sprung carriage tilted alarmingly. He held his tongue, however. He knew better than to comment when His Grace was in one
of his black moods.

With a sigh Jeffers tightened his grip on the boot and prayed
that he would live to see the sunrise.

Chapter Six

A few hours later the sun slid from the gray ocean and cast a luminous net of silver toward the chalk cliffs of Seaford and Beachy Head. Along the coast to the east the Seven Sisters slept on, their great white bluffs veiled in clinging dawn mist.

A single sloop bobbed in Seaford harbor, a sleek beauty whose stern bore the word *Sylphe*. Almost as soon as the sun appeared, a stout figure emerged from below deck and began briskly laying thick coils of rope in piles to be mended.

It was not a task Captain Augustus Scott relished. He'd greatly have preferred to weigh anchor and set sail for the Azores or beat south across the Channel to Dieppe.

With a frown the stocky seaman turned to survey the clouds piling up along the horizon. Fair weather turning nasty, he predicted, relying on the sure instincts of a man thirty years at sea. Aye, there'd be stiff offshore winds and a cold spell before morning.

With a shrug the captain returned to his monotonous task. Without rope there could be no sailing, he knew full well.

In the distance faint puffs of white began to smoke along the Sussex coast road from Brighton. It was a carriage traveling fast, the captain thought, his wide brow knitted for a moment. Unusual to have visitors to the sleepy hamlet of Seaford at such an early hour. The captain's nimble fingers continued to work the frayed coils, splicing in new rope to mend the broken sections, but every few minutes he raised his eyes to the northwest, watching the white clouds grow larger.

Ten minutes later, a neat post chaise and four bowled up the deserted road toward Seaford's lone pier. The captain's brows twitched sharply when he recognized the Duke of Hawkesworth's coat of arms.

How like His Grace to come tearing hell for leather to the coast after not visiting the *Sylphe* once in the past year. The man was reckless to a fault, the captain thought disapprovingly.

Briskly tossing aside the frayed ends of rope, he strode across the deck and along toward the end of the pier. Aye, the Quality had their whims all right—but Captain Scott was paid well to accommodate those of the Duke of Hawkesworth.

Even before the carriage had plunged to a halt, Jeffers jumped down from the boot and moved to quiet the cattle. The duke's face was lined and tired, but there was a reckless excitement to his step when he sprang down from the box and tossed the ribbons across to his groom, meeting Jeffers's anxious eye with a frown. "You need not stay long, Jeffers—only to unload. Then you may return to the inn we passed over the hill. Make the cattle—and yourself —comfortable."

But long years in the duke's service had given Jeffers certain privileges. A question was written large on his face, although he dared not speak it aloud.

"Don't be a mother hen, Jeffers!" Hawke snapped, frowning. "It suits you ill. And as for the question you're champing at the bit to ask—you may expect me when you see me, and not a bloody minute sooner!" With that hard utterance Hawkesworth turned, flung open the carriage door, and disappeared inside.

As his eyes adjusted to the dimness of the coach's interior, the duke studied the limp form twisted uncomfortably on the morocco seat. Reddish-gold hair had escaped the woman's hood and lay in wild disarray around her unnaturally pale face. One hand was curled protectively around the top of the woolen throw that

Hawkesworth had tossed over her the night before. Her other hand trailed limply across the edge of the seat.

Hard to believe she was not the innocent she appeared, Hawke thought cynically. His eyes were hard as he knelt beside his wife and slid his hands beneath her hips and back, pulling her pliant form against his chest.

Without warning the faint scent of jasmine assailed him, carried on the rising heat of her body. The woman moaned slightly and nestled closer against him, causing Hawke's breath to check sharply. He felt a sudden tightening in his groin and cursed the immediacy of his response. One more proof of her power over him! he thought angrily, fighting the old hunger.

Stifling a curse, he clutched the woman in his arms and turned to make his way back outside. When he saw the captain on the pier waiting for him, Hawke was thankful that her motionless form covered his arousal.

"An unexpected visit, as you see, Scott," he said curtly. "My wife is ill and must be taken below immediately. Jeffers will help you with our things, though we haven't many. After that you may see to provisions—one week's worth should do, I imagine. Jeffers will assist you. Then chart a course for"—his hesitation was only momentary—"for the Isle of Wight, I think."

With that the duke strode past the impassive captain and over the wooden planks onto the lightly rocking sloop. At the top of the passageway he turned, and the look he shot the captain was shuttered and hard. "One last thing. My wife and I are not to be disturbed, Scott—not for any reason. Do you understand me?" The duke's voice was harsh with exhaustion and tension.

The captain nodded expressionlessly, and a moment later Hawke's feet echoed down the passageway leading below. Captain Scott caught Jeffers's eye and raised an expressive brow; then he bent to help the groom unload a battered wicker hamper from the boot. In their concentration, neither man noticed the small figure dart from the carriage and hide behind a stack of barrels on the dock.

Below deck the Duke of Hawkesworth stopped before the door at the end of the narrow passage. It was the only door on the vessel that could be locked, he knew. Smiling grimly, he pocketed the key and stepped inside.

The cabin was smaller than he remembered. A narrow bed stood at one end of the room, flanked by a small wooden chest and a simple armchair. The cabin had served Hawke well enough on his sailing expeditions as a boy. Now he was going sailing again, the duke thought bitterly, but for a very different sort of prey.

With cool deliberation the tall man kicked the door shut behind him and moved to deposit his sleeping wife onto the bed. He must have given her too much laudanum, Hawke thought, for she should have begun to waken by now. Her thick lashes fluttered like a bronze veil against the pallor of her face, and she turned and burrowed slightly into the pillow, as if searching for a comfort suddenly denied. Unaware of the alluring picture she made, the woman parted her lips and sighed gently.

Looking at her now, Hawke found it hard to remember her contempt and her taunts—even harder to believe she had seduced one of the young grooms on his estate. Yet this was the woman who had regaled the bewildered servant with a mocking description of her husband's anatomy and skills as a lover!

Yes, the duke thought coldly, the time had come for a reckoning. His plan was quite simple, really. He would bring her to the ragged edge of passion, stirring her blood until she was mad with wanting him and begging him to finish what he had started.

Then he would leave her, humiliated and vulnerable—just as she had left him. And that was only the start of what he meant to do to her.

A vein throbbing in his forehead, he studied the woman on the bed, savoring the confrontation to come. He'd had a great deal of experience in the two years since Isobel had left him—probably too much, the duke thought cynically, remembering only some of the bodies and even fewer of the faces.

He had learned a great many things in the arms of those pouting flirts, bored wives, and energetic Cyprians. Perhaps the most important was that his endowments and abilities filled no other woman with disgust. Quite the opposite, in fact.

Why was it, then, that Isobel's mocking laughter continued to haunt him through the long nights?

The boat rocked rhythmically as the wind fluttered the damask curtains over the open porthole. Dim light filtered over the hard, angular planes of Hawke's face. His eyes were like smoke when he shrugged out of his dust-spattered coat and crossed silently to the bed.

For some reason, now that the moment of reckoning was at hand, he was curiously hesitant. His jaw flexed below the deeply etched lines of his face as he silently lifted his wife's hands free of the pillow. He did not trust himself to touch the curls of her rich hair, nor the pale curve of her cheek. Especially not the blushing swell of her lips, which rounded in protest when he lifted her against his chest.

His large hands sought the tiny buttons at the back of her simple gray kerseymere gown, and he wondered once again why she wore so unattractive a garment—she who had always prided herself on being entirely in step with the latest Paris modes.

With a faint rustle, her gown opened before his impatient fingers, and Hawke pulled the gray material lower to untie the ribbons of her chemise, sliding the tucked white linen away from her whiter skin. He feasted on the pale curve of her exposed shoulder, and then his eyes turned lower, where the full swell of her breasts was offered to him so sweetly. Her nipples taunted him, peach-colored, tightening in the cool damp air.

She seemed somehow more delicate than the Isobel he had known, her skin more translucent, like poured silk traced with faint blue veins. Perhaps the years apart had changed her, just as they had changed him.

Then Hawkesworth allowed himself no more time for thinking, for desire snaked through his loins again. He raised her hips to slide the gown and chemise from her languid body, his fingers quick and wary as if moving over hot metal. With hooded eyes he watched her hands clutch at the coverlet, twisting the wool between her fingers as her mouth moved to form restless, silent words.

When she was totally revealed to him a moment later, Hawkesworth caught his breath at her perfection. By God, she was even more beautiful than he remembered, her waist slimmer and her tapering thighs crowned with auburn curls a shade darker than those that framed her face. He grimaced, cursing the desire that hardened his manhood.

The desire she always knew exactly how to invoke. The desire she had always scorned and used against him.

The desire he meant to summon within her now.

Just then, he saw her smile and its sweetness jarred his resolve dangerously. In that moment he wavered, knowing a sudden distaste for what he was about to do, but just as quickly he mastered his reluctance.

The agony must be ended, and soon, or he could not vouch for what violence he might do her.

Or himself.

No, he could not turn back now.

Hawke's eyes glinted like cold steel as he leaned down and caught once again the faint fragrance of jasmine drifting up from her soft skin. Suddenly, she curved toward him, and her hand sought his comforting warmth. When her fingers threaded through his, she pulled his broad palm closer, breathing a tiny sigh of pleasure. Good, he thought, very good. This would be easier than he had imagined.

But Hawkesworth had not counted on the fierce desire that her touch provoked. Without thinking he turned her face and bent to meet her lips. Her mouth was achingly sweet, and after a moment her lips parted before his delving tongue. Slowly he slipped within her, seeking out hidden corners, teasing her gently and then more forcefully as she twisted against his intimate caress.

He gave her no quarter, pursuing her ruthlessly, teaching her his power. When a tiny breathless moan broke low in her throat, he stroked deep, initiating the primitive play of man against woman.

She whimpered and tried to escape him, but he captured her face and held her motionless, never ceasing his relentless invasion until she weakened and received him fully.

So, Isobel! the Duke of Hawkesworth thought coldly. That lie is laid to rest! You are no more immune to my touch than I am to yours.

Then the battle was engaged in earnest. Soon, Hawke told himself, very soon, he would brand her with the fire of her own passion.

That same fire would burn her poison from his blood forever.

Lying on the narrow bed beneath him, Alexandra smiled gravely. She tossed upon hazy dreams, fleeing toward a distant continent. In her mind whirled the thousand lights and colors of another place and time, a country where white mirages shimmered and twisted in the breath of a dry, searing wind.

She frowned, studying the high Indian plain before her. Two figures were outlined against the mirage, but she could not make them out. When she heard the proud neigh of a horse, she ran toward the black shape of her hunter with a cry of delight, slipping onto his unsaddled back and twisting her hands deep in his ebony mane.

Ah, Fury, you were worth every sovereign of the fortune the Nawab of Bengal demanded for you! Black and silent as the night, you carried me falconing in the foothills of the Himalayas and tiger hunting in Bengal. And when I froze in fear before the pair of king cobras rising out of the dust, their baleful black hoods spread for attack, it was you who lashed out to save me.

Her ankle had been shattered when the frenzied horse threw her from the saddle. With the acrid taste of death in her mouth, Alexandra had crawled on elbow and knee to the great suffering creature. The long minutes had passed while she stroked Fury's neck, her tears blending with the sweat welling up over his black body.

Each surge of that proud heart had swept the cobras' terrible poison farther through the horse's helpless body. Death was certain—there was nothing to do but wait, and they both knew it. Helplessly, Alexandra watched the slow death creep closer until finally the deadly toxins attacked the heart.

His eyes wild, Fury shuddered one last time and then stirred no more. Even now, the memory still haunted her.

But suddenly, in this place out of time, this place of dreams, Fury was with her again, and Alexandra accepted this as naturally as she accepted the other phantoms she had met in this netherworld. How good it felt to be free again, the wind sleek in her hair,

Fury powerful beneath her as they pounded across the white plains!

"Ah, my love," she whispered breathlessly, "where have you been these long years?"

Her lips curved into a ghost of a smile as she slid her hands into Fury's mane, tangling her fingers in the thick sable hair and dropping a kiss on his tensed neck. She exulted in his speed and effortless motion, in the flex and play of rippling muscles beneath her legs. All her pain, all her regrets were forgotten, and she lost herself in the flight toward white peaks beckoning on the distant horizon.

But a hint of warning clouded her happiness. Restlessly, she shifted, shaking her head. Why did she drift so oddly from thought to thought? Why did her body burn with its own life, a thing apart?

Dimly, then, she perceived that she was not alone. The stranger was with her—the man from the fog. She flinched before that hard, bitter face etched with dark shadows. How had he followed her here to the Indian hill country?

The air shimmered with heat and began to hum as the man's image solidified. Slowly, his arms surrounded her. Strong hands circled her waist and pulled her from Fury, slanting her against a broad male chest. His eyes were dark gray flecked with silver, and when she looked down at him, she saw they were smoky with desire.

She wanted to fight him, but the effort was great. Their breaths caught as they faced each other, foe and captive held immobile while their silent struggle raged on. Then slowly he slid her to the ground, drawing her down along the hard, muscled length of his body.

She tried to look away from the smoky pull of his eyes, but he caught her chin in his hand and forced her to face him. Long and hard she fought him, using all the desperate strength of a small animal cornered by a savage predator.

Even as Alexandra fought fiercely, she knew with terrible clarity that she was losing. For in that unforgettable moment she felt the first stirring of a woman's passion. In rich heavy waves it broke over her and swept her along in its relentless path.

Strong hands tightened upon her waist and forced her closer against the saddle of her captor's thighs. With every inch he broke her, teaching her the hot need of his manhood. His lips slanted down, warm and heavy, drinking in her very soul.

Fight! her mind screamed, but her body rebelled.

She had wandered for so long, friendless since her father's death, an outcast from all she had known and valued. Now something promised to blot out her pain and replace it with keener pleasure than she had ever known.

Suddenly, she frowned, fighting the warm waves that licked at her so seductively.

No! She could not yield. Not ever! Not to this man.

As if in a dream, the Duke of Hawkesworth heard his wife's ragged little sob, followed by his own groan of pleasure. Drugged with the magic taste of her, he struggled back and dragged his mouth free, the husky rasp of his breath mingling with her whispered sigh of regret.

Hawke had a sudden feeling that he would never be the same after what he was about to do. He had to fight an urge to turn and leave the room.

Not yet, he told himself. Not when there was so much at stake.

With a frozen sense of inevitability he watched his hand slip to his wife's breast and coax her nipple to aching hardness. Then, as he saw her twist restlessly against him, he spread both hands and spanned her breasts, feeling the taut crests tease his palms.

She murmured softly and arched against him. Hawke's breath caught at this unmistakable invitation, and all his doubts were forgotten.

His broad palm burned where he touched her, and his breath was ragged in his own ears. *Get a hold on yourself, you fool! You've come too far to lose everything for a moment of hot-blooded abandon!*

The duke's eyes narrowed, and his mouth formed a thin smile. This time she would dance to his tune! In the throes of the drug she would hide nothing from him.

His strong fingers skimmed her perfect white skin, playing across the curve of her ribs and down to her taut belly. Slowly, as if he had all the time in the world, Hawke tangled his fingers in the auburn triangle at the top of her thighs.

When he ranged deeper and parted her, he found the liquid fire that confirmed what he already suspected. She wanted him. Triumphantly, he teased her to offer her honeyed sweetness, smiling when she arched slightly against his hand. With a reckless laugh he brought his lips to explore the hollow of her neck and then moved lower to nip the proud peaks of her breasts, forcing her toward the explosive release she had long denied him.

As if in a dream, he felt her struggle and twist against his hand.

Her muted gasp echoed in the small room. "No," she whispered raggedly, tossing beneath his masterful touch. But each movement only pinned her against him more intimately.

The boat lurched suddenly, and Hawke felt the world shrinking around him until all that was left was the little room and the wild sweet abandon of her response.

"Please," she moaned achingly, and this time Hawke heard the fear in her voice.

"Yes, damn it! This time you won't stop me, Isobel!" His caressing fingers eased deeper within her, and a moment later he heard the tiny moans torn from her parted lips. With a raw surge of primal male triumph, he exulted in her cries, in the way her hands bit into his shoulders, urging him ever closer. Then he felt her shudder and watched her eyes flutter open, only to cloud with surprise when the convulsions began to take her.

"No!" she cried, her body arching away from him. "Not—" But the words died on her breath, torn from her lips as her choking cry spilled through the quiet room.

It was over, Hawke told himself.

Small beads of sweat dampened the black hair at his brow as he watched his wife's shuddering release. He had found the passion Isobel had mockingly denied him. Her hold on him was broken at last.

But as he looked down upon her vivid beauty, sunset hair wild against ivory skin, watching her ragged breaths drawn through full lips still swollen from his kisses, Hawkesworth discovered it was he who felt drugged.

He would not have recognized this woman beneath him, a woman who responded with such sweet fury to his urgent fingers. With masculine pride, Hawke told himself it was he who had changed her, claiming her this way.

In that moment, reckless with one triumph, he knew he had to have another. Driven to the brink of exhaustion, he felt the gnawing hunger of the old obsession.

Only this time he did not fight its angry heat. Urgently, he stripped away his neckcloth and pulled his shirt free of his breeches. An instant later he flung the tangle of white cloth behind him, revealing a broad expanse of muscle lush with mahogany hair. His chest rippled as he bent to tug off his boots and send them flying after the shirt. His fingers were already at the buttons on his breeches by the time his boots hit the wooden floor.

Then he was naked, sliding down beside his wife, slanting his hard muscles across her fragile skin. He turned her face into his neck, their bodies fitting together perfectly, softness against aching hardness. With a groan Hawke moved over her, dizzy with the heat of her breath playing across his neck and chest. His face was taut with desire as he checked his passion, feathering kisses across her sweet curves and hollows, readying her for his entry.

She was pliant beneath him now, still burning in the afterglow of the passion he had just aroused. Hawke felt himself slide into the dream that shimmered around them, the same dream that had tortured him for years. Only this time it was real and no illusion when he looked down to see their bodies slick with sweat, his wife softly yielding beneath him.

"Isobel," he commanded raggedly. "Open your eyes and look at me, by God! Look at our joining."

Through a haze of passion, Hawke studied her pale face. Her skin was alabaster, so translucent that a vein showed clearly where it pounded at her neck. For a moment her delicate auburn lashes fluttered restlessly, but even then she did not wake.

He lifted himself above her, his thoughts whirling as he fought to control his raging desire, the hard heat of his body crying out for release in her honeyed softness.

With a harsh curse, he pulled himself from her just in time.

Any longer and he would be lost, Hawke realized. Too far gone to stop himself. Too far gone to prove his mastery over his wife once and for all.

And by God, he wanted her awake and exquisitely aware when he took her to the brink of passion, plunging deep within her again and again until she cried out her need to him.

Fighting against the hot tide of passion, he struggled upright and stood looking down at his errant wife, his face a taut mask. She was beautiful beyond belief, Hawke thought bitterly, studying the alabaster skin still flushed from his heated touch. Her fiery hair cascaded about her like a burnished halo, and he found himself twisting a vibrant curl around his fingers. Abruptly, he caught himself, jerking his fingers back as if he were burned. He of all people knew that this was no haloed angel before him.

Unsteadily, Hawke lifted his breeches from the floor, tamping down the still-flaming embers of desire. He forced himself to look away, for her beauty was a torment to him now. With quick, angry steps he plunged across the room to the porthole, looking out at—but not quite seeing—the sheer chalk cliffs to the east glinting stark and white in the morning sun.

For long hours Hawkesworth paced the narrow room, his anger swelling as he awaited the final bitter confrontation with his wife. Forward he strode along the room's narrow length and then back again, over and over, his face dark with barely contained wrath, sullen like a Channel gale about to break.

But he knew no release—for either his passion or his fury.

For the woman on the bed did not wake.

Chapter Seven

For Alexandra, tossed upon the tide of dreams, the turmoil was already fading. With weary fingers she steered her little dhow, angling the small sail to capture a shifting wind. In the wake of the storm's fury she felt only wretched emptiness.

Briefly she had been buffeted by waves of burning pleasure so sharp they verged upon pain. Mindlessly she had fought the tides, only to feel herself spiral away into darkness.

Now the storm was over. All she felt was the gentle rock of the sea beneath her and the sun pouring down like warm honey.

Tired. Why so tired?

With a muted sigh, Alexandra let herself slip back into the rhythm of the waves that slapped softly upon the sides of the dhow. Beside her, Rajah squeaked demandingly, and she reached to soothe his sleek, warm fur. Gently, she gathered him against her and closed her eyes, sliding down into the peace that beckoned so seductively.

Sleep, sleep, the darkness whispered, and so she did.

For Hawkesworth, the minutes crept by with excruciating languor.

On through the gathering twilight he paced, tense and silent as he wore a path in the still, small cabin. The captain brought him food, but he could not eat. So he drank instead, a glass of claret and then another and another, until the bottle was nearly empty. Then he changed his travel-stained clothes and began to pace once more.

After another quarter of an hour he could contain his impatience no longer, stalking to the bed to study his captive closely. It was then he noticed that her pale skin had grown whiter. Her breathing had slowed, so slight that she seemed not to move at all. Lying on the bed, her hands limp at her sides, she suddenly seemed to Hawke more dead than alive.

She was slipping away from him, he realized abruptly. He chafed her cheeks and called her name, but still she did not respond. For the briefest instant he thought of letting fate decide the outcome. If death was her due, he might as well let it come without a struggle.

But the Duke of Hawkesworth found that the beliefs of a lifetime were not easily forgotten. With a curse, he began to shake his sleeping wife, calling her name and damning the old fool of an apothecary who had told him that two tablespoons of laudanum in half a cup of brandy would do the trick nicely. Briskly, Hawke slapped her pale cheeks and lifted her to her feet, only to feel her legs crumple uselessly a moment later. Again and again he lifted her, trying to force her to stand and walk.

"Wake up, damn it!" he ordered, trying to penetrate her drugged sleep. "I'll not lose you now, Isobel!" Her eyelids flickered open for a moment, but immediately closed. The duke cursed long and fluently then, for he had the terrible premonition that if he did not catch her and hold her soon, she would slip away from him forever.

In his desperation, Hawke recalled a young housemaid who had slid into just the same lethargy after being dosed with too much laudanum. He frowned, remembering his mother's crisp orders to fetch a tub filled with cold water.

A second later he was at the door, bellowing orders as he tossed a blanket atop his wife's pale body. "A tub, Captain Scott, and fill it full with seawater!" The startled seaman's face appeared at the top of the stairs. "Hurry, man! Have Jeffers bring coffee, too, black as he can make it!"

The captain knew an order when he heard one, and something in the duke's flinty eyes made him bite back the question he'd been about to ask. "Aye, Your Grace!"

Minutes later a brass hip bath was wedged into the cabin's narrow length, freezing seawater still sloshing against its rim. On the chest nearby stood a steaming tankard of coffee. With a curt nod, Hawkesworth dismissed the captain, who studiously avoided looking at the motionless figure on the bed.

As soon as the door closed, Hawke lifted his wife's limp form and plunged her into the freezing water. Still she did not move, and he grew close to despair.

His eyes closed, Hawke dropped his head against her reddish-gold curls and found himself praying awkwardly, something he had not done since his youth.

Outside he heard the dry whisper of the wind and the cries of circling gulls as the *Sylphe* pitched at her mooring. He smelled her faint scent of jasmine, cursing himself and the bitter fate that had driven him to such extreme measures. His shoulders sagged, and his hands tightened around her back.

It was then that he noticed the faint stirring, the merest quiver in her shoulders. With a surge of hope, he lifted his head.

Again it came. In feverish desperation, Hawkesworth caught a handful of water and tossed it across her face. The auburn lashes fluttered, and she moaned slightly. Again he splashed her face, this time slapping her cheeks and calling her name.

"Wake up, damn it! Fight, Isobel! Fight me!" Once more, Hawke struck her face with a stinging slap, followed by another dowsing, and finally he was rewarded when a weak fist rose to block his hand. With a gasp, Hawke caught her palm to his lips, breathing a prayer of thanks against the wet skin. His own cheeks were damp as well, and he could not have said whether the source was her wet body or his own tears.

Heedless of the water he sloshed over himself, Hawke lifted his wife dripping from the brass tub and carried her to the armchair, where he settled her in his lap. Briskly, he drew his coat of blue superfine across her shivering skin and lifted the tankard to her lips, all the while watching for her eyes to open.

"Open your mouth and drink this, damn it. It will warm you." He tilted a bit of the bitter drink into her lips, waiting as she was racked with coughing. "No more laudanum, I promise you," he added grimly. When her coughing subsided, he forced another drink upon her and held her face until she swallowed it.

Slowly the color returned to her cheeks. He felt her begin to shift restlessly on his lap and smiled grimly at the bolt of desire that shot through him as her hips kneaded his thighs.

The cease-fire was nearly over, he vowed.

In his lap Alexandra Maitland began to make the long climb back to consciousness.

She awakened slowly, her senses only gradually attuning to the world around her. Dimly, she registered the rocking of the sloop, the sharp tang of seawater, and the cry of hungry gulls. Too cold to be Madras, she thought hazily. The smells were all wrong as well.

And then she noticed something else. A man's taut thighs beneath her, his solid arms anchoring her while one large hand coiled in her tangled, half-soaked hair.

With a frown she struggled to pull free of his hold, shaking the ragged fragments of sleep from her mind.

"Hold, Isobel. It will not do to walk just yet."

There was something deep and compelling about the voice flowing over her with such cool authority. She remembered that voice. She remembered the chiseled face that went with those rough dark tones.

And then Alexandra's struggling hands met naked skin. *Her* naked skin!

Her eyes flashed open, and she took in the small room, the open porthole, the rumpled bedding.

Last of all, the tanned, unsmiling face with brooding gray eyes.

"Dear God, what have you done?" Her voice was an anguished cry.

This time, Hawke held her for only a heartbeat longer before he allowed her to struggle out of his grasp. From the chair he watched her, silent and unmoving, as she backed unsteadily toward the wall.

Alexandra sensed the currents running fast and deep beneath his frozen exterior. Even then, she sought out the dark pools of his eyes, silently begging him to tell her that what she feared had not taken place.

"What have I done?" Hawke laughed grimly. "I've saved your life, it seems. And the question, my dear Isobel," he said slowly, "is more rightly what have *you* done."

Alexandra clutched the meager length of wool to her shivering damp frame, vainly striving for decency, unaware that it was his coat that covered her. "I? I've done nothing but been driven and hounded by you since that ill-fated moment when our paths first crossed. And now you have—" Her voice broke, and she could not utter the words. To say them aloud would make them too real.

"I've done nothing but prove your lie, my dear. You were very close to death, and I must confess that the temptation to let you slip on was great. But it seems, Isobel, that not even for you can I break the habits of a lifetime." The tall man lounging in the armchair ran a coldly deliberate look across her bare thighs, which were exposed beneath his coat. "Perhaps it was the thought that when I got to hell I would find *you* there, waiting to torture me for all eternity."

"Then you did not—"

The man interrupted coldly. "Did not what? Bed you? Really, my dear, such delicacy of speech is not at all your style. You are much more believable when you stay closer to reality."

"You still insist that I am your wife? Mindless, brutish creature!"

His face hardened at her words, and he continued as if she had not spoken. "The answer is no, I did not bed you, though I cannot imagine why one more man between your legs would make the slightest difference at this point."

Shock and hysteria warred in Alexandra's whirling thoughts. Suddenly, she felt an overpowering urge to laugh. What would one more violation mean now, after all that had happened to her? She was as good as ruined anyway, she thought wildly.

Seeing her relief, the arrogant man before her smiled a lazy, knowing smile. "No, my dear, today's performance was all on your part, and it was most affecting indeed. Your uninhibited display of passion surpassed my wildest expectations." He stopped, and his eyes narrowed as he watched her response.

Alexandra's eyebrows rose, and once again she fought the urge to laugh. Really, the madman was making no sense at all! If he had not violated her, then what was he talking about?

He smiled impersonally. "Nymph or temptress, I ask myself? Natural harlot or just a poor, tormented creature—as you have made of me? Perhaps, in the end, it does not matter." His voice dropped to a taut whisper. "For I find you still in my heart, God help me—like a parasite burrowing ever deeper." His voice grew uneven for a moment, and he did not speak. He was close enough to touch her now, but he did not; he only sat rigidly across from her, his burning gray eyes locked upon her face. "Shall I spell it out for you then? It was a little test, you see, to determine whether that habitual coldness of yours was a pretense to torment me. And your response was everything I'd hoped for. Oh yes, the cries of passion were entirely beyond faking, my dear, especially when you begged me to complete what I had so carefully begun. I believe that now we may dispense with this fiction that you find me—how did you once put it?—'repellently clumsy, more huge brutish animal than man.' "

Alexandra finally began to glimpse his meaning. He had touched her while she slept a drugged sleep—dear God, he had more than touched her. And she—she had . . .

The idea was unthinkable.

She stood before him, swaying, and suddenly, from deep in her mind, came memories of the erotic sculptures that decorated the temples of India. Scenes of gods and goddesses intimately entwined flashed before Alexandra's eyes, their bodies boldly merged. Scenes that the English memsahibs had whispered about disapprovingly and had walked past with rigidly averted eyes. "Disgusting!" they had snapped in outrage. "Degraded!"

Once Alexandra had asked her Indian ayah about the odd sculptures. The brown woman had smiled, telling her the story of how the world began, flowering from the passion of Shiva and his consort.

But Alexandra had never quite understood. She was untutored in the ways of man and woman, her imperfect understanding gleaned only from the giggling and whispers of Indian servants overheard as a child and later from the furtively shared imaginings of the other girls at the colonial school.

If it was true, then this implacable stranger had—

The blood rushed to Alexandra's face in a hot tide. She felt his unrelenting gaze upon her, knowing that he triumphed in her mortification. Was this the way of man and woman? she wondered desperately. Her father had never spoken of such things, of course, and her mother had been lost to her so young.

The tall man ran his odd silver-flecked eyes across her sensitive skin, burning her as surely as if his long fingers were grazing her.

"What kind of monster are you?" she cried. "Will you not hear reason?"

"I fear I am beyond reason," her captor replied dispassionately. "If so, it is you who have made me that way."

"Please," she whispered hoarsely, "release me now. You have kidnapped and degraded me—what more can you want of me?"

"Only one thing more, Isobel," he said slowly. "Then you will be released. More important, I shall then be free of *your* curse."

As he spoke, he uncoiled his muscular body from the chair and moved toward her. Too late, Alexandra saw the smoky determination in his eyes. Too late, she turned and plunged toward the door.

Her hand met cold metal, frantically twisting the knob, but he had been careful to lock the door and pocket the key. In a frenzy, feeling him close behind her, Alexandra struggled with the knob and jerked it furiously until she lost her footing and fell to the floor.

Hot tears burned a trail down her face as she flung her hands upon the floor in anger. He let her pour out her fury for a moment before catching her clenched fists in one hand and sweeping her effortlessly against him with his other arm.

"You're the Devil's own son!" Alexandra spat in impotent rage, flailing against his hard grip. Her head fell back to reveal a sprinkling of tears beneath the tangle of red-gold hair.

Her captor's eyes burned with gray flames as he carried her across the room, pulling his jacket from her trembling frame and tossing her naked upon the rumpled bed. His eyes narrowed as he studied her pale beauty.

"And you are his daughter, my dear. Yes, you really are quite exquisite," he said coolly. "But how disobliging of me to remain clothed when you are so fetchingly bare."

Deep in her throat Alexandra fought down a sob of rage and fear. His large hands slowly rose to work his neckcloth free of its knot. In shock but unable to look away, she watched him loosen the snowy folds and then pull the shirt from the waist of his breeches. Moments later, he flung the shirt behind him, revealing a rippling wall of muscled flesh thickly matted with dark hair. In a daze Alexandra watched fluid muscles flex across tanned skin as he bent to remove his boots and tossed them carelessly to the floor.

Even when his fingers went to his buckskin breeches, she could not drag her eyes from the muscular breadth of his body. "You cannot mean to . . ." Her voice trailed away in horror.

"But I mean precisely that, Isobel! I mean to exercise a husband's rights and then teach you how it feels to want something you can never have. To teach you to suffer as I have suffered."

The buttons of his breeches were freed, and in an impatient gesture he stripped them off, dispensing with the supple leather as carelessly as the rest of his clothes.

Alexandra choked, unable to tear her eyes from his body. Bands of muscle rippled across his powerful arms, chest, and broad shoulders.

She tried, but failed, to keep her eyes from dropping lower, and she saw with shock and fear the rampant length of muscle at the crown of his thighs. Dear God, he was huge! Two spots of color stained her white cheeks—the only color in her face except for the great aquamarine pools of her eyes.

How remarkable, Hawkesworth thought as he walked toward the bed. Her eyes flame like seafoam in a spring storm, green and blue churning into white froth. A muscle began to flash in his jaw when he saw her curl into a tight ball, her arms clutching her knees.

"I am not your wife, damn you, nor will I pay for her sins,"

Alexandra rasped unsteadily. "I will claw your eyes out before I let you so much as touch me!"

"But you mistake the matter, Isobel. This will be no rape. You'll be begging me to take you before the night is over."

"Never," Alexandra whispered raggedly.

His eyes fixed her within their smoky depths, and Alexandra thought of the king cobra, which seduced its prey to immobility before the final strike. Like the cobra, this man's control was a palpable thing, his command total; already he was beginning to cast his black spell over her.

Her back pressed against the wall, Alexandra fought the dark power of those unwavering gray eyes.

His voice was teasing, dark with unspoken promise as he watched her. "Are you wondering how it will be between us after all these months? Quick and savage or slow sweet torture? Which way, Isobel?"

Alexandra felt her skin burn with the memory of his hair-roughened chest and the rigid line of his thighs. Choking back a little moan, she closed her arms tighter around her nakedness.

"Ah, how very ill suited you are for the role of innocent virgin," he added mockingly. "Not when nature gave you the body and soul of a harlot."

"And you the morals of a foul toad! For twenty years and more I have lived in safety among people you would no doubt call heathens. Only when I came to England did I meet with true savagery!" she cried. "And you are the vilest of savages!" She flung her head back, her dark eyes flashing. "No, worse than a savage, for you come from a society that teaches you to know better."

His shuttered expression did not change and Alexandra realized he'd heard nothing she said. Even if she could prove her identity, he would still ignore it. Panic washed over her with suffocating force as she saw there would be no reasoning with this man.

"L-let me go!" she cried then, hating the fear that caught the words in her throat.

"Not just yet, I think." Something checked his advance, and the quiet pad of his feet stilled. "Though for now it will suit my purpose well enough to let you suffer awhile longer. Yes, wait and suffer as I have done. It may do you good," her dark captor added with a hard, mocking laugh.

"I am lame! A cripple, can't you see? Not the woman you married. You cannot want me!"

"Oh, but I do," her captor said flatly. "More than I have ever wanted anything in my life." His voice dropped, its taut fury revealing the man's inner torment. "And I damn your soul for that too."

He turned and tossed on his discarded breeches, white shirt, and boots and then he left. She saw the door close behind him; she heard the click of a key turning in the lock outside.

"Are you so witless that you cannot see your error even now?" Alexandra screamed at the locked door. "What sort of arrogant ass are you?"

But there was no answer, only the angry ring of boots upon the narrow stairs.

In the empty cabin Alexandra slid slowly to the floor. Bereft, seared by the fires of fury and shame, she felt hot tears slide down her cheeks.

Could nothing make this madman see reason? Dear God, how much more could she take?

A rough, mocking voice whispered that the greatest humiliation was still to come.

Chapter Eight

Somewhere in the long hours of darkness Alexandra fell into a fitful sleep. When she awoke, it was nearly dawn, and gray light had begun to steal in through the room's open porthole. The cold clutched at her stiff muscles, and she grimaced with pain when she tried to rise from the hard floor where she lay curled.

She did not know how long she had slept, or when her reckless captor would return, but she knew that this would be her only chance to escape. Desperately, her eyes ranged across the room, seeking a way out. Her teeth chattering, she moved to the porthole and pulled aside the fluttering curtains. Below her stretched a rippled expanse of iron-gray sea. Farther out, a line of breakers snarled in white fury. *Blaze and bother!*

Turning, Alexandra saw they were moored only fifty yards from the great stark face of the chalk cliffs—fifty yards from the sandy beach.

Her heart began to pound. She could make it, she knew she could. She was a strong swimmer, for this exercise had hardened her after the accident in India, when her ayah had insisted on a daily regimen to strengthen her wasting muscles.

With growing hope, Alexandra turned back to the room. Thank God she was small, for the porthole would be a tight squeeze.

Now, what to do about clothes? Her eyes flashed to the small wooden chest next to the door, and she threw open the lid, barely stifling a crow of victory when she saw neatly folded clothes inside.

Quickly, Alexandra pulled out a simple white cambric shirt, slipped it over her head, and folded back the cuffs, which drooped almost to her knees. Next came a sturdy pair of brown homespun breeches, equally oversize. Deeper down, she found a thick piece of knotted rope—some sort of keepsake, she supposed. Quickly, she looped the rope around the breeches to anchor them at her narrow waist. Last came a jaunty boy's sailor cap which she jerked onto her head, stuffing her tangled curls up beneath the brim.

She looked wistfully at the boots nestled at the bottom of the trunk but realized they would be impossibly large. She would just have to go barefoot.

Her fingers trembled as she pushed the armchair to the porthole and climbed up. For a moment she hesitated, one leg over the chair as she studied the angry sea churning below. The leaden depths reminded her of her captor's eyes, and Alexandra knew she had no choice but to jump.

Then she heard the slap of a bucket riding from a stout rope on the other side of the porthole. Her eyes widened, and she leaned out farther, straining for the rope, which hung just out of reach.

The boat swayed as a wave captured it from astern, rocking the bucket close for a moment. She'd almost touched it that time! Tensely, she waited for the exact moment to stretch out, perilously poised over the water.

This time she had it! Her fingers closed on stiff coils, and she gave thanks for the knots at even intervals, which were designed to make a full bucket easier to raise to the deck.

She took a gulp of air and pushed through the narrow porthole, barely able to force her way outside. With one last kick she leaped free, but was left dangling for a heart-stopping instant before her legs closed around the rope. Then slowly she began the agonizing climb up the knotted strand, inching ever closer to the brass rails that bordered the deck above.

Her energy was almost gone and she had ripped off two nails by the time her fingers met cold metal. With the last of her strength she kicked out and found the deck's narrow ledge. A moment later, her head came even with the rails.

The sun had not yet broken above the horizon. On deck, all was silent, for which Alexandra breathed a prayer of thanks to Indian deities and English saints alike.

Carefully, she slid a leg over the railing and dropped to the wooden deck. For a moment she crouched there, motionless, regaining her strength before making a dash for the planks that led to the narrow pier and terra firma beyond.

From the far end of the sloop came the murmur of quiet voices. Immediately, Alexandra recognized her captor's rough, commanding tones. Her heart hammering, she uncurled from the deck and plunged unsteadily toward the row of uneven planks that bridged the gap between ship and pier. Her ankle began to throb, but she barely noticed.

So far, luck was with her. The voices continued in a low murmur. When she was almost at the wooden bridge, she lunged unsteadily, bringing her lame ankle down against the uneven boards with a sharp crack.

She cursed beneath her breath and forced herself forward over the narrow bridge of planks, resolutely avoiding the sight of the water churning below. And then her feet touched the solid pier.

Almost free, she told herself. All her energy was focused upon the gate at the end of the pier and the barrels stacked clumsily nearby. As she fled wildly forward, a small shape darted from behind the barrels and Alexandra recognized the crooked smile of the urchin who had guided her through the London streets.

Jauntily, the boy raised a hand in greeting, and a half-delirious laugh broke from her dry throat. She started to speak, but Pence immediately stilled her with an urgent finger directed toward several horses tethered a few yards up the slope. Nodding grimly, Alexandra followed him across the dock toward the still-sleeping hamlet of Seaford, quiet beneath the curve of the green downs.

They were halfway to the nearest cottage when she heard an angry voice roar from the boat. Discovered!

Wildly, Alexandra looked for a place to hide but saw only open ground flowing away from her on all sides. Move, move! her mind screamed.

She pressed on fiercely, though her stiff ankle made her clumsy. When Pence raised his thin, sturdy arm, she was happy to take it.

Angry voices snapped in the gray leaden dawn, and she heard the hollow ring of boots on wood. Running feet pounded along the wooden pier, drumming cruelly in her ears. As her heart hammered in her chest, she tried to block out everything but the cottage ahead.

Behind her came a shouted curse, then a horse's wild neighing. She heard the flat thud of great hooves striking the chalky white earth, pressing closer with every heartbeat.

Blaze and bedamned! So close now! She could almost see the moist petals of the red roses climbing up the side of the nearest cottage.

Even when the great bay plunged beside her, she still did not slow her headlong rush.

"I'll teach you to run from me again, by God!"

The man's voice cracked across her like a whip, but she pressed on, her face a white mask of pain. Then rough hands seized her waist, jerking her from Pence's grasp and tossing her roughly up and across the unsaddled horse. She fell face-down across the beast's back, gasping as the horse's spine cut into her stomach. Through her pain she caught a sudden glimpse of powerful thighs tightened against the horse's flanks, and she looked up into a face etched with fury, eyes flashing like gray flames.

"I'll make you sorry for this day's work!" her captor vowed through clenched teeth. "There'll be no escape this time—not until I'm finished with you."

She could not answer, for she was breathless, exhausted, and dizzy from the blood that churned down to her head. Abruptly, they turned, and she glimpsed the face of an astounded groom and her young friend.

"Take the guttersnipe below, Jeffers! If he makes so much as one move to escape, thrash him within an inch of his life!" Her captor's voice sounded unnaturally loud to Alexandra, ringing mockingly in her ears, a cruel counterpoint to her hammering pulse.

Pence only snorted. "Don't frighten me, ye villain! Been whipped by far worse than yer gentry lot, nor ever gave in to him. Won't never give in to ye neither!"

The faces began to swim before Alexandra's eyes. Dear God, she hoped the boy would be all right. Listening to the forced bravado of that young voice, she felt something snap deep inside her, stripping away the last layers of her proud reserve.

"Blackguard! Whoreson! May the fires of hell consume you!"

As if from a great distance, she heard his raucous laugh.

A gruff voice cut him off. "What about Your Grace's young urchin?"

The Duke of Hawkesworth laughed recklessly, triumphant at the sight of his treacherous wife sprawled ignominiously before him, her slim buttocks twisting as her dirty bare feet kicked at thin air. "This one goes with me, Jeffers! I mean to teach the wretched creature some manners, by God!"

With his harsh laughter ringing in her ears, Alexandra closed her eyes and fought black waves of vertigo. She felt the bay stallion turn, then surge to a gallop. A moment later, the drumming in her ears reached a shrill crescendo, and she was swept into darkness.

Above the riders the sun rose higher, flashing off the white chalk cliffs that plunged into the gray-green ocean. East they rode, along the top of the cliffs, criss-crossing shepherd and hunting tracks but passing no human habitation. Their only company was a pair of noisy jackdaws who surveyed them from a perch near the crest of the downs, while the restless sea hurled itself against the rocky base of the cliffs below.

Hawkesworth knew the way well. On this day he took a fierce pleasure in the magnificent landscape that stretched before him. Soon they would pass the towering cliffs of Beachy Head and then curve north toward Hawkeswish.

Hawke felt a primal power surge through him as he rode above the crashing ocean. It had been too long since he rode bareback with the wind sharp and fine in his face. His eyes flashed silver as he looked down upon his wife, slung before him in the style of the ancient Saxon warriors who had savaged this part of Sussex.

Had she given up her fight so soon? he wondered. When he looked down some minutes later and saw her eyes still closed, he pulled her upright before him. She fell limply against him, swaying before her eyes jerked open. Immediately, she began to fight his grip.

Hawke responded by releasing her so abruptly that she nearly fell from the horse before righting herself. After that she stopped struggling and leaned stiffly back against him, hugging Aladdin with her breeched legs and tangling her fingers in the reddish-brown mane to steady herself.

She was as proud as ever, Hawke thought, and still a fine rider —perhaps even better than he remembered. She sat the horse easily, flowing with every surge, not fighting the powerful rhythm.

Just as she had been a superb lover on their first night together, Hawke thought, remembering the way she had fitted herself to him and half followed, half urged him to what had turned out to be delirious completion.

The memory made his large, hard fingers tighten unconsciously around her waist and splay across her flat belly. She tensed, and Hawke felt the muscles bunch and pull sharply away from his touch. He forced her back against his thighs, kneading the taut concave of her abdomen and then lifting his thumb to graze the lower swell of her firm breasts, outlined so pleasingly against the thin cambric shirt she'd stolen from the boat.

He heard her gasp of surprise and saw her nipples outlined against the white fabric. His eyes narrowed as he thought of her resourcefulness in trying to escape in his old clothes. Totally brazen—and yet somehow the clothes suited her, Hawke thought, watching the wind comb her hair into wild disarray against the loose white garment.

She was not exactly in a position to fight him now, he realized suddenly. His thumb rose higher and raked her taut nipples through the fine cambric.

"Let go of me, you arrogant ass," she hissed, breaking her proud silence and prying angrily at his hand.

"As you wish," he muttered, releasing her so quickly that she lost her balance and swayed sharply. She would have fallen had she not thrown an arm around his broad shoulders.

Almost immediately, her hands dropped away, and she stiffened her shoulders. A second later, Hawke spanned her waist and pulled her back against him. When she tried to jerk away, the effect was only to push herself closer to his hand.

"More, my love? You had but to ask." With a hard laugh Hawke pulled her shirt free from her breeches and slid his hand underneath to claim the silken ivory skin of her belly.

"You black-hearted, pig-headed—" The proud beauty tossed her shoulders angrily in a vain effort to evade his touch, but she could do no more without falling from the pounding horse. Relentlessly, Hawke captured both breasts in his large hand and raked his nails against the flushed silken crests until he felt her shudder.

Desire stabbed through him, and Hawke felt his manhood swell. Recklessly he released his hold on Aladdin and brought both hands forward, coaxing her nipples erect between his powerful fingers. She gasped and flailed wildly at his relentless touch.

For a moment they swayed crazily, almost falling. Hawke's body was on fire, and he felt an overpowering urge to throw her down onto the soft green turf at the top of the cliffs and take her then and there, with the wild salt wind rushing across their naked skin.

Urgently, he dipped past the knotted belt, seeking her dusky curls.

"Release me, you filthy swine!" she cried, twisting helplessly before him.

His only answer was a groan when he found her woman's heat and turned his mouth into the hollow of her neck, sliding his tongue wetly across her velvet skin. When he heard her shuddering breath, he kissed her punishingly, nipping her with his teeth.

By God, he wanted to leave his mark upon her, to see her carry a red welt on her neck from his teeth! He wanted to plunge deep inside her, to fill her with his seed and know the triumph of her breathless sounds of pleasure.

A tiny sob escaped from deep in her throat. Hawke pulled his hand away abruptly. "Sorry, my dear, but you'll have to wait for what comes next," he whispered tauntingly.

"I hate you!" she cried, adding a most unladylike curse beneath her breath.

"Never fear, when this ride is completed, I promise you a different sort of ride, one where I shall put myself totally at your . . . service," he said against her ear.

"The only service you can provide is to release me, you braying ass!" she hissed.

Hawke threw back his head and laughed. Her face was hidden, but he smiled at her back, stiff and ramrod straight before him.

Yes, by God, it would be a pleasure to break his wife to his bit, even if it took a week of starvation and a horsewhip to do it.

Then the duke smiled cynically. Somehow he did not think the taming would be nearly as difficult as he had thought.

Chapter Nine

With dazed eyes Alexandra studied the unbroken line of green hills and the plunging white scar of the cliffs before her, seeing none of them.

Blaze and bother! she raged at herself. Why do I give him exactly what he wants? Inconspicuously, she reached up to brush angry tears from her cheek. What manner of devil *was* he?

Against all reason, she had felt the exquisite power of his hands. For a moment she had even wanted him to continue, Alexandra realized, sick with fury and shame. Even now, her hips burned where they were pressed against his powerful thighs.

Had he done this aboard the *Sylphe*? she wondered, feeling her face stain red. A jeering voice told her he had done this and far worse.

Her chest heaving, she sought to focus on the wild beauty of the downs, watching a pair of noisy sea birds plunge over the edge of the chalk cliffs down to the churning waves below. Thyme and verbena drifted on the salt wind. Gradually her vision focused, and she began to see the powerful, stirring beauty of the place.

It was a harsh, unforgiving landscape, quite unlike anything she had seen in India. Yet even the stark ridges were dotted with tiny yellow and purple wild flowers. And always before her was the wild mystery of high cliffs plunging in a reckless dash to meet the sea.

Like man and woman, Alexandra thought, implacably opposed, fighting yet ever bound. Maybe that was what her ayah had been trying to tell her, she realized suddenly.

But she would neither yield nor be bound to any man, Alexandra vowed. Not until her father's reputation was cleared, and maybe not even then.

They pressed on, kicking up little puffs of white powder where they crossed bare scars of chalk. Suddenly, they veered almost to the edge, and Alexandra gasped to see the sheer drop of three hundred feet to the angry sea below.

Just then, with a low rumble, the edge of the cliff gave way. Only her captor's instant reflexes saved them, as he slapped the great bay to jump the widening chasm. An instant later, the white ridge separated in a sickening crack and plummeted to the waves below.

"You might have killed us both!" Alexandra cried, the taste of fear acrid in her mouth. "Does your recklessness know no bounds?"

"Exhilarating, was it not, Isobel? Or have you lost your nerve as well as your virtue?"

"For the last time, my name is Alexandra! If you could pry yourself free of this obsession for even a moment, you'd recognize I'm telling the truth."

"I cannot begin to tell you how moving it is to hear your concern. Freeing myself from this obsession is exactly my purpose."

Alexandra had just checked an angry snort when she felt the man's hand clench abruptly where it rode against her waist.

"Slow, Aladdin," he crooned, an odd tension in his voice. "Steady now."

Something in his tone made Alexandra turn with unwilling curiosity. She followed his narrowed gaze across the downs, to where the high ridge dropped sharply into a wooded valley. Mellow gray walls rose in the hollow, surrounded by an ancient forest of beech and sycamore. An intricate series of Elizabethan towers and parapets crowned altogether the most imposing structure she had ever seen.

It was Alexandra's first glimpse of the great country house, that mainstay of English aristocratic life her father had recalled so fondly while in India. Seeing the cool green lawns and weathered stone walls, Alexandra began to understand for the first time the sadness that had occasionally settled upon Lord Maitland as he peered out upon the shimmering white heat of a Madras afternoon.

Landscape and house evidenced the perfect blend of human ingenuity and natural beauty. Everything was the work of man but had been cunningly designed so that the structure seemed to have grown up by a trick of nature—even the twisting sheath of water, smooth as a silver ribbon against the green slopes.

White sheep dotted the meadow all the way to the horizon, filling the valley with their soft bleating. So cool, Alexandra thought, so peaceful. Had she ever seen so many shades of green?

In the afternoon sun a long facade of mullioned windows blazed like a thousand mirrors, and the beauty of the place tugged at her very soul. " 'Earth has not anything to show more fair,' " she breathed, unaware that she had spoken aloud.

"Hawkeswish," her companion said, more to himself than to her. "I'd forgotten just how lovely it was."

Alexandra laughed quickly to cover her emotion. "Hawkeswish? What a ridiculous name, to be sure!"

"You never had any aptitude for language, did you? *Wisc* is the old English word for 'wet place,' as I've told you times past counting."

"You told Isobel, not me!" Alexandra snapped unevenly. "And I'm sick to death of hearing your wife's name." Her shoulders stiff, she turned toward the badly scorched trunk of an ancient oak. "Why don't you remove that eyesore?" she snapped, searching for some point of criticism to wound him.

"Eyesore!" the man thundered behind her. "The Sussex oak that has flowered since Elizabeth's time? By God, that shattered tree is more worth saving than you are!"

Her captor kneed the horse suddenly, and they surged beneath a drifting veil of willow fronds toward a shadowed coppice of beech and sycamore. As they entered the semidarkness beneath the canopied branches, Alexandra saw a flash of movement. Behind her she felt the man stiffen slightly and turn his horse in that direction.

For a moment she frowned, unable to make out the pale tangle of arms and legs among the low greenery. Gradually, her eyes grew accustomed to the darkness, and she heard a grunt. The expanse of white skin separated into the bodies of a man and a woman clothed in no more than what nature had given them.

With horrified fascination Alexandra watched as the man arched and then began to thrust wildly between the woman's open legs while she moaned and twisted restlessly beneath him. Suddenly, with a groan, the man plunged one last time and then collapsed. Abruptly, the woman stiffened and tightened her legs around his waist. Then she, too, lay still.

In the small grove all was quiet until Aladdin nickered; the gentle sound echoed loudly in the sudden stillness. After a moment the weary lovers recovered enough to raise their heads and stare up at the intruders. Amazed comprehension tightened the young man's face, and he jumped awkwardly upright.

"Yer Grace!" he mumbled in confusion, bowing jerkily—whether in respect or to cover his nakedness, Alexandra could not say.

"Do I keep you so idle then, Briggs, that you must occupy yourself with such activities?" the man behind Alexandra asked in a bored voice. "I shall have to remedy that."

In fearful fascination Alexandra watched the red-faced servant mutter something beneath his breath and scramble into the underbrush in search of his cast-off clothing. His deserted lover showed no such signs of embarrassment; she only sniffed angrily and reached for the shift and gown she had so lately shed.

Alexandra knew she ought to be horrified by what she had just seen, but somehow she was not. Maybe she was approaching hysteria, for the coupling had seemed more comic than scandalous.

Beneath them the horse slowed, then stopped to sniff the grass. The copse was silent, the sylvan lovers having scrambled off, and now the only noise came from the rhythmic crunch of Aladdin's teeth. Against her better instincts Alexandra turned back to see how Hawkeswish's proud master was reacting to the little drama.

"You find it amusing, my dear?" His mouth was set in a thin

smile, and a muscle flashed at his jaw. His eyes were hooded, their expression unreadable as they stared at the surprised circle of her mouth. "Perhaps I can offer you a source of further entertainment."

Before she could move, he slipped from the horse and turned to pull her roughly down after him so that she stumbled into his arms. Angrily, he jerked her along to the spot where the two lovers had so lately trysted.

"Does this spot suit you? Of course, it has the advantage of being time tested."

Alexandra's heart hammered as she envisioned the frozen image of the sylvan lovers, their bodies naked, urgent, and plunging. Was this the joining of man and woman then? Was this what the madman planned for her?

Suddenly, Alexandra saw herself stretched out beneath her captor's muscular body, pillowing his hard length between her thighs as she met his powerful thrusts, branded indelibly with the fire of his passion.

Fear and rage jolted through her at the image.

"Yes," he murmured darkly, "let us turn back the pages of time. Let me teach you what torment is."

Wildly, Alexandra fought against the narrowing prison of his arms. "Cur! If I had a knife, I would truly teach you the meaning of slow torment!" Again and again she lashed out at his chest but without the slightest apparent effect.

"How fortunate for me, then, that I have no knife for you to steal! Only a different sort of blade—one that leaps gladly to do battle with you now."

His face came closer with each heartbeat. The hard, angled planes hovered over her, singeing her with his heat before he crushed his lips against her open mouth, slanting her head between his unyielding hands so that she would meet the total force of his invading tongue.

For long minutes he did not release her—not until she ceased struggling, not until she was giddy from lack of air. When his fingers lifted at last, Alexandra wrenched away, gasping as her aching lungs rushed to replenish themselves.

Hawkesworth studied his flushed captive coldly, tangling his fingers in her hair as he forced her face up to meet his harsh gaze. "I am glad to see that young Briggs's faithlessness pains you not. Perhaps I should have turned him off the day I found him here with you. I guess even then I knew it was entirely *your* doing." Then, as his captive stiffened, Hawkesworth tightened his hands hold, pulling her head back roughly. "You promised me one day you'd teach me the meaning of the word *torment.* Now it's my turn to repay the favor."

He watched her face turn pale, and his eyes narrowed as he remembered coming upon his wife as she seduced the young groom in this same spot three years before. Just as he had then, Hawke felt a murderous surge of anger swell over him. The blood drained from his face, and he brought his fingers to his wife's neck.

For a moment his vision turned black, and he fought the impulse to tighten his grip until she fell to her knees and begged him for her life.

But the woman in his arms begged for nothing, only swung her balled fists vainly toward his face. "Oh—let me go, you great lackwit!"

A vein beat heavily in Hawke's forehead. So she still defied him, did she? "God damn you, Isobel—Alexandra—whatever you style yourself these days." His fingers twisted in her red-gold mane, and through a haze of fury he heard her bite back a moan of pain.

For the merest instant fear flashed through Alexandra's widened eyes, and then her lips tightened. "Do you sink so quickly to your wife's level?" she cried, her sea-green eyes snapping in fury. "If you are so easily brought to your knees, then you are as contemptible as she!"

Hawke blinked before her fiery glare, maddened by her mocking contempt. His long fingers slipped around her neck.

So she meant to bring him to his knees, did she?

With a growl of fury he flung her down upon the mossy ground. By God, they would see who yielded first!

But Alexandra was quicker. With a little sob she pushed herself upright and began to run blindly, parting the willow fronds in her headlong flight. And that was where he caught her, there beneath the canopy of drifting fronds by the side of the silver stream, his hard hands capturing the tail of her shirt and reeling her in like an exotic burnished trout.

Vainly, Alexandra strained against him, until without warning the fine old cambric split from neck to waist and slipped off into his hand. Released, she fled sightlessly forward, only to feel his iron grip at her ankle. An instant later she sprawled face-down in the mud at the stream's edge.

"Savage!" she sputtered. "No gentleman would hold a lady thus, against her will!"

"What would you know about matters pertaining to ladies, Isobel?" Even as he spoke, Hawke's iron fingers slid up her twisting body. All the while, her straining fists met empty air, as useless as buzzing mosquitoes, her frenzied movements only serving to smear wet clay over her ivory skin.

"You wouldn't know a lady if you saw one, damn your eyes!" Wildly, she pressed against the wet earth, forcing her way to her knees but even then unable to escape his cruel touch.

"Now who is on her knees, love? But perhaps this is your preference?" Hawke's long fingers bit into the tender hollow of her stomach, slamming her back against his thighs. "Nothing would suit me better."

Pinioned between his rigid thighs, Alexandra gasped to feel the searing length of his manhood. *Would this humiliation never end?*

"Is this what it takes to give you pleasure?" he snarled, mud-slick fingers capturing a rose-tipped breast.

"Filthy rodent!" she countered, thrashing wildly. "Nothing you can do will ever give me pleasure!"

Hawke spat out a mocking laugh. "Something more in the traditional style then? Too bad—I'm certain you could have taught me a thing or two about this position." His breath was like fire against her neck when he began to press her down, pinning her slim body beneath his crushing weight.

Blaze and bedamned! Trapped! Alexandra twisted in helpless fury. But maybe not. . . .

Desperately, she rolled sideways, turning to aim a blow at that place where her father had told her a man—even the strongest man—was always vulnerable. Even as she struck out, however, her tormenter parried her knee with his own.

"You do not catch me twice with the same trick, *my love*"—the endearment was a curse on his lips—"as I warned you the last time you tried that." Relentlessly, he trapped her plunging body, capturing her beneath the solid, rippling length of his thighs. "But now it comes to me—perhaps it is the fighting itself you most enjoy."

"Give me a pistol and I'll show you a fight, by God!"

"First knives, now pistols! 'Tis a bloodthirsty bitch you've become, Isobel. But today it won't be my blood that's spilt, nor yours—though I've contemplated that possibility often enough in the last months." His large mud-stained fist pressed her cruelly against the wet bank, while his eyes forged over her, opaque like smoke, missing no detail of her nearly naked form. "You see, in Spain I learned what it takes to kill a fellow human, and it's far more than you might think—as well as far less." His mouth twisted into a cold smile. "Remember that, my dear. And be glad that today's not for dying, only for the little death—the release that comes from desire burned away to its ashes."

"You're the Devil's own henchman! Nay, the very Fiend himself!" Alexandra screamed, struggling impotently beneath his massive body.

"Pretty words, my dear," he said tightly, catching her fists in his palms and forcing them down on each side of her head until his face was only inches from hers. "Very pretty words from the one who made me what I am. I wonder, will you still be so smug after I've had you a thousand times and a thousand different ways? After I've thrown you away without a second glance, like yesterday's rubbish?"

"It will take more than a miserable swine like you to break me —Your Grace!" Alexandra added in reckless fury.

One sable eyebrow climbed assessingly. " 'Your Grace,' is it now? Your timing is exquisite, as always. But don't let your hopes grow. I don't mean to cast you off for quite a while yet. When I do, however, I promise to leave you with excellent references for your next provider."

Suddenly, his fingers twisted at her makeshift belt, forcing the knot free and tearing the rope from her waist.

Dear God, Alexandra thought. *He cannot do this! How can I reach him?*

His face a taut mask, her captor dragged her upright and pushed her backward until she felt bark cut into her side. Without a word he caught her wrists and forced them around the tree trunk, careless of the pain he caused as he secured them with the rope.

Despite her angry attempt to squeeze them back, tears began to slip from the corner of Alexandra's eyes.

Not even this did Hawke notice. He was already striding up the grassy slope, his fluent curses carried down to her on the wind. "Damned bloody horse! Where's he gone?"

A shrill whistle rent the air, then another.

Bound to the tree, Alexandra shivered as the cool wind played across her chest, forcing her to excruciating awareness of her nakedness. Scarlet with shame, she struggled against her bonds, but they held fast. Her humiliation was complete when the baggy breeches, released from their makeshift belt, began to slide down her slim hips. No matter how she twisted, she could not halt their progress.

What was the black swine about now? She had her answer a moment later when she heard a questioning neigh followed by the muffled drumming of hooves.

"Bloody time you came back, Aladdin!"

Before Alexandra's dazed eyes swam the image of a bronze mane tossing in the wind. A moment later, she felt hands at her back, freeing her wrists from their restraints. Awkwardly, she stumbled away from the tree, rubbing her rope-burned skin. Her captor's silver-gray eyes raked over her body, missing no detail.

A tangle of white came sailing through the air, and Alexandra caught the fine fabric by reflex. Her eyebrows rose in sharp slants when she saw the remains of the cambric shirt in her hands. "What maggot have you taken into your twisted brain now?" she demanded, clutching the shirt to her chest.

"For now, it pleases me to see you dress. I find I have no desire to feel a layer of slime between us when I mount you," he said brutally.

Alexandra choked at his coarseness, shrugging on the tattered shirt while her thoughts whirled at this sudden reprieve. Abruptly, her captor tossed the rope toward her, and she grabbed it before he could change his mind. With trembling fingers she looped a knot at her waist and tucked in the shreds of her shirt. Then she straightened warily and thrust her tangled hair over her shoulder.

"You were not always so quick to cover your nakedness," Hawke said softly, menacingly.

Before Alexandra quite knew what he was about, he had grasped her hand and pulled her to a line of rocks a little way up the hillside, where Aladdin was waiting patiently. Roughly, he forced her before him, onto the rough stones, and tossed her onto Aladdin's back. A moment later, she felt his hard thighs brace her hips.

"Wh-where are you taking me?" she rasped through dry lips.

"You ask too damned many questions. You always have, come to think of it. Haven't you learned that too much thinking is bad for the female brain?"

Alexandra snorted. " 'Tis a trait no one could fault you for! You think not with your brain but with your—" With a little gagging sound she caught herself, horrified by what she had been about to say.

"Come—don't stop now, Isobel," Hawkesworth said silkily. "This begins to grow interesting. Exactly what part of my anatomy were you about to describe? My stomach? I've a fondness for good food, certainly, but not to an inordinate degree. My mouth? I enjoy spirits well enough, I suppose. But perhaps you were referring to my—"

"Stop!" Alexandra shrieked, dragging her hands across her ears.

"Shaft? Manroot?" He ground the words out relentlessly against her ear. "My—"

"Filthy coarse beast!" she cried, twisting away from his mocking laughter.

"How very amusing you have become, my dear! I could almost believe that you're afraid of me." His arm was like a steel band around her waist as he spurred Aladdin forward across the thick grass. "Of course, we both know that is impossible."

Alexandra was too angry to speak. It was pointless anyway, for he twisted whatever she said. She sat stiffly before him, hating the rough pressure of his thighs against her hips, hating the long fingers that gripped her stomach.

Hating most of all her painful awareness of those things.

She would find some way to escape, she vowed. But before she did, she would teach this braying ass a lesson he would not soon forget!

The hot afternoon sun poured down as they rode beside the winding stream. They crossed another coppice of beech trees and climbed steadily until Hawkeswish burst upon them in all its splendor. The weathered gray stone was stained with the run-off of centuries of rain, while one section of the towers and parapets had cracked and fallen to the roof. Somehow, the effect only added to the power of the great house.

Strong and proud, the stones seemed to say, *we bend with the ravages of time but never break.*

Just like its master, Alexandra thought bitterly. But then, the Duke of Hawkesworth had been born to every privilege. How could he be anything but strong and successful?

The perfectly raked pebbles of the circular drive clattered beneath Aladdin's hooves. How manicured the lawns and drive! Alexandra thought. Even in Madras, with a veritable army of Indian servants at her disposal, the grounds of Government House had never looked so immaculate.

Yes, she decided unwillingly, *immaculate* was the only word to describe Hawkeswish, and probably it was fear of the duke that kept the servants so vigilant.

When they were still some yards from the house, the carved oak doors opened upon a short, black-suited figure. For a moment the man's face creased with shock, but almost immediately careful impassivity settled in its place.

Alexandra's heart began to pound. "Help me, for God's sake!" she implored of the motionless figure at the top of the steps. "You must! I am not his wife! Indeed, I have only just arrived from India. My father—" She stopped abruptly. Her father's name would carry no weight in England.

"Your father was a blackguard, a bigamist, and a gamester, I'm afraid," the duke finished dryly.

Furiously, Alexandra clawed at the fingers gripping her waist and somehow managed to pry them free. She hurled herself from the horse and stumbled toward the servant. "Help me, please, I beg of you!" she cried, throwing herself on her knees before the stunned man and catching his arm in a desperate grasp. "If you have even a shred of Christian decency—"

Black eyes flashed at her, and an expression of unmistakable dislike tightened the servant's narrow lips. "Your Grace will not be wishful to make a scene," the man said icily, looking down with distaste at the fingers clutching his sleeve. "Now, if Your Grace would be so kind as to release me."

He pulled himself straighter and looked up at the duke, rigidly ignoring the woman kneeling before him. "May I say how delighted we are to see you back, Your Grace?" he said tightly. Not in any way did he acknowledge the fingers still gripping his forearm. "I shall fetch Briggs immediately."

"I rather fancy Briggs is unavailable just now."

"Your Grace?" Once again surprise sharpened the well-trained steward's features.

"No matter. Any one of the grooms will do." Hawke jumped down, and immediately the steward moved to take charge of Aladdin, jerking his arm from Alexandra's grasp. "We will require the Venetian Chamber to be readied."

"Very good, Your Grace. I shall send Shadwell to you directly. Does Jeffers follow?"

"Not until tomorrow, I expect."

"Are you both mad?" Alexandra cried wildly, still kneeling upon the marble steps. "Have I come to a *country* of madmen?"

The steward stood rigid, his eyes trained somewhere above the duke's head.

Suddenly, long tapered fingers gripped Alexandra's arm like a manacle and pulled her stumbling to her feet. When she looked across at the duke, she read a warning in his hard silver eyes.

"And *you* may take yourself to the Devil, Your Grace!" she flashed back, her eyes snapping with blue-green fire.

"You must be weary, my dear. I fear you have overtaxed yourself. Let me help you upstairs." Hawkesworth began to haul her up the broad marble steps. "We will be in the Long Gallery, Davies."

"Very well, Your Grace."

Stumbling in her captor's hated grip, Alexandra saw nothing, heard nothing, felt nothing. *It is all a dream,* she told herself. *In a moment I must wake up.*

But the steps were high, and the pain in her ankle was very real —as real as the cruel bite of the iron fingers upon her arm.

For the first time Alexandra realized she would find no ally in her escape. Her grim jailer had seen to that.

With a sick feeling she faced the possibility that there might be no escaping him.

Chapter Ten

Even as the terrifying thought flashed into Alexandra's mind, her proud spirit rebelled: She would never give in—*never!* Somehow, she would find a way to free herself from this lunatic.

Relentlessly, he towed her over the threshold and into the great house. She was dimly aware of a dark-beamed ceiling, a massive oak staircase, and polished wooden walls hung with ancient tapestries that shone like jewels in the late afternoon sun.

She grimaced as pain shot through her ankle. The beast was nearly dragging her!

"Hurry up! In a minute you'll have all the time you need to contemplate the treasures of my house, Isobel," Hawke said curtly.

She did not answer, saving her energy for the steep flight of steps ahead. As she had feared, she was gasping with pain by the time they reached the top. Still the hateful duke pressed her forward, hauling her down a carpeted corridor into a long room lined with casement windows.

Down the length of the room he dragged her, their feet thundering across the polished wood floor. He did not rest until they stood before a huge portrait at the room's far end.

"There," the Duke of Hawkesworth said coldly, pushing her

closer to the gilt-framed painting. "Now you may give me your opinion of my latest acquisition. Very good, is it not?"

Exhausted, Alexandra raised her head and looked up.

And stared into her own face.

Her indrawn breath grated sharply in her ears. *It was impossible!*

And yet. . . .

Red-gold hair fell in thick coils around a pale face lit by half-closed aquamarine eyes. Sensual rose lips curved up in a seductive smile. But it was not her own face, Alexandra saw. The nostrils were too wide and flared, and the brow was rather smaller than her own.

As she continued to stare at the portrait in horrified fascination, she saw other differences. The hair was a shade darker than hers, its tones less vibrant. The eyes were set a trifle closer together, which seemed to emphasize their cold hauteur.

But it was nevertheless much like looking into a mirror. Something about those cold, proud eyes held Alexandra, refusing to release her. And that was when she felt the chill hint of evil radiating from the woman in the portrait. Suddenly, Alexandra shivered.

Mesmerized, her eyes flashed lower, toward the white expanse of skin stretching unbroken from neck to navel. Sweet heaven, it was her own image but unclothed, every curve wantonly displayed.

The Naked Bacchante, or so Lawrence called it. Truly he outdid himself for you. In fact, he was very loath to part with his masterpiece, although the man who commissioned it offered him a fortune for the finished canvas." The hard voice hammered on relentlessly in Alexandra's ear. "In the end I had to offer terms that neither man could refuse." The menace in his voice left Alexandra with no doubt of those terms. "And then Prinny threw himself into the fray, determined to have the painting for Carlton House. Unfortunately, *he* was not dealt with so expeditiously. Now, do you mean to persist in telling me there are two such as you upon this earth? Go ahead," the duke ordered flatly, "convince me! Tell me how to deny the evidence of my own eyes."

But Alexandra could find no words to begin. How could she

argue with such incontrovertible evidence—with a portrait that was the very image of herself?

The duke's low laugh taunted her. "I thought not. Not even you are so brazen."

It was then that Alexandra noticed a dark stain upon one lush, high breast. Frowning, she bent closer to examine this single imperfection in Lawrence's masterpiece. To her horror she saw it was no blotch that marred the firm ivory curve, but the slim jeweled hilt of a dagger protruding from the woman's heart.

"Dear God!" Alexandra whispered, her startled eyes flashing to the duke's drawn face.

"I'm afraid *he* had nothing to do with it," Hawke said with a harsh laugh. "I'd been drinking rather heavily that night, but it was the sight of Robbie's tear-stained face that finally—" His mouth twisted in a grimace, and long seconds passed before he could speak. When he continued, his voice was taut with his effort at control. "But do not congratulate yourself, my dear, for it won't happen again."

"And who is Robbie?" Alexandra asked sharply.

"Who is Robbie?" Hawke repeated in disbelief. Then it was as if all his hard-won control shattered. His teeth grated audibly, and he sprang toward her with a look of raw fury blazing on his face. "By God, does your perversion know no bounds?" he thundered, shaking her until his features swam before her eyes. "Robbie is our son, damn your black, unnatural mother's heart!"

He drew back, and his hand flew up to strike her. His fingers tightened, his face contorting with rage as he looked down at her, revulsion set in every hard angle of his face. Then his jaw froze into a relentless line, and his fist dropped to his side. "You pollute everything you touch, don't you? You can never rest until all good is destroyed. Well, not this time! The game here is of *my* making and played by *my* rules." He swept her up and tossed her over his shoulder before she had time to realize what he was about. "Yes, by God! This is a lesson long overdue."

"Put me down!" Alexandra cried, her mind still whirling at what he had just told her.

"In my own good time," Hawke answered, striding down the long gallery. His fingers tightened painfully, crushing her hands, forcing her into submission. His boots thundered across the wooden floor, then swept outside to pound up the stairs three at a time.

Alexandra's heart surged crazily. "I demand that you put me down this instant!"

"As you wish, madam," Hawke countered a moment later, storming through a door near the end of the corridor.

Alexandra was roughly flung down upon a wide bed veiled by rich velvet hangings. Her breath caught in her throat as she stared up at her raging captor through the wild tangle of her hair. "You can't do this!" she cried raggedly.

"I can do anything I wish. You will find you have no friends in this house—no allies of any sort." He towered over her, his face set in harsh lines that bespoke his unlimited hatred.

"What do you want of me?" she rasped.

"Want, my dear wife? I want to break you, piece by tiny piece. Until you beg for mercy. And I mean to begin here and now." His hand swung down in a powerful arc, tearing first the fragile shirt and then her threadbare breeches from her trembling body.

For a long moment he stood staring down at her, a vein pulsing at his temple. Then, abruptly, he spun on his heel and thundered to the door, where he stopped and turned back. "We can do this the hard way or the easy way. It's up to you. Either way, the result will be the same. The only way you'll ever leave Hawkeswish is when I've broken you to my bit and you've learned to wear my saddle."

His words were still ringing in Alexandra's ears when the door crashed shut, and she heard the mocking echo of a key grating in the lock.

"You'll be sorry for this!" she screamed as she jumped from the bed and hurled herself against the solid oak door.

"No more than I shall make you," she heard him answer from the other side. "And you may scream as much as you like, for most of the staff is in London. As for the rest—suffice it to say, they are entirely loyal to me. After the things they've witnessed in this house, you would find it difficult to shock them. They all hate you, you see." He laughed harshly. "Although not nearly as much as I do, my dear."

Then his muffled steps drummed across the carpet and back down the corridor.

Chapter Eleven

Caged like an animal, Alexandra thought furiously, turning to glare at her prison. Sunlight streamed through high mullioned windows, casting a golden glow upon walls of aqua silk, fine oil paintings in gilt frames, and armchairs of aqua Genoa velvet.

Even to her feverish eye, the objects in the room attested to good taste and the unlimited wealth to indulge that taste.

For the first time Alexandra looked at the bed where Hawke had thrown her minutes before. From the ceiling overhead was suspended a vast canopy of aqua velvet that looked as fragile as it was magnificent, while the opposite end of the room was dominated by an intricately carved oak armoire. The arrangement was complemented by a cherry Queen Anne highboy and matching chairs. Beside the highboy a cheval glass winked back at her.

Unconsciously, Alexandra brought her hand to her neck, where the dried mud had begun to itch unbearably. With revulsion she regarded the dirt ground beneath her fingernails.

She was tired, dirty, sore, and hungry. But she was not broken, by God! He would learn that soon enough.

With an angry snort Alexandra crossed to the window, where she saw the green sweep of the downs and a faint flash of water in the far distance. Suddenly, her gaze narrowed, and she reached over to finger the aqua curtains thoughtfully. Her lips curved into a smile.

She would soon teach the hateful duke a thing or two, she vowed furiously.

A moment later, she jerked one side of fabric from the window. Deftly, she ripped off a short piece and tied it about her waist like a sash. Then she draped the rest of the long curtain about her slim frame, just as she had seen her ayah do so many times in India, and tucked it into the sash at her waist to form a gathered skirt. When there were no more than two yards left, she brought the end up and over her left shoulder and secured it behind her.

There! she thought triumphantly, studying herself in the cheval glass. Her hands slid down the thick fabric swathing her from shoulder to ankle in aqua folds, even though she had no under-blouse. Her ayah would have been proud of her.

The next problem would not be so simple to solve, Alexandra knew. She studied the view from the window and gauged the distance to the ground. It had to be at least thirty feet, she realized in disappointment, which rendered her first plan impossible. Even if she tied together every scrap of fabric in the room, they would never reach so far.

Blaze and bedamned! Well then, if she couldn't go down, she would just have to go up. With tense fingers Alexandra jerked open the window and stuck her head out, then swiveled to stare up at the roof.

Six feet above the high window ran an indented stone parapet.

Yes! Alexandra thought wildly, her heart beginning to pound.

An instant later, she disappeared inside the room and began to shove the highboy toward the open window.

Twilight was just settling upon the downs when the Duke of Hawkesworth threw open the long French doors of his study and stepped out onto the terrace. This was his favorite time of day, that precious interval after the afternoon's heat and before the bleak loneliness of night.

Drink in hand, Hawke crossed the flagstones to stare toward the west, where the sky was streaked with lavender and aquama-rine. Something about the pure, translucent colors made him think of startled eyes that flashed imperiously, eyes that reached out to haunt him even in his dreams.

A pebble skittered across the roof and dropped to the flagstones with a high *ping*. Bloody owls nesting on the roof again, Hawke thought, cursing silently. A frown set his lips as he turned to look up at the darkening line of the parapets.

Another stone came hissing down to strike him in the forehead, and this time the duke's curse was far from silent. But the oath froze upon his lips when he saw a slim figure suspended in midair, her pale ankles thrashing as she climbed up the curtain that was draped over a notch in the crenelated roof.

By God, she would be killed!

Hawke's glass slipped unnoticed from his hand, crashing upon the flagstones. For a horrifying moment the woman suspended overhead froze, looking down at him, her eyes huge and haunted. Even at this distance he could see that she was waging a battle with her fear.

"Bloody little fool!" The words were barely out of his mouth when she twisted about and resumed her desperate struggle up the taut fabric, her forearms flashing silver in the gathering dusk. She lost her hold for an instant, and Hawke froze. She sobbed and spun crazily down the twisting fabric, and he felt her pain almost as if it were his own.

He did not move, paralyzed, as she broke her fall at the very last moment and dangled high overhead. Only when one fist climbed awkwardly and her knees closed around the length of fabric did he breathe once more.

And that breath woke him fully. He leaped across the terrace in two great running strides. Damned if he would let his wife kill herself while escaping—not when so much was still unfinished between them!

High above, Alexandra dragged herself inch by inch along the groaning velvet. Already a jagged tear had rent the center of the fabric, and she prayed she could reach the roof before the old cloth disintegrated.

But she refused to consider failure. Nor would she think about the granite-faced man staring up at her even now from the terrace below.

Beneath her fingers the fabric grew taut, and she realized she was nearing the point where the curtain was anchored to the roof. A shuddering heartbeat later, she felt rough stone beneath her fingers. Her whole body racked with tremors, she clawed her way up and over the crenelated border and collapsed in an exhausted heap on the rough pebbles of the roof.

She looked up into a twilight sky that burned radiant cobalt above the roof's gathering shadows. Unsteadily, she rolled to her feet and like a hunted animal began to search desperately for an escape route, knowing that her grim pursuer would not be far behind. She crossed the roof toward the southeast corner of the house, touching a line of chimneys and carved parapets still warm from the sun's heat.

Out of the twilight shadows behind her came a muffled snap, and Alexandra swung around to find her fear a reality.

"Do you hate me so much that you'd risk your life to escape?" the Duke of Hawkesworth asked in a deadly voice as he stepped from behind a snarling stone lion. "Or can it be that I have finally broken through that marble shell and made you know the taste of fear?"

"S-Stay back!" Alexandra hissed unsteadily, creeping backward, never taking her eyes from his angry face.

"Why? So that you can break your neck when you stumble over the loose stones by the south front? So that you can fall down the ruined shaft there by your left foot? No, that I will not. I'm not about to let you go so easily. This storm's been a long time brewing, and we'll have it out between us here and now." As he spoke, Hawke moved closer, and his voice rolled across the darkness in unbroken waves. "You've fire enough, Isobel, which is something I forgot. Either that, or you're half mad—and there we might find something in common. But one thing I never thought was that you were a coward. Right now, that's what you appear."

Alexandra, already nearing the small domed tower at the southeast corner of the roof, gave a hard laugh. "You're a fine one to talk of cowardice, Your Grace, here on your home territory with a staff to do your bidding. Put us down on open ground, and I'll teach you fear soon enough." Her foot slipped on a fallen chimney tile, and she swayed awkwardly before righting herself.

"What's wrong with right here?" Hawke asked silkily. "It's all very well to talk about open ground, but now we have the whole roof before us. Why don't you stop running and face me?" He kept his movements slow and unobtrusive, but all the time he steadily closed the distance between them.

"Because it would be no contest, as you well know! So stay away from me, I warn you! I've had enough of your treachery." She felt the warm stone of the circular tower touch her back, and she fought down a trill of wild laughter. She only had time for a quick glance at the stone parapet bordering the roof and the ancient gnarled oak beyond before the sound of falling stones brought her around sharply.

He was less than a yard away, his eyes pinpoints of silver in the navy twilight.

Alexandra kept her back to the warm stone, afraid to look away from him for even an instant now. Her trembling fingers searched the wall of the tower, seeking an opening in the stone face but finding only the regular lines of stone and mortar.

There had to be some opening, either window or door, she told herself frantically.

"You're out of luck, my dear. We closed off the stairway from the south tower three years ago, after Davies took that bad tumble there. Perhaps you'd forgotten," the duke added, faintly taunting.

No! Alexandra thought. Not when freedom was so near! Her fingers closed upon a loose granite slab, and she struggled to wrench it free. "Stay back!" she threatened, raising the block before her chest.

Hawke stopped and held his rage in check, for he saw that she was now dangerously close to the edge of the roof. "Very well," he said, crossing his arms carelessly at his chest. "What next?"

In the darkness to Alexandra's left the oak leaves rustled softly in the wind. "Move back," she said hoarsely, praying that he would obey. He had to, she thought. She needed time to think and space to maneuver.

"Or what?"

"Or I hoist this stone atop your great witless head!"

His soft chuckle carried easily in the stillness. "I think not, my dear. It's an artful bluff and I congratulate you, but now it's time to admit defeat."

"Not while I can yet draw breath, damn you!" Without warning Alexandra hefted the square of granite and hurled it toward that rough taunting voice, for in the darkness she could see little more than the outline of his white shirt. She heard the thunder of falling rock, a brief silence, then a score of small, muffled explosions far below.

Without pausing, she turned and flung herself over the stone railing where the green oak leaves trembled in the night wind.

"Stop!" Hawke's hoarse shout rent the air, bouncing back and forth between the chimneys, echoing like thunder.

But Alexandra's ears were full of the fury of her own heartbeat and the roar of the wind until she could hear nothing else.

A storm of angry branches bit into her face, and her right shoulder cracked against a massive bough. She cried out in pain, clawed by a thousand wooden fingers as she plunged down through the thick foliage.

Her thigh struck wood, and the force of the impact ripped a piercing cry from her throat. Even then, she continued to fall, whipped by twigs and branches, flailing about desperately to grasp anything solid. When finally her fingers met rough bark, she clung with all her strength and swayed crazily up and down until the unseen branch beneath her fingers finally came to rest. A moment later, she felt the outline of a limb at her feet.

Coughing, she spat out a mouthful of bitter leaves and began to work her way in toward the trunk, elbowing aside twigs and foliage. It was hard going in the dark, and she nearly fell more than once, relying upon touch alone for guidance. Then her hands found the oak's wide trunk, and she sank down to her knees with a sigh of thanks.

But there was no time for rest. She hiked up her makeshift sari and slid down along the trunk, lowering herself bough by bough until she hung no more than five feet above the ground. She let herself dangle for a moment, then fell with a muffled thump, gasping at the pain that seared her ankle.

It was one more thing that she would repay the foul toad for someday, Alexandra vowed, picking herself up and stumbling toward the brow of the hill where a grove of beeches shone silver in the light of the rising moon.

The wind was singing across the meadow, and the moon had just lifted over the treetops, providing her a dim path. She knew she could not go far, for her ankle was throbbing savagely. She had not noticed it before, caught in the desperation of her escape, but the pain could no longer be ignored.

She had to find a place to hide, for he would certainly come looking for her, and probably others of his staff as well. But where? Alexandra wondered, studying the open grassland criss-crossed with pale lanes of moonlight. She clambered up the crest of the hill and stopped to listen for sounds of pursuit.

All was quiet save for the rustle of the grass and the answering whisper of the leaves. With a sigh of fatigue she leaned back against a broad oak, paused for a moment, then moved to explore the valley before her.

It was then that she saw a gnarled beech tree halfway down the slope, where twisted roots emerged and then plunged back into the earth. Almost afraid to believe her eyes, she fled down the hill until the great trunk loomed before her, twisted and nearly hollow where it had split and reformed decades before.

Exhausted, she sank to her feet, then curled up into a ball and drew back into the shadowed cave.

Two hours later, after slipping quietly down the grassy slope, the Duke of Hawkesworth came upon his elusive quarry curled like a woodland animal, a sprinkling of red primroses and wild orchids at her feet. He had come alone, unwilling for any of his staff to witness what would follow.

Luck had been with him, or he would have missed her. The rising of the moon had sent a bar of light through the branches of the beech tree, so that he noticed her pale arms and one slim ankle.

He caught his breath at the picture she made, a silver nymph nestled in the tree's dark bower. She did not look frightened now, Hawke thought. She looked neither proud nor venal, but other-worldly and infinitely fragile. She looked, in fact, as though she *belonged* in this place of enchantment, and Hawke felt his heart twist painfully.

With savage force he stamped out the dangerous beginnings of tenderness. It was midnight—time for Titania to wake, Hawke told himself coldly.

Chapter Twelve

Something smooth and solid prodded Alexandra's outstretched leg. She stirred restlessly, mumbling a sleepy protest. Almost immediately, her dark eyes flew open.

She concealed her fear well, Hawke thought grudgingly. Only the slim fingers twisting in the cloth at her shoulder betrayed her.

"Get up," he ordered.

Alexandra swept the last traces of sleep from her mind and fought to control her fear. "Go to hell!"

Hawke did not argue. He reached down and caught the length of cloth at her shoulder, tore it from her chest, and jerked her cruelly to her knees before him. His eyes were silver fire branding her very soul, and all the while he forced her relentlessly closer, reining her in by the ragged edge of her sari.

"Offspring of a snake!" she cried hoarsely, fighting to hold the length of fabric around her. "I'll see you hang for this!"

And then she was slammed against the hard wall of his chest, his fingers digging into her shoulders. Wildly, she fought him until her teeth found his hand, and she bit down with all her strength.

With a savage curse, Hawke released her. Immediately, Alexandra scrambled away, stumbling over the roots that caught at her feet. Even as she moaned with pain, she clawed her way up the slope.

But she didn't go far. His booted foot slashed out and caught her ankle, knocking her forward against the ground and driving the breath from her lungs. Gasping, she watched a curve of polished black leather descend before her face. When she tried to rise, his boot fell upon her hair, grinding down the fragile strands to hold her captive. As she twisted helplessly, his boot inched closer to her scalp, until even the slightest motion caused her savage pain.

"Stop!" she screamed, watching the taut fabric of his breeches descend before her, the throbbing evidence of his male power clearly outlined before her frightened eyes.

Slowly, he slipped to his knee beside her, all the while keeping his boot pressed against her tangled mane so that she could not look away. "You'll pay dearly for that, Isobel," he vowed, reaching a bloodied hand up toward the white linen at his neck. With cold deliberation he loosened the folds and tugged the cloth free.

Before she understood his intent, hard fingers trapped her wrists in the neckcloth and tethered them to a gnarled root above her head. Alexandra's heart pounded like thunder in her ears as a wave of fear crashed over her. "I beg of you," she rasped, "do not do this terrible thing! You are wrong about me—so wrong. Stop now, before you destroy us both with your recklessness!"

"Too late," Hawke answered hoarsely, for the fire was already snaking through his groin. "It was too late the first moment I laid eyes on you."

Alexandra felt the last shreds of her pride shattered by the trace of smoky madness in his gray eyes. "Listen to me. Please!"

Impatiently, Hawke ripped a piece from her skirt and wrenched it across her mouth, gagging her. "No more talk," he said flatly.

Wild with fear, she thrashed beneath his boot, tears slipping down her cheeks. A heavy thigh fell across her flailing legs, anchoring her to the grassy slope.

"Stop fighting me," he warned. "You only make this harder for both of us."

Her protest was caught by the folds of velvet at her mouth, and she twisted in vain against the knots cutting into her wrists. She was helpless before his unleashed fury, and they both knew it. She shuddered, tossing wildly when he began to strip the velvet from her body.

"You really *are* afraid," Hawke whispered, still half disbelieving. "How could I have failed to see it sooner?" Relentless fingers tugged at her skirt, peeling away the heavy folds to free the silver beauty of her skin to his fevered gaze. "You should thank me for this service, Isobel, for I shall free us both this night."

Alexandra closed her ears to his words, knowing the awful certainty of what was before her. Darkness licked at her eyes, and she struggled for breath, feeling hysteria creep over her.

His silver eyes raked over her flushed face and heaving chest. "Yes, by God, even wrapped in that curtain, you contrive to look magnificent," he muttered. With a curse he swept his fingers along her trembling length. He forced his knee between her thighs as he sank down to taste the hollow at her throat. "And your pulse is as ragged as mine," he muttered roughly. His warm breath taunted her ear as his tongue measured her ragged pulse. "Yes, burn for me!" he said grimly. "Since it's you who bequeathed me this hell, it's only right you join me there."

Black waves of panic washed over Alexandra, and she felt her hold on reason crumbling. His lips were like fire, searing her raw skin. Suddenly, she felt a new sensation, a strange tension that gripped her body, warring with her fear.

She shivered as his teeth nipped her neck, then trailed relentlessly lower, leaving a damp trail of fire across her shoulder. Against her will, from somewhere deep within her came an answering restlessness, an unfamiliar stirring of blood and nerve and muscle.

In that fiery moment the last traces of Alexandra's childhood fell away. Innocence gave way to awareness, and her healthy young body began to respond to his relentless, driving need.

Suddenly, little flames leaped to life wherever his mouth branded her skin. She was a candle melting beneath his flame, she realized in horror, racked by angry sobs beneath the gag.

Hawke's fingers hooked around the loose fabric at her waist. Impatiently, he lifted her hips and swept the rest of the concealing cloth away. The sash about her waist was next to go. His fingers traced a dark bruise upon her thigh; then he rose to his knees to look down at her, so naked and fragile, painted by moonlight.

By God, she looked innocent, Hawke thought, lost in a blaze of desire. She who was the breath of depravity!

His eyes raked her ivory skin, her full peach-tipped breasts, her red-gold hair flung like a precious silk tapestry against the green carpet. No wonder he could never drive her image from his mind through the long years of her absence! She could drown a man with her satin skin, with her exquisite taste, with the sweet yielding sounds that tumbled from her lips.

The grove was silent around them. Over the slope the wind sighed softly, carrying the sounds of bleating sheep and the tinkling of little bells, but neither person beneath the gnarled beech seemed to notice.

"Yes, love," he rasped, "this is the beginning. Tonight I break you. Tonight you will lie beneath me and give me whatever I ask."

Never! Alexandra thought wildly, but his hand closed over her furled nipple, and then his mouth took its place, tugging powerfully, urging her to aching hardness with his teeth. He used her expertly with his hands and lips, forging a breathless, exquisite torment, until she was reckless and urgent, her blood on fire. Her eyes closed and her head twisted helplessly as wave after wave of raw molten pleasure buffeted her. She felt him shudder in the same instant that her traitorous body answered his dark call.

Triumph leaped through Hawkesworth as he heard her choking moan. Impatiently, he rose to strip jacket, shirt, and breeches from his heated skin.

Terrified, Alexandra felt the brand of his taut flesh and the rasp of sable fur at his chest. Gently rounded clumps of moss tickled the tender skin of her back and buttocks where he pressed her into the damp ground. Her small hands twisted against their bonds, desperate to shove him away, knowing he would soon fill her with the hot pulsing muscle that pressed against her thighs even now.

Hawke's breath was labored and his face hard and hungry as he tasted the curving line of her furled nipples and her taut belly, his unshaved jaw rough against her sensitive skin. "Your body, at least, is honest. It tells me what all I need to know, madam," he whispered. When his heated breath fluttered against the dusky curls that crowned her thighs, Alexandra wrenched wildly at her bonds, desperate to escape this unthinkable invasion. But escape was impossible.

Hawke felt the thundering of her heart beneath his arm when he parted her and found her damp heat. "Here's my first answer," he said huskily. With excruciating slowness his fingers invaded her velvet darkness.

Wildly, Alexandra arched away from his touch and twisted her body, trying vainly to dislodge his taut, muscled weight. The bonds at her wrists cut deep as she cried out her rage against the cloth over her mouth.

"Now I mean to have a second." Skillfully, he stroked her, building a fire that raged within the deepest recesses of her straining body. "Your fire—give it to me now!" he said roughly, pushing her relentlessly, filling her with his driving touch. "There will be no more holding back between us. 'Tis the Devil's own fire you feel, but tonight it will break this cursed spell that holds us both."

Sobbing, Alexandra tossed helplessly beneath him, her mind fighting his fiery assault at the same time that her body spun out of control. She arched her back as velvet waves of pleasure crashed over her. As if from a great distance, she heard a strangled cry and realized too late that it came from her own throat.

And then she was swept past pride or thought of any sort. The maid struggled and finally gave way to the woman, as her world shattered into a vortex of quicksilver.

"Sweet Jesus," Hawke muttered. Then with a hoarse groan he slid to his elbows and entered her. As if in a dream, he heard her gasp. He felt her stretch to receive his swollen manhood and struggle to fit herself to its throbbing length. His mind and body on fire, he did not wonder at her tightness but plunged on toward her hot, honeyed darkness.

His blood was pounding in his ears and his body screamed for release when he met the fragile barrier and swept fiercely past it. By then he was beyond stopping, beyond thought of any sort.

A searing blade of pain ripped through Alexandra. Wild-eyed, she cried out in shock and pain, but the sound was trapped by the gag at her lips. Blindly, she wrenched against the massive body that pinioned her, arching her back and bucking, desperate to dislodge his weight.

Anything to be free of the pain and shame of this invasion!

But her jerky, frenzied movements only flayed the tender skin at her bound wrists and in the end forced Hawkesworth over the edge.

With a harsh cry he tightened and drove one last time, exploding deep within the narrow recess, filling the woman beneath him with his warm seed. Not until long moments later, when he lay spent against her shuddering body, did he hear her dry, choking sobs.

Slowly his head lifted. For the first time he saw cold tears glistening on her cheeks.

Deep lines furrowed the translucent skin of her brow.

A trail of crimson stained the velvet at her mouth.

Only then did the Duke of Hawkesworth realize that pain and not frenzied passion had twisted the body of the woman beneath him.

Not the sullied curves of a seductress named Isobel but the unwilling body of a maiden who had never before known a man's intimate caress.

The pale, violated body of a stranger named Alexandra.

Chapter Thirteen

Through the chaos of his whirling thoughts Hawke heard her terrified cry come back to haunt him.

You are wrong about me! Stop now before you destroy us both with your recklessness!

Too late! his mind sang back in answer, and the words coursed in his blood, in the tremors that still shook him.

Too late the first moment I laid eyes on you.

Around them the wind stirred restlessly, raking through the leaves overhead, while a jackdaw cried plaintively somewhere in the distance.

What had he done? Hawke thought, sick with revulsion. How could he have made such a terrible mistake?

Because of his colossal arrogance, of course. And because of his savage obsession with Isobel.

The slim body beneath his tensed, and Hawke realized his weight must be adding to the pain she already felt. Slowly, he pushed himself to his elbows, horrified to see drops of blood upon the velvet that bound her mouth.

The same color as the blood that must now dot her thighs, he thought, sick at the realization of what he'd done. I'll make it up to her, he vowed. Somehow, I'll find a way.

His fingers trembling, Hawke untied the gag and carefully lifted it from her mouth. Even then, she did not move or look at him, her face a white mask as she stared blindly toward the hill. Her whole body was rigid, in shock from his cruel assault. Only her huge frightened eyes revealed her inner torment.

With a touch of infinite gentleness, the Duke of Hawkesworth reached down to smooth a wayward strand of reddish-gold hair from her cheek.

His captive recoiled as if he had struck her, and low, racking sobs escaped from her taut lips. When he saw dark blotches where her teeth had bit into her lips, Hawke flinched. With a curse he slid to the ground beside her and cradled her face unsteadily, forcing her to look at him. Dear God, how could he have done this mad thing?

"Who in God's name *are* you?" he whispered, his mind still rebelling against the enormity of his blunder.

Suddenly, Alexandra began to laugh, but the sound emerged as stiff, ragged sobs that shook her whole body. She tried to hold herself rigid, hating the sight of this madman who had violated her without remorse. Her mind yearned for darkness, afraid to think, afraid to face the awful truth of what had just occurred. Even when the salt of her tears began to sting her bloodied lips, she did not move to wipe the cold drops away.

"Go . . . away," she whispered raggedly. "Just l-leave me alone. You've g-got what you wanted." She curled into a ball, her arms circling her knees protectively.

Protection? It was far too late for protection, she thought wildly. Her beautiful blue-green eyes were wide with hysteria as she tried to fight free of the hands cradling her face.

But she could not. Hawke's thumbs skimmed over the faint traces of blood where her teeth had gashed her lips. When he saw her tense and recoil, his hands dropped. What could he do or say now that would not bring her more pain? he wondered grimly.

"N-now are you satisfied?" she sobbed. "Dear God, what sort of man are you to do such a thing?"

A muscle leaped at Hawke's jaw. What sort of monster, indeed? Had he finally lost his mind? She'd tried to warn him, time and again, but he wouldn't listen.

His face was harsh with revulsion and self-disgust as he looked down at her. "The worst sort of fool, it appears."

Caught in the dark grip of a nightmare, Alexandra shuddered uncontrollably, praying that now, at least, he would let her go. Praying that she would sink into numbness and forget the horror of the last days. All around her, beads of dew flashed like diamonds in the moonlight, their beauty unnoticed.

With leaden fingers, Hawke freed her wrists, frowning at the raw welts that emerged from beneath the cloth. He slipped to his knees beside her, running shaky fingers through his dark hair, still unable to take in the irreparable harm he had done.

"My God, what have I done?" he breathed.

His hoarse cry finally shocked Alexandra from her dark tunnel of pain. Anger slashed through her, keen as a Moghul blade, and her proud Maitland blood roiled, crying out for vengeance. "You've ruined me, that's what you've done! Destroyed my l-life with your cursed obsession! I hope the thought gives you all the pleasure you hoped for!" she rasped, straining to cover her nakedness with her trembling hands.

"Your pain gives me no pleasure, I assure you," Hawke said roughly. "My God, I don't even know your name."

"It can make no difference now," Alexandra answered bitterly.

"No? There are things to be considered, arrangements to be made—God knows, a thousand problems to be faced!"

And yet even as Hawke spoke, a hard voice taunted him. *Don't be a bloody fool,* it warned. *Women are all the same. She was the one who came hurtling toward him out of the London fog. She was the one who had driven him to this madness, jeering at him, taunting him with every breath.*

But Hawke knew the cold excuses were false, that the mistake was his and his alone.

"Oh, yes," his white-faced captive cried, "I forget that you are the great and august Duke of Hawkesworth! Of course, you can sweep all this under the carpet with a flick of your finger! 'Davies, see that the wench is cleaned and taken care of,' " she said mockingly. " 'Give her a few shillings and some of my wife's old clothes. That should keep her happy.' Well, I'll take nothing from you, Your Bloody Grace, not one damned thing, for you disgust me! 'Tis *you* who are the real cripple!"

The insult struck home with sickening force. The duke reared up, his face a blaze of fury. "You take a risk, woman! Pray explain how you came to be wandering the London streets alone. No decent female would go careering about without an escort. You could only expect the worst in such a case!"

"And I damned well found it, didn't I?"

Hawke's eyes glittered like beaten silver in the moonlight. "You flaunt yourself in the streets and wonder that you're taken for Haymarket wares? By God, woman, you may count yourself lucky to find yourself with me and not some other sort of man."

"You have insulted me, threatened me, and kidnapped me, Your Grace. You have drugged me and r-raped me," Alexandra cried, her voice rough with pain and anger. "Do you now try to tell me that *I* am to blame for your w-wretched behavior? I suppose you consider any unescorted woman fair game."

Hawke reined in his fury, his silver eyes suddenly narrowing. "But stay," he murmured half to himself, reaching down to grasp her chin in iron fingers. "The likeness is remarkable and must have occasioned comment before this. Perhaps it was *you* who did the hunting, thinking to turn the resemblance to your advantage. It would be too great a coincidence otherwise."

Alexandra recoiled from his hard grip. "On the contrary, I have no designs upon you. I don't even *know* you! My only wish is to leave this place and never to set eyes upon your vile face again."

"I'm not sure I can allow that," the duke said slowly, an edge to his voice. "You see, I have yet to decide what I am to do with you."

"*Do* with me?" Alexandra repeated furiously. "I'm not your chattel to be disposed of at a whim!"

"Have a care, woman! I'm trying to meet you halfway in this damnable coil. Don't force your advantage."

"Ad-advantage?" Alexandra repeated wildly, hysteria rising in her voice.

"Get a hold on yourself, damn it! This is no time for the vapors."

"Why not?" she cried wildly. "What better time than now?"

Even as she spoke, Alexandra began to laugh—low, wrenching noises that came from the very edge of sanity.

Hawke's long fingers dug into her shoulders. "Stop it!" he ordered hoarsely.

"You're hurting me!" Alexandra blazed back, hate flashing from her stormy eyes. "Or do you enjoy inflicting pain?" she cried, oblivious to the way his jaw tensed at her words, oblivious to the deathly pallor that swept over his face.

With a sob Alexandra began to rain wild, frenzied blows upon his arms and chest and neck. Her breath grew ragged, and her hands stung, but still she lashed out at him. Strangely, the man beside her did not move but accepted the full fury of her fists, watching her unblinking until the storm of pain and shame had burned itself out of her system.

At last she fell away from him, sinking to her knees and covering her face with her hands. "Dear God, what will become of me?" she whispered brokenly. "I've nothing now—nothing left at all. Not even my pride." As she spoke, Alexandra rocked back and forth, shivering uncontrollably.

Only then did Hawke move, rising without a sound to sweep her into his arms and draw his discarded coat around her shaking shoulders. "Hush," he whispered fiercely against the flaming tangle of her hair. The soft scent of jasmine filled his lungs, and the soft hills of her breasts pressed against his chest.

Abruptly, he felt a sharp stirring in his loins, the fierce onslaught of returning desire. Like a damned randy beast! he thought, cursing himself soundly.

"You're not alone," he said gruffly, his voice rough with desire. "I've brought this upon you, and I'll make it up to you." His lips brushed her warm fragrant curls, their touch so light that Alexandra did not feel it. The vow Hawke made then was for his own ears only.

Somehow I must make it up, he told himself grimly.

Straining against his strong hands, Alexandra clutched at the last tattered remnants of her pride. "No you won't! I'll take nothing from you, do you hear?" she cried, summoning up the angry fire that had carried her through too many tragedies in her short life. "There's nothing you could do anyway," she sobbed. "Even you, the great Duke of Hawkesworth, can never put this to rights! So just go away. Take yourself off to hell!"

Hawke did not answer her. What could he say when every law of man and nature was on her side?

His only response was a tightening of the hard mask his face had become.

He carried her up to the house, along the great carved stairway and into the bedroom which adjoined his, thankful that his staff had learned to make themselves scarce until summoned. The woman in his arms did not relax against him at all, although Hawke saw that she was near to breaking. When he settled her upon his wife's bed, she turned away immediately, keeping the tense line of her spine between them.

"If it comforts you, Alexandra," he said, using her name for the first time, "you need not waste your curses. I am more than familiar with the torments of hell. We are old friends, in fact."

"It does *not* comfort me," Alexandra answered, her voice no more than a hollow whisper. "My only comfort will be to see you hang." A shallow tremor shook her shoulders.

Hawke stood up, muttering a curse. He studied the stiff set of her body for long minutes, then turned away. His mouth pressed in a thin line, he pushed the heavy armoire in front of the window, effectively blocking any further escape attempts by that route.

Even then, Alexandra did not turn.

In the hours that followed Hawke paced back and forth in his bedroom, listening to her muffled, inchoate sobs from the adjoining room. Once he went to her door, and his hand was on the knob before he could stop himself. At the small metallic click her choking sobs ceased.

He would be the last thing she wanted now, Hawke realized, walking slowly back and sinking down into the chair that faced the connecting door.

Sweet Jesus, who was she? Hawke wondered for the hundredth time. How had she come to be wandering the London streets alone? Had she no parents or brothers to protect her? Or was she a different sort of female entirely, a woman who found her employment in the darkened corners and narrow streets?

Her innocence ruled that out, he conceded reluctantly. But why, then, had she been walking alone at night? No decent female did such a thing. As he thought back over the scene of their first meeting, Hawke's suspicions reawakened.

Perhaps he'd been *meant* to discover her in the fog. Perhaps the whole episode had been carefully arranged by someone who knew precisely how to penetrate his defenses.

Hawke's face darkened as he thought of the only two people who were capable of such calculated treachery.

And if that was true, what was Alexandra's place in the scheme? Her pain and fear seemed real enough, but perhaps she was a very accomplished actress. Haymarket and Holborn were full of such women, after all—women who would feign any emotion for a price.

The thought did not shock him as much as it should have, for the Duke of Hawkesworth had long since lost any shred of trust where women were concerned. Had his father's numerous infidelities not been enough to kill his idealism, then the flagrant behavior of his acquaintances among the *ton* certainly was.

Five years ago, he had been the target of every matchmaking mama in the land. Dowagers and debutantes had watched him hopefully for the slightest sign of interest, but he had never been more than coolly correct.

Even today, leg-shackled as he was, a bevy of females waited hopefully for news that his profligate wife had departed this earth. The debutantes were the worst, he thought grimly; some tittered and affected coy familiarity, while others merely smiled vapidly and lapsed into tongue-tied silence. One and all, Hawke had treated them equally—with politeness and total indifference.

It had been Isobel's own indifference, in fact, that had first attracted him, even more than her beauty and confidence—he was, after all, well used to the company of beautiful and accomplished women. Probably Isobel had planned that as well. She was capable of anything, as Hawke had discovered in the three years they had lived beneath the same roof. Anything that amused her, anything that brought her pleasure.

Anything, as he had finally learned, that caused pain to another.

Hawke had learned his lessons in manipulation from a master. And after she left him, he'd continued his studies on his own.

His flirtations had been carefully reserved for widows and calculating wives in search of discreet amorous diversions—experienced women who understood the rules governing such *affaires.* He was a careless lover, bestowing expensive baubles on his temporary partners, but never did he offer the slightest sign of tenderness or affection. And if any of his partners showed signs of wishing to make a more lasting connection, Hawkesworth instantly gave her her *congé.*

So how had it come about that after all his experience, he had been gulled into thinking the unknown woman in the adjoining room was his wife?

Long into the night he pondered that question, his fists plunged deep in the pockets of his dressing gown while he paced the dark room.

The only answer was that he had been meant to do precisely that. That the whole episode had been carefully planned from the very beginning, and that once again he was the dupe of his wife and her treacherous brother.

Hawke's silver eyes narrowed as they studied the door to the adjoining room. The quiet sobs had subsided, he noted grimly. Probably this Alexandra was right now congratulating herself on a scene well played! Recalling his bitter sense of shame and self-hatred after discovering the evidence of her virginity, Hawke felt his anger begin to build. How she must have enjoyed that!

Isobel and her brother were not the only ones who could lay traps, he decided, his eyes glittering like ice. The woman in the adjoining room would soon discover that two could play at such games.

Chapter Fourteen

Alexandra did not awaken for nearly twenty-four hours. When she finally stirred, the afternoon sun was slanting through heavy crimson curtains. Blinking, she tried to recall where she was.

She stretched tentatively, wincing at the dull ache in her ankle and the strange tenderness between her thighs. Where a man had lain and forced his entrance. . . .

And then anger and savage shame crashed over her.

She who had overseen a household of one hundred servants, who had been treated as an equal by her father and admired by all who knew her! She who had known only respect from every man she had encountered in India.

Violated savagely. Taken like a common dockside trollop.

In cold fury she dragged the heavy coverlet away and sat up in bed. With a sense of disgust she saw faint traces of blood upon her thighs.

Mistaken for another woman by a madman!

Ruined! There was a deadly ring of finality about the word.

Tears glazed Alexandra's eyes as she stood and walked toward the armoire that now blocked the window. Only a crack of glass showed behind the heavy piece of furniture, just enough space for her to make out the elms and oaks scattered against a lawn of piercing green. From the corner of her eye she saw a formal garden laid out with topiary trees and hedges carved in fantastic shapes. At one edge of the drive, set back from the road, was a stone structure that she judged to be the stables.

Suddenly, Madras seemed a lifetime away.

At that moment there came a gentle tapping at the door. Alexandra fled back to the bed and drew the coverlet protectively to her neck.

"Leave me alone!" she cried, dashing hot tears from her eyes.

The door opened a crack. "Beg pardon, Your Grace. 'Tis only me, Lily."

To Alexandra's intense relief, her visitor was a young maid carrying soap and towels in one hand and a black lacquer box in the other. Behind her trailed two liveried footmen with a brass tub full of water.

"His Grace said as how you'd be wishing for a bath, Your Grace," the wide-eyed girl said shyly, dropping a curtsey and then carrying her box to the bed.

Sensual floral fragrances taunted Alexandra's senses as the girl opened the lacquered box to reveal an assortment of soaps and bath powders in colored-paper packets. "Mrs. Barrows, the housekeeper, makes 'em, Your Grace. Uses our own roses, she does. Jasmine, magnolia, and lily of the valley. Ever so nice, they smell. But you must know all about that, Your Grace." Suddenly, the girl blushed crimson, dropped a curtsey, and scrambled from the room.

Which was just as well, seeing that Alexandra had neither the means nor the energy to explain that she was not the Duchess of Hawkesworth and that she had been kidnapped. The girl would certainly find that incredible, Alexandra thought grimly.

No, it was easier to stare into the clear water and allow the swirling steam to scour her mind free of painful memories. With a curious, trancelike motion Alexandra lifted a pale yellow packet rich with the scent of lilies. Slowly she slit the paper and emptied its contents into the steaming water, dispersing the powder and crushed petals into a fine froth with her fingers, letting the fresh steam envelop her.

With a sigh, she slipped the green ribbon from the paper packet and twisted it around her hair, gathering the red-gold strands high upon her head. A moment later, she stepped into the tub, armed with a little brush to scrub away the dirt ground into her feet.

If only the other stains could be erased so easily! she thought bitterly as the water slid across her tired limbs, hot and soothing. She rested her neck against the rim of the tub and filled her lungs with perfumed mist.

She had almost forgotten such comfort. The last time she had had a bath in anything approaching such luxury had been almost two years ago, at Government House.

Remember who's providing it, she reminded herself.

Her eyelids fluttered against her gently flushed cheeks. A tendril of burnished hair escaped from her hastily tied bow and coiled down across her shoulder into the gently steaming water.

Somewhere down the hall she heard Lily speaking quietly with Mrs. Barrows. From the wall behind her came a scratching sound.

Rodents at Hawkeswish? The thought gave her infinite pleasure. Perhaps there were creatures beyond even the grand seigneur's control.

Farther down the hall, a door closed with a snap and footsteps padded along the corridor. With a deep sigh Alexandra blanked out the turmoil and confusion of the day before and let herself dream for a moment that she was back at Government House.

She imagined the gentle click of the punkah wallah fanning thick, humid air rich with ginger. She almost expected to see her smiling ayah emerge through the door, laden with back brush, gauzy wrapper, teapot, and tantalizing gossip about who had lately been seen with whom, doing what.

"Will you be needing anything else, Your Grace?"

Alexandra's eyes flashed open. The shy maid had returned, mindful of her duty. "Only that you cease to address me as Your Grace."

"Beg pardon?"

"I am not Your Grace," Alexandra said furiously, sloshing water out of the tub onto the floor.

"Then how shall I address you, Your Grace? I mean—"

"Yes, what else would you have the girl call you?"

Alexandra's eyes hardened when she saw the duke settle his

broad shoulders against the doorframe. Immediately, she lurched lower, dashing a wall of water onto the carpeted floor. "Miss M—" she started to say, but something held her back. "Anything but Your Grace," she snapped, "for I'm not your infernal wife, as you well know!"

"Leave us," Hawke ordered the startled maid.

"Stay, Lily!" Alexandra countered desperately.

For long moments the young girl stood poised between the two antagonists, her eyes wide and uncertain. Then the force of habit won out. "Yes, Y-your Grace," she stammered, dropping a curtsey to Hawkesworth and turning to flee the room.

"The Devil fly away with you!" Alexandra snapped. "Do you always get what you want?"

He did not move from the doorway. "Invariably. In everything that counts." There was a dangerous edge to his voice that disappeared as quickly as it had come. He inhaled slightly. "I see you chose lilies. Isobel wore a heavier fragrance, I'm sorry to say. The roses soon began to grow cloying."

In her anger Alexandra had almost forgotten that she crouched before him naked in the bath. With a scowl she tightened her arms about her chest and slid to the bottom of the shallow tub. "I did not make the selection to please you. Now leave me alone."

She was good, Hawke thought coldly. *Very good.* "And if I don't?"

"I'll ring for Lily," she said. "For all your rakish ways I doubt you'd care for the staff to know what happened last night. Even your blackened reputation would suffer if your villainy became known. And such things have a way of getting about—perhaps even back to your son. Abduction and rape are such unpleasant words. I don't think you'd care for them to be used in connection with you."

The expression in Hawkesworth's eyes hardened. "Could that possibly be a threat, my dear?" His voice was fine and sharp. "If so, then I will give you some advice. Never threaten me. You'll find that I make a very bad adversary, especially where the well-being of my son is concerned."

Alexandra stiffened before the cold fury of his gaze. He'd make a bad enemy, would he? Well, he would find the same held true of her! she vowed silently, meeting his gaze with cool disdain. "As you see, I am terrified, Your Grace."

"I see only that you have regained your spirit. A remarkable recovery, considering how bereft you were last night," Hawke said mockingly. "Or perhaps a fine performance. I also see that naked, you are every bit as delectable as I remembered, Miss—what is your name, anyway? In all the high drama last night, we never got around to introductions."

Alexandra's eyes fairly crackled with anger. "None of your cursed business!"

"Shall I come and shake it out of you? I will, you know."

Alexandra felt his fury wash across her. "M-Mayfield," she lied. "When are you going to let me go?"

Slowly, like a wolf stalking his prey, the duke crossed the room. "Odd, the name little suits you," he said silkily.

Alexandra stiffened, feeling his finger touch an errant curl and pull it from the water, twisting and tucking it up into the knot at her crown.

"As for when I mean to release you, the answer is not for a while yet."

Furious, Alexandra lurched upright in the steaming water. "You bloody—"

"Yes, Miss Mayfield," he said, *"quite* delectable."

The sight of the duke's eyes running over the exposed curves of her breasts and the top of her knees sent Alexandra swirling back down in the tub. "Why not, you bloody bastard? Aren't you content with what you've done to me already?"

"Because, my dear, I detect my wife's fine hand at work here," Hawke said flatly. All his suspicions had been confirmed by her threat of blackmail. So that was Telford's game, was it? "Until I know exactly how you're involved, I mean to keep you here with me at Hawkeswish. Now, let's dispense with this pretense of enraged innocence, shall we, and get right to the point. How much is Telford paying you—fifty pounds? One hundred? Whatever it is, I'll double the amount if you tell me where he is and exactly what he's planning."

"You can't hold me here, you swaggering satyr!" Alexandra

hissed. In her wrath she paid no heed to the rest of what he had said.

"Just see if I can't—that, and a great deal more!" Without warning, his long fingers slid down to cover her neck and shoulders.

Alexandra felt a jolt of awareness when their skin met. "Get out!" she raged, furiously eyeing the towel draped just out of reach on a low stool. But she was powerless to move, as he well knew, for the slightest motion would give him an unrestricted view of her naked anatomy.

"I might find other forms of payment, you know." His breath teased at her ear, while his hands slid smoothly across her back and shoulders.

"You—you—" Mutinously, Alexandra tightened her arms across her chest, glowering up at him. "Words desert me before your villainy."

"There is a first time for everything, my dear—as you discovered last night. For myself, this is the first time I've been used as a lady's maid." His warm breath stirred the fine hairs at her ear. "Consider my offer—you will find me a far more pleasant companion than Telford, for his delight is pain, while mine is pleasure." As if to prove his point, the duke dipped to taste the delicate skin at the back of Alexandra's neck.

"You can take your pleasure, your precious wife Isobel, and this man you call Telford, and hie yourselves off to the Devil!" Alexandra cried. "Speaking of which, don't you have work to do—saints to tempt? Souls to torment? Believers to harrow?"

Hawke threw back his head and laughed, his fingers never ceasing their drugging rhythm upon her neck and shoulders. "Who knows? Perhaps I'm doing all those things right now. But then, you are no saint, are you?"

Angrily, Alexandra reached into the water and sent a great wave flying toward his still smiling face, feeling a blaze of triumph as he was drenched from head to thigh.

"That was a very bad idea, Miss Mayfield," he said quietly, hauling her from the water and slamming her against his chest. A moment later, his damp mouth came down to crush her in a punishing kiss, forcing her to taste his fury, burning her with his violence and heat. His fingers dug into the slim curves of her buttocks, driving her into the saddle of his thighs.

A whimper escaped Alexandra's lips. She could not breathe, she could not think clearly. She feared she would faint.

Miraculously, his mouth lifted and she was free.

"Blackguard!" she cried as soon as the capacity for rational thought returned. "You have the morals of a snake!"

"But my point is made. We can be civilized about this, my dear, or we can be very primitive—the choice is up to you. If you choose to play by the rules of a savage, you'd better expect the same treatment in return. Now, which is it to be?"

"No rules," Alexandra rasped, hating the raw edge of panic in her voice. "I won't play your filthy games!"

"Oh, but you will," Hawkesworth said icily. "It's far too late to change your mind now. And you'll begin by dining with me. Shadwell will escort you down in forty-five minutes. We keep country hours here, and I do hope you turn out to be a punctual sort of female."

"I'd rather sup with a scorpion!"

"Suit yourself, my dear. But if you do not join me, you'll remain locked in this room."

"Gladly, if your company is the alternative."

He studied her from the doorway, his massive strength dwarfing the dark timber frame. "You may have won the battle, my dear, but don't think that you can win the war."

Alexandra's eyes flew to Hawkesworth's face, and the dark mix of desire and raw male power she saw there made her gasp. Her whole body tingled with the awareness of that force.

As if he read her thoughts, Hawke drew one sable eyebrow up in a mocking slant. He was smiling faintly as he pulled the door shut behind him.

An instant later, a bath brush cracked against the wooden frame like a thunderclap. In the silence that followed, Alexandra heard the duke's lazy laughter echoing down the hall.

He could take his title, his wealth, and his base suggestions, and go straight to hell, Alexandra fumed as she stepped from the bath and toweled herself dry. She would teach him soon enough that she was *more* than his equal.

In every way.

Chapter Fifteen

True to her captor's word, Alexandra was left alone in the room. Her furious pacing was interrupted only much later, when Lily came bearing a dinner tray, a sheer lace peignoir draped over her arm. For a moment Alexandra was tempted to send both back with a suitable message for the duke; then common sense took control. She realized she must eat. And even a sheer nightgown was better than none at all.

The wide-eyed little maid left with a promise to return in a half hour's time.

One half hour.

Alexandra looked at the pea soup, cold beef, shaved ham, and lemon curd upon the silver tray.

One half hour.

Suddenly, she found her appetite miraculously restored.

Hawke jerked the door to his study closed and stalked to the massive desk at the opposite end of the room.

Women, he thought furiously, are inveterate liars!

Angrily, he poured a small amount of brandy into a large crystal goblet, then doubled the amount.

Who the hell did the chit think she was, and what was it about the irritating creature that brought out a granite streak of possessiveness in him?

He emptied the glass and poured himself another.

She had a great deal to learn, this one, and he was just the man to teach her. But who was she? She claimed she was from India, and her air of hauteur suggested that her father had been a man of some importance there.

But that was always the way with these colonials, Hawke thought cynically. She was probably no more than the daughter of an insignificant East India Company drone.

The truth would be easy enough to find out.

Which still left the question of how she had run into Telford. And how much Telford was paying her.

Hawke smiled cynically. There might be ways of shaking her loose from Telford. Ways that Hawke would find totally enjoyable. His eyes narrowed as he recalled her momentary whimper beneath his punishing kiss.

Oh yes, Miss Mayfield was not as unfeeling as she pretended. He could make her want him—Hawke knew it as clearly as he knew his own unmistakable desire. So why did she continue to defy him, damn it?

And who was she to be talking about morals?

Hawke's silver eyes narrowed, studying the amber spirits in his glass. What did women know of honor or morals? They were far too busy spending their husbands' money, rigging themselves out in the latest fashion, and ensnaring their latest lover to concern themselves with honor.

Maybe this woman is different, a nagging voice answered. Ruthlessly, Hawke cut it off.

Women were all the same. Isobel had taught him that.

Precisely to the minute Lily returned, announcing herself with a quick tap at the bedroom door.

"Come in, Lily," Alexandra said, her voice muffled.

When the maid entered she found the curtains drawn and the room in semidarkness. The duchess was lying in bed with the covers drawn over her head.

"Are you feeling poorly, Your Grace?" the girl asked anxiously.

There was no answer from the bed.

Warily, the girl stepped closer. "Your Grace?"

When the sleeping form still did not stir, Lily moved across to the foot of the bed.

Suddenly, the door was wrenched open and Alexandra sprang from her hiding place. Her heart pounding, she slammed the door and twisted the key in the lock. Down the hall she fled, the long trail of her ivory peignoir fanning out over the azure carpet. Lily's muffled cries were barely audible as Alexandra reached the end of the corridor and halted, listening for sounds from below.

He must be at table, she realized, which meant that the servants were occupied as well. With bated breath she stole down the curving staircase to the Great Hall, her fingers gripping the oak banister. She sighed in relief, realizing the muffled cries from her room could not be heard so far below.

She had just stepped onto the marble floor when she heard approaching voices. Heart pounding, she slipped beneath the vast spiral of the staircase and waited.

"Eaten almost nothing, he has. Oh, a bit of ham, but little else. Never been the same since his wife—well, you know all that as well as I do. Odd, though, this one he brought with him from London. He says as how she's the duchess, but Lily says she's changed. Not so cold nor haughty no more. If I didn't know better, I'd think—"

A tittering voice cut off the first housemaid. "You'd think? And who are you to be settlin' the duke's affairs?"

Two young women walked briskly through the hall, hands full of freshly ironed linens, too occupied with their argument to pay any attention to the dim figure hiding beneath the staircase.

"No law that a person can't hold an opinion, is there?" the first said testily. "Leastways, not so far as I know." Abruptly, she stopped, shoved a hand on her hips, and confronted her companion. "Let me tell you, I remember Her High and Mighty Grace only too well. Slashed me with a carving knife, she did! Said I was dawdlin' about my work—can you credit that? And what she did to Briggs—well, that's a tale best left untold. So I'm tellin' you now, it's kind to me the duke's always been, and I'm sorry to see him in such a state, that's all. Been drinkin' heavy too. Footman told me so."

"Heavy?" Another titter. "Steady, maybe, but not heavy. Got a powerful head for spirits, does our duke. Drink any man beneath the table, he could. In fact," the saucy housemaid added smugly, "Briggs says as how the duke ain't generally considered *dangerous* till he's broached his fourth bottle."

"Well, if he hasn't already, he soon will. Lord help us, that means we'd best shake a leg. The footmen will be back from servin', and us still here gabbin' with the bed linens not changed. Mrs. Barrows will sack us for sure."

The pair bolted toward the narrow rear stairs reserved for the servants. Only then did Alexandra release the breath she'd been holding so tightly for the last minute.

So he was drinking, was he? Good! Maybe he would drink himself into a stupor. For all she cared he could drink himself to death!

For a moment she studied the corridors leading from the great hall. Blaze and bother! Which way? The cursed house was a maze.

A door opened somewhere to her right, and she decided in an instant. She fled down the marble corridor on the opposite side. The passage soon narrowed, twisting at a right angle, and she found herself in the rear of the house. The smells of roasting meat and fresh bread told her she was near the kitchen.

A door opened in front of her, and she caught a quick glimpse of Davies' trim black-suited figure, then slipped through the first door that presented itself. She heard his feet scurry past, whispering on the cold marble. Turning, she saw she was in some sort of storage room off the pantry lined with potatoes, turnips, and onions. At the end of the room was a heavy door with grillwork at the top.

To the stables, Alexandra thought hopefully.

She shoved open the heavy door and shivered in a blast of cold air. Stone steps led down into the gloom beneath the house.

Damn! Behind her she heard Davies returning, this time at what was as close to a run as the decorous servant would ever come. Lily was with him, speaking quickly, very frightened.

Alexandra plunged forward and swung the door closed behind her, just as loud voices exploded in the corridor.

In a panic she fled down the rough-hewn granite steps, feeling the cold dampness of the air beneath the house. Her way was lit by torches whose flames danced in the shifting air currents. At the bottom of the steps she halted, studying the vast cavern before her. All was stone—floor, roof, and walls. The ceilings were huge, with vaulted arches, and below stood row upon row of massive oaken casks. The cider rooms, Alexandra realized, where the estate's beer was brewed.

Her bare feet were silent as she ran beneath the shadowed vault. Before her was a second, narrower room, intersected every three feet by thin wooden frames. Hundreds of bottles were cradled within the racks, which ran from floor to ceiling.

The wine cellars. No way out. She was trapped!

She shivered suddenly, the cold damp air beginning to penetrate her thin peignoir. Behind her came the clang of a door and the heavy stamp of feet.

"You search the still room and the conservatory. I'll check the wine cellars."

He was coming! With a hand to her lips, Alexandra fled into the shadows, shrinking back behind a wall honeycombed with bottles. Angry steps thundered across the large room she had just left, the sounds echoing beneath the vaulted ceiling.

She caught her breath, struggling for silence. The footsteps halted. At the far end of the room she saw a low door in the wall, probably a storage area of some sort, she decided. Slowly, she began to creep toward it.

But the long dangling sleeves of her nightgown pulled taut, caught on a sliver in the wood. Alexandra twisted away, shredding her sleeve, only to feel her skirt catch in a metal support jutting from the wooden struts. Throwing caution to the wind, she jerked wildly to free her skirt, for she had heard the echo of her pursuer's indrawn breath in the adjoining room.

She ripped free, but in the process the offending piece of metal came loose and the whole frame tottered crazily.

"Where the hell are you?"

In answer came a deafening boom as the wine rack collapsed

onto the stone floor, followed by a host of smaller reports as hundreds of wine bottles toppled free to meet a similar fate.

With the duke's furious curses ringing in her ears, Alexandra fled along the narrow aisle between the wine racks, shivering as she passed through a thick veil of spider webs. Dust lay heavy on the floor at the end of the room, and she was coughing by the time she reached her goal. She tugged at the knob, but the little door would not budge. Wild-eyed, she turned and pressed her back against the cool granite wall.

She heard the crunch of his boots upon the broken glass and inhaled the rich, sweet scent of grapes and decay.

"By God, when I get my hands on you—"

Alexandra's heart was hammering wildly when Hawke's taut features appeared. His eyes were silver fire as he closed the distance between them. "First you attack my roof, and now you demolish my wine cellar. I'll make you pay for every damned bottle!"

"Stay back!" Alexandra cried, her voice high pitched and unnatural.

But Hawke did not stop, nor did she imagine he would.

She turned, desperately tugging at the thin strips of wood that cradled dust-covered bottles. The rack began to sway.

"Stop! Those bottles are forty years old!"

The whole frame gave way, and Hawke barely had time to duck before wood and glass crashed explosively to the floor.

From the other side of the wreckage Hawke studied Alexandra, tight lines of fury etching his face. "You little bitch," he said softly, the sound more frightening that any bellow.

Slowly, he stepped over the fragments of glass and wood. Alexandra sank back against the wall, trapped once again. Hard fingers circled her wrist and hauled her out of her hiding place.

"What kind of hellcat are you? Oh, yes, I'll make you pay for every one, Alexandra," Hawke said roughly, his eyes burning across her slim shoulders and heaving chest. "It will give me almost as much pleasure as the wine."

He pushed her roughly back toward the wall, trapping her against the hard line of his chest. Without taking his eyes from her face he reached behind him and lifted a bottle from one of the last remaining racks. His eyes played across the dusty glass for a moment. "1776—a bad year for English sovereignty but a very good year for brandy." His muscled thighs ground against Alexandra while he lifted the bottle and pulled out the cork with his teeth.

"Try some, Miss Mayfield."

Alexandra's face was white, drained of any color as he forced the bottle into her mouth.

"Drink, damn it!"

"I won't, you arrogant—" She choked as the fiery spirits rushed into her mouth. She clawed at his chest, coughing violently as more brandy flooded down her throat. The fumes were thick in her nostrils, and she swayed dizzily.

Abruptly, the bottle left her lips. "Not so greedy. Leave some for me." Effortlessly, Hawke pressed closer still, capturing her hands between their straining bodies. Carefully he raised the bottle to his lips and drank long and hard, stopping only when no more than an inch remained at the bottom of the vessel.

"You waste good brandy, sir," Alexandra hissed, twisting helplessly. But his massive body could not be shifted. In the struggle the sleeve of her nightgown was pushed low on her shoulder, and the sheer fabric parted to reveal the pale curve of her breast.

Hawke's eyes were molten flames as he feasted upon her ivory beauty.

"Not at all, my little hellcat." With cold deliberation he tilted the bottle, splashing the remaining brandy across the white expanse of her skin. He chuckled, low and coarse. "I prefer to sample the rest from a different vessel."

Dizzy from the spirits he had forced upon her, Alexandra felt the room sway. The lanterns suspended at intervals from the ceiling danced crazily. Suddenly, she felt his warm lips upon the curve of her breast, plundering her skin, licking away every drop of the brandy he had poured there.

"Stop," she gasped as his lips traced a fiery path across her heaving chest. Lower they dipped, tracing the furled bud of her nipple through the sheer veil of lace. "Please," she moaned. But then he tugged powerfully, and suddenly nothing stood between her and the exquisite torment of his teeth and tongue.

I must not give in! Alexandra thought wildly. Not to this vile, arrogant devil. She might have been bested, but she would never surrender willingly. "You cannot force desire, you cur! All the wealth in the world cannot do that!"

The fingers at her shoulders tightened sharply. Then his tongue surged beneath the lace edge of her gown and freed the rest of her skin to his touch. "Shall we see about that, my dear? How much did Telford offer you—one hundred pounds? Two hundred?"

His lips suckled her tight bud, pulling fiercely until she felt a flash of lightning shoot out from the aching point of contact. "Nothing," she moaned. "I know no Telford."

She felt as much as heard his sharp laughter. "Three hundred, then—and all the pleasure your silken body can take." He did not wait for her answer, and his lips dipped again to their relentless torment.

Fire licked at the edges of her consciousness as she freed one hand from between them. She ran trembling fingers along the shelf at her back. "I don't want your money. And you can take your pleasure and—"

His head lifted, and Alexandra checked herself, afraid that he had discovered her hand was free. Then his full lips curved. "Liar! I can feel the answer in your heartbeat. You feel the fire just as I do." His eyes were cynical, for he did not doubt the outcome. "What is your answer, Miss Mayfield? Do you stay with my wife's brother, or do you throw in your lot with me?"

At that moment Alexandra's fingers closed upon a dust-covered rim of glass. She blinked, and hope surged through her. "My answer, Your Grace?" she repeated, her voice high and unsteady. "Why, that even hawks must sometimes sleep."

The man at her breast had barely raised a questioning brow when a heavy glass bottle crashed down upon his head. He studied her with a stunned look, and Alexandra panicked, afraid that she had not hit him hard enough. She should have known he would have a thicker skull than a normal human being!

And then, very slowly, he sank to his knees and pitched forward against the curve of her belly, where he collapsed with a ragged groan. For a moment Alexandra could not move. She'd done it! Nor had it been so very difficult, she thought exultantly.

The duke's full weight was upon her now, his head resting

against her waist, his arms dangling uselessly around her shoulders.

Blaze and bother! What was she supposed to do with the big oaf now?

With a fierce effort she struggled to push away his dead weight. He was heavier than she had expected, and she was panting by the time she maneuvered him into the corner and propped him against the wall.

With a sigh of relief she stood back and wiped the fine haze of sweat from her brow. She felt a prickling on her chest where the brandy had dried to a sticky sheen. Carefully, she stepped over the wreckage of the wine cellars, wincing when her bare feet met fragments of glass.

The long shredded remains of her peignoir billowed out behind her as she ran through the vaulted room to the narrow stairway, and victory sang through her delirious mind like the fiery spirits he had forced upon her.

Her step was light as she sprang up the rough stone stairs and back down the corridor to the Great Hall. Then, at last, the massive oak door was before her.

Stifling a cry of happiness, she sprang forward, twisting the knob sharply. The door opened with a loud metallic squeak, and Alexandra threw caution to the winds. As she scuttled down the front steps through the globes of light cast from the large lanterns on each side of the door, her feet fairly flew in the still night.

The stables loomed up before her in the darkness, a single lantern burning at the open gate. Warily, she crept inside.

Shifting shadows played across the planks of the empty stalls. From somewhere to the rear came a snort, then an answering neigh. Carefully, she made her way across the straw toward the closest stall.

"Kin I help ye, Yer Grace?"

Alexandra jumped and spun about. A dark-haired groom was studying her with a puzzled look. Immediately, she drew herself to her full height and studied him haughtily. For once, she would use her cursed resemblance to the infernal duchess to her own advantage. "Get me my horse," she said curtly.

The servant's eyes flashed across her sheer peignoir for an instant, and then he looked away, his face flooding crimson. "Blue-bell?" he asked nervously. "Don't know as I should—that is, the duke didn't say nothing about—"

Alexandra cut him off imperiously. "If you value your position here, you'll get the horse and be quick about it!"

"Yes, Yer Grace," the man mumbled, then lurched off toward the rear of the stables with Alexandra close behind. They stopped before an open stall, where a fine roan mare was contentedly chewing oats. Big brown eyes looked up at Alexandra with interest.

"Leave me," she said icily, desperate to be away, knowing Hawkesworth might appear at any moment.

The groom disappeared, and Alexandra moved closer, running a hand down the mare's silky back, crooning gently. The animal danced skittishly for a moment, then settled down, whistling happily through flaring nostrils as Alexandra stroked her soft neck.

Good, Alexandra told herself. Now all she needed was a bridle. On the far wall she saw a series of wooden pegs hung with bridles, crops, and blankets. Her fingers trembled as she chose a bit, and some instinct made her take down the riding crop that hung nearby before turning back to the docile mare.

"Steady, Bluebell," she whispered. "Let's take a little ride, shall we?"

Anxiously, she picked up a saddle and slung it over the horse. With quick fingers she tugged at the girth, tightening it to fit, feeling the loss of every precious minute.

"Going somewhere, Miss Mayfield? With my horse?"

Alexandra gasped when she heard the angry voice behind her. The animal was between them, her last chance at escape. With raw energy born of desperation, she pulled herself up into the saddle and drove the surprised Bluebell toward the black mouth of the stables, forcing the duke to step back as she passed.

"Not with my horse, damn you!" Hawke's hesitation was only momentary, and his long legs soon closed the gap. Disturbed by the threat in her master's voice, Bluebell slackened her pace. Hawke's fingers caught Alexandra's ankle and tore her from the horse.

"Now at least I shall know how to treat you—like the conniving trollop you are!" His hands circled her fragile wrists, and he jerked her against him, forcing her arms painfully behind her back. "I should have left a guard at your door. A few days without food and water would have made you a more amiable companion."

"Let me go, damn you!" Alexandra struggled vainly against the bite of his cold, iron fingers. "Are you afraid to use the word? 'Tis no *companion* I am, but your *captive*. Your *prisoner!*"

"*Prison* is such an unpleasant word, Miss Mayfield. Have you any notion of the unspeakable things that go on in a place like Newgate? Life with me, on the other hand, would have certain— compensations. But first—" He studied her appraisingly for a moment, then slung her up over his broad shoulder with appalling ease and stalked toward an empty stall.

"Damn your black heart, let me go!" Alexandra cried fiercely. Dear God, she had been so close to freedom!

"Not until it suits me to. We've some unfinished business, you and I, and now is as good a time as any to settle it."

"I'll get away!" Alexandra shouted as she arched her body and pummelled his back. "You'll never hold me! This is England, not some isolated caliphate in the Hindu Kush. There are laws against such barbarity!"

"On my lands you will find that I am law and rajah, my dear. No one will challenge any order I give. Only *you* have yet to accept that fact. But I mean to teach you now."

With a smooth ripple of his powerful muscles, Hawke flipped Alexandra forward and tossed her down into a bed of straw lining the freshly cleaned stall. From the floor she looked up at him, contempt, dismay, and fear playing across her features.

Hawke's lips were set in a thin white line. Slowly, he reached to the wall beside him and took down the leather strap that hung there.

Alexandra felt the last drop of blood drain from her face. "You wouldn't dare!" she whispered hoarsely.

"Oh, but I would, Alexandra. In fact, in your case it's a positive necessity. I'd be doing my fellow man a disservice if I let you roam about inflicting your willful ways upon an unsuspecting populace." As he spoke, Hawke brought the leather strap down sharply against his open palm.

With a little moan Alexandra jumped up and tried to scale the wooden planks of the stall, desperately searching for a toehold so she could climb out of his reach. But her weight fell suddenly onto her weak ankle, and she swayed and slid back down to the straw.

Then her fingers touched the smooth leather of the riding crop hidden in the folds of her skirt. Frozen, she waited as Hawke closed the distance between them. When he reached for her, she whipped the crop savagely across his face, watching in horrified fascination as a line of blood sprang from the wound.

With a snarl Hawke tore the crop from her trembling fingers, caught her waist, and flung her down in the straw. In the next instant he hauled Alexandra prone across his knees, and she fought his efforts to drag the full skirt of her nightdress above her head. But her flailing feet lashed out in vain.

"Let me go, blackguard!"

For a moment Hawke did not move. Her breasts were crushed against his thighs, and he could feel the firm crests at their center. Her straining hips were smooth and slender, the ivory skin silken to his touch. He went rigid as a savage burst of desire ripped through his groin at the sight of her nakedness.

In spite of everything he wanted her. He wanted to take her there in the straw, to turn her over and feel her long legs wrapped about his waist.

To make her shudder and pant with pleasure as he filled her. Again and again.

"You really are a cripple, aren't you!" she cried, the sound muffled by the straw at her face. "Do you blame *that* on her too?"

Hawke's face darkened with fury, his desire abruptly forgotten. A moment later, the last fragile vestiges of her gown ripped beneath his angry fingers.

White with shame and rage, Alexandra felt a cold draft play across her buttocks.

Thwack! Without warning the crop snapped down against her tender skin. She bit her lips sharply to keep from crying out, feeling hot tears splash over her cheeks. "Bastard!" she cried angrily, writhing against him. Dimly, she realized it was Hawke's hard hand and not a riding crop that set its burning brand upon her tender flesh.

Somehow this realization made the ignominy ten times worse.

"You'll soon learn to obey me, little hellcat!" Hawke growled.

"Never!" she screamed hoarsely, fighting the burning pain.

Thwack! Hawke delivered another stroke just below the first.

"You may go s-straight to hell, Your Grace!" she choked out.

Half blinded by tears of rage and pain, Alexandra struggled vainly against the iron grip that pinned her against his thighs. "Do you need this to make you feel like a man?" she cried. "You enjoy inflicting pain, don't you? Maybe that's why your wife bolted!"

Suddenly, the duke's thighs went rigid beneath her chest.

Alexandra flinched and tried to twist away from the next blow, but Hawkesworth ruthlessly held her where she was. Her choked sobs echoed in the sudden stillness as the seconds stretched out, but the blow never came.

"Who spoke to you of such things?" Hawke demanded harshly. "Telford?"

She was crying now, sobbing openly. "The Devil take you and your bloody brother-in-law! It doesn't require a monumental intellect to see that you're nothing but a shell of a man."

"Who?" Hawke repeated fiercely, all his suspicions aroused. He turned her across his rigid thighs until her tear-streaked face blazed up at him. "But we both know that only one man would twist the truth so," he growled. "And that's Telford, of course. But he's no match for me. I bested him once already, when I caught him selling secrets to the French, and he'll lose this round as well. Where will that leave you?" Hawke's fingers dug into Alexandra's forearms. "Here with me, that's where, and you'll soon find I'm very much a man, Alexandra—all bone and fire and hungry muscle."

Alexandra's laugh was half wild. "I'd like to grind those bones to dust!"

"That, my dear, might be a highly pleasurable experience, judging by the success of the last time I bedded you." His eyes glittered as they studied the dim streaks on her cheeks. "Perhaps even now you carry my child," he said, an odd tension in his voice.

Alexandra's face creased in ludicrous dismay as she grasped his meaning. Her wet lashes glistened against eyes as angry as the Channel in a spring storm. She was too furious to speak; she could have done no more than croak at that instant.

Unconsciously, her fingers stole to her slim waist and fanned out over the gentle hollow of her stomach. "Impossible!" she whispered.

"Not at all," the duke answered. "Unlikely perhaps, but hardly impossible."

She had never considered this. Right now she might be carrying a child—the Duke of Hawkesworth's child.

His bastard, rather.

"You'll get no bastard child from me, Your Bloody Grace!" she cried when she could once again speak.

A vein drummed at Hawke's temple, and his hand bit into her fingers. Suddenly, he gripped Alexandra's wrists and pulled her up until her face was only inches from his. "But perhaps that is precisely Telford's intention. Perhaps he means to use a child against me."

Alexandra's aquamarine eyes were huge with disbelief. "You think that—you believe—" she stammered, then continued in a ragged voice. "Know this then. If I do carry a child, the babe will be mine and mine alone. Neither you nor anyone else will ever take it from me to play your infernal games!"

She was telling the truth, Hawke realized, mesmerized by the sea-green fury of her eyes. "I hope you mean that," he said finally. "It will go hard with you if I find you've lied." His grip on her wrists loosened fractionally.

"Remember what *I* have said, as well. My child—if I carry a child—is mine alone, not your chattel!"

"*Our* child, Alexandra. Yours and mine." A strange light pierced the changeable silver depths of Hawkesworth's eyes, and his voice dropped to a murmur. "Man must fill woman, planting his seed deep so woman can hold and ripen. Two are needed to create a new life, you know."

"I'm not likely to forget that fact, Your Grace. No matter how hard I try," she added bitterly.

It was then that Alexandra realized Hawke's hands were no

longer restraining her. Immediately, she struggled upright in his lap, her face fiery red as she tugged at her tattered garment. She tried to rise, but the flimsy cloth was caught between his thighs. "Release me, knave, so I can return to my cursed prison."

"To stay, or to plot your next escape?"

Alexandra's buttocks were burning. At that moment she wanted nothing more than to escape this relentless scrutiny and tend to the welts rising along her tender skin, but something in his challenge made her answer with angry bravado. "You can't keep me here by force. I'll never rest until I've found a way out!"

Hawke's eyes narrowed, and his mouth curled into a lazy smile. "Is it very uncomfortable?"

Would she ever be able to hide anything from this cursed man? Alexandra wondered. "Not nearly as uncomfortable as the slash upon your face, I hope."

Slowly, Hawke's fingers traced the fiery welt that ran from his temple to his chin.

Alexandra watched the silver fire playing in his eyes, a vein beating wildly at her neck.

"You might have been killed," he said roughly. "We're not so far from the chalk cliffs. In the dark you and Bluebell might have fallen to your deaths, with no one the wiser."

"That might have suited you very well."

"On the contrary. I have much better uses for you." His eyes glittering, Hawke freed the lacy fabric from beneath his thigh, and immediately Alexandra pulled away. With lazy grace he rose and extended his arm to her. "Now you will accompany me back to the house—before we give the servants anything more to gossip about."

"What choice have I?"

"None at all." His hands circled her wrists, pulling her to her feet. " 'Tis a dangerous game, Alexandra, and you're far out of your depths. I don't know what Telford has promised you, but you'll find it a bad bargain. My offer is infinitely better."

Not for the first time, Alexandra felt as if she'd stumbled into a nightmare. "Offer bedamned! As always, you twist everything to suit your suspicious imagination! I want nothing to do with either of you, nor this infernal game you play."

Hawke's fingers tightened on her wrists. "Then tell me your real name."

"I—I've already told you." Even now, some instinct warned her against revealing her identity. "Alexandra Mayfield."

"Which leaves us precisely where we started," Hawke said flatly.

Chapter Sixteen

That night a footman stood guard outside Alexandra's room. She could see his tall shadow flickering beneath the door in the dim light of the hall lantern. The sight filled her with fury, and once again she cursed her fate as a pawn in a cold-blooded game between two madmen.

Finally she dozed. She slept fitfully and awoke more tired than when she had first closed her eyes. There was no sound from the adjoining room, and the pale light behind the armoire told her the sun had barely crossed the horizon.

She went to wash her face in the basin on the dressing table, eyeing her shredded, wine-stained nightgown with disgust.

The morning passed slowly. Lily brought a breakfast tray and returned later with an elegantly trimmed gown of sapphire muslin, presented with the duke's compliments.

Alexandra dressed slowly, and the long minutes began to grate upon her nerves. A footman brought a luncheon tray, and she ate mechanically. A housemaid came to change the linens.

Sometime later, she heard the sound of approaching horses. Looking through the crack behind the armoire, Alexandra saw the duke standing below on the drive hailing a pair of mounted riders. One man was rather tall and sallow faced; his companion was quite astonishingly beautiful, Alexandra noted, and gave every appearance of being fascinated by her host.

Probably admiring neighbors who'd heard the great sahib was once more in residence, she thought angrily.

From the corridor came the sound of voices.

"This looks like the room," came a man's burly country voice. "Reck'n the whole structure up to the parapet'll have to go. Be a damned nuisance to replace, I kin tell ye."

Startled, Alexandra turned as a key twisted in the lock. The door opened on a footman, followed by two stocky laborers clad in heavy woolens.

"Beg pardon, Your Grace, but these gentlemen"—the footman said the word with an audible sniff—"have come to repair the broken parapet. Perhaps you'd care to wait in His Grace's room."

Alexandra turned and followed the footman into the duke's room, which was dominated by a huge bed hung with brown and gold tester and hangings. Just like the duke, she thought furiously —overblown and overwhelming.

The room was large and airy, occupying the southwest corner of the house. One entire wall was lit by high mullioned windows that opened onto a sweeping view of the downs, and Alexandra fancied she could make out the glint of the Channel coast far in the distance.

Mesmerized by the view, Alexandra barely heard the workmen commence their hammering. The footman closed the connecting door, and outside in the hall she heard Lily's quiet voice, followed by the muffled pad of feet down the corridor.

Several minutes later, the connecting door opened. Assuming it was the footman, Alexandra did not immediately turn.

"Beg pardon, Yer Grace."

Alexandra turned to see one of the workmen standing on the threshold, wooden mallet in hand. "Do you require this room as well?" she asked in surprise.

"No, Yer Grace," the man said. He took a step closer, then another. Suddenly brash, he scanned the low bodice of her sapphire gown, his narrow-set eyes tightening with interest.

Something about his look made Alexandra shudder. "In that case I suggest you return to your work," she said coldly.

" 'Tis my work that brings me here now. Aye, 'tis fer ye I've come. Yer Grace," he added, almost as an afterthought.

Alexandra's eyebrows rose. "For me?"

"Yer lookin' fer a way out of this pile, so I hear, and I've got it." His eyes flashed once again to the creamy swell of her chest.

"Out? But how—"

"No questions. We ain't got much time before that bleedin' footman returns." He crossed the floor quickly, taking her arm and pulling her toward the adjoining room, where a large wooden crate stood open, its heavy wooden lid supported by the second workman.

"There's yer ticket out o' here," the man beside her said, pushing her toward the door.

Alexandra's thoughts were whirling wildly. "But—who sent you?"

"No bleedin' questions, I said!" The narrow-set eyes hardened. "Ye want to get out o' here or not?"

"Yes, of course, but just tell me—"

"Then shut up and get in. Ye'll have all the time ye want fer questions once we're away from here."

Alexandra's spine prickled with uneasiness. She took a step back, noticing that the man's teeth were rotten and foul smelling. Then his hand clamped down hard upon her shoulder, and she felt the rigid outline of a pistol at her back.

With a muffled curse the man thrust her toward the crate. At the threshold Alexandra lost her footing and swayed unsteadily.

"Help me," she said weakly, raising her arm to clasp his shoulder for support.

His black eyes widened speculatively as she fell against his chest. "Wouldn't I like to do just that, lovey. Give ye somethin' to remember me by, wouldn't I just!"

Ruthlessly, he dragged her across the room. When Alexandra felt the crate at her back, she twisted furiously, knocking his pistol to the floor and kicking it back under the bed. But she had time for no more before thick hands picked her up and flung her into the dark wooden interior.

With a choking cry Alexandra struggled to rise. An instant

later, a dirty hand slammed over her mouth. Twisting wildly, she sank her teeth into the man's fingers.

"Bloody bitch!" The man's palm crashed down on her cheek, throwing her back against the side of the crate. For a moment blackness closed over her and a strange high-pitched whine rang in her ears. "Get the gag!" A filthy cloth was crammed between her lips and jerked tightly around her neck. "Move again, and I'll hit ye hard enough to set ye sleepin' fer a week!"

The man's leering face swam before her as she tried weakly to rise. The next moment his mallet crashed into her skull. The cold cruel smile continued to mock her, the last thing she saw before blackness exploded behind her eyes.

Sequestered in his study, Hawke pushed aside a pile of papers and spun the large globe beside his desk. Before him lay two envelopes sealed with the Hawkesworth crest. As he turned the globe thoughtfully, one forefinger touched the smooth wood. Finally the globe came to a rest, and the duke looked down and saw his finger upon the green spike of India.

What was it about her? he wondered. Was the woman what she seemed, or was she part of Telford's cunning maneuvers?

His letters would soon yield an answer and he would find out everything he needed to know about his beautiful captive—including her real name, for he didn't believe her story for a moment.

A quiet tapping came at the door, and Davies entered. "Luncheon is served, Your Grace. I trust you will not be disturbed by the noise, for the stonemasons have come to repair the roof, as you ordered."

Hawke spun the globe idly, strangely unwilling to let go of that small space in the middle of the Indian Ocean. "Masons?" he said absently. "I ordered no masons. When did they arrive?"

"Not more than twenty minutes ago, Your Grace."

An instant later, the duke's silver-gray eyes darkened and he leaped across the room toward the gun case. "How many were there?" he demanded sharply.

"Two, Your Grace," Davies answered, totally bewildered. "But I thought—"

"Go and get Hardy," the duke interrupted, taking down a pair of Swiss precision target pistols. "Then meet me on the third-floor landing of the servants' stair."

Alexandra felt a sickening pain at her temple, followed by a wild lurch of the floor beneath her feet. Something sharp and heavy banged against her shoulders. She tried to scream, but the cloth at her mouth prevented any sound from escaping her raw lips.

Again and again the crate lurched, and each time, she was dropped with savage pain against the rough wooden slats. She tried to move, but her hands were bound behind her.

I'm helpless, she thought furiously, trussed like a chicken for slaughter. She pounded the wall of the crate with her feet, but the muffled sound was lost in the deafening crash of the crate being dropped down the steps.

Boots crunched upon rock, and she knew they had left the stairs and were now upon the drive.

Where was the damned duke when she needed him?

The crate tilted sharply. Wood splintered against wood, and suddenly she was jerked upright once more. A horse whinnied somewhere nearby.

"Let's get out o' here!"

With a sickening lurch they began to move down the drive. They were in some sort of wagon, Alexandra realized—a farm wagon, judging by the protesting creak of the heavy wooden wheels. The crate shook unpleasantly, the vibration piercing her very bones.

The air closed in around her, dank and suffocating. Sweat broke out on her brow. She could feel the drops run down her cheeks, but she was powerless to wipe them away.

"Spring 'em, man!"

A whip cracked, and the wagon lurched crazily, rumbling across the gravel.

Too late! Alexandra thought wildly, and felt a strange desire to laugh. What would the proud Hawke say when he discovered his precious hostage gone, stolen from under his nose?

She tasted hot salty drops upon her lips and knew that they were tears.

"Stop!" Running feet hammered across the drive, and a pistol exploded somewhere to her left.

"Please!" she cried, the sound no more than a ragged whisper. Again a pistol thundered, closer this time.

"Stop, or I'll put the next ball through your bloody heart!"

Her own heart lurched as she heard the driver's graphic curse, and a moment later, the brake was thrown, wood grinding in protest against wood.

Before they even came to a halt, she heard the sickening sound of flesh meeting flesh, followed by a dull, muffled thump. A heartbeat later, strong fingers hammered at the wood above her head.

"If the woman's hurt, by God, I'll—"

The crate sprang open. Suddenly, Alexandra was surrounded by light and space and clean, fresh air. Warm bronzed hands removed the cloth at her lips. At first she could not see; then her vision cleared, and she looked up into piercing silver eyes.

Eyes that burned over her face and twisted body, as if to assure himself that she was alive and unharmed.

Tormented eyes.

Alexandra tried to speak, but she was racked with a dry spasm of coughing.

"Don't talk," the Duke of Hawkesworth said, reaching down to cut the rope at her wrists. "Tie them up, Davies, and lock them in the ice house until the riding officers come. That should cool the bastards off."

Strong fingers closed upon Alexandra's shoulders, and she felt herself lifted against a broad chest. Warm muscles shifted beneath her cheek, and she heard the muffled hammering of Hawke's heart. A tiny whimper escaped her gritted teeth.

Without a word he strode across the drive and into the house, carrying her as easily as if she were a child. She felt weightless and mute, as if caught in that numb state between waking and sleep.

Hawke kicked open the door to her room with his boot and deposited Alexandra into a chair.

On his lap.

His long fingers pushed the tangled curls from her face and traced the angry bruise along her cheekbone. "Here—drink this."

A cold glass touched her numb lips, and something twisted

inside her. Something that banished numbness and fear, making this coercion the final blow. "No!" she screamed, twisting away, then fighting in earnest, balling her hands into fists and striking wildly. "I'm sick to death of being ordered about, do you hear? Sick to death of being shut in, of having foul things forced down my throat!" Alexandra was shouting now and tears streamed down her face as she rained frenzied blows across his massive chest, his forearms, his shadowed face. "Most of all, I'm tired of being a pawn in this unspeakable game between you two madmen!"

Again and again, she pummelled him while he sat motionless beneath her flying fists. He did not try to protect himself. Finally, the long frenzied outburst passed, and Alexandra's choking wrath subsided.

Her tired, stinging fists slowed their wild flailing. Her heart pounded as she waited, expecting him to pin her hands behind her and force the drink down her throat at any moment.

Surprisingly, he did not.

"It was only meant to make you more comfortable." There was a curious tension in Hawke's voice. "You're safe now. I'll force nothing upon you." His voice cut into her whirling thoughts—soothing, coaxing.

Listlessly, Alexandra let her hands fall to her lap. She turned and stared into smoky eyes alive with molten flecks of silver. Eyes almost tender, just now. His lips twisted, and she wondered suddenly how they would feel against her raw, swollen mouth.

Hawke's head moved, and for a moment she thought he meant to kiss her. To her infinite fury she felt something very much like a stab of disappointment when he did not.

Dear God, was she losing her mind?

Abruptly, strong hands lifted her from his lap and settled her back against the cushions of the chair.

"I've got to see to those two. Stay here and rest," he ordered gruffly. "I'll send Lily up to stay with you until I return."

But I don't want Lily.

Alexandra's haunted eyes followed his broad back as he crossed the room, and she felt a moment of raw terror at his leaving.

Never! she cried in silent rage. That way lies madness!

"I don't want Lily," she rasped then. "I don't want you or this house or the safety you promise. I want only my freedom!"

"I'm afraid that's not possible, Alexandra," Hawke said roughly. "Especially now that Telford knows you're here." He pointed to the window, which framed green rolling lawn and trees beyond. "There's probably someone out there watching us right now, awaiting Telford's next orders. Perhaps he even has a spy here in the house, recruited from among the staff. He's a desperate man, Alexandra, and he'll stop at nothing to destroy me. You must see that by now. I might release you, but *he* never would, and you'd soon be broken to his will, forged into an instrument of his revenge. Understand this—he would use you against me in any way he could, and his cruelty knows no bounds. Your only protection is to stay here with me."

"No!" Alexandra cried, for she had begun to glimpse a greater peril, one more dangerous than cruelty at the hands of a stranger. "You can't watch me every second. Someday you'll blunder, and I'll be gone before you notice."

"Then, my dear," her captor said flatly, "you are a greater fool than I could imagine."

Hawke was in a foul mood when he thundered down the stairs. By the time he finished interrogating the two ruffians in the ice house, his fury was white hot.

As he had feared, the men had no idea who'd paid for their services. Once again, Telford had outmaneuvered him, cleverly concealing any connection with the kidnapping, careful to keep all communication through intermediaries.

Hawke did not immediately return upstairs, feeling a curious reluctance to face the woman waiting there. Somewhere in the back of his mind, he still wondered if Alexandra had been in league with Telford all along and whether her abduction was part of their plan. Perhaps Telford had sent the two hirelings to bring her back without arousing the duke's suspicions. Perhaps the bastard had meant to bait a trap using Hawke's lovely captive.

But Hawke did not really believe that. Not anymore. Alexandra's pain and fear had been too real, and the bruise on her cheek was genuine.

And so at last the arrogant Duke of Hawkesworth was forced to face the fact that sheer coincidence had brought Alexandra Mayfield across his path. From the start she had been an innocent victim of the deadly game of cat and mouse between him and Telford.

But now the contest was nearing its finish. Telford's funds must be growing low, driving him to take ever greater risks. Yet Hawke knew his old enemy, the man who had already tried twice to kill him, would never stop until he finally succeeded.

Unless Hawke killed him first.

Alexandra was sitting in the wing chair when Lily knocked at the connecting door a few minutes later. The red-haired beauty frowned when she saw a swirl of green silk and white lace draped over the maid's arm.

"His Grace explained about the misunderstanding," the girl began hesitantly. "Your resemblance to the duchess and all, I mean. Proper frightenin' to think two strangers could look so much alike. He said as how you'd be joinin' him at table and would be needin' these, Your—beg pardon, Miss Mayfield." As she spoke, Lily held up the shimmering length of bottle-green silk.

Alexandra did not move, still stunned by her encounter with the coarse intruders. If Hawke had come a minute later . . . if Davies had not alerted him to the unplanned visitors . . .

A tremor shook her, then she raised her chin defiantly. Damn the lot of them! It would take more than two ruffians to frighten her. And as for the Duke of Hawkesworth, Alexandra would show him that fear was foreign to her nature.

Through the southern windows the sun flashed upon the gossamer tissue satin in Lily's hands. Thoughtfully, Alexandra reached for the dress, which settled as light as a butterfly's wing against her shoulders. The long sleeves were caught in tight tiers of emerald ribbon from the elbow to the wrist. The dress was stunning, Alexandra thought, but very décolleté, caught in a low square neck that looked as if it would expose almost as much as it concealed. There was no question whose dress this was.

Alexandra stroked the delicate fabric thoughtfully. "Did the duchess often wear dresses so . . . ?"

"Skimpy like? This is actually the best of the lot, if you'll pardon me. A bit tame, by her standards. You should o' seen—" The girl halted suddenly, catching her lip in her teeth. She'd be sacked for carrying gossip if she weren't careful.

"Is there nothing else I might wear?"

The girl snorted. "You'd like the others even less than this, believe me."

Reluctantly, Alexandra reached for the chemise, a flimsy confection of white lawn trimmed with row upon row of lace. The low-tucked bodice fitted Alexandra tightly, forcing her bosom unnaturally high. With bated breath she slipped the emerald dress over her head, hearing the rich whisper of silk as it fell.

The large cheval glass winked back at Alexandra, showing a woman of exquisite beauty, a woman made for a man's pleasure.

She blushed at the expanse of creamy skin revealed by the low neck. An untoward movement might push her entirely from the dress, she thought in horror. Her brow furrowed, she bent to finger the lace at the bottom of the chemise.

Soon a length of filmy white trim lay on the bed. Scarcely ten minutes later, thanks to Lily's dexterity with a needle, Alexandra's décolletage was discreetly covered by sheer lace. Lily also discovered a length of embroidered ribbon, which she skillfully wove through Alexandra's hair, hesitantly confiding that this was the first time she had dressed a lady's hair. Her fingers were nimble, however, and the resultant Grecian style suited Alexandra to perfection. The careful disorder of ringlets cascaded upon her shoulders like a warm fire against cool, creamy skin.

"Oh, miss, you look ever so—so nice," the little maid confided impulsively, before stammering to a halt in confusion.

"Do you think so, Lily?" Alexandra gave her a warm smile. "The lace has given me a great deal more confidence, I must say."

"It's funny—you look the very picture of *her,* only ever so genteel like."

From the hall came the muted chime of a clock. Lily cried softly and caught her hand to her mouth. "Oh, miss, those be the chimes. Mrs. Barrows will be *that* angry if I've made you late!" She was already dashing toward the door.

Shadwell, the impassive, slightly stooped butler, was waiting to escort Alexandra to the duke. His lips seemed to tighten for an instant as Alexandra swept from the room. Then he turned and followed her down the richly carpeted corridor.

The sun filtered through the long windows of the Great Hall, lending a warm glow to the gleaming marble and fine old wood. Imperiously, Shadwell led her to the end of the north wing, stopping finally at the last door of the corridor. He knocked once, then entered at the quiet command from within.

A broad-shouldered figure stood silhouetted before the long French windows at the far end of the book-lined study. Slowly, the Duke of Hawkesworth turned, revealing buff breeches molded to muscular thighs. An elegant coat of dark blue superfine encased his wide shoulders perfectly, revealing the touch of a master tailor. His linens were snowy white, their sole adornment one small diamond.

Even from where she stood in the doorway, Alexandra felt this man's raw male power, barely concealed in his exquisitely tailored garments. He did not move, and she could not quite make out his expression, silhouetted as he was against the sunlight. She heard his words clearly, however, and they made her tremble.

"My God," Hawke said roughly. "It is as well that Isobel is not here. If she were, she would claw your eyes out in jealousy, Miss Mayfield."

Chapter Seventeen

By God, the woman was lovely, the Duke of Hawkesworth thought, stunned. Her burnished hair gleamed like molten bronze in the sun, a perfect counterpoint to the rich green of her gown. She looked far more beautiful in the garment than his wife ever had.

The duke frowned, trying to identify the exact differences between them. Perhaps it was her easy grace and the animation of her features. Isobel had always been cold and reserved, and her pride stemmed only from self-importance. But this woman's fire owed nothing to social position or fortune, Hawke decided; it sprang from her strength of mind and her self-possession.

Yes, the two were fire and ice, he decided, unable to tear his eyes from the vision before him. They grazed her creamy shoulders and her bodice. A tiny smile played across his lips as he saw the modest scrap of lace she had somehow secured across the gown's décolletage. Entirely enchanting, Hawke thought. Vitality burned within her fine eyes.

Suddenly recollecting his surroundings, Hawke nodded to dismiss the butler. "Thank you, Shadwell. I shall ring if we require anything further." Hawke watched her eyes travel across the book-lined walls to the desk littered with paper work.

A clear breeze wafted into the quiet room, and a green-winged butterfly floated through the French windows down a bar of late afternoon sunlight. It circled aimlessly for a moment, then settled on Alexandra's outstretched hand. The delicate wings slowed and fluttered closed.

Hawke's breath checked. Was he wrong to hold her longer at Hawkeswish? He'd ruined her already with his recklessness, and it was too late to change that. Yet without his protection, she would be easy prey for Telford.

And here, a mocking voice asked, *is she not in greater danger here?*

From the lawn came a raucous shriek, and a round shadow darkened the floor.

Alexandra drew closer to the open window but stopped short, out of reach of the motionless man who watched her so intently. Her skin prickled under his scrutiny. She had never known such a man, so potent, so disturbing. He infuriated her. He confused her.

Remember what he has done to you, Alexandra thought bitterly. Remember that he has violated you and would do so again.

On the lawn a peacock fanned open its feathers in a blaze of color. "I might have expected you to own peacocks," she said stiffly, watching the butterfly sail away to freedom.

"I'm afraid you can't lay the blame at my door. The damned creatures were Isobel's sole contribution to Hawkeswish, and they make an infernal racket day and night. I've tried to give them away, but no one will have them."

His eyes were bright as he studied her bodice measuringly. Alexandra's cheeks grew warm with embarrassment beneath his scrutiny.

"You've modified the dress, I see. Such a pity."

Get a grip on yourself, she thought furiously, turning back to the golden room, mellow with fine old wood and glowing leather. On the floor stretched a rich Aubusson carpet in tones of apricot, gold, and smoky crimson. She moved past a huge wooden globe to the claw-footed mahogany desk and lifted a slim leather volume that lay open among the papers.

Her eyes darkened, and she snapped the book closed sharply.

"You are interested in the Vellore mutiny?" she demanded. "Why?"

Hawke raised a questioning brow. "I am interested in many things, among them Indian affairs. I had no idea it was a crime." He moved to the desk, cutting through the ray of sunlight, and took the volume from her numb fingers. "*An Inquiry into the Mutiny at Vellore, with a Consideration of the Strange Customs of the Indian Sepoy,*" he read slowly. "But perhaps you could tell me more than this book."

Alexandra's expression hardened. "Perhaps I could, but you would not care for what I told you."

"And why is that?"

"Because the raw, unvarnished truth is rarely as pleasant as the exotic tales of starry-eyed travelers."

"You intrigue me, Miss Mayfield. Exactly what *is* your father's position in that country?"

"Was," Alexandra said bitterly. "He's dead now." A wave of regret washed over her, and she turned away, refusing to reveal any emotion to this man. "And I do not choose to discuss this further." Feigning coolness, she lifted a large volume from the bottom shelf of a nearby bookcase and placed it on the desk.

"I shall be delighted to hear your judgment of that particular book," Hawkesworth said silkily.

The face Alexandra raised a few moments later was a rich shade of crimson. "But these are—they show—" she stuttered.

"One of my grandfather's peccadilloes. The work of an obscure Italian genius, I'm told. Very rare. Quite valuable now." The duke's silver eyes glinted with humor as Alexandra thrust the book away from her. "Prinny's offered me a fortune for those prints," he added meditatively, "but I think I must suffer the royal displeasure and deny him. One never knows when they may prove . . . instructive."

"Have you no shame, Your Grace!"

"My father taught me that shame is for lesser mortals, Miss Mayfield," Hawke said quietly, suddenly serious. "A duke may count himself safe from such frailties."

"I see you are determined to be impossible. Perhaps it would be better if I returned to my room with a tray."

"Come," Hawkesworth said, an odd light in his eyes, "can't we call a truce? The evening will stretch long without company. And I have yet to offer you anything to drink." He walked to the crystal decanters arranged on a small chest behind the desk. "Will you have something before dinner? Sherry, perhaps? Unfortunately, I have very little in the way of brandy left to offer you," he added dryly.

"This is all a source of vast amusement to you, isn't it?"

The duke's eyes snapped with fury as he swung around. "On the contrary, Miss Mayfield! I am merely trying to make the best of a damnable situation. I suggest you do the same."

Alexandra stiffened. "I do not care to drink, Your Grace. It might be drugged."

"I give you my word as a gentleman that it is not."

"The word of a nobleman, perhaps. But a gentleman . . . ?" Her voice trailed off suggestively.

"I have called men out for less provocation than that," Hawkesworth said. "If I thought you meant it—but you have nothing to fear from me, Miss Mayfield," he added with soft mockery.

"I am not afraid of you!"

"Then it must be yourself you fear." Amber liquid spilled into a fragile goblet of etched crystal. Hawke held the goblet out to her in a silent challenge.

Alexandra rose to the bait, as Hawke had known she would. Two spots of color appeared in her cheeks. "A glass of sherry would be delightful, Your Grace," she announced defiantly, reaching for the glass.

The drink was sweet and wonderfully smooth. Immediately, she took another sip and then gracefully drained the glass, never taking her eyes from his face.

Hawke's eyebrows rose in a lazy slant. "You'd better go slowly there. This particular vintage has a deceptive smoothness."

She answered by holding out her glass to be refilled.

"Is it to be pistols at dawn then, Miss Mayfield?" Hawke asked as he poured her more sherry.

"I rather fancy swords, Your Grace. Exceedingly sharp swords."

"We might find better ways to resolve our differences, you know."

"I doubt it." Did his silver eyes narrow for a moment, or was it Alexandra's imagination? Damn the man! she thought, draining her glass rebelliously.

"Liar," Hawke said with soft violence.

"Let me go," she demanded. "That would resolve our differences."

"Impossible."

"I will go where this man Telford can never find me—up north, to Scotland perhaps."

"You have family there?" Hawke's tone was deceptively casual.

"No, but—"

"Then how do you expect to live?"

"What business is that of yours?" Alexandra asked, twisting the empty glass in her hands.

"You have become my business, Miss Mayfield, like it or not. Now, how do you plan to support yourself? Or would you rather not voice your methods aloud," he added cynically.

"As a governess! A decent enough occupation—something you would know little about!"

"Ah, but that is one thing you'll never do, my dear. Not now."

"And why not?" Her whole body was stiff with anger. "I am the daughter of a gentleman, the recipient of a sound education. I shall make an admirable governess, for I've more maturity than most females my age, and I've seen a great deal more of the world."

Hawke's look was lazy, knowing. "Your skills, unfortunately, are not in question. Rather, it is your beauty—and your association with me—that makes you unsuitable for any position as governess or companion. In a decent household, that is."

Alexandra blinked. "What association have I with you? None but Pence and your staff is aware of . . ." Her voice trailed off.

"Yes, Miss Mayfield? Do go on. Aware of what? That I kidnapped you, that I drugged you"—his voice hardened—"that I bedded you, believing you to be my perfidious wife?"

"None of them would tell," she whispered.

"But you forget that there is one other who certainly shares this secret. James Telford, a man who misses nothing. The one person more vile than my wife," the duke said with a tone of flat finality.

"But why—"

"I've never told anyone else about those years." Hawke's silver eyes probed her face for a moment, and then it seemed he came to some sort of decision. Without warning he turned and paced the room restlessly, his half-filled glass still in hand. "It's a long story, but I shall try to make it brief. I was at Corunna in 1808, did you know? It was . . . a nightmare. We were caught among the high passes in the driving snow. In the end six thousand men died between Astorga and the sea. The memory will haunt me always, I think. Perhaps that is why I agreed to become an unofficial adviser to the War Office upon my return from the Peninsula. In that capacity I often received communications of a strategic nature. Unfortunately, there were other things on my mind at the same time, and I was not as vigilant as I should have been," he added, his voice harsh with self-recrimination.

"Those 'other things' being Isobel, I presume." Suddenly, Alexandra understood a great many things about Hawke, including his obsession for Isobel.

He made her an ironic little bow. "Congratulations, my dear. You are very astute. Yes, as I was slowly being drawn into her web, Telford availed himself of his access to my house and stole military documents, which he sold to the French." Hawke's face was dark and lined, and his hand clenched and unclenched at his side. "When I realized what he had done, I very nearly killed him. As it was, he must have passed a very unpleasant six months recuperating from the beating I gave him." Hawke's eyes shone with savage satisfaction at the memory. "But you still do not understand, do you? I can see it in your eyes. James Telford is Isobel's brother. He has already tried to kill me twice, and he will not stop until he succeeds. I have become *his* obsession, you see." Hawke's mouth twisted in a mocking smile as he raised his glass. "So let us drink a toast, Miss Mayfield, to a truce and a new beginning. To your long and happy stay in my house. And perhaps, in time, to an end of Telford's meddling."

"I will drink," Alexandra said finally, horrified by the tale he had just told, "but I'll make no truce." With nerveless fingers she raised her glass and drained the sweet spirits, watching Hawke warily.

"Now sit down and tell me about India. I understand that it's worth a man's life to see the sun rising over the Himalayas." In a split second Hawke's mood had changed, and he was the urbane, unruffled host once more.

Stiffly, Alexandra seated herself in a gilt chair of apricot Spital-fields silk. She swirled her glass distractedly as she studied its pale contents. "Sharp colors. Clear light. Yes, they take the breath away," she said at last. "One does not easily forget such things—nor the sight of the sick and hungry in the streets. Yet even those people retain a certain dignity, a calm acceptance of their lot."

"Your parents?"

"Both dead," she said flatly, concentrating on the glass in her hand.

"I'm sorry."

Alexandra did not trust herself to look up then, afraid he would see naked pain in her face. Her fingers tightened on the fragile glass rim, and a moment later, with a high-pitched ring, the delicate crystal shattered in her hands.

Dumbly, she watched blood drip upon the golden flowers. Scattered glass fragments glistened in a bar of late afternoon sun.

Then the ragged glass stem was lifted from her hand. The duke's breath stirred her hair, and she felt his long powerful fingers raise her palm to his mouth and draw off the beads of blood.

Warm lips, she thought bitterly. Hated lips. The lips of her enemy.

A choked cry escaped from her throat. When she tried to pull away, he held her fast, and after a moment he drew a white square of linen from his pocket, pressing it firmly over her thumb.

"It's not a deep wound, fortunately."

How little you know, Alexandra thought. The wound is as deep as my life, and will surely never heal—for when I lost my father, I lost all I value most in the world. He was the best friend I ever had.

She wrenched her hand from his grasp. "Why do you not offer me another glass, Your Grace?" Yes, alcohol might clear her turbid thoughts and rouse her for the battle to come. For there would be a battle between the two of them, she had no doubt of that. He would not let her go without a struggle.

For a moment Hawke did not move. Did the little fool realize what she was doing? he wondered. Seeing her determined look, he offered her a new glass.

Alexandra promptly emptied half, enjoying the pleasant warmth that filled her stomach.

"Where did you make your home in India?"

"Everywhere—nowhere," she answered, unwilling to reveal much about herself. "We moved about a great deal. Later, we settled in the south, where we lived the longest. Sometimes at night I wake and still listen for the cries of the parakeets in the garden. But they do not come, and I—" She stopped abruptly, angry that she had revealed so much.

He stood before the empty grate, one boot upon the fender, studying her thoughtfully. "You miss it dreadfully." It was a statement rather than a question.

Alexandra shook her head, angry that he had seen so much. "It was a long time ago. Another lifetime, it seems now. The Hindus believe we live many lives, did you know, returning over and over, until we perfect our souls. Perhaps it's true—perhaps it would take many lifetimes to accomplish perfection."

The duke's sharp eyes swept across Alexandra's face. "So I've heard. It seems a strange way of thinking to me. But I suppose we all must find our own paths."

In spite of herself Alexandra felt a stab of curiosity about her enemy. He was a cold predator one minute and a witty host the next, asking the right questions to trigger a chain of memories. His attention was flattering and even seemed sincere, she thought curiously. Perhaps that was why she found herself answering at greater length than she intended.

She drained her third glass before she quite realized it, and the room began to radiate a hazy golden glow.

"Yes, this is a tolerable sort of room," she said, "even though it lacks punkahs, verandas, and nesting parakeets."

And so it was, Alexandra decided, enjoying the warmth that enveloped her and helped her to forget she was not there by choice.

Before she realized it, Hawke had crossed the room and replaced her empty glass on the silver tray.

His face was deeply lined as he stood above her. "And you are a great deal more than tolerable," he said, an odd tension in his voice.

"While *you*, as we both know, are an immoral scoundrel and a blackguard," she replied, driven by some inner demon to taunt him, to torment him as he had tormented her.

And at that precise moment Alexandra discovered she was not without weapons in this strange silent war that raged between them. She saw it in the tightening of her captor's jaw and in the fire that leaped into his smoky eyes. "Your eyes betray you," she said mockingly, glorying in the stiff set of his lips, "as does your mouth, for all that your upper lip is fine and correct. It's your lower lip that declares your real character, you see—arrogant and sensual—along with that unruly lock falling across your brow. Yes, bad character will out," she concluded mockingly.

A muscle flashed in Hawkesworth's jaw. "Since I am a scoundrel, I need feel no remorse for what I mean to do next, Miss Mayfield."

Alexandra did not move, lost in the raw passion that flared in his eyes, unaware that the battle lines had subtly shifted.

A discreet cough sounded from the doorway, where Shadwell hovered. How long he had been there, Alexandra could not say.

"Dinner is served, Your Grace."

The meal was long and unhurried. From pheasant, saddle of mutton, and ragout with truffles to feather-light soufflés, Mrs. Barrows had outdone herself. At some point the dishes began to blur, and Alexandra had to concentrate to respond to the duke's questions. All the while, she did little more than toy with the sumptuous fare, for her appetite had deserted her.

Dessert was simple, in keeping with the duke's custom. There were strawberry meringues and pears steeped in red wine and offered with thick cream. Vaguely, Alexandra wondered how their cook obtained such things out of season.

And always there was an array of wine—Burgundy, hock, and claret. Later came sweet, rich dessert wines—brandy, port, and muscatel. The duke made no demur when Alexandra consumed

several glasses. When his arrogant black brows rose in a questioning slant, the effect was only to spur Alexandra on in her determination to show she was not afraid—of him *or* of herself.

Oh, yes, I shall beat you at this game! Alexandra vowed. She
had often taken wine and after-dinner liqueurs with her father,
who enjoyed discussing government affairs with his keen-witted
daughter.

But Alexandra forgot that she had eaten very little and that she
had soon consumed more spirits than she had ever been allowed
to consume before.

Across the lamplit table, Hawkesworth frowned. What was the
chit about? She'd drained glass after glass, straight through the
evening, in answer to his challenge. Did she really think she could
remain impervious to so much alcohol?

His eyes narrowed when she smiled up at the liveried footman
who was offering her a meringue. The poor man flushed, Hawke
noted with grim amusement.

And who would not, faced with that glorious smile, that flaw-
less skin? She was an exquisite flower and no man was safe from
her charms, he thought. In her own way she was as dangerous as
Isobel.

"And what did you do with the bear, Your Grace?" she demanded then, disturbing his musings.

"I took him to class with me, of course. He was at least the
equal of any of the junior scholars. The don, unfortunately, did
not see the matter in quite the same light, and I was sent down for
the rest of term."

"I trust your father taught you the error of your ways."

"I do not care to remember it, Miss Mayfield, even now. But as
he felt it was a useful occasion to begin educating me in estate
matters, the affair had a satisfactory conclusion. And now I believe I've bored you with my stories long enough. Come, I have
something to show you."

Alexandra was still smiling as she, too, rose from the table.
Only somehow, her feet were not where they were supposed to be,
and she swayed dizzily. Frowning, she accepted support from the
footman behind her.

The duke was at her side in a moment, circling her waist and taking her arm.

"Bother!" she said. "It is too infuriating! Why must my ankle begin to plague me now."

Hawke studied her with concern. "Is the pain considerable?"

"No, it's the clumsiness I detest. But I thank you for your assistance." As she spoke, Alexandra tried to pull away from him. Her heart hammered wildly when he did not immediately release her. "I do not believe I asked for your assistance," she said coldly.

Hawke's fingers tightened.

"You, Miss Mayfield, are foxed," Hawke said softly.

"Don't be *ridaculous!*" she snapped. "You, sir, are a liar! As well as a black-hearted scoundrel. Now release me this instant!"

"So that you can crack my skull once again? Or perhaps this time you mean to destroy my dining room."

"How soon you revert to your true detestable self!"

"What else do you expect of a rogue?"

"Nothing! Indeed, I infinitely prefer you thus—callous and ill-bred—for it is then so much easier to treat you precisely as you deserve."

The servants had left, and now only the two of them remained in the candlelit room.

"And how is that, Alexandra?" Hawke asked softly.

"As a common criminal."

"Neck stretched before a cheering populace? You'd enjoy that, wouldn't you, little hellcat?"

"Blishfully."

"I can think of a better sort of bliss."

"Not while I live and breathe!" she spat. Realizing she was being drawn inexorably closer, Alexandra twisted and swung wildly at her captor's chest. But her vision was oddly blurred, and suddenly she saw two jeering faces before her instead of one.

Hawke caught her hands with ease and trapped them between their bodies. "You have only begun to live, sweet Alexandra. I could teach you things that would make you forget how to breathe."

"Let me go!" she said unsteadily, caught by the silver flame of his eyes, by the shadows that danced on the chiseled planes of his face.

Still he held her, unwilling to relinquish her. "But then whom would you spar with?"

"A point well taken. 'Twould be difficult to find anyone as odious as you."

"Are you always so blunt?"

"Are you always so frightened by honesty?" she countered. "Men often are, I've discovered. Honesty cost me a great many suitors in India, but I count myself well rid of them. They were interested only in my—" Suddenly her mouth twisted in annoyance. "Blaze and bedamned!"

"In what, my dear? Your enticing body? Your sweet fire?" Hawkesworth could not pull his eyes from her enchanting face. Unconsciously, his grip tightened upon her arm. "If not, they were fools!" he muttered, his voice low and smoky.

The silver glints in his eyes danced crazily, and Alexandra wondered if she had indeed had too much to drink. Her pulse seemed ragged and unsteady, she noted with detachment. "No more than you are!" she retorted, and suddenly forgot what they were arguing about.

"Perhaps I am." Abruptly, the tension of his hands relaxed and, he turned to push her gently toward the door. "Come, Alexandra, I have something to show you."

"More of your indecent prints? No, thank you."

Hawke studied her soberly. "A thing of great beauty, of beauty nearly equal to your own."

"I do not trust you, Your Grace."

"Hawke," he whispered. "Call me Hawke."

"A fitting name for such as you—lean and cruel. A predator."

The dark lock of hair was once more upon his brow, Alexandra noted. She wondered how it would feel against her fingers. There was something about his scent, too, she decided, her brow furrowing in concentration. What was it? Light, spicy soap and old leather. The crisp smell of good wool. The dusky sweetness of wine. Unconsciously, she inhaled again, filling her lungs with the distinctive smell.

"So serious, Miss Mayfield? Are you afraid that under the wine's influence your true feelings will emerge?"

"You would *like* to see me slash you to ribbons?"

A reluctant chuckle escaped his lips. "Vixen," he said softly.

"Where are you taking me?" Alexandra demanded, disturbed by the dark intimacy of his tone. He was guiding her through a long narrow corridor to a part of the house that she had never visited.

"See for yourself." Hawke pushed open a door and steered her across a dark courtyard.

In the darkness she could see nothing. A door creaked before her, and then a gust of warm, damp air ruffled her hair, carrying the rich scent of flowers.

A moment later, Alexandra caught her breath. She saw before her a high vault of glass lit with hundreds of candles. Everywhere around her was greenery—a mad profusion of trees and plants and flowers.

"The greenhouses," Hawkesworth explained. "We grow our own vegetables here, as well as flowers and trees, so that we have fresh provisions nearly year round. The lilies for your bath were grown here too." He led her down a row of trees to a long workbench covered with tubs of white lilies.

"How lovely!" Alexandra cried, bending down and inhaling their rich fragrance. Suddenly, she felt dizzy. When she straightened, Hawke was close behind her, his warmth penetrating her thin silk dress. Slowly, she turned, as if caught in a dream. Around her the candles began to sway and leap, hundreds becoming thousands. Her throat was oddly dry. "What—what are you doing?"

"Something I've been wishing to do all evening," Hawke whispered, his voice low and urgent. Very carefully, he caught her flushed cheeks in his hands and smoothed their warmth with his thumbs.

Alexandra meant to fight him—indeed, her small hands curled into balls and rose to his chest. But once there they did not move, for somehow her being split, and suddenly she was two women— one proud and aloof, the other yearning for the touch of his mouth.

With infinite care he pulled her to him, pressing her against his muscled length, allowing her to feel his arousal. "God, how I want you!" he growled as his thumbs slid across her trembling mouth. "The taste of that sweet mouth on mine. The warm weight of your impudent breasts spilling into my hands."

Hawke's eyes glittered as he leaned close and slipped his warm lips over hers, brushing and kneading her mouth, letting her know his strength and his barely contained desire.

Blackguard! a dim voice warned. *Slap him!* But Alexandra paid no attention. Her thoughts were focused on the velvet texture of his mouth as he parted her lips and teased her with his tongue until she moaned slightly.

Suddenly, the world shifted upon its axis, and she would have fallen had Hawke not caught her in a hard grip.

"You've told me you're honest," he said. "If so, admit how you feel."

Alexandra's eyes were huge and luminous in the glow of the candles. When she spoke, her voice was no more than a whisper. "Foxed, actually." She licked her dry lips and saw his eyes flame at the unconscious seduction of the gesture. "That is, not foxed, precisely, but . . . I fear I ate too little at dinner. Perhaps I should have something more—"

Slowly, Hawke traced the lush curve of her lip with the pad of his thumb. "Ask, and I'll make you forget your hunger."

The candles danced and spun overhead, and rich-scented air filled Alexandra's lungs. Flushed, dizzy, and strangely languid, she closed her eyes. "And if I do not ask?" she said unsteadily, afraid of his answer, afraid of herself.

"You have said I'm a scoundrel. A scoundrel would not hesitate to plunder such enticing sweetness."

Alexandra's breath caught in her throat. She was not even aware that her hands had slipped behind his neck to comb through the dark locks nestled against his collar.

A moment later, she was swept up into impatient arms and crushed against his chest. He cursed, stumbling over some hidden obstacle in the dark, and her lips curved with wanton pleasure at his reckless desire, knowing it was she who had provoked it.

The night was rich and sultry with the perfume of flowers as he carried her to the far end of the cavernous room. Through a wall of glass Alexandra glimpsed a silver crescent moon riding low on the horizon, casting a pale bar of light upon a wicker chaise surrounded by potted orange trees.

Carefully, Hawke slipped her onto the soft cushions and knelt before her, his eyes like silver fire in the moonlight.

Alexandra blinked dizzily. She felt his warm breath against her bodice, then a current of cool air.

"This is the second damned thing I've been wanting to do all evening," Hawke muttered, cutting the thread on the dress with his teeth and pulling the wisp of lace away from the low neckline.

The curve of her chest rose and fell erratically, pale silver in the moonlight.

"So beautiful," he said softly, and traced her silken skin until he found her nipples against the tight bodice and slipped beneath to free them. Then his lips fell where his hands had been, and she moaned as a fierce wave of pleasure broke over her.

"Stop, please!" she moaned. "You make me dizzy. I will surely faint!"

Hawke laughed and caught her closer, teasing a taut nipple with his teeth. His lips curved with pleasure when he felt her slip back against the chaise.

Impatiently, he stood and shrugged out of his coat. Fires were kept burning here even in spring to protect the sensitive plants, and he was too damned hot. Sweat stood out in little beads upon his forehead. With a curse, he swept the moisture away and tossed his coat down onto the floor.

"I'll make you faint, by God!"

She did not answer.

"Alexandra?"

She sighed raggedly. Her bronze lashes fluttered; then closed.

"Alexandra!" he repeated sharply.

This time there was no response whatsoever.

"Hell and damnation!" Hawkesworth muttered in quiet astonishment, unable to believe the evidence of his eyes.

The wine had done its job too well. His impudent captive had fallen asleep on him!

Chapter Eighteen

The tavern was small, smoke filled, and very noisy. In every corner hung the stench of unwashed bodies and cheap gin. A ruddy woman with powerful forearms moved through the room dispensing tankards to man, woman, and child alike, snatching her patrons' money, careful to bite even the smallest coin before stowing it away in the pocket of her filthy, voluminous gown.

"More ale, Rose!" a drunken voice rose above the din.

"Hold your water, Jocko!" she bellowed back, to the merriment of the raucous patrons at the surrounding tables.

Just now, her attention was focused upon the richly dressed gentleman who sat by himself near the stairway to the upper floor. She must go lightly there, thought Rose Watkins, for there was a great deal of money to be made from this one.

"A message for yer hand, milord." She held out a single folded piece of paper. When the man did not bestir himself, she laid the note before him upon the rough-hewn table.

His long tapering fingers lifted the ivory sheet and scanned the crude handwriting. A rough expletive escaped the man's lips. "The bungling bastards!" James Telford whispered hoarsely. He'd have to try something even riskier now. Something that would force him to ride to Sussex this very night. But first . . .

The burly proprietress of the Lion frowned, seeing her dreams of profit going up in smoke. "Be wishin' anything else, Yer Lordship?" she asked quickly. "Anything at all, Rose Watkins can fetch it."

Cold, colorless eyes studied her for a moment, and in spite of all her years and experience and callousness, Rose Watkins shivered.

"I shall keep that in mind," he said, his soft voice in odd contrast to his sharp, expressionless eyes. "Perhaps you will tell me more about this man called Digger. In the meantime where is the girl?"

"Waitin' above, Yer Lordship, just as ye asked."

The man rose and carelessly tossed several gold guineas upon the greasy table. "See that we are not disturbed—for any reason."

Once again, the burly woman shivered, glad that she was too old and too blowsy for the flesh trade. Certainly not with *this* one.

The gentleman smoothed the crimson-silk folds of his waistcoat and slowly mounted the stairs. When he came to the room at the end of the hall, he turned the knob carefully, making no noise as he opened the door.

The shivering young thing inside did not immediately see him, but when she heard the light step, she spun about, thrusting a slim hand to her mouth.

The colorless eyes narrowed and ran down the girl's bony body, ill concealed beneath a grimy shift. Young enough, he thought. Skinny enough to be a boy. And terrified.

James Telford's spirits lifted fractionally.

The girl did not stir, for Rose Watkins had told her what would happen if she left this room before the rich gentlemen had finished with her. Even when the man reached into his pocket, she did not move. When she saw what he held in his hand, however, she began to whimper.

In a few short minutes her soft cries rose to shrill, terrified screams.

And then, miraculously, her prayers were answered. The door was thrown open to reveal the angry features of a beautiful angel.

"What's going on here?" the woman demanded, her blue-green eyes glittering as she took in the scene before her.

The man shrugged indifferently.

"But how unkind of you, James," the red-haired beauty named Isobel said silkily, closing the door and moving toward the bed. "You've begun without me."

Thunder rolling in the distance. Suffocating heat. Gunfire.

Alexandra bolted upright in bed, staring into darkness and dreams. . . .

Into the old Terror.

Her heart pounding, she heard a distant crash and waited for phosphorous fingers to slit the clouds a moment later. The Devil's fire, she thought wildly. It had come again—the roaring fury of the monsoons erupting across the Indian plain.

And just as it always did, one nightmare gave way to another; the distant peal of thunder dragged in its train grotesque visions of that night ten years before when Vellore had run red with English blood.

Rigid with fear, unable to move or even to cry out, she waited for the hammering thunder to call up pounding feet and harsh cries in the night.

Overhead the thunder rolled, cracking and roaring above the howl of the wind.

Paralyzed, she heard the dim cries of the house servants, the angry hiss of musket fire. Her eyes huge with fear, she saw plumes of smoke rising from the silent outbuildings.

And the blood, dear God, the blood everywhere, staining the white linen, splashed upon the white walls.

No! Vainly, she screamed in the dark silence of her mind, twisting before the ghostly shapes lit in each stroke of lightning.

The houseboy crumpled by the stairway, pristine in white muslin even as his neck was broken. The young soldier still grinning, fallen in the hall, a musket ball through his neck. The captain of the house guard motionless in the dust, a great crimson stain wetting the back of his coat.

The sickly smell of death everywhere.

She screamed and thrashed, shredding the covers that trapped her legs, fighting the invisible hands that caught her and dragged her inexorably down.

Overhead, the angry thunder raged on, plunging her into the

terror of the uprising as if it had been yesterday. With each explosion her fear grew until it reached a savage crescendo, suffocating her, stripping her of pride, of sanity itself.

From the darkness nearby she heard a wild, unnatural keening, and the sound filled her with unreasoning panic.

Cold fingers ripped her skin. She cried out, fighting blindly in the darkness.

And then she was trapped against a hard body, held immobile as her slim frame was racked with uncontrollable shudders.

"Ayah?" she sobbed in panic. "You lied! The Devil's fire has come again! Father? Where are you? The guns—dear God, the blood!"

"Only a storm," a new voice said, far away.

The smell of death was acrid in her nostrils, mingled with the smoke of the burning house. "Must get out," she mumbled. "Fire everywhere." Still the iron claws gripped her. "Let me go!" she screamed, recognizing for the first time that her nightmare was strangely altered, that this voice was a strange and unfamiliar element among the shadows of her old fear. "Please," she moaned, "else we burn to death in here!"

"Hush," the dark voice whispered. "The storm will soon pass. 'Tis only a spring squall rolling in from the Channel. Hush—hush now."

Silver eyes narrowed and glowed for an instant in the lighting's flare. What madness was upon her? the duke wondered, watching her trembling fingers rake the empty air.

A bolt of lightning exploded directly overhead and threw the room into ghostly brilliance. At the same moment the woman on the bed wrenched herself free, her eyes blind with terror.

And then she sank back into darkness, screaming as if the very bowels of hell itself were torn open before her.

Chapter Nineteen

At five o'clock the next morning Alexandra awoke to the sound of drums pounding in her head. With a low moan she rolled onto her side and dragged the feather pillow closer around her head. But the pounding continued, worse than before.

What were the servants about? she wondered, grimacing at a stab of pain that bit into her temples. Repairing the roof at—one watery eye cracked open to ascertain the hour—at the first gray light of dawn?

Her tongue was dry and felt like the ragged stuffing inside a well-used quilt. Her red-rimmed eyes sank closed, and she burrowed back beneath the cool sheets.

Too late. Her stomach twisted with nausea.

Then she felt the hoarseness in her throat, the heavy ache of her arms and shoulders. *The dreams!* They had come again in the night with the tempest, sweeping her once more back in time.

Into darkness. Into the Terror.

First the lightning, always the lightning. *Kolimin,* the villagers called it, but Ayah was a superstitious woman, and to her it was the Devil's fire—the fury of nature at its most savage, blazing across the plains.

Afterward, Alexandra never remembered anything. Only the

tension and aching of her body remained the next day, dim reminders of the war she had waged with her fear.

The war she always lost.

But something had been different last night, she realized, unable to remember what it was. Frustrated, she racked her mind, but as always the memories eluded her.

She sat up with a start and immediately regretted it. This was pain, she discovered, as her temples throbbed in earnest and the vague terrors of the night were forgotten in the grating agony behind her eyes.

The wine, of course. What a fool she'd been. And to have eaten so little!

With a growing sense of uneasiness Alexandra tried to recall exactly what had happened the night before. She remembered only scattered images—a cozy study. Warm laughter. Lilies. Dancing candles. And Hawke's demanding mouth on hers, his teeth moving to her neckline, his lips upon her breast.

She heard the doorknob click and in her misery did not even turn.

"Whoever you are, go away," she whispered.

"Why, it's only Lily, miss. Beggin' your pardon for intrudin' so early, but His Grace said you was wishin' to be wakened for an early ride. But first he said as how you'd be wantin' coffee and a cold wash. Though how he did know is beyond me. . . ." The girl's voice trailed off when she saw Alexandra's hands covering her cheeks and forehead. "Are you feelin' poorly, miss?"

"Dear Lily," Alexandra said very slowly and very carefully, "not ill—dying at the very least. Now please go, and let me die in peace."

The girl stood frozen, her face tense with worry. "I'll fetch Shadwell—there's a doctor in Alfriston. He could be here in an hour." She turned and started for the door.

A feeble moan from the bed stopped her. "Please! No doctor."

"But, miss—"

"Oh, my cursed head! Quiet is all I need—blessed quiet and darkness."

Lily fell into puzzled silence. Alexandra had just begun to conquer the feeling that she was swimming in swells of black ink when the maid exclaimed, "So that's the way of it! Cup-shot, are you? Well, His Grace was in the right way of it then. All you'll be needin' is a cold wash and a spot of coffee to make you more the thing."

A muffled groan emerged from beneath the pillow, followed by an inaudible order.

"Aye, it's hurtin' now, but you'll see soon enough. Coffee's what you're needin'. So if you'll just sit up . . ."

Alexandra sighed. There would be no getting rid of her determined helper if she didn't comply. "Very well. But one drink and then"—she winced as she sat up—"then leave me to expire in solitude."

Lily smiled sympathetically, holding out a heavy earthenware cup. Alexandra's nostrils flared in rebellion as the bitter smell of coffee assailed her. Her face twisted with distaste, but the maid held firm.

"Just a sip or two. 'Twill help you, believe me. My da was one to swear by it, and he should know, bein' as how he was three sheets in the wind once a week."

Eyes closed, Alexandra found the cup, grasped it with nerveless fingers, and forced down a mouthful.

"Now one more, miss."

She sighed and took another. The hot liquid burned her throat, and her stomach lurched in protest. "Sweet heavens! Lily—the basin!"

The deed was done, and almost immediately the nausea was gone. Slowly, Alexandra opened her eyes. Her head still hurt and her eyes were watery, but the awful pain and dizziness had begun to lift.

By the time she finished the coffee, Alexandra felt restored to something partially resembling normalcy. She went to the window, threw open the pane, and filled her lungs with cool, crisp air. Pink and purple clouds streaked the sky in the east, and a low mist hung across the downs.

All in all, a fine morning for a ride, she decided.

With a slight smile, Lily produced a riding habit of russet velvet with matching boots and gloves. The habit was a novelty to Alexandra, cut in an archaic style with a tight fitted jacket and a full skirt, in two separate pieces. But the effect would be quite lovely, Lily assured her. Twenty minutes later, feeling like a new woman, Alexandra descended the wide staircase, smiling to the footman holding the door open for her.

The duke was waiting by the stable block, one polished boot propped with lazy grace against a wooden fence rail.

Alexandra's heart took a slow dive at the amused speculation on his face, and she wondered again exactly what had transpired the night before.

"You knew!" she said accusingly. "You knew how it would be!"

Silver eyes traced her face, lingering upon the faint smudges beneath her eyes, the angry bruise at her temple, and the slight pallor of her cheeks. "Of course I knew, for all you put up a gallant fight. Although not as gallant as the fight you made upon arising, I expect."

"You must be very familiar with the condition!" Alexandra said indignantly. "You might have warned me!"

"Would you have accepted a warning from me?" For a moment the air between them sizzled with tension.

"No," Alexandra admitted at last. She raised wide, slightly hesitant eyes. "What—what exactly happened last night?"

Hawke's mouth slowly curved into a smile. "You don't remember?"

"Obviously not, or I wouldn't have to ask, knave!"

"What a blow to my ego! For me the earth shook, while you have no recollection of the event." Hawke shook his head sadly.

"Liar!" Alexandra whispered, horrified.

"Am I? Have you no memory of my hands, my lips . . ."

Alexandra gritted her teeth, only too aware of her aching recall —but only up to the point where he deposited her on the chaise; after that, all was a blank. "You didn't!" she rasped, choking. "I wouldn't! Im-impossible!" she hissed finally.

"Are you so certain?" Dancing silver eyes taunted her.

"No, damn you, I'm not! For you, scoundrel that you are, would be quick to—"

"Take cruel advantage of your inebriation? No, hornet, that I did not, for I like my bed partners to do more than snore. You passed out and I took you upstairs, where I deposited you chastely in your bed. Remember this," Hawke growled. "When I bed you, you'll be awake and entirely aware beneath me, I assure you."

"Never!"

"It's only a matter of time. We both know it."

"I know nothing of the sort, you cur!" She spat.

"You're repeating yourself, my dear," Hawke answered negligently. With his mocking eyes fixed on Alexandra's furious face, he bowed slowly and with elaborate courtesy, waiting for her to precede him to the stables.

She did not move. "Why don't you leave so that I can enjoy my ride in peace?"

"You have nothing to fear from me, Miss Mayfield. I want the very same thing you do—if only you were honest enough to admit it."

"Rubbish!" Alexandra tossed her head angrily, her blue-green eyes darkening. "A very wise man once warned me never to trust anyone who promised he was harmless, Your Grace." How much she missed that man! Alexandra thought.

"Hawke," her companion corrected, taking her arm and starting up the graveled path. "Who was he?"

Alexandra wrenched her arm free and stalked toward the stable. "I'd rather not say," she said stiffly. She knew she would have to get used to questions about her father one day, but his loss was still an open wound. Perhaps she had never really faced his death.

Iron fingers circled her wrist, holding her motionless. "Who?" Hawke repeated coldly.

"Very well, damn you—my father!" she snapped, struggling to free her hand.

"Tell me about him."

"Why would a man like you be interested in my father?"

"A man like me?" Hawke repeated, his fingers tightening. "I fear you know nothing at all about me, Miss Mayfield. But we are going to change that soon enough, for I find I am interested in everything about you." To Hawke's astonishment, it was true. He had never before felt the slightest interest in the lives of the women he'd bedded. "And no matter how cleverly you deflect me, I mean to have an answer."

Alexandra's chin rose proudly. "Very well. He was wonderful.

He taught me to ride, to hunt, and to read Sanskrit. He taught me to judge horses—and people. He knew everyone and everything." She spoke defensively, as if she expected an argument. "The Indians loved him and the English did, too, all except for—" She stopped suddenly.

"Except for whom?"

"The *kala nag,* the black snake. There are always black snakes," she added flatly. "But it's of no consequence now." Alexandra was suddenly aware that she had said far more than she intended.

"Remarkable," Hawke said quietly. "But you do not mention drawing, French, or deportment. You'd make a sad governess, I fear."

"Oh, I'd a string of governesses for those things," Alexandra said dismissively. "My father taught me all the *important* things."

"Quite astonishing." Hawke's silver eyes narrowed upon her face.

They had reached the stables, Alexandra noticed in surprise. A sleepy-faced groom emerged from the shadowed interior, bits of straw clinging to his jacket.

Hawke released her arm. "Saddle Aladdin and bring him around. Then have Bluebell brought for Miss Mayfield."

Just then, a high-pitched voice hailed them, and Alexandra turned to see a small figure fly from the rear of the stables. She frowned, unable to make out the boy's face.

" 'Tis me, Pence! Just got back from London we did, me and Mr. Jeffers."

Alexandra laughed with delight to see that impish smile once more. The urchin looked older, she thought, for his face was fuller and less pale. Things had gone well for him. Nor did she miss the telling note of respect in the boy's voice when he spoke of the duke's groom. "And very fit you're looking too. So Mr. Jeffers is treating you well, is he?"

"Ain't he just! Teachin' me how to care for the cattle, how to blow up the yard o' tin. Hasn't let me hold the ribbons, yet, o' course." The small pang of regret vanished almost immediately. "Says I got light hands, though. Says as how I'll make a good coachman someday if I keep to it!"

The boy's enthusiasm was infectious. "'Tis fine to see you, Pence, and fine to know things are going well."

"Better'n I ever dreamed," the boy said frankly. "Only hope things be half so good for you, Miss Ma—"

At that moment Alexandra developed a sudden paroxysm of coughing. Pence darted a bright, curious look, first at her and then at the duke, who was leaning against the open stable door.

"We brought your things, too, miss. Thought you might be missin' them." After waiting for a nod from Jeffers, Pence flew back to the rear of the stables, returning a moment later with a bulky object beneath his arm.

Alexandra stiffened, her eyes riveted on the battered wicker hamper he carried. "Rajah!" she cried, springing across the gravel.

The Duke of Hawkesworth's gray eyes widened, and he frowned. With sharp curiosity he watched her spin about and set the container down upon the ground. His frown deepened as a flurry of scratching erupted from the battered case, followed by a series of odd, high-pitched squeaks.

"Yes, my little love," Alexandra crooned, oblivious to the rapt stares of Pence and the two men. "Never think I forgot you! I'll have you free in a trice!" Her trembling fingers gently slipped the hempen clasps free of their closings, and she raised the lid.

With a shrill squeak a small circle of brown fur shot out from the hamper and landed in Alexandra's outstretched hands, which promptly enveloped him in a careful embrace.

"I know, my love," she whispered against the sleek fur. "I've missed you too."

"Tried to take care of him, I did," Pence said anxiously. "Wasn't overly pleased with me, I can tell ye. Pecked at his food an' whimpered fit to break a person's heart. Reck'n he was wantin' ye."

So this was her Rajah, Hawke thought curiously, studying Alexandra's delighted face as she stroked the creature in her arms.

Suddenly, Richard Decimus Sommerton, the Duke of Hawkesworth, peer of the realm and inheritor of 100,000 acres, with ancient estates and vast holdings in Sussex, Derbyshire, and Scotland, was pierced with a sharp stab of jealousy.

Jealousy for one tiny quivering mongoose.

"I take it this is some sort of pet?" he inquired coolly.

Alexandra looked up from the sleek line of fur. "Oh, infinitely more than a pet, Your Grace. A friend. Yes, the very best friend one could ever hope to have."

"My friends are generally of the two-legged sort," Hawke said, irritated and still oddly jealous of her loving attention to the skittish creature in her hands.

"Perhaps that is your loss."

Hearing the tension in their voices, Rajah looked up curiously. His pink eyes darted to the tall man beside his mistress, and his little pointed head tilted to one side. A sharp squeak emerged from his throat.

"Longing to explore, are you, Rajah?" Alexandra asked, and was immediately answered by a burst of staccato sounds.

Carefully, she lowered Rajah to the ground. His head aslant and his tail bristling, the little mongoose picked a careful path to Hawkesworth's feet. Intently, he sniffed one of the duke's gleaming black riding boots.

Four pairs of eyes watched with differing emotions as the mongoose analyzed the sight and smell of those immaculately polished creations. And then as swiftly as the investigation had begun, it was over. The curious mongoose turned to pursue a more intriguing scent that led toward the rear of the stables.

The Duke of Hawkesworth, it seemed, had been summarily dismissed.

Alexandra could restrain herself no longer, and her laughter spilled out in a rippling wave. An instant later, she was joined by Pence, while Jeffers abruptly pulled a cloth from his pocket to nurse a sudden cough.

Only the Duke of Hawkesworth appeared unamused. "Rajah, is it? The name appears well chosen," he commented dryly.

"He is most particular about his friends," Alexandra explained sweetly.

"I expect Rajah and I will come to terms." Hawke leveled a quelling glance at his suddenly discomfited groom. "A spring cold, Jeffers?" At the old man's mumbled denial Hawke's eyebrows rose. "Perhaps you'd better go and tend to it then. And take that damned creature with you," he ordered.

Suddenly, Alexandra was alone with Hawkesworth, even Rajah having deserted her for the challenge of new terrain. "Rajah stays with me!" she began mutinously.

"Even when you ride?"

As the duke spoke, Bluebell, the duchess's horse, was brought out of the stables, and Alexandra felt her irritation melt away. The roan had a skittish disposition, and a great deal of action. She might as well ride, she told herself, since she would not be able to pull Rajah from his exploration so soon.

She accepted the groom's help to mount, and with a challenging look back at Hawkesworth, she was off.

The ground was cloaked in gray patches of low-lying clouds. When Alexandra galloped through the mist, the world seemed to disappear. She was caught inside a soundless white room, only to burst out a moment later and find color and form miraculously restored. On she galloped, ignoring the rider beside her, focusing on the beauty of the morning.

For almost an hour they rode, climbing steadily to the east. The sun rose over the downs and had burned off the last of the fog when Hawke reined in Aladdin and pointed directly ahead.

Following his hand, Alexandra turned and saw a narrow, sheltered valley bordered by deep green pines and low bushes. Down through the center flowed a twisting ribbon of silver.

"Did your father teach you to fish?" he asked thoughtfully.

"We often fished together. Why?"

"Because I mean to offer you a wager." Then, as if in afterthought, he shook his head. "But it is out of the question, of course. You are merely a female—and still cup-shot from last night."

"I am not cup-shot!" Alexandra said indignantly. "And what has being a female got to do with it?"

"Everything, I should imagine," Hawke said, his eyes burning insolently across her chest and down her thighs. "It would really be too unfair of me—"

"Make your wager, damn it!"

"Very well. You claim to have a great many skills, Miss Mayfield. Let us see which of us has the more useful ones—specifically, who can come up with breakfast first. Follow me—if you dare."

As Hawke had known she would, Alexandra did follow, turning Bluebell and plunging down the slope to a clear, rock-strewn stream. Hawke dismounted and tied Aladdin to a beech tree. His eyes were expectant as he turned toward Alexandra.

She did not wait for him but dismounted quickly by herself.

Hawke's eyebrows rose mockingly, and Alexandra felt her face redden, but she refused to be ruffled. "I believe you mentioned something about finding us breakfast, Your Grace."

"Follow me then, and prepare to swallow your words."

"Never! Prepare instead to swallow your pride, braggart!"

Hawke snorted as he made his way down the grassy slope, thick with long-stemmed water plants and leafy ferns. At the stream's edge he stopped to study the clear waters. A trio of swans swept gracefully down the crystal currents, their necks high and proud. When Alexandra came to stand beside him, he pointed to the exquisite white creatures. "You see before you the Hawkeswish swans, a royal bequest dating back to Elizabeth's time. We used to pay a tax on each one. A great deal of time and effort has been spent over the centuries separating the broods. Each owner has his own mark, so that his swans may not be taken up by others."

"And what is the Hawkeswish mark, Your Grace?"

"A small crescent moon on the right leg. You'll see for yourself at the swan-hooking ceremony."

"Swan-hooking ceremony?"

"When the creatures are caught with a staff and taken from the water for marking. An ancient ritual—and one I haven't seen for far too long," Hawke added, almost to himself.

"I fancy the swans don't enjoy it half as well as you do," Alexandra said soberly.

"If they are wise creatures, they realize where their protection lies. And now, Miss Mayfield, behold your breakfast." One long, tanned finger pointed out a moving shape in the clear depths of the swift-moving stream. A large fish darted from behind a rock and raced downstream.

"A fish, Your Grace?"

"Hawke," he corrected offhandedly, his eyes on another darting shadow. "And not just any fish, little cynic. A red-spotted trout—a fat, tasty Hawkeswish trout." Abruptly, Hawke began to unbutton his jacket. "They breed in these clear gravel beds, you know. They winter in deep waters higher upstream, then come down in summer to the shallow fords here at midlevel."

Alexandra watched in amazement as the exquisite duke began to shed his sartorial splendor. First his jacket and crop went flying, then his gleaming boots. "You're serious?" Her tone was sharp with disbelief.

Hawke merely chuckled and returned to his task. With slow, careful steps he entered the stream and worked his way gradually up against the current. A red-flecked oval tilted by the opposite bank, followed by another. Hawke waited, immobile. A dark cloud of minnows flashed past, then a slow-moving eel. Several seconds passed, and a larger fish darted down the center of the stream, its red-spotted body outlined sharply against the mottled gray bottom.

In a flash the duke's hand pierced the water and reappeared an instant later with the fat trout thrashing in midair. He gave a loud shout of triumph.

"You did it!" Alexandra's shock was obvious.

"Yes, by God. I haven't lost the touch! Old Havers would be proud."

"Havers?"

"The water bailiff of Hawkeswish. He knows everything worth knowing about these streams. About all the streams in Sussex, I'll warrant. Taught me as a lad to fish without benefit of a net or pole. Said it might come in useful sometime, and he was right."

Alexandra eyed the flapping shape in his hand with distaste. Fish, particularly when they were uncooked and wriggling, were far from her favorite creatures. "What do you mean to do with the thing now?"

"Cook it, of course. You shall skin it for me."

At Alexandra's croak Hawke hid his laughter no longer.

"You—you—" Alexandra sputtered.

"Arrogant blackguard?" Hawke suggested with mock politeness. "Come, admit you're bested, Miss Mayfield. You claim to be an honest creature. Now prove it."

Much to her dismay, Alexandra felt a tiny smile play about her lips. It was the sight of the usually exquisite duke that did it. He stood knee deep in water, his breeches wet, his cuffs soaked, and his hair disarrayed by the wind. He looked, in fact, like an entirely different person from the cold stranger who had accosted her on a foggy London street.

He's still a dangerous man, Alexandra reminded herself. Remember what he's done to you.

"And what devilish plans are you weaving now, little hellcat? The last time you had such a look, you fractured my skull with a bottle."

"Something you richly deserved. I'm merely thinking that this fish, like all your other dependents, has been trained to obey his master's every whim."

"And thus you reduce my triumph to nothing! You are hard, Miss Mayfield." His silver-gray eyes narrowed. "You make me wonder what it would take to teach *you* to obey my every whim."

Alexandra merely shrugged and looked down at the fish still flapping in Hawke's hands—anything to avoid the smoky depths of his eyes. "Very well. I concede that you have your uses. I shall make certain to look you up should I ever become lost beside a stream without food or fishing pole. You would be a great comfort in such a case."

The two horses tethered on the bank looked up from their grazing and sniffed the air, sensing a sudden tension. Aladdin neighed softly, questioningly.

"Oh, I would provide you with a great deal more than *comfort,* in such a case. You may be certain of that." Hawke looked down at the fish still twisting in his hands. Suddenly he stiffened. "Here!" he cried, at the same instant tossing his wriggling catch toward Alexandra.

By reflex, she reached for the object hurtling toward her and gasped when she touched its cold, wet scales. An instant later, she cast the trout back into the silver current, where it spun about and darted downstream.

Hawke raised a sable eyebrow. "You are cavalier with our breakfast, Miss Mayfield. I shall enjoy seeing you come up with another."

His lazy arrogance goaded Alexandra to fury. "With pleasure! After all, if you can manage it, how hard can it be?" Quickly, she sat down and slid off her half-boots, then hiked up her skirt to her ankles, studiously avoiding the duke's eyes. She made her way down to a large boulder jutting out over the stream and slowly lowered herself until she could trail a hand in the clear water.

From the sand and pebbles at the bottom of the stream, a carp rose to the surface in a cloud of bubbles but darted away before she could move a finger. Cautiously, she brought her other arm around the rock, inching forward until both shoulders were extended over the water.

She saw him then—black speckled and fat, cruising lazily within a cloud of minnows. She waited tensely, eyes narrowed, as the minnows brushed past, nibbling her fingers. The fat trout drifted only inches behind.

Suddenly, she thrust her hands down into the water, her eyes trained on the slow-moving shadow. Then she had him, cold and wriggling in her grasp.

She stood in triumph, displaying her catch to a stunned Hawke, delighting in his look of surprise. "What do you say now, braggart?"

His eyes narrowed. "I say bravo, Miss Mayfield—and I hope you know how to swim!"

A moment later, the surface of the water shattered as Alexandra swayed, then plunged into the freezing crystal currents.

Chapter Twenty

Alexandra gasped in shock as the frigid waters closed over her head. A moment later, her hands struck gravel, loosing a cloud of sand and water plants from the stream bed. Swiftly, she tucked her body and turned in a tight circle, then sputtered to the surface just as Hawke's large hand snaked around her waist. His laughter rang in her ears as he hoisted her from the stream.

She could feel his ribs heaving with laughter as he toppled her onto the fern-covered bank. Angrily, Alexandra tossed the sopping curls from her face. "Oh, to blazes with you!" she snapped, shivering slightly when the wind played down the narrow valley. "I had him in my hands. You saw it!"

"If only you hadn't decided to take a swim. Yes, you weren't half bad for a beginner," Hawke finally conceded. "But you'd better take off that jacket before you catch cold."

At Alexandra's mutinous look, Hawke held out his elegant brown coat. "This will do until yours dries." He looked up at the cloudless azure sky. "I shouldn't think it will take too long."

"My habit is sodden," she said stiffly. "I'd prefer to ride back now." Her aloof air was shattered abruptly by a sneeze.

"And sit a horse in those wet clothes for an hour? Out of the question!"

"Very well," she said through gritted teeth, reaching for his jacket. "You may take yourself off to the horses while I change."

"Isn't it rather late for such delicacy?"

"Then I'll go back to the house without you!" Abruptly, Alexandra's nose twitched in preparation for another sneeze.

"All right, damn it!" Hawke barked. "One of us must be sensible, or we'll be here all day arguing. My God, your teeth are chattering already." Smothering a curse, he turned and stalked up the bank to the horses.

When she was sure he'd gone, Alexandra began to work the tiny buttons of her jacket free, cursing the modiste who had invented the style of tightly fitted garments with dainty buttons. Of course, they hadn't been designed to swim in, she thought ruefully. When the buttons were finally freed, she darted a suspicious glance at the duke.

But Hawke was busily rummaging in his saddlebags, oblivious to her plight. Quickly, Alexandra wriggled out of her jacket and chemise and tossed Hawke's dark brown coat around her shoulders. With stiff fingers she worked the buttons closed, then slid her arms about her waist for warmth. The sun was warm on the bank, and she settled down onto a large flat rock, smoothing her skirts around her to dry.

His scent clung to the coat—the smell of horses, old leather, soap, hay, and some other elusive element. The primal man-smell made her wish she'd never taken the cursed thing. It might as well have been his arms around her, she thought, infuriated.

"All clear, I take it?" Hawke's voice, close to her ear, made her jump.

"Quite." To cover her nervousness Alexandra settled back against the rock and wrung out the wet fabric over her ankles.

"I've found you a towel. Turn onto your side so I can dry your hair with it." Alexandra did not move. Hawke opened his leather saddlebags and impatiently held up a wrinkled length of cloth. She sneezed once again. "Hurry up, damn it! Or do you fancy catching a contagion of the lungs? It will take us well over an hour to get back, you know!"

Alexandra eyed the cloth uncertainly. It smelled strongly of horses. She sneezed again, then reluctantly turned to her side.

Hawke's strong, hard hands gathered her hair and began to blot it with the towel. Hands firm and gentle. Hands that held their strength in check just now. Hands clearly experienced in such matters.

Alexandra stiffened.

"What's wrong now?"

"Nothing," she snapped.

His hands tightened around her hair for a moment, then resumed their brisk rubbing. "It disturbs you to think I've done this before—is that it?"

Alexandra snorted and tried to twist away, but he caught her damp bronze tresses and held her immobile. After a moment he spoke, his voice very low. "The other woman, in this case, was my mother. She had an inflammation of the joints, you see, a condition that rendered her acutely uncomfortable whenever it rained. It used to ease her pain to have a hot bath, and afterward she liked me to dry her hair like this. She suffered far more than she let any of us know, I believe."

"She sounds very brave," Alexandra said quietly.

"She was a rare woman. My father, on the other hand—" Abruptly, Hawke's voice changed. "Now that your hair is finished, let's see about the rest of you." Before she could frame a protest, he was kneeling and drying her feet. "You seem to favor the barefoot state, Miss Mayfield. Is it these boots you dislike, or footwear in general?"

"You must bring out the worst in me, Your Grace, for it's been years since I've gone barefoot."

"Then you ought to thank me. Don't your feet feel better now?"

Unconsciously, Alexandra arched her feet and stretched her toes. Immediately, Hawke's hands slid down over her sensitive soles, and her eyes closed at the sheer pleasure of his touch.

Suddenly, Alexandra remembered where she was—and with whom. She stiffened and tried to kick away from his grasp.

Hawke's fingers tightened. "Don't fight me, Alexandra, or I might come up with better ways to spend our time here."

Alexandra blinked at the dark command in that voice. Once again, his fingers moved, sending flames along her spine, making her remember other things he'd done with those large strong hands, other places he had stroked.

"How did it happen?"

"Happen?" she repeated unsteadily.

Hawke's fingers raised her skirt and traced the ragged scar that snaked around her ankle. "This."

"A-accident—" Alexandra swallowed, suddenly hoarse. The pressure of his hands sent her pulse racing. She coughed and began again. "A riding accident in the hill country. The cobras came out of nowhere, and Fury was down in an instant." She stopped then, shivering as the memories washed over her. She looked away from the deep silver of Hawke's eyes, twisting her habit restlessly. "I can still hear the sounds of his thrashing. Dear God, the dust and sweat! The smell of fear!" Suddenly, it was all there before her again. "Fury," she whispered.

Hawke's thumbs stroked her ankles in widening circles. "You were thrown?"

" 'Twas a pair of king cobras, their black bodies hidden in the dust. I didn't see until—until it was too late. Fury saw, though. He reared and trampled upon the hooded death, but not before their venom had found its mark."

Alexandra's eyes were hazy. She could suddenly hear the great horse's anguished thrashing. She could feel the angry sweat that frothed along his tortured body. Unconsciously, her voice took on a singsong lilt. "Yes, love, it will be over soon now. Rest, Fury. Dream of Simla and cool green fields."

A heavy tear slid from her eye. The movement seemed to rouse her and she blinked, covertly brushing her cheek.

"Is that part of the nightmare?"

"How do you know about that?" Alexandra demanded, her whole body tensing.

"Because you had one last night. You were still asleep, but you were screaming and fighting something—something that existed only in your mind."

"I don't care to talk about it," Alexandra said curtly. She realized that his fingers were climbing up her calves. She stiffened, but as she tried to twist away, Hawke's fingers tightened sharply.

"What—"

"Don't move." His voice was no more than a whisper, but its harsh command halted her protest. Her eyebrows climbed when he inched one hand from her leg and reached slowly for the saddlebags beside him on the grass.

Suddenly, from the ground near her head came a dry rustle, the very breath of evil. Alexandra shivered, and Hawkesworth's hand clamped cruelly against her ankle. The rustling grew louder, and she felt the cold whisper of wind against her neck. Her nerves began to scream.

Drawn by a terrible compulsion, she tried to twist her head over her shoulder. Immediately, Hawke's fingers cut deeper into her skin, and when she looked up, his face was a white mask. She kept her eyes on his face, too afraid to see the pale death that lurked just out of view in the grass.

She looked helplessly at Hawke, seeking the comforting reality of his broad shoulders and iron frame, seeking his silver eyes, which glinted just now with fear. She watched his fingers dip inside the leather saddlebags and emerge with a pearl-handled pistol.

From the corner of her eye Alexandra saw a shadow part the tall grass. A draft hissed across her cheek, and she felt the cold kiss of death. Desperately, her eyes searched Hawke's face.

Don't move! his slate eyes commanded. *Trust me this once.* Slowly, his hand lifted; slowly, the cold metal barrel inched above her leg.

The pistol thundered, and at the same instant a shrill hiss exploded by her waist. Alexandra heard a muffled thump and then the wild slap of a twisting body. A moment later, the movement ceased, and all was quiet except for the gentle murmur of the stream.

Her eyes asked a silent question of Hawkesworth, who slowly straightened. For long moments Alexandra scoured his face, unable to move. She heard rather than saw his boot scrape the grass and turn something over.

Then the duke released his breath in a long, explosive burst. "Close, by God! Too close. A black viper's poison can—" He caught himself suddenly when her face blanched. Then Hawke noticed her hands were clenched so tightly that the joints were white.

"It's all over now," he said roughly. "This one will never stalk anything again." When she still did not move, Hawke tried again. "Look!" Carefully he lifted a black length of scaled muscle that flexed slightly in the rigor of death.

It was the worst thing he could have done.

Alexandra choked. "No! Not here! You have the great blacks here?" she mumbled hoarsely, her nostrils wide with terror. "I placated you at the shrine beneath the great banyan tree with mice and bright ghee! You've taken Fury from me! You've taken Rajah's firstborn! Leave me alone!"

With a curse Hawke sent the dead snake flying into the creek, then dropped on his knees beside her. "Stop it!" he commanded, his voice rough and caressing at the same time. " 'Twas no cobra but a Sussex black viper, and he is no more. You are safe, Alexandra," Hawke said gruffly, pulling her stiff body into the circle of his arms. "Safe, do you hear? Nothing will harm you. I swear it!"

His fingers slid around her back and urged her closer, seeking a softening in the rigid muscles that resisted him still. "Safe," he whispered into her damp curls. "Safe, by God," he breathed into the cool hollow beneath her jaw. "Do you hear me?"

Slowly, the warmth of his body penetrated her numbness. She felt his hard, muscled thighs at her hip. "Am I?" she whispered. "And who will save me from you?"

With a curse the Duke of Hawkesworth forced her back against his chest. "No one," he rasped. His eyes were gray like scudding seas as her breath played against the triangle of skin where his shirt opened to his neck.

And suddenly, it was not enough for him—not nearly enough.

Not enough freedom. Not enough joining of warm naked skin. Hawke's eyes closed and his hold tightened until he was raw with the awareness of her unsteady heartbeat, the husky timbre of her voice, the sweet fire of her body against his.

His fingers slid deep into her hair. He gazed down into the haunted depths of her aquamarine eyes and felt himself drown. There had been another pair of blue-green eyes once, he remembered, but this time Hawke was drowning in a way he had never known with Isobel.

"No one at all." Half dreaming, he turned so that his lips traced the lines of her tears and his tongue tasted the warm salt upon her cheeks. This time he knew he wanted all of her and must have her assent in the taking.

Alexandra heard his rough whisper, heard the ragged note of passion, as well as something else that eluded definition.

"Let me go!" she cried.

"Even now you ask that?"

"Now and always! I will never stop fighting until you release me!"

"And I will never stop until I've made you mine. Till I've put my mark upon you." Hawke anchored her face with his strong bronzed fingers. "Until you admit that you feel this passion flaring between us."

"Never!" Alexandra cried, struggling wildly against his touch.

"Shall we put the matter to a test?" As he spoke, his hands slipped inside the gaping neck of her borrowed jacket. His long fingers traced the delicate hollows of her collarbone. "Prove to me you are indifferent, and I'll let you go," he dared.

Hope surged in Alexandra's heart. Here, at last, was her way of escape. "And you will honor your promise when I do?"

"If you do," Hawke corrected. His eyes shimmered with silver flecks, as fluid and changeable as the stream that flashed by their feet. "Yes, in that case I give my word I will release you. Now you must give yours; if you fail, you will cease this pretense and come to me willingly, as my woman."

"You will certainly lose, Your Grace!" Alexandra said defiantly.

"Then give me your word!" Hawke demanded.

"I give it," she snapped impatiently. "Now begin, that we may the sooner be finished with this farce."

Slowly, Hawke smiled, his hands gently grazing the upper swell of her breast. "What's the hurry, my dear? Do you fear to lose?"

"Bastard!" she rasped through gritted teeth. "I have nothing to fear from you!"

His smile widened and his hands dropped, tracing her breast to find the impudent bud at its center. To her fury, the crest immediately furrowed and grew taut beneath his fingers.

"You will lose, my little hellcat. And the loss will give both of us infinite pleasure."

"Never!"

His touch grew demanding. "Tell me, Alexandra. Tell me you feel this fire as I do."

"I don't!" she cried angrily, twisting beneath his hands, her breath coming hard and jerky.

Immediately, Hawke's fingers spread, capturing her entirely within their span as his thumbs rasped her nipples to raw awareness.

"Liar," he taunted, his silver eyes inches from her face.

"Nothing! I feel nothing! You can't force desire!"

"Ah, but in your case force is not necessary." His fingers tightened, and each hand captured a taut nipple, sending agonizing flashes of pleasure through her body. "Tell me, little hellcat," he whispered, "tell me this pleases you." Slowly and very deliberately, he pushed her back against the grass, capturing her beneath his thighs.

To Alexandra his voice sounded thickened and strangely uneven. She strained away from him, terrified of the flood of feeling his hands provoked. Dimly, she realized that their bodies had become the field of a battle older than time.

He straddled her fiercely, a primal aggressor, every inch rigid, throbbing male as he anchored her wrists to the ground. And his granite challenge brought Alexandra's stubborn pride flaming to life with an equal fury.

She forced her eyes closed, unwilling to give Hawke a glimpse of the embers he had so expertly stirred to life. But sightless, she felt him in a hundred new ways—the warm musky fragrance that was uniquely his, the hot rushes of breath that stirred a curl across her collarbone, the dark force of desire that strained his own breathing.

The touch of his skin became a torment. Almost as if he knew this, Hawke did not move, branding her at wrist and thigh where their bodies met. She struggled once against his iron grip, but it was ineffectual, and they both knew it.

She was like a small night creature caught in the jaws of a hardened predator.

Suddenly he shifted, and his breath warmed her chest. Then there was only searing pleasure as his hot tongue circled and covered the hungry aching crest of her nipple.

Alexandra cried out at the sudden assault, stunned by the scorching waves that shot through her body. "No," she moaned, but her point was lost because at the same moment she arched beneath him.

Hawke's tongue missed nothing in its expert tracing—hard and wet, then smooth and stroking. "You will tell me," he whispered against her silken skin. "This time I'll have the words, by God."

She shuddered, twisting beneath him—whether to evade or meet him, she dared not consider. Her young vibrant body burned inside and out, awakened by his masterful touch to a shattering sensuality.

He turned her body traitor again and again, until she had to bite her lip to hold back the moans that threatened to burst free. His mouth forged an exquisite pleasure, so keen it bordered on pain. Alexandra felt all her inner barriers threatened by the silken bonds of passion that danced between them, breast to mouth, thigh to thigh.

"Torment and my delight," Hawke whispered against her burning skin. "Give yourself to me, swan! Give me your fire. I promise I will return it twofold."

"Never!" she whispered, her body twisting wildly beneath him, her struggle more eloquent than any words. "Stop—"

"Say the words, Alexandra," Hawke ordered hoarsely. "I will have them this time."

Her body shifted urgently, fighting his fire and his power, desperate to escape his drugging touch. Her fingers strained against his iron grip, and for a moment she did not know whether they fought to bring him closer or to push him away.

"Tell me," he said raggedly, and Alexandra suddenly knew that this was as hard for him as it was for her.

A moan escaped her throat. "I cannot. After the things you've done, I must always fight you!"

"Look at me, swan."

Unwillingly, Alexandra obeyed the dark pull of his rough voice and saw his eyes were smoky with passion and a torture of his own.

"There are no reasons. There is nothing else but this power, this rare and wonderful fire that flames between us. It is as old as the earth itself, and as natural. You feel it as I do."

"Release me," she whispered raggedly. "Don't do this."

"I must, my exquisite swan. You *will* be mine." With excruciating slowness he turned her wrist over and brought his lips to taste the pulse that throbbed wildly there. "A woman of fire and ice." His lips traveled up her sensitive inner arm to the hollow of her elbow, which he teased with his tongue. "All damnable pride one moment and shattering vulnerability the next." He raised his head and studied her flushed cheeks, unable to hide the smile of triumph that curled his lips. *"My* woman."

Alexandra trembled at the relentless command in his smoky eyes. "I belong to no man!" she cried.

"Acknowledge it, my beautiful swan. You belong to me now." Deliberately, he surveyed her creamy skin, which flushed beneath his rough scrutiny.

She was drowning in his clear silver gaze. But a person is never truly captive, Alexandra told herself desperately. There is always some remnant of strength—some vestige of will, however small. A spirit never belongs to another unless given freely in love.

Love? How could love enter into this harsh bargaining? What room was there for love in the angular lines of that hard, tortured face above her?

When finally she spoke, it was the voice of a stranger—fierce, hoarse, ripped from the very core of her being. "You are a liar and a rogue, the very scum of the London streets! I admit nothing, do you hear, nothing except that I loathe you to the very depths of my being!"

Long fingers wove through hers, clenching tightly, pinioning her against the grassy bank. His eyes had gone gray and bottomless. They missed nothing—not the darkness that trembled in her eyes, not the hoarseness of her voice, not the delicate flush upon her ivory skin.

"You will," Hawke vowed roughly. "Before we've finished I'll have the words, even if I have to wrench them from your lovely throat."

Slowly, he lowered his powerful body. Alexandra shivered as she felt the rugged imprint of his taut manhood against her thighs. Unconsciously, her mouth softened for his touch, yet he did not give it. Her tongue came out to moisten her lips, and she knew a raw hunger for the taste of him.

Still he did not move. She felt his warm breath and the throbbing of his heart long moments before his lips took hers in fierce, hungry domination.

His mouth was sweet and hard upon her, marking her in the thousand indefinable ways that a man marks his woman. She was liquid fire beneath his tongue as he surged deep, then retreated, a sensual imitation of the greater joining to follow. Alexandra moaned raggedly, molding her mouth to his even as she twisted against his iron frame.

Hawke's hand slid to her knees, lifting the skirt that was by now only a little damp. Long, masterful fingers swept her inner thigh. "Goddess, you are. Queen of my swans," he whispered as his teasing fingers rose higher. "I must give you my brand. Here. And here. No one else will ever taste you." His weight shifted, and he pushed up her skirts, bringing his mouth to the satin skin at the top of her inner thigh. "My swan mark, here. You'll be for no other man." His lips were restless fire as he pulled the soft skin into his mouth, sucking roughly, then nipping her with his teeth.

Alexandra moaned at the dark erotic strokes. She thought of his mark upon her, and against every instinct it set her aflame.

There was a tiny snap as he released her and pulled away to survey his work. "A crescent moon. That shall be your swan mark. And only I shall know where you carry it." Hawke's voice was raw. "See my mark upon you, Alexandra."

Alexandra lowered tremulous eyes and saw the small wine-colored crescent upon her pale thigh. She gasped at the power of that erotic sign and felt suddenly the power of his claiming.

Branded by his passion. Marked, forever. His woman.

Madness! Unthinkable!

Her eyes were tormented when she raised them to his face.

"No," he rasped, "this will be a new beginning between us.

Forget the past and everything before this moment. Give yourself to me," he whispered. "Let me teach you the ways of love. I'll keep you safe—and well satisfied." Strong fingers stroked her thigh, then climbed to find her wild tangled silk and the honeyed depths beyond. "Ah, love, at last! So sweet. So hot. Let me taste your sweetness."

His velvet tongue was upon her, coaxing, tormenting, driving the last shreds of reason from her mind. "Let me go!" she begged.

Then she thought no more, for her whole being gathered into a shimmering core of raw nerve endings, and with a choked cry she shattered beneath his demanding touch, fighting him even as he swept away the last barrier of her pride.

And then Hawke set his swan mark upon her—unseen, immutable.

For all time.

Chapter Twenty-One

The flimsy wooden door of the Lion smashed in two, and fragments of wood flew across the whole width of the crowded room.

"Where is 'e? Where's the bleedin' bastard?" an angry voice bellowed. The owner of that voice came into view a moment later, a stocky man, dressed all in black, his bulk vast muscle without the slightest ounce of fat. With a graphic curse he kicked away the splintered wood and stepped into the smoky room.

Like restless shadows the occupants of the nearby tables scuttled away from his angry glare. The room grew totally still.

"Where's the nib cove?"

Rose Watkins had heard the explosive crash from the next room, where she'd been busy watering a tub of gin. Now she strode into the uneasy silence, her hands balled on her hips. "What the bleedin' hell've ye done to my door, Tom Taylor?"

"Ye'll be worryin' about the hole where yer head used to be if ye don't tell me where Telford is!" the man in black snarled. Just then, two more men stepped through the ragged hole where the Lion's door had once stood.

"Stow the whids," Rose snapped, sliding her hands into her pockets and feeling the comforting outline of the pistol concealed there. "Follow me to the back room, so we can discuss this proper like!"

In the silence a new voice was raised—a soft flat voice from a table near the foot of the stairs.

"I fancy these persons must be looking for me, Mrs. Watkins. Bring us some brandy—unwatered for once, if you please."

The nervous onlookers squeezed toward the door, opening a clear space down the middle of the room.

The man at the far table carefully straightened the lace at his cuff, then turned to study the three men before him. "I am James Telford. But I cannot conceive what business you claim with me."

The man in black strode across the room and leaned over to stab the table with thick, scarred fingers. "Did a job for ye, cove. Reck'n ye figured we'd not be comin' back fer payment. But we did. So ye better pay up. Here and now, if ye know what's good fer ye."

Telford's flat, emotionless eyes surveyed the stocky man. "But I've never seen you before in my life. You must have taken me for someone else." He shrugged dismissively, and his slim fingers dropped to the arms of his chair.

"Like hell, I have! Hired us to crack a crib over Alfriston way. Lost my two best men in the bargain. Now ye'll pay up, or I'll—"

"Or you'll what?"

The man curled over the table blinked at the cool, dispassionate tone of that strange voice. "Why, first I'll stuff that fine lace down yer bleedin' throat, and then I'll—"

A trill of lilting laughter halted the man's angry tirade. Infuriated, he turned and looked up into the most beautiful face he had ever seen.

Her eyes were the color of the morning sky, Tom Taylor thought dimly, and her hair the color of sunset. He could not draw his gaze away as the woman moved gracefully behind Telford and laid a slim hand tipped with bloodred nails upon his shoulder.

"Dear James, you do associate with some of the oddest creatures. What is it the man is threatening to do?"

Tom Taylor blinked, suddenly recalling his mission and his betrayal. He shook his head, cursed crudely, then focused on the gentleman in the crimson waistcoat once more. "Five hundred pounds, ye bastard! On the table. Now."

Telford smiled gently, a thin quirk that barely touched his lips. "Very well. I see I have no choice but to reward you as you deserve."

The man in black waited silently. His two companions sidled closer behind him, greedy for their share of the purse.

Without warning three blasts rocked the room. The table splintered and human blood and skin and bone sprayed from the spot where seconds before, three greedy men had stood an angry vigil.

For long moments no one moved. Then slowly the gentleman in the crimson waistcoat lifted his hands from beneath the table. Carefully, he laid two silver-handled pistols side by side upon the scarred wood.

The woman behind him quietly added a third pistol to the line. "A very good shot, James," she said silkily. "I rather fancy we both are."

Rose Watkins was the first to move, stepping over the grisly red debris staining her floor.

"Sorry to cancel my order, Mrs. Watkins," Telford said with a faint smile. "But I fear that Mr. Taylor and his friends won't be joining me after all."

"Yer a bleedin' cool one," the Lion's mistress said with reluctant admiration.

The flat eyes of the man before her registered no emotion at the compliment. "And now, Mrs. Watkins," he said softly, "I believe you once told me you might fetch me anything in London." The colorless eyes narrowed, suddenly very intent. "Anything at all."

Chapter Twenty-Two

For long minutes the two people on the bank did not move. A soft wind stirred the long grass, and beside them the stream murmured on. A bird trilled from a shadowed hedge. A large fish darted sharply from the water and fell back with a rich plop.

Alexandra's eyes fluttered open.

Her skirts were bunched up to her waist, and a man's heavy body slanted across her, pinning her to the ground. Silver eyes plumbed her very soul.

She remembered where she was, and with whom. Suddenly, all the color drained from her face. "What have you done to me?" she cried, her voice raw and tormented.

Hawke did not move. For a moment it was as if he had not heard. His hand did not waver, nor his gaze, but through his fine cambric shirt she felt the wild drumming of his heart, echoing her own. Only a muscle flared against the hard line of his jaw.

"I've won our wager, Alexandra," he said at last, his voice oddly gentle. "You are mine now, marked with the fire of our passion and with the ecstasy I will bring you again and again as my woman."

An errant beam of light played across her unruly curls, turning them a blushing gold. How impossibly lovely! Hawke thought. How unbelievably responsive!

Fire in his hands, after years of Isobel's ice.

He studied her eyes, the color of the dawn sky, cloudy and haunted, shadowed in the wake of her passion. Her fire was everything he had ever dreamed of, and Hawke knew then that he had to have her.

Forever.

From the bank above them a pebble rolled free and slapped hollowly into the streaming current. Somewhere beyond, a horse neighed restlessly, then another pebble spun into the water. For a moment neither of them heard, their world drawn too taut to permit intrusion.

A shadow fell over them.

Hawke was the first to raise his head and stare with narrowed eyes up the bank.

"What in the Devil's own name is goin' on here?" a hard voice rang out above them.

Hawke smothered a curse. He should have been faster, he thought grimly. He would have been if he hadn't been caught in the spell she wove. Yes—and if he hadn't been in torture from the fiery ache at his groin. His head reeling, he struggled to pull his jacket around Alexandra, shifting his hard body to cover her nakedness.

She gasped when she felt the full swell of his arousal, and that made him curse again, more explicitly this time.

Who the devil dared to come here? He'd left strict orders with Davies that no one was to disturb them. This morning the stream was off limits to even the prince regent himself, by God!

He stared up at the dark figure silhouetted against the sun, irritated that he had to clear his throat before he could speak. "Who the hell wants to know?" Whoever had disobeyed Hawke's express orders was going to be very, very sorry.

"The water bailiff of Hawkeswish, by God—and ye'll answer to His Grace for this encroachment!"

The harsh words died in Hawke's throat, and savage anger turned to black amusement. He threw back his head and laughed.

"Havers, you old curmudgeon! What are *you* doing here? You were confined to bed, the last Davies told me!"

The voice turned uncertain. "Yer Grace? Never tell me that—" There was a low, muffled curse. "Forgive me! I thought—" More throat clearing. "Reck'n I'll be gone then, seein' as how—" The other man stopped again, then plunged desperately on, gruffly trying to be matter-of-fact. "Downstream sluices been in need of checkin' this age."

"Have they?"

"Oh, aye, Yer Grace."

"An excellent idea then, Havers."

Abruptly, the shadow fell away, and light bathed Alexandra's face once more. She felt Hawke's chest rumble when he looked down at her.

" 'Tis only Havers—the man I mentioned earlier, who taught me to fish these waters. A rare hand, he is. Always a stickler for his responsibilities, even though Shadwell reported him nearly on death's door last week."

His words dropped like hollow coins into the pool of wary silence between them. Alexandra rose to her elbows and struggled to push him away. "You've won nothing, do you hear?" she cried. "Whatever happened was forced, not given willingly. I shall never be yours!"

Instantly, the duke's hand flattened on her shoulder and pinned her, squirming, against the cool earth.

"I won, Alexandra. Do not try to deny it. I won, and you stay."

"No, damn it! You've won nothing! I hate you too much to feign indifference. I'll always hate you—for what you are, and for what you've done to me!"

Her fingers raked his cheek, drawing blood. With a savage curse Hawke captured her flailing hands and wrenched them above her head. "So this is the value of your word?"

"I keep no bargains with the Devil!" Alexandra spat back, twisting furiously beneath him.

"Cold-blooded little bitch," Hawke said with soft menace. "Perhaps you're like Isobel after all. Perhaps I should take you as I meant to take her. Since you call me the Devil, let me act the part."

Something twisted in his face, something that made Alexandra know a moment of raw panic. "You wouldn't," she whispered.

The sneer that contorted his chiseled features was cruel and very ugly. His fingers dropped to the buttons of his breeches.

Alexandra moaned, shamed by the hot tears upon her cheeks.

"Are you afraid, my lying little whore? Does the fear make you hot and hungry for my throbbing shaft?" he growled. "You'll have it soon, I promise!"

A wild sob broke from Alexandra's lips. "Madman! Monster! Release me!"

"You've struck a bargain with the Devil, woman! He never goes back on his promises."

He freed his rigid manhood and pressed her down beneath him, grinding savagely against her thighs, letting her taste the full force of his fury. "Here I am, all at your bidding. Open your legs for me, harlot!"

With his free hand he wrenched up her skirts, seeking the hot tangled curls at the junction of her thighs.

"Please," she pleaded raggedly, beyond pride or shame.

"Please continue? Nothing will stop me, I assure you!"

"Stop, Hawke! Don't do this. *Not again!*"

Something in her voice cut through Hawke's fury. He froze, looking down at her face and seeing the tears glinting on her pale cheeks—just as he had that night in the forest, after he took her for the first time.

Hawke's face twisted and he cursed viciously.

The next thing Alexandra knew, he had rolled off her and risen to his feet.

"I'll stop, alright. You're not worth the struggle. Why should I fight with a cold little bitch when there are hundreds of women eager to share my bed? Experienced women, who know how to pleasure a man! Women honest enough to give their passion freely!" His boots squished up the damp bank, across the thick ferns and water grass. "I've had my fill of manipulative females like you, by God!"

A moment later, Alexandra was alone.

Slowly, she sat up and smoothed her skirts with numb fingers.

Damn you, Hawkesworth! she thought. And damn me for falling into your trap! Again!

With wobbly legs she stood and stumbled down the hill toward the stream, where she cupped her hands and dashed cold water to soothe her burning cheeks. At that moment she looked down and saw her face, her eyes dark and cloudy, her lips still swollen from his savage touch. So different from the youthful innocent who'd angled with her hands for trout an hour before!

From her thigh came a faint prickling, and she remembered the mark he had set upon her. With terrible consciousness she thought of all that had followed. An angry tear tumbled silently into the darting silver currents, currents that just now reminded her of the Duke of Hawkesworth's cold eyes.

Another tear splashed quietly into the restless stream. She sneezed.

I've shamed myself. I've betrayed the man I will marry.

At that thought, Alexandra's mind rebelled. It was her captor's fault, damn him! Everything had come of his recklessness, his colossal arrogance.

With a surge of bitterness, she shrugged on the damp jacket of her habit. Her eyes narrowed when she saw at her feet the garment Hawke had loaned her. Suddenly, she chucked the soft wool into the swift current and watched with smoldering fury as it disappeared downstream.

If only she could drown the *man* so easily!

Five minutes later, Alexandra stood at the brow of the hill, her stiff, angry spine turned to the wind. Below her feet the downs spread out like a green patchwork quilt.

As she had expected, the horses were gone.

Blaze and bedamned! The man meant to allow her no chance to escape, did he?

Her mouth was set and determined as she studied the stream's silver curve where it dropped away to the south. For a moment she saw nothing but grass and meandering thickets; then she noticed Aladdin's russet coat in the shadow of an oak tree. Two men stood speaking animatedly beside the horse.

Yes, Your Bloody Grace, Alexandra thought, this shabby scene is played. Tossing her skirts angrily, she turned and walked quickly along the hill in the opposite direction.

In other circumstances Alexandra would have found the setting delightful. A fresh wind rustled the grass, redolent with the scent of verbena and sea salt. Overhead, a pair of jackdaws wheeled gracefully. But on this occasion her eyes fell unseeing upon the fragile blue gentians that danced against the springy turf.

She had gone no more than fifty paces when she heard the thunder of horse's hooves. She broke into a run.

"Yer Grace! Stop! You must not—" The quavering voice behind her halted. "The duke is waitin' for ye downstream." Only the bailiff's obvious discomfort made Alexandra slow her steps.

The old man was breathing heavily by the time he came abreast, mounted on Bluebell. His honest, ruddy face was creased with concern. "And ye're goin' in the wrong direction! 'Tis nine miles over the downs to the great house, as Yer Grace must recall. Ye must not attempt it!"

Alexandra's lips twitched angrily as she spun around, hands thrust upon her hips. "You err in your address, sir. I am not the Duchess of Hawkesworth. And I do not mean to return to that house!"

She turned and resumed her determined march. Behind her came a sharp intake of breath. "But Yer Grace—madam— miss—" Havers sputtered off uncertainly.

Alexandra merely continued walking.

Several minutes later, she came to a narrow white trail—probably a shepherd's path—which she followed along the crest of the downs. As she moved north, the smell of the sea began to fade. Her habit was only a little damp now, although the chill had penetrated her bones, for she was still accustomed to the heat of Madras. Her ankle was stiff; by the time she reached her destination, she knew it would be far worse.

With narrowed eyes she studied the ground until she found a long gnarled branch to use as a cane. It was not much to look at, she thought wryly, but it would take some of the weight from her ankle.

Behind her came the drum of hooves once more. The old man was nothing if not diligent, Alexandra thought. This time, when the horse thundered closer, she did not stop. "Go back and tell your master that his swan has swum away!" she called over her shoulder.

"Where the hell do you think you're going?" Hawke growled, his face a frozen mask of anger.

Alexandra thrust her hands upon her hips as Aladdin's muscled flank cut off her advance. "So you deign to come yourself this time, instead of sending a tired minion! Do you mean to throw me across your saddle again? I warn you not to try it, for this time I have nothing left to lose, and my nails are very sharp!"

Aladdin danced uneasily, raising small clouds of chalk in the white track, but Alexandra refused to step back. She'd rather be trampled than show any sign of weakness before this brute.

"I should have known that you're exactly like the rest of your sex—an inveterate liar! But that changes nothing. You *will* stay."

"I'd rather face the lowest slime of the London docks than stay a moment longer in your company!" she hissed.

"God's blood, woman! What will it take to make you understand the danger you run? *Your only protection is with me.* Somewhere out there, Telford is waiting. Until I've flushed him from cover, you have no choice but to remain."

"As your prisoner!" Alexandra cried furiously, stamping her foot. Immediately, a bolt of pain shot through her ankle, and the makeshift cane fell unnoticed to the ground.

"*Prison* is such an unpleasant word," Hawke sneered. "You can have no idea of the life you would lead in a place like Newgate."

"Enduring Newgate would be infinitely preferable to enduring *your* company."

"The choice is not yours to make! Now, will you stop thinking of yourself for once, damn it? It's almost ten miles to Hawkeswish. In any other circumstances I would be delighted by your stubborn insistence to attempt it, for the walk might cool your damnable temper. But Havers is still weak from his illness. *He* cannot make the trek with equal impunity."

"What concern is that of mine? He has Bluebell," Alexandra snapped, her arms crossed stiffly against her chest.

"He will not take the horse while you walk, of course," Hawkesworth said impatiently, as if addressing a simple child. "If you walk, he must insist on walking too. To ride would be unthinkable."

"Well, of all the cockeyed—! I suppose you let him believe I'm your wife too!"

Hawke's eyes flashed with irritation. "No, I did not, but Havers's code is strict. He would never allow a woman—any woman—to career across the downs on foot while he rode."

"Very well. In that case I shall take Bluebell, and you may ride with the old codger."

"Impossible," Hawke said flatly.

"Why not? Because the great sahib wishes otherwise, of course."

"Because, little fool, the poor man would be mortified."

Abruptly, Alexandra had another idea. "Then let him ride with me."

"Out of the question!" Hawkesworth said sternly. "He would be just as mortified riding with you as he would with me. You will ride in front of me, damn you, and there's an end to the matter. I won't see an old man made ill because of your stubborn pride."

Anger flashed from her aquamarine eyes as Alexandra made an elaborate mockery of a curtsey. "But, of course! I am only an unworthy slave who bows at your feet, master!"

"If Havers weren't nearing collapse over that hill, I'd take you across my knee and—"

"Just bloody try it!"

Hawke's smoky eyes narrowed suddenly. "How did my jacket come to be floating in the stream? Or do I dare ask?"

Alexandra's gaze dropped to Aladdin's twitching tail. The horse expertly flicked a fat black fly from his hindquarters. "I threw it there," she snapped.

Hawkesworth shook his head in disgust. "I might have known." What a fool to have thought the hellion might be in danger! he thought grimly. "Well, you may congratulate yourself. Havers insisted on hoisting the damned thing out and nearly drowned himself in the process. Do you now mean to decimate my staff?"

"Of all the abominable, blockheaded, *bovine*—"

"Get on the horse, damn it!"

Alexandra shot him a fulminating look. She thought briefly of running, but the open downs offered little chance of concealment.

"Forget it," Hawke warned roughly. "I'd run you down before you topped the rise." His tone grew sharp with impatience. "Can't you swallow your damnable pride for even a moment? For a man who might well be your grandfather's age?"

"That's unfair!" she blurted out. "By the sands of the Ganges, you twist everything!"

Hawke did not wait any longer. He drove Aladdin forward, reached down, and swept Alexandra up into a crushing embrace. Then he pulled her before him in an awkward imitation of the sidesaddle position.

Aladdin danced skittishly as Alexandra turned slashing fists against Hawke's chest. "Let me go, you vile creature! This game is played!"

"So you think it's a game, do you? Telford plays no games, and neither do I, as you'll soon discover." He cursed when Alexandra's nails raked his cheek, then twisted her hands behind her back. "Now sit still and stop squirming, damn it, before Aladdin throws us both!"

"I am not squirming," Alexandra answered furiously as he nudged the great horse into a gallop. With every movement of the animal beneath them, Hawke's taut muscles flexed and forced her back against the saddle of his thighs, leaving her in no doubt of his potent masculinity.

"Then stop whatever it is you *are* doing!" Hawke's right hand circled her back to take up the reins, and his lips grazed her ear for a fraction of a second. "At least wait until we're in bed, when you may exercise your passion to its fullest! In fact, I shall insist upon it."

Alexandra's face flamed crimson in anger. Every motion of the horse threw her back against Hawke's broad chest and muscled thighs. Even worse, she had nowhere to put her hands. When she tried to clasp them in her lap, Aladdin's spirited gait threw her off balance.

She simply refused to consider the other options.

Suddenly, Hawkesworth reined in his mount. "My dear Miss Mayfield," he said with the exaggerated clarity one used to address a simpleton or an impossible child, "you must do something with your hands. Hold on to my shoulders or circle my waist—grasp my head, if you must. But do something! I promise I'll read no more into it than a very prudent desire not to fall from the horse and take me with you."

His eyes were an unsettled gray when Alexandra shot him a scorching look. Curse the man, she fumed.

Gingerly, she lifted her hand and positioned it at the very edge of Hawke's shoulder, keeping their contact as slight as possible.

"Come, come—you can do better than that."

Alexandra seethed, remembering the last time she had sat a horse with him. Suddenly, at the duke's urging, Aladdin reared, his great hooves pawing the air, and she was thrown crazily off balance.

Desperately, she grabbed Hawke's shoulder for support, her fingers just below the long hair at the back of his neck. Immediately, she felt the rumble of his mocking laughter.

"If only I had my cane!" she cried in helpless fury.

"Don't worry, you won't be doing any more walking today."

When they neared the lower stretch of the creek, Bluebell's questioning neigh echoed on the wind. A moment later, Havers appeared, wet clothes plastered to his rangy frame.

"Aye, that's more the thing. Now here's Bluebell, miss, and ye'll be back at Hawkeswish right and tight in a quarter hour. I've the weirs to check anyway before I wind my way home."

"Take the roan," Hawke ordered, "and leave the weirs for tomorrow. Then it's dry clothes and a warm fire for you."

"But Yer Grace, it's barely midday!" the old man protested. Suddenly his face darkened. "If ye think I'm not up to the work then—"

"I mean to keep an eye out for vipers, and I'd like your assistance on the way back," Hawke explained quickly.

"Well, if ye put it that way. . . ." The bailiff frowned uncertainly.

Hawke decided to end the discussion. "That's settled then. Now let's be off, for I'm famished and you must be numb to the bone. On the way back you can tell me how the trout are doing."

Reluctantly the old man mounted Bluebell and followed Hawke

over the hill. Suddenly, a smile lit the bailiff's face. "Yes, real beauties they be in the high stream hereabouts. None to match them anywhere else in Sussex."

"Miss Mayfield caught one."

The bailiff frowned and scratched his head. "But I saw no poles. How did she—" The bailiff directed a shocked look at the grinning duke. "Never say ye were tryin' to teach the young miss to stroke a trout, Yer Grace! A fine way to go on, and I don't mind sayin' so!"

Alexandra slanted a look at the arrogant duke to see how he accepted this rebuke from a servant, albeit a respected one.

He seemed in no way put out. "She was actually rather good at it, Havers. With a little practice she could become your star pupil."

"Was she now? Comin' from ye that's high praise indeed, for ye had the quickest pair of hands I ever saw."

Alexandra couldn't contain a tiny sniff at Havers' words.

"It's been a long time, Yer Grace," the bailiff said quietly. Was there a touch of sadness in his voice? Alexandra wondered.

"Eight years," Hawke answered. A silence fell between them, and Alexandra had a feeling that both men were grappling with memories—and judging from the set of their faces, they were not pleasant ones.

Finally, Havers cleared his throat. "This may not be the time to speak of it," the old bailiff said uncertainly, "but I must be tellin' ye there's matters needin' your attention here, Yer Grace. The downstream weirs fierce in need of repair. Lower stretches of the stream siltin' up, and the swans . . ." The old man's voice trailed off sadly.

"What about the swans?" the duke asked sharply.

" 'Tis dyin' off they are, Yer Grace. What with the siltin' of the shallows and problems with the weirs, the cygnets can't pass. 'Tis trapped in the marshes they are. Aye, trapped there, until they die." Havers' ruddy face took on a fierce look. "Royal swans have swum the high stream here for eight generations of Hawkesworths, with all the grace and purity we mortals will ever know this side of paradise." His voice hardened. "I only hope they'll be here for the ninth generation to enjoy as well!" Abruptly, the old man broke off, done in by the unaccustomed strain of so much talk.

"Why was I not told of this sooner?"

" 'Twas not for lack of tryin', Yer Grace. Davies's had my warnin's time and again, and he promised to pass them on to ye in London. Maybe ye never had them. Maybe ye'd other things on yer mind." The bailiff's voice was flat with reproach.

Frowning, Hawke thought back over the turmoil of the last two years. Two years since Isobel's departure. Two years during which he had forgotten just about everything else in his desperation to find his wife and rid himself of his reckless obsession.

He didn't recall hearing anything about the problems at Hawkeswish, but he couldn't honestly say they hadn't been mentioned. In the last two years he'd given his steward's monthly reports only scant attention.

With a feeling of shame Hawkesworth realized how far out of touch he had become with his staff and the conditions at Hawkeswish. The problem with the swans, he saw suddenly, was only one example of how he'd allowed things to slip while he was preoccupied in London.

"Then there's the matter of the vipers," the white-haired bailiff continued gruffly. "Somewhere they're breedin'. Tracked 'em time and again, I have, but can't find their nest. More than I ever saw before. What with the mild winter just past, we can expect even worse. Fairly worries me to death, Yer Grace, though I don't count myself afraid of much in this world."

This time, the reproach in the old man's voice was patent. The snakes were a menace at the best of times, Hawke knew. With their numbers swelled . . .

"Have you searched the lowlands near the grotto?"

"Where ye caught yer first viper on yer tenth birthday? That I did right off. Caught one family there, but no more. The rest must've found a cool protected spot—a cave maybe. If only I had a few more men I could—"

"Why were not a dozen assigned to you?" the duke interrupted impatiently.

For long moments the bailiff did not speak, hesitating uncomfortably.

"Well?"

" 'Twas not Davies's place to go against yer orders, Yer Grace. 'Footmen to keep to the house, stable men to keep to the stables, and gamesmen to the park.' Those were yer last words on the subject."

Hawke felt a cold weight in his stomach as he remembered saying those words. Words spoken in anger and bitterness. Words spoken after he'd come across Isobel and that fresh-faced groom panting in the shrubbery.

"All that is about to change," Hawke said curtly, burning with anger at himself for his gross negligence over the last years. "You'll soon have all the help you need, Havers. We'll find the nesting grounds and rid Hawkeswish of this black menace. And hereafter, you have my permission to take whatever steps are necessary to protect the swans. Hire a hundred stout men from Alfriston, if necessary, and build new weirs. I mean to lose no more swans," he added harshly. His vow was as much to the woman riding before him as to the old bailiff.

Alexandra stiffened at his words. They would soon see about that!

"That I will, and promptly, Yer Grace! 'Tis a pleasure to have ye back again. And I'll be beggin' yer pardon for sayin' so, but 'tis at Hawkeswish ye belong. Yer no more the Marquess of Derwent. Two years it's been since yer father died. Yer the seigneur now. 'Tis Hawkeswish that needs ye."

And you need Hawkeswish. Although the white-haired bailiff did not say the words, he might as well have, Hawke thought.

Overhead, a kestrel hung in the wind, cried shrilly, then darted toward the cliffs to the south. Hawke watched blindly, feeling a crushing weight of guilt, recognizing how close he'd come to disturbing forever the beauty and order of his ancestral home.

He'd never take Hawkeswish for granted again, by God! "One more thing, Havers."

With a look of dismay, the old man abruptly halted his joyous plans for the new weirs.

Hawke's face was unreadable. "These grand projects are not to commence until tomorrow. Today it's still warm clothes and a fire for you."

"Aye, Yer Grace," the bailiff said happily.

Engaged in his thoughts, Hawke did not notice the sudden stiffening of the woman riding before him.

"Marquess of Derwent?" Alexandra asked sharply.

"My courtesy title before my father's death. You know the name, I see. I wonder if I ought to be complimented or offended that my reputation has preceded me. Do I dare ask what exaggerated tales you've heard?"

Alexandra did not speak. The green downs swam crazily before her staring eyes, which darkened with a flash of blind hatred.

"As bad as that?"

Her teeth grated as she struggled to choke back deadly rage. He could laugh about his reputation! This blackguard, whose lazy, careless signature had endorsed her father's recall notice?

Marquess of Derwent? Now the Duke of Hawkesworth?

Her father's murderer!

Riding in taut silence, Alexandra clutched her bitterness to her like a cache of bright golden coins and pondered the future. Gone was her fury, and in its place stood cold determination and a raw hunger for revenge.

Unseen by her captor, Alexandra's aquamarine eyes hardened. Yes, it would be sweet, she told herself, so very sweet to see this man suffer. It would be her pleasure to make him taste the torment her father had experienced during the last days of his life.

A tight little smile twisted her mouth as she saw the great house in the distance.

Yes, she would stay—and gladly! She would study him. She would learn everything about him.

And when the time was ripe, she would ruin him, as cruelly and decisively as he had destroyed her father in India. It would give her pleasure as nothing else could. The thought of revenge had been all that kept her going through the bitter weeks after her father's suicide.

It seemed that fate had brought her on a long and twisting path and delivered her into the keeping of her worst enemy, then presented her with the means to mete him the savage punishment he deserved.

Perhaps, she thought grimly, there was justice in the world after all.

Chapter Twenty-Three

The shadows outside Alexandra's window grew long and spindly.

Behind the wooded hill the sun faded, and the shaded lines bled together into the gathering gloom of twilight. Then blackness fell upon the downs.

Night. A time for dark imaginings. A time for revenge.

She stood motionless at the window long after the moon had climbed over the trees, and she saw before her not the rolling English countryside but images of a harsher plain.

To her dreaming eyes came the vision of tall schooners rocking at anchor while the sun climbed bloodred from the Bay of Bengal. She saw white stucco houses, quiet in the blazing noonday sun. In her ears was the rhythmic click of the punkah wallahs at their ceaseless fanning, while mint and ginger drifted in the window with the white dust of the bazaar.

She saw faces, too, some known and some unknown—her mother's fragile beauty, now no more than a dim memory. Her ayah's unlined walnut skin. Her father, his bearing stiff and regal to the end, only the pain in his eyes and the tenseness of his jaw hinting at an inner torment.

Alexandra reached out to him, but he looked right through her and marched off with his hands clasped behind his back, as he used to do when pondering some difficult question of government policy.

Father! Alexandra called vainly, but he was gone. He could not help her anyway. She was a woman now and revenge would be hers alone.

Across the room a doorknob clicked loudly.

"Why are you standing here in the dark?"

It was a rich voice, Alexandra thought impassively. A voice of dark compulsion. The voice of a man used to giving orders and being obeyed. The voice of a man who got whatever he wanted.

Except this time.

Behind her came the grate of a flint and the hiss of flame along a wick. His scent filled the room, the rich smell of the outdoors, of leather and wool and a faintly spicy soap.

She felt a tug at her hair as his bronzed hand circled a red-gold coil that spilled over her shoulder.

"Let go of me," she said coldly. "Before—" She stopped herself just in time.

Immediately, the duke's face changed, hardening. For an instant Alexandra saw surprise sharpen the deep gray eyes; then his cold mask dropped in place. "Before what?" Hawke's hand tightened, capturing the lock of hair.

"You're hurting me. You are a man who will always hurt people, I think."

"That was not what you thought this morning. This morning your body twisted with a different sensation, although you are loath to admit it. Why do you fight me, little hellcat?" he demanded roughly. "I offer you my protection and the myriad comforts that my wealth can provide. I offer you the pleasure of my body. At this moment I can think of a hundred women who would give anything to be in your position."

"Then make your offer to one of them, for I won't join the ranks of your besotted mistresses!"

Alexandra wrenched away from his hand, turned her back to his mocking face, and paced to the other side of the room. Looking down, she saw the lantern gleam on a dark shape protruding from beneath the bed.

Her eyes narrowed thoughtfully; then her breath caught in her throat. When she turned back toward her visitor a moment later, a smile curved her lips. "But perhaps I've been hasty," she said softly. "I shall think on what you offer. And perhaps tomorrow you will do me the honor of showing me some more of this charming countryside. Someplace distant and very secluded?" Her eyelids fell, and she studied him beneath a veil of lashes.

"What are you up to now?" Hawke growled, closing the distance between them in two strides to capture her shoulders. "One minute you're a termagant, and the next—" He dragged her roughly against his chest, his silver eyes blazing across her face. "The next minute, you employ the tricks of a practiced harlot. Which are you?"

"Take me riding tomorrow, and perhaps you'll find out," Alexandra challenged, running her tongue delicately across her upper lip.

Hawke's breath checked abruptly. Mesmerized, he watched the soft pink skin play across her damp lip. His groin twisted painfully with a hot stab of desire.

By God, he wanted her! Right there on the carpeted floor, her long ivory legs gripping his waist!

Right now.

Alexandra's mocking voice cut into his fevered thoughts. "Tomorrow, Your Grace. Unless you admit you cannot wait. A wager, let us call it."

"You little bitch," Hawke growled. Then abruptly, his hands dropped from her shoulders and balled into fists. "I can wait, Alexandra. Believe me, what I do to you tomorrow will be worth waiting for."

Long after Hawke had left her, Alexandra lay awake in bed watching his shadow move back and forth in the light beneath the connecting door. But he did not return, as she had known he would not. The wager and his twisted male honor prevented him.

No, the duke would not return before morning, and that would give her all the time she needed.

Carefully, she slipped from the bed and knelt on the floor, then searched until she found the heavy length of metal. Her trembling fingers caressed the cold barrel of the pistol that Telford's thug had used against her the day before. In the chaos that followed, it had been forgotten.

Alexandra crept to the window. In the dim moonlight she could make out a lead ball rammed home in the barrel. A long narrow barrel, she saw, rifled for precision. The weapon used the new style of copper percussion cap, she noticed, her eyebrows rising sharply. Hardly the sort of weapon one would expect to find on the beefy-fingered brute who had assaulted her.

But this was not his weapon at all, Alexandra realized. It belonged to James Telford, Hawke's deadly enemy.

How appropriate, then, that it had fallen into her hands.

Carefully, she tore a piece of cloth from her habit and wrapped it around the pistol's hammer. She didn't want the damn thing to go off until she was ready, Alexandra thought with a grim smile. She took another length of cloth, ran it through a hole she'd made in her chemise, and knotted the weapon securely in place at her knee, where it would be well concealed.

Then she stood up and surveyed her handiwork, her face set with cold determination.

She did not regret that she would have only one shot. Her father had taught her well. One would be enough.

In the gray dawn Hawke opened the connecting door, his face lined and shuttered. He was surprised to find Alexandra already dressed and ready, but he was careful not to show it. Her face was very pale, Hawke thought, and there were dark smudges beneath her eyes. She seemed very distant, almost preoccupied, which infuriated him.

They did not speak as they descended the broad stairs and found their saddled horses waiting.

Aladdin carried two full saddlebags, Alexandra noticed, looking questioningly at Hawke.

"We don't return until tomorrow." His slate eyes were hard and mocking.

She merely shrugged and did not look at him again, lest he see her tension and the bitterness that lurked just beneath the surface of her cool exterior.

Hawke's goal was a low hostelry near the coast, the haunt of sailors, smugglers, and trollops—a place where he would flaunt her and make her see exactly what he thought of her. He did not plan beyond that, although the idea of taking her back to the *Sylphe* hovered in the back of his mind. That would be decided in its own time, he told himself grimly.

He kept to a brisk pace—fast, but not so fast that it would tax the horses over a long distance. Steadily on they rode, and he did not rein in Aladdin until he saw the high crest of the chalk cliffs and the Channel glinting beyond. By then, the morning was well advanced.

"We stop here," he said curtly. As he spoke, he leaned back in the saddle to stretch his shoulders and neck, enjoying the warmth of the sun on his back.

"Where are we?"

"Someplace very remote," he answered mockingly. "The Channel is just beyond that rise, in fact. On a very clear day you can just make out the coast of France." He frowned, squinting against the sun, eyeing the line of offshore clouds. "But not today." Abruptly, he turned back, grasped the reins loosely, and crossed his hands before his chest. "Get down."

In spite of her resolve Alexandra felt a moment of fear. But she steeled herself to ignore it and held her thoughts upon the moment of perfect, burning revenge soon to come. The pistol was a cold weight upon her knee as she looked up at Hawke. "You do me too great kindness, sahib."

Grim faced, Hawke dismounted and removed the leather satchels from Aladdin's back. Then he set the horse free to graze.

"Won't they run away?"

"Aladdin won't stray far, and if I know Bluebell, she'll stay close to Aladdin."

Hawke took a blanket from one of the satchels and spread it on the ground. He lay back, propped on one elbow, and studied her coolly. "Come here, Alexandra," he ordered.

She jumped slightly, and their eyes locked. She was still standing next to Bluebell, her fingers gripping the reins. She could feel the horse at her back and was strangely loath to leave its comforting warmth. The mare nickered, sensing the strange tension between the two riders. For a long moment Alexandra did not move.

"You'll have to come a great deal closer than that for what I have in mind, my dear. Or have you lost your nerve?"

Alexandra's breath came fast and jerky as she saw the predatory silver gleam of Hawke's eyes. A moment later, she raised her chin defiantly and moved to sit on the corner of the blanket farthest from his reclining frame.

His hand shot out with lightning speed and dragged her sprawling across his chest.

"Much better," he whispered as his fingers slid across her back, molding her to his powerful body. "Why do you look so frightened, my dear? This outing was at your request, as I recall."

Alexandra clenched her teeth, steeling herself for the encounter to come.

Hawke's eyes narrowed. "I mean to have an answer. Which are you, my dear? Harlot or termagant?" Slowly, his hands moved down her back, curved to cup her buttocks, and forced her against his thighs.

She caught her breath as she felt the hard outline of his manhood hot and insistent against her belly.

Hawke laughed, but there was no trace of warmth in his hard, mocking glare. " 'Distant and very solitary,' " he reminded her. "Is this what you had in mind?"

Alexandra's mind was racing. She shifted her knee slightly, edging the pistol closer to her hand. "Someplace where we won't be disturbed, Your Grace," she answered, never taking her eyes from his face, afraid he might notice her preoccupation. "Someplace where we could get to know each other better without fear of interruption." As she spoke, her fingers searched vainly for the knot that held the pistol in place.

"And then?"

Alexandra twisted slightly. "And then?" she repeated, her voice faintly unsteady.

"Well? Is this another of your tricks, woman? There's a word for your sort of female, you know." Hawke's voice was jeering.

Suddenly, Alexandra found the knot. Her fingers trembling, she attacked the last obstacle to her long-dreamed-of revenge.

Just as the strands loosened, Hawke rolled over and pulled her beneath him. Feverishly, she grabbed the pistol and steadied it only a second before it would have fallen against his knee. Her heart lurched, and she prayed he had not noticed the telltale motions of her hand at her skirt.

"I don't know what you're about, Alexandra, but understand this—there'll be no more running. No more interruptions." Hawke's eyes were like a cold winter sea as he studied her. "I've a mind to teach you a great many things today. I'm certain you'll make an apt student."

The devil take him and his teaching! If only he would move his knee and let her finish! The pistol was nearly free.

Suddenly, Hawke reached down and swept Alexandra's hands above her head. "This will be what the first time should have been. Long and fierce, swan, until you beg me to end the sweet torment and plunge us both over the edge. Then you'll talk no more of running or freedom."

The wind whipped down over the hill and tossed Alexandra's red-gold curls until they lashed Hawke's face. An electric tension sizzled between them, shocking in its raw intensity. For a moment neither moved. Suddenly, a fat glob of water hit Hawke's face, followed by another.

Frowning, he looked up and saw a dark line of clouds running in toward the coast.

Damn it! Hawke thought. They'd have to seek shelter. Cursing long and fluently, he stood up and jerked her to her feet. With a shrill whistle he summoned Aladdin from the far side of the hill.

"Wh-What are you doing? Where are we going?" Alexandra demanded hoarsely. So close to revenge!

"Didn't you notice the storm? Or was your nightmare just another act?"

Alexandra looked to the south and shivered imperceptibly as she took in the black slash of clouds above the Channel.

"Come on," Hawke ordered, already dragging her up the slope.

The wind built quickly in force, tossing Alexandra's hair wildly and hurling rain into her face. As they crossed the hill, she saw a weathered barn set in a slight depression of the downs and a rough shed made of slanting planks behind it. Abruptly, Hawke released her and grabbed the horses' reins.

Out over the Channel a ragged finger of lightning leaped from the darkening sky. The horses tossed their heads and danced skittishly until it was all that Hawke could do to hold them.

"Go inside, while I tether the horses!" he shouted against the roll of thunder that followed.

Alexandra jerked open the heavy barn door and darted into the shadowed interior. She turned and put her shoulder to the door, struggling against the wind to close it. When it was at last latched in place, she tossed up her skirt and ripped the pistol free with trembling fingers. The binding around the hammer was the next to go.

Now! she thought wildly. Let him come now! She was ready.

The door creaked behind her, then crashed shut.

He was soaked, Alexandra saw in the brief flare of light from the door. His hair was plastered to his head like a dark pelt. He shrugged out of his jacket and strode to the wall behind the door, where he dug deep into the hay.

With a grim laugh Hawke exposed a hollow section of wall near the dirt floor. "Just where it used to be, by God!" From a hidden chamber behind the wooden plank he lifted a tinder box and an old lantern without panes. Next came a small wooden keg. "Smugglers use this place to land their silks and brandy," he explained. "When the excisemen aren't nipping at their heels, they rest here by day and move inland with the darkness."

He did not turn around but struggled with the flint to light a candle for the lantern. After several failed attempts he finally succeeded and rested the flickering light on an upturned barrel.

Once again he dug into the hiding place. This time he brought out two blankets, a length of French lace, and a pair of fine crystal goblets. "Run goods—specially ordered for a bride's trousseau, no doubt. Everything we need to be comfortable until the storm passes, including brandy direct from Paris."

Alexandra's cold fingers cradled the gun concealed in the folds of her skirt. "I should have expected you to know about such things," she said bitterly.

"The smugglers' comings and goings are common knowledge on the coast," Hawke said, shrugging.

"Yes, a murderer would know of such things."

"Murderer?" He frowned then, his attention caught at last. "What are you talking about?"

"You. The Marquess of Derwent. A murderer!" Alexandra said shrilly, finally giving voice to the words branded upon her heart so long ago: " 'We hereby order your immediate recall to London, where you will answer charges of bribery, corruption, and gross irresponsibility which led to a sepoy rising and the subsequent loss of 200 lives.' Do those words sound familiar, Your Grace? Do you remember signing your name to that document?"

Hawke frowned. What was the woman about now? "The recall of the governor-general after the suppression of the Vellore mutiny, I believe. I have some notion of the document. Why should it interest you?"

"Did it give you pleasure to grind a man into the gutter?" Alexandra cried as if he had not spoken. "To destroy twenty-five years of unstinting service to the Crown in one stroke of the pen? You, who had never done an honest day's work in your whole cursed life!"

"The letter was a joint decision by the whole board of control," Hawke said slowly. "A decision reached after two months of debate. Someone had erred: someone had to take the blame. Maitland was in charge; therefore it was his responsibility."

"As simple as that? Neat and clean and settled." Alexandra laughed, a cold, dead sort of sound. "But it's not so simple after all, Your Grace. For that man was my father, and you're going to feel the pain he felt, the burning jolt of the ball that ended his life!"

Slowly, Alexandra drew the gun from within the folds of her habit and raised it until the barrel pointed directly at Hawke's temple.

"Well, I'll be goddamned," he said softly.

"Without a doubt."

"Are you mad?"

"Perhaps I am," Alexandra cried, laughing recklessly. "But it's a happy sort of delirium to have you in my sights at last! To see you begin to suffer as he did!"

Hawke took a step forward. My God, he thought—she was Lord Percival Maitland's daughter?

"Don't move," Alexandra warned. "I can shoot the eye of a jack at ten paces."

"Your father again?"

"My father. A man whose name you aren't fit to utter."

"A man who nearly lost his garrison. A man who refused to take responsibility for his flawed decisions at a time of crisis."

"No!" she screamed, and the wind echoed her shrill protest. " 'Twas not his fault, but the fault of men who ordered him to do the impossible. Men who knew not the slightest thing about conditions in India. Men like you, damn your soul!"

Hawke moved slightly closer. "And you planned this whole thing for revenge? You were searching for me that night in the fog?"

"Of course," Alexandra lied. "I came to make you crawl. To make you right this obscene injustice against an honest, decent man." A bolt of lightning crashed overhead, and her hand quivered slightly.

"Ah, but I won't crawl." Slowly, he stalked closer. "But I think you will. Hear that, Alexandra? The storm is nearly upon us. Hear the drum of the thunder." His eyes were silver pinpoints in the gloom. "The Devil's fire."

"Stop!" she cried furiously, hating the tremor of her hand, which soon grew to a visible shaking. "Storm or not, I'll put a ball through your skull. At this distance I can't miss—not with a weapon like this."

"Did Telford arrange this too?" Hawke asked in a tone of cool dispassion.

"I plan my own revenge!" Alexandra screamed. "I need no one's help! I've been planning this ever since the night I found my father's shattered body."

Hawke's eyes were shadowed and unreadable. "Have you ever shot a man, Alexandra?" he asked softly, taking another step closer. "Have you heard the last rattle of breath, been close enough to see the eyes go flat and vacant when the life is ripped out of them?"

"I'll see it soon!" she cried. "I'll laugh when you die!"

"I think not. You don't have what it takes."

A ragged bolt of lightning lit the room, and in the sudden flare Alexandra saw his mouth set in a thin line.

In the inky darkness after the lightning bolt passed, she saw a different room, bloodred, rank with the suffocating smell of death. Her father's body sprawled across the neatly stacked papers on his desk.

Alexandra's hand shook uncontrollably. "No!" she screamed. "You'll die for what you did to him! You and the two others who signed his death warrant!"

"The storm's nearly overhead now. Can you hear the wind?"

"Shut up, you bastard! It won't work!"

"Won't it?" he asked, taking another step until he stood no more than four feet from her. "Listen, Alexandra," he ordered with silken violence. "They call to you. Like the fiends of hell clawing at the door." As if in answer, the wind screamed and lashed the barn with sheets of rain.

"Stop!"

"They're coming, Alexandra. Can you hear?"

"Murderer!" she cried to drown out the sound of the storm. She shuddered as the Terror began to creep along her spine. "You might as well have shot him in the back! At least I'll face you when you die!"

A bolt of lightning crashed directly overhead, exploding like a giant fist across the wooden roof, hammering and rattling the whole building in the storm's unleashed fury. And then there was a new sound against the wind—a wild, ragged keening.

"I must do it!" Alexandra screamed helplessly, but her finger would not move.

"Go on then," Hawke growled. "Do it. Now."

Suddenly, there was a flare of light, and the lead ball exploded down the barrel, hissed past Hawke's ear, and neatly shot out the candle inside the paneless lantern.

"Forgive me, Father," Alexandra cried brokenly, throwing the gun away from her as if it burned her fingers.

The next moment, Hawke's hands were upon her shoulders, shaking her savagely. "So you meant to put a ball through my heart, did you, Alexandra Maitland? You'll wish you did before

I'm done with you," he said cruelly, pushing her down upon the hay.

She lay white-faced before him, her hands twisting at her waist. The storm was upon them in all its fury now, and without the lantern they were plunged into semidarkness.

Her breath came in little choking bursts as she fought the tremors that shook her limbs. Her beautiful eyes were wide and staring. "No," she moaned. "No more."

"Much more," Hawke vowed, dropping down to slant his hard body across her in the hay. "But this time it will be me and not a dream."

"Ayah!" she muttered, twisting madly to escape.

"Wake up," Hawke growled, trapping her restless body beneath him. "This is no dream. You're here, not back in India! Wake up, damn it! Fight me!"

Another violent bolt rent the air. Suddenly, Hawke heard a horse's wild neighing, then the muffled drum of hooves. Damn! They'd bolted even though he'd tethered them well!

His captive forgotten, he jumped up and ran to the door, throwing it open just in time to see Aladdin and Bluebell disappear into a gray wall of rain. Hawke cursed long and fluently.

He did not hear the rustling in the hay behind him until it was too late. As he turned, he saw his captive dart blindly past him into the fury of the storm.

Sharp, tiny nails ripped her flesh, and a thousand stabbing fingers pulled her down. Hungry teeth snapped at her legs.

Wildly she struggled, only to feel more hands claw her neck and scalp. Still Alexandra fought, for dimly she knew that to yield would be to die.

"Father?" she screamed, but only the shrieking wind answered, flinging her terror back at her.

The Devil's fire slashed through the sky and sent its ghastly light dancing over the earth. Long fingers wrapped around her neck and tightened relentlessly. Choking, she struck at the rigid fingers but met only air.

Black waves of fear crashed over her, and a queer whine rose in her ears.

They screamed her name in a thousand voices, and above the din she heard the sound of her own terror. She choked, desperate for air, and fell to her knees, flailing crazily.

The iron bands tightened until blackness licked at the edge of her dreaming mind. Then the wind roared and tore the last racking sob from her throat.

Cursing, Hawke struggled up the hill against the slashing rain, unable to see more than a few feet in front of him. He ran stumbling toward where he had seen Alexandra disappear, praying he would find her before she reached the cliffs.

At the top of the hill he stopped, hunched into the wind, and flung the rain from his face to peer into the unrelenting curtain of gray before him.

That was when he heard her scream.

He plunged forward, half stumbling, and nearly fell over her in the streaming rain. She was caught against a dwarf hawthorn, struggling wildly, her glorious mane caught by a thousand tiny thorns. The more she fought, the tighter she was impaled. Yet like a crazed animal she thrashed, until tears soaked her face and her eyes were dazed with pain.

Suddenly she fell to her knees, screaming in blind terror.

"Stop fighting!" Hawke ordered, but the wind flung the words back at him, mingled with her wild hysterical laughter.

He tugged at her hair, then reached down into his boot for the knife he'd hidden there. It was five minutes' work to cut her free and throw her stiff body over his shoulder. Strangely, she no longer fought him.

She was shivering by the time he got her back to the barn. He tossed her down into the hay, and there she lay, her body rigid, her eyes glazed and unseeing. Grimly, Hawke jerked off her skirt and torn chemise and wrapped her in one of the blankets. He chafed her cold skin roughly, but she gave no sign of noticing.

With a savage curse, he reached for the keg of brandy, filled a glass to overflowing, and forced a small amount upon her. She took it without demur, unmoving in his arms. Again he tipped the glass against her mouth, more this time, and she coughed when the high-proof smuggled spirits burned down her throat.

Weakly, she fought the iron fingers forcing more of the liquid fire between her lips. "C-couldn't do it," she muttered brokenly. "Too much d-death already. Forgive me, Father."

Hawke smiled grimly. He stripped off his own clothes and pulled the blanket around them both. Soon he would give her something to beg forgiveness for, by God!

He slid his hand between their damp bodies and massaged her skin, forcing warmth back into the rigid muscles. Rain hammered on the roof like the hollow sound of his heart, and he asked the one question still gnawing at him. "Who sent you, Alexandra? Telford? Was this his idea?"

She mumbled something between short, jagged breaths, and Hawke bent closer to listen.

"Who?" he repeated sharply.

"No one. Me. M-my revenge. Against them all."

Hawke felt a harsh, blinding sense of relief. She was not lying this time, he knew, for the madness was upon her, and she could not lie in its grip.

"So this thing is between us alone," he whispered. His fingers massaged her spine and buttocks, and he pulled her into his body's heat, never ceasing his powerful strokes. "Wake up, Alexandra. The storm is nearly over. A new storm is about to begin, by God."

He drew slightly away, bringing his hands around to the cold, taut crests that teased his chest. His thumbs played over her nipples mercilessly, circling and closing again and again. Then his warm caressing fingers slipped lower, tracing her navel and massaging the hollow of her belly.

When she cried protestingly, Hawke brought his open palm to the junction of her thighs and forced her legs apart as he flattened his hand against her soft fur.

He recognized the exact moment when her whimper of fear became a moan of desire. Instinct and vast experience told him, even though she had not yet recognized it herself.

He knew and did not stop. He might have, had he been capable of rational thought, but by then the madness was upon him as well.

Searing muscle probed Alexandra's thighs. Suddenly, her eyes widened, and the ragged edge of dreams gave way to harsh reality. Her breath caught in a sob, and she pounded clumsily against his chest. "Let me go, m-murderer!" she cried. "Haven't you done enough?"

With a bitter smile Hawke trapped her fingers in one large hand and rose above her, his manhood rampant between them. "Not nearly!" He found what he was seeking, and his smile was thin and cruel as he parted her. "Not for you. Certainly not for me." She twisted wildly, but he captured her beneath a muscled thigh while his finger slipped inside, stroking deep and then retreating, over and over, until she arched blindly. "Not yet," he taunted.

Alexandra felt lightning play over her, exploding along her raw nerves and bathing her in silver fire. Her body was a thing apart now, molding itself to those expert hands, her taut muscles desperate for the release he held just out of reach.

And still she fought him.

Hawke's fingers circled, plunged deep, then quickly retreated. "Now?" he growled.

"N-never!"

"Say it!" he ordered.

"Oh, God, stop!" It was a last desperate plea.

"Tell me, Alexandra! No more lies."

It was madness, it was savage, blinding pleasure, and she could fight it no longer. "Please!" she cried in a voice not her own but a stranger's.

Abruptly, Hawke knelt and cupped her buttocks. He watched her face as he lifted her and plunged inside, filling her with living fire and hard throbbing muscle.

A moan broke from Alexandra's lips. "Damn you!" she cried. "I hate you for this!"

But he only laughed and pulled away until she twisted helplessly, desperate for his return. "Yes, Alexandra, like that, with little pleasure sounds upon your lips. Like this." His hands caught her ivory legs and pushed them apart so that their bodies met with savage, stunning force. "Feel it! Feel my fire."

Her mind poised on the edge of darkness, Alexandra moaned hoarsely. Still Hawke toyed with her, never giving her what he had taught her to need so desperately.

"You're not fighting me now, swan. You're struggling to get closer." He slipped his hand between them and found the tiny ridge of her desire, stroking her with an exquisite touch, careful not to push her over the edge as he relentlessly heightened her pleasure until she panted and tossed wildly beneath him.

"This way," he rasped. "This is how it will be between us! Always. Whenever I love you."

Again and again he brought her to pleasure's threshold, shredding the barriers between them, learning the things that made her moan and twist beneath him. He remembered it all and turned the knowledge against her a moment later, driving her again and again to the ragged edge of passion, only to pull back and prolong the raw torment.

For them both.

No regrets! Hawke told himself in black fury. No aching sense of loss! Only this fierce, gnawing blade of need. Only a man who used a woman as she was meant to be used, teaching her who was master before taking his own pleasure.

As if from a great distance, Alexandra heard his ragged groan and felt his thighs tense against her flanks.

"Now, swan!" he cried.

And then the velvet fury was upon her. The ground fell away, and she screamed, only to feel his strong fingers surround her. She forgot to breathe, she shattered, she rent the clouds. Through the sky she rode him, feeling the rain that was sweat dampen their skin, seeing the sparks of living lightning leap from his eyes.

Beyond the thunder he took her. Beyond the storm to a greater fury until the lightning played around her and plunged deep within her.

Until she was the storm itself, and only he could tame her.

And then Alexandra fell into the maelstrom, scattered into a million charged particles. She died in blackness and in silver, and there he taught her how to be reborn and rise once again from the ashes of their spent desire.

Chapter Twenty-Four

Later, much later, they slept, while the rain beat a steady drone overhead. The wind dropped, and heavy plumes of mist curled around the corners of the weathered barn. Inside, the smell of hay hung heavy upon the cool damp air.

Hawke was the first to wake. For long moments he did not open his eyes, enjoying a dark, drowsy contentment, warm still from passion kindled and spent not once but many times. He was not yet ready to face the harsh light of day with its crushing burdens of duty and responsibility. Instead, he flexed his shoulders, his mind and body satiated, smiling faintly as he listened to the rain tap upon the roof.

He yawned and lazily stretched out a hand, only to meet warm silken skin beneath his fingers. The effect was immediate and riveting. He jerked as if struck by lightning, and desire scorched a path along his groin. He felt himself swell with a burning hunger to possess her again—his proud, defiant captive asleep beside him.

Lord Percival Maitland's daughter, by God! Wealthy, cosseted, and high born. A tempestuous beauty who had stunned him with the fury of her passionate response. A woman who'd nearly murdered him for God's sake!

A grim smile played across Hawke's chiseled features as he

recalled how close he'd come to dying in the seconds before she shot the candle's flame off the wick. A damned good shot—she could have put the ball just as easily through his heart, he knew.

And yet she had not.

Careful, Hawke told himself. Women were God's curse upon men, created to dazzle and betray. Not one of them could be trusted. He had forgotten that once in his reckless obsession with Isobel.

It was not a mistake he intended to make again.

A muscle moved at his jaw as he looked down at the willful creature asleep in the straw, her glorious hair scattered like sunset clouds across her ivory shoulders. She was like no woman Hawke had ever known.

Perhaps it was her rare vibrancy that had taken him by storm. Perhaps it was her bold, flaming spirit after the cold, corrosive years with Isobel.

He did not know. He didn't want to know, afraid to explore his feelings too closely. It was enough for now that he wanted her, that he would hold her and have her, again and again, as long as his desire remained.

Whether she liked it or not.

It was the least the wench could do after tracking him to London with the express intention of murdering him! Hawke scowled as the insistent throbbing in his groin began to build. Smothering a curse, he rose on one elbow so that he could see her face when she came to consciousness. Then he waited.

Something sharp tickled Alexandra's nose, and she batted it away.

Warm. Soft. So tired.

Again came the tickle at her face, but she twisted to her side, unwilling to leave the snug cocoon of sleep.

Then her nose twitched sharply. The smell of straw, damp air and sea salt filled her lungs. Leather and horses. Once more she sniffed. A man's smell?

She smiled slowly, a delicious golden languor heavy upon her limbs. Then her fingers met a broad chest furred with dense, springy hair. Abruptly, her eyes flashed open, and she jerked upright in the straw, sending dry strands flying everywhere. Two bright circles of color stained her cheeks.

"Titania awakes," the man beside her said coldly. "I see that you slept well. A good tumble in the hay often has that effect. My compliments, Miss *Maitland*. Bedding agrees with you."

"You—you—" Alexandra sputtered. An instant later she was overcome by memories, shameful memories, that made her breath check in horror. Memories of exquisite, aching torment, followed by fierce and unfettered pleasure. She flinched and pulled a trembling hand before her eyes as if to ward off thoughts too painful to face.

Suddenly aware of her nakedness, Alexandra fell back, clutching straw to her trembling body. Streaks of crimson slashed across her cheeks, the only color in her pale translucent skin. "Savage!" she hissed. "Cruel, vicious savage!" Vainly, she tried to edge away from him, but he rolled smoothly and pinned her beneath a muscular thigh.

"If so, I am a savage who holds your father's reputation in his hands. And it was you who came in search of me, may I remind you. You were the one thirsting for my blood, intent on revenge and righting what you term a cruel injustice." His eyes were mocking. "I can only wonder what you meant to offer me in exchange for my help."

"I meant you first to crawl, to suffer as he did. Then, if you did as I asked and cleared my father's name, I would have let you go, worthless as your life is!"

"But you lost your chance when you discovered I wouldn't crawl and you hadn't the stomach for killing. So what's left for you to bargain with?" Hawke jeered, his face only inches from hers.

Alexandra glared back, her fingers balling into fists. Oh, if only she had a pistol to level between those hard mocking eyes!

"You do not answer?" Hawke growled, trapping her hands and crushing her beneath him in the warm straw. "This, perhaps?" With cool deliberation he scrutinized the creamy skin of her neck and shoulders, which flushed crimson beneath his taunting eyes.

"Stop, you contemptible snake!"

"Stop?" A dark eyebrow climbed mockingly. "But we're just

getting started, Miss Maitland. Now *you* are the one who must beg. For such a thing as you ask, I must have something of value in return. If not your body, then what?"

Alexandra twisted helplessly. Her breath came fast and jerky between clenched teeth. Wretched bloody man! She was fed up with his mockery and cold manipulation. A few hours ago, he had bent her to his will, taking cruel advantage of her paralyzing terror during the storm. But it would never happen again! she vowed, fighting the dark memories of his savage lovemaking.

"The satisfaction of correcting an injustice done to an innocent man!" she cried, forcing her thoughts away from those shameful images.

"Unacceptable, I'm afraid. All the evidence pointed to your father's guilt."

"Evidence offered by liars, by men who hated and envied him! Men he had punished for corruption and who sought to have their revenge by raising spurious charges against him!"

"Very stirring, my dear," Hawke said softly, his eyes narrowing. "But why, I ask myself? Why would a rich and desirable young woman devote her life to the bitter task of restitution and revenge? Why would she give up the chance for a home and family to pursue such a thankless quest? There is something unhealthy about all this."

"Love!" Alexandra snapped. "Loyalty! Things you would know nothing about, Your Bloody Grace!"

"Love?" Hawke repeated cynically. "Love and what else?"

"For honor's sake too! But I forget—a miscreant like you wouldn't know the meaning of that word either."

"And you would?" he scoffed. "No, to others you may lie—to yourself, even—but not to me. You're hiding something, Miss Maitland, and I'll have it out of you, mark my words. But until I do, we have terms to be set. What have you to offer in return for my help in clearing the charges against your father?"

Alexandra struggled furiously against his iron grip. "D-damn your depraved heart!" she sputtered, hating the silver eyes that probed her so relentlessly. With a cry of inchoate anger she twisted sideways and tried to sink her teeth into his wrist.

Hawke only laughed and moved his hands out of range. "I see

that I must answer for you then," he growled. "You have only one thing of interest to me, and that is your exquisitely responsive body, which would tempt a saint to transgress his holy vows. And that, my sweet, *dutiful* Alexandra, is how you'll repay me."

"Never, you bastard! You can't force me to—"

"Ah, but I don't propose to *force* anything. It's your assent I require—your passion willingly given when you come to my bed. You'll come to me of your own free will or not at all, my dear. I'll have all your passion and all your fire, not one spark less. If you want your father's case reopened and his honor restored, that is my price," he finished roughly.

"Never, you fiend! Never will I do such a thing!"

"So Lord Maitland's daughter is not so loyal after all? Not willing to overcome every obstacle to restore her father's reputation? Was all that talk of love just a sham too?" he sneered.

Alexandra strained wildly against his cruel grip, but she could not loosen those rigid fingers. "No, I won't listen! You twist everything! Even white you turn into vilest black." She tried to drag her hands toward her ears, but Hawke pulled them roughly away.

"A coward, too, I think," he continued ruthlessly. "Afraid to face your own passion. You know such an arrangement would bring pleasure to you as much as to me, for you have the fiery sensuality of a born courtesan. It shows in a thousand ways— every time you drop your lashes instinctively, every time you moisten your lips with your darting tongue. Every time your eyes burn upon me, I see your true nature revealed, my dear Alexandra. And yet not long ago you chided me for lacking honesty. Are *you* so afraid to face your own passion? Or has dishonesty become a habit with you?"

"The only thing I feel for you is passionate hatred," Alexandra hissed furiously, "along with an overwhelming desire to claw that insolent smile from your face!"

"Liar!" he growled. "Just like all the rest of your sex. I was a fool to expect you to be any different. But I'm a fool no more," he added, his voice hardening. "Today I collected my first installment against the payment you will make me for resurrecting your father's reputation."

Alexandra shivered as his words pounded over her like crashing waves—relentless, cold, and unforgiving.

"Mark me well—I will continue collecting as long as I choose to. Whenever I want. Wherever I want. *Whatever I want.* And you, Miss Maitland, had better pray that my desire for you lasts until our business is concluded."

"P-pray that your desire lasts?" Alexandra choked in fury. "What sort of foul insect are you? Does your treachery know no bounds?"

"Save your histrionics for a more appreciative audience," he said scathingly. "You were the one with murder on your mind. If we're to talk of treachery, we should begin with that."

"But I—" Abruptly, Alexandra bit back her denial, refusing to justify herself to this insolent blackguard. Never would she admit that their meeting in London had been the work of fate rather than her own design. That her plans for revenge had not included murder.

"Now, which is it to be?" her slate-eyed captor continued relentlessly. "Lord Percival Maitland reviled as a scoundrel down through history or hailed as a hero who walked the precipice and made the best of a dangerous situation? Everything depends on you, Alexandra—you warm and yielding in my bed. So give me your answer. I'll accept your pledge on our bargain, for I believe that you harbor some twisted notion of honoring your word."

"While you have no honor and offend every law of man and nature in making such a demand!" Her eyes were storm-tossed, sea-green against her white face.

"Ah, but you've said I'm the Devil himself, so you must not expect anything better of me. Now, give me your word, or I'll wash my hands of the whole affair."

Alexandra ground her teeth in helpless rage, but she was trapped, and they both knew it. She looked up at his shuttered face, hating this man who would give her no quarter. Long she studied him, repulsed by his cold arrogance, his insolent assumption of control over her life.

She was helpless before him, and once again revenge was to be denied her. Worse yet, she would be made to yield to her greatest enemy, so that her father's innocence might be proved at last. The irony of the situation suddenly struck her: her own innocence would be bartered for her father's.

But how could she do otherwise? What price was too high to ensure that her father was finally at peace?

"How unspeakably vile you are!" she cried. "But of course, you already knew that." She struggled to be as cold and merciless as he was. "Very well, blackguard, you may do what you will with me. But know that I'll be far away from you during those moments. That I come to you only because I love my father more than I hate you. Know always that the only thing I'll ever feel for you is raw hatred," she promised from between drawn white lips.

Hawke's eyes glittered as a small smile twisted his mouth. Alexandra did not know it, but there was nothing cool about his feelings for her. His lazy indifference was only surface deep, a habit learned after years of practice. "You challenge me exceedingly, Miss Maitland. Yes, it will be an exquisite pleasure to prove you wrong on both those counts."

"I don't give a damn what gives you pleasure!"

His eyes turned smoky, and Alexandra saw that one rose-tipped breast was revealed amid the scattered stalks of hay. With a stifled curse she burrowed down into the straw away from his mocking scrutiny.

Hawke's laugh was low and dark. "You ought to care, for my pleasure ensures your own. Luckily for you, however, I am not at leisure to pursue the question now. Darkness will soon be upon us, and I must find those damned horses before the light goes. So get dressed, and stop this wanton teasing lest I lose all my fine resolve."

"Teasing bedamned!" Alexandra cried furiously. "The only teasing I've in mind for you is with the end of a whip!"

Hawke smiled cynically and shook his head. "Such language from the lips of a lady!" His eyes scoured her face for a moment; then he stood up and shrugged into his clothes. After he sent her habit and chemise flying toward her face, the heavy planked door crashed shut behind him.

How dare the man? Her mind seething in impotent rage, Alexandra dropped her clothes. She grabbed the leather satchel that lay beside her on the straw and hurled it with all her might against the door. If only lightning would strike the cursed man down!

But the duke appeared to lead a charmed life. Alexandra heard no clap of thunder, only his mocking laughter carried on the wind. She shrugged on her chemise and habit, then sat down to tug furiously at her boots.

The loathsome reptile! He was indisputably the lowest form of life on earth! If only there were another way. . . .

But he had left her none. So, she decided grimly, she would do as he demanded. She would go to the man's bed and accept his advances without protest, but he would never have one iota more than that from her. She would be present, and nothing else. And maybe, after a while, he would tire of her and leave her alone.

She was considering the pleasure it would give her to watch the Duke of Hawkesworth suffer an old and particularly vicious form of Sikh torture when she heard an unfamiliar voice outside the door.

"Hands up, ye bastard!"

There was a muffled thump, followed by the report of a gun. Alexandra jumped up and threw open the door just in time to see Hawke's tall form stagger. A stocky man with a pockmarked face stood before him on the crest of the downs, his pistol still leveled at the duke's chest. With a roar Hawke straightened. He plunged toward his assailant, mowed the man down, and tossed the gun behind them. Hypnotized, Alexandra watched the two men grapple, their straining bodies rolling back and forth on the wet grass.

A snap at the far side the barn roused her, and she slipped back into the shadows just as a second man, pistol in hand, rounded the corner and headed straight for the pair at the top of the hill.

Desperately, Alexandra scanned the desolate landscape, calculating her chances for escape. But she realized that without Hawke, she had none. Unwillingly, she turned and searched the barn for a weapon, knowing that she had used her only shot. The steps outside grew louder. Then her eyes fell upon Hawke's open satchel and the barrel poking from beneath its leather flap.

A pistol! she thought wildly. So he had not come to this deserted place unprepared. Soundlessly, she stooped to examine the weapon more closely. It was beautifully made, with silver-mounted butt and breeches. Most important of all, it was loaded, and within the satchel was a small mahogany case full of percussion caps and lead balls—enough for at least thirty shots, she calculated.

"Stand apart!" a hard voice ordered, outside the barn.

Quietly, Alexandra drew back against the wall and inched toward the open door.

"We could deliver ye dead as well as alive, Yer Grace. Reckon it makes little difference to us!" the newly arrived accomplice warned.

Alexandra studied the scene before her. The new arrival, tall and lanky, stood no more than three feet away from her and was motioning nervously with his pistol for Hawke to release his accomplice.

"Now, damn it! I won't tell ye again."

Reluctantly, Hawke released his pockmarked enemy, who sprang to his feet and lurched out of reach.

"Tie him up and let's be off, damn it, before the tide turns!"

Without warning Hawke threw himself forward and knocked the pockmarked man to the ground.

The lanky man closer to Alexandra cursed furiously and braced himself to fire.

An instant later, her shot sent his pistol flying from his hand. He turned swiftly, surprise and fear darkening his thin face. Then he bolted for the cliffs above the beach, his stocky companion only a few steps behind him.

Grim faced, Hawke struggled to his knees. His forehead was furrowed with pain as he wobbled onto his feet, and a faint patch of red darkened the side of his white shirt.

Slowly, he stumbled down the hill, one arm pressed to his ribs. Only pride held him upright. His face was pallid and set as he wavered through the door and knocked it closed with his boot. Awkwardly, he fumbled with the bolt, which dropped home just as he collapsed onto the straw.

At last he looked up at Alexandra, his mouth drawn in a hard line. "You have a steady hand, Miss Maitland, and although I don't much relish the thought, it seems I owe you my life. What I don't understand is why you helped me." His eyes were unreadable in the semidarkness.

"Nothing more than self-preservation, I assure you. With you gone my own chances for survival would be slim indeed. But don't let it go to your head, Your Grace," she added bitterly, her hands on her hips. "Murdering you would give me the profoundest pleasure."

"Then I must find another source of pleasure to distract you." Hawke's attempt at a smile suddenly twisted into a grimace.

"What do we do now?"

"First, you give me the gun." Beside her Hawke waited, his hand outstretched and trembling slightly.

Alexandra looked down at the finely balanced weapon and felt a keen reluctance to part with it, for all that it was unloaded. Suddenly, she saw that the dark stain now covered the entire side of Hawke's shirt and half of his chest. "You're bleeding like a pig!" she gasped.

"Crude but correct, I'm afraid. But never mind about me—I'll hold. Give me the gun. Those two will soon be back, and this time they'll bring company. They've probably got a boat waiting directly below on the beach. When they return, we must be ready."

"When? Not if?"

"They'll be back—you can count on it. Telford will have promised them a fat purse this time. He must be growing desperate."

"Why don't we find help?" Alexandra demanded impatiently.

"Damn it, woman, we have no choice! The nearest village is five miles hence, and without horses we'd never make it." His eyes darkened. "In time, that is."

He was right, she realized. In his condition he could not go far. Alexandra now understood that the next few hours would decide her captor's fate as well as her own. He might very well bleed to death before her eyes, in fact.

More blood, one more death—after so many.

Reluctantly, she handed over the pistol.

His brow creased with pain, Hawke bent and clumsily reloaded. "You are a lucky woman, it seems. You may soon find yourself rid of me forever," he said grimly. Then, the loading done, he sat back to wait. Careful to keep the pistol balanced on his lap, he extended his left hand and explored the wound at his side.

"If you fell asleep, I could take the gun and leave you here alone," she said defiantly.

For an instant Hawke's fingers stilled at their probing. "You could. But will you?" His face was very pale, drawn with lines of pain.

"I don't honestly know."

"In that case"—Hawke fought down a groan when his fingers found the ragged edge of the wound—"it's a chance I'll have to take."

Just then, something brushed softly against the planks outside the door. Hawke stiffened and raised his pistol toward the sound.

Swaying slightly, he fought the searing waves of pain that lashed his side. His fingers tightened against the silver-mounted butt.

There was a whisper of movement near the ground, and a shrill squeak exploded from the far side of the door.

"Your Grace! Are you in there?" It was Jeffers's voice, harsh with anxiety.

"Thank God!" Alexandra breathed.

A moment later, with a jerky groan, Hawke collapsed insensible upon the straw.

Chapter Twenty-Five

"Damn it, man, must you drag us over every stone between here and Hawkeswish?"

"I beg your pardon, Your Grace," Hawke's grizzled groom answered stiffly, "but I'm not in the habit of conveying my passengers in farm vehicles."

They had commandeered the clumsy old wagon from a farmer near Alfriston, and it was an unpleasant mode of transport at best. At every rut and incline the old wooden wheels grated protestingly and shook Hawke until his teeth rattled.

"Then make allowance for the cursed bumps!" Stifling a curse, Hawke fell back weakly against the straw heaped around him. "Forgive me, Jeffers," he announced a few moments later. "I know you're doing your bloody best."

His eyes were bright and glassy when he looked across at Alexandra, seated beside him in the back of the wagon. "It seems you have me where you want me at last, Miss Maitland."

"Not quite, but almost," she answered crisply. Her eyes took in the wide strip of cloth secured across his chest. He had lost a great deal of blood, and he was beginning to grow feverish. Despite all her anger at the man's insolence and treachery, Alexandra realized she did not want him to die.

Not today anyway, she told herself grimly. Not unless it was her ball that lodged between his ribs.

A moment later, Hawke's eyes fluttered closed and did not re-open. He had drifted into unconsciousness, which was just as well, she thought. With all the jolting, some of the straw slid away from his side. Alexandra soundlessly pushed it back into place. "How far to Hawkeswish?" she asked the groom seated before her.

"Two hours, I reckon. Is His Grace—"

"I'm afraid he's unconscious."

"Hardy should be back with the doctor soon after we arrive. Has the bleeding stopped?"

"I can't be certain." Alexandra frowned, wondering at the loyalty the duke had won from all his servants. Rajah was curled beside her, sleek and comfortable in the straw. She stroked his warm fur. "It was fortunate that you came when you did, even though those two ruffians got away."

"I'd give a year's salary to get my hands on those bas—" Jeffers cleared his throat. "Thank the lord Rajah was with us. A good man, Hardy, but he lost track of you in the storm. If we'd arrived even an hour later—" With a smothered curse Jeffers broke off to steer the stolid work horses around a heavily eroded stretch of road.

Beside Alexandra the little mongoose squeaked quietly and his tail arched with pleasure at her smooth caress.

"The duke's a hard man," the old servant said gruffly. "But he's a fair one, too."

Not with me, Alexandra longed to say, but it would not do to discuss such things with Hawke's servant. "This isn't the first time Telford has sent someone after him, I take it?"

"No, by God. The villain will never stop until he has everything that belongs to the duke. And as for *that woman,* she's been be-hind her miserable brother every step of the way."

Aware that he had probably said more than Hawke would like, Jeffers lapsed into a moody silence. Alexandra realized she would get no more out of him that day.

The downs stretched before them, a green sea flowing all the way to the horizon. With a sigh Alexandra settled back to wait.

For what, she was not exactly certain.

* * *

Contrary to the groom's expectation, they arrived to find the doctor waiting, flanked by a crowd of anxious servants. The duke was still unconscious, and his eyes barely flickered as four footmen carried him up the front steps under the doctor's stern eye.

Seeing that everyone's attention was focused upon the wounded duke, Alexandra decided this was her chance to escape. She took several cautious steps backward, then rammed into a large, unyielding body.

"The duke would be a mite disappointed to find you gone when he awoke, miss." It was the brawny footman, Hardy.

"Let me go," she pleaded quietly. "It's better this way, believe me. If only you knew—"

"I know enough to be certain His Grace would draw and quarter me if I let you leave now." He was not unfriendly, but his brown eyes held an unmistakable warning.

Reluctantly, Alexandra turned back toward the house. It had been a pointless exercise anyway, since she couldn't leave before her father's name was cleared.

Frowning, she watched the footmen carry the Duke of Hawkesworth's heavy, unmoving form up the stairs. Until their bargain was fulfilled, she knew she would remain Hawke's captive.

The London streets were crowded with afternoon strollers undeterred by lowering gray skies. A small figure with a half-melted Gunthers ice in hand skipped along busy Oxford Street while his old nurse struggled to keep pace.

Unnoticed by the boy or his nurse, a carriage with shades drawn followed close behind, careful to maintain a discreet distance.

Where was the silly brat headed now? the woman inside wondered. Her brow creased in irritation. They'd already dragged her back and forth across London, from the Botanical Gardens to Astley's Amphitheatre and then to Gunthers for ices. The whelp was still as fresh as ever, the woman thought, but Nurse was showing her threescore years and the two brawny footmen in attendance were slower on their feet than when they'd left Bedford Square that morning.

Bloodred nails traced the barrel of the pistol in the woman's reticule. Trust her cursed husband to have the brat well guarded! But the net was growing tighter, and soon she would have everything she'd ever dreamed of—wealth beyond imagining and sweet, boundless freedom.

Her long fingers stroked the lush curve of her breasts and her flat belly. Yes, she knew well how to enjoy all of it. Her body was still as lithe and smooth as the day she'd taken her first lover.

Her dark aquamarine eyes glittering, she recalled her tutor's unexpected expertise with his hands and his delicious penchant for violence. Oh, she'd gone to her exalted husband a virgin, all right, but only in the strictest sense, for by that time she'd learned many techniques of pleasure that spared the membrane of maidenhood. Good God, what a fool Richard had been! the woman thought, smiling smugly as she recalled all the other men, all the other nights of savage, stolen pleasure.

Across the street the boy who was her son slowed in response to his nurse's scolding.

What was the old bitch about now? If they delayed much longer . . .

Isobel's beautiful eyes narrowed. Everything had been precisely calculated; James had seen to that. Her brother was indeed a master of detail. But not even he had counted on the last stop at Gunthers, nor the slow pace necessitated by the nurse's aging limbs.

Chastised, the boy turned, and the little party resumed their progress up the street. One more block, Isobel thought exultantly. One more block, and her husband would never again stand in her way!

On the far side of the street the young marquess lagged behind to study a granite gargoyle, whose repulsive features held endless fascination for a boy of five.

It gave Isobel all the time she needed.

"Robbie, my love, over here!"

The boy whirled about, his features transfigured with joy and disbelief to hear that long-awaited voice. *"Mama!"* The word had scarcely left his mouth before he was bolting down the street, gargoyle, Gunthers, nurse, and home forgotten in one wild, convulsive heartbeat.

"Master Robbie, what are you about now?" his nurse called urgently, motioning for the footmen to follow her impetuous charge.

Too late, the nurse saw the door of a nearby coach swing open. A slim, red-haired beauty stepped out into the street, her arms outstretched. Robbie was nearly at the curb when a runaway hackney lurched from a narrow side street, pitching wildly. The angry hooves of the team thundered toward the boy, who froze with panic and watched helplessly as the horses knocked the beautiful woman to the ground.

Isobel's shrill cry rent the air, echoed an instant later by her son's tortured scream. The hackney plunged to a halt. When, at long last, the horses quieted, a slim figure lay face-down upon the cobblestones, her bright hair flung out like a tangled halo around her slack features.

White faced, the boy crumpled to the ground, his hands reaching vainly for his mother.

The long night passed. The Duke of Hawkesworth drifted in and out of consciousness for several hours, while everyone in the great house hung suspended, waiting for some sign of his rallying. The doctor was in constant attendance, but his stiff features gave little indication of his patient's condition.

Two more days passed in equal tension. There was some improvement in the duke's condition, it seemed, but the doctor's optimism was guarded.

On the following afternoon Alexandra walked to the window, lifted the edge of a curtain, and stared out over the rolling lawns of Hawkeswish. In the wake of the storm all was lushly green, and the sun sparkled against the wet grass, covering the blades with tiny diamonds.

England, Alexandra told herself. The country was nothing like India. The smells were strange. The climate was different. The people, too, were different from those she had grown up with on the other side of the world, possessing none of the easy Indian acceptance of fate and their calm habit of procrastination.

Her father had belonged to India more than he knew, Alexandra realized. The tales he had told her of England came more from his idealized memories of youth than from reality.

Studying the piercing green of the lawn, Alexandra saw that she would have to change to suit this new place. She had been in England for only a few weeks, yet so far she had made a dismal mess of everything she had set her hand to. Yes, perhaps it was time to begin anew, to look at everything with fresh eyes.

There was a chill in the air, and she turned to pull a fine cashmere shawl across the dress of lapis silk that Lily had laid out for her. She studied herself impartially in the cheval glass, relieved to see that the shawl covered the scandalously abbreviated neckline.

What Alexandra did not see was that the rich colors of the shawl set off her hair and made her red-gold curls burn like living flame against her shoulders, or that the vivid lapis hue of the dress lent creaminess to her skin and made her eyes shine with blue-green fire.

When Lily arrived to dress Alexandra's hair before dinner, there was a worried look on her plain round face. "I'm that worried, miss, I can tell you. Shadwell's been as quiet as the grave, and the doctor no better." The girl's fingers tightened abruptly on Alexandra's hair. "Oh, I do beg pardon, miss, but it's just that we're all so worried. I know I shouldn't be tellin' you this," she added impulsively, "but a footman arrived from London yesterday. In the middle of the night, mind you! He's been closeted with Davies all mornin' and then the doctor was called. It's all very strange. I only hope it isn't more bad luck for His Grace."

"It's probably only business concerns requiring a prompt decision," Alexandra said soothingly. "I'm certain the duke will be recovered very soon."

"I wish I could believe that," the worried maid said, shaking her head.

When Alexandra stepped out into the corridor on her way down to dinner, she heard angry voices from the room next door. A moment later, the duke wobbled into the hall, only to find his way blocked by a bristling Shadwell.

"Enough of this damned quacking!" Hawke said angrily. "The

wound is on the mend, and the only danger I face now is going off my head with boredom. Out of my way, Shadwell!"

He appeared much healthier than Alexandra had expected. His eyes had lost their glassiness, and most of his natural color was restored to his face. But there was a sharp tension in the set of his shoulders, and he seemed gripped by restlessness.

"You are up, I see," Alexandra said blandly. "Your friend Telford will be delighted to hear it."

"The Devil take Telford!" Hawke growled. "Give me your arm down the stairs."

Alexandra's eyebrows rose.

"Very well—*please* give me your arm, damn it!"

Hawke swayed slightly, and Alexandra reluctantly did as he asked. "You are as impatient and unruly as a spoiled schoolboy, you know."

"Far worse, I should think. Are you surprised to see me up and about?" he demanded, his dark eyes intent on her face.

Alexandra was strangely discomfited by his scrutiny. "Not in the least. I was certain it would take a great deal more than one pistol ball to kill you."

"Disappointed?"

For all that she should have been, Alexandra was not. Of course, she would never admit as much to him. "That all depends on how you behave. Ask me again after dinner."

Hawke continued to lean upon her arm as they made slow and halting progress down the steps and on to a comfortable sitting room in the south wing.

Ignoring Alexandra's penetrating eyes, Hawke poured himself a drink; she refused his offer of a glass for herself. Then he stretched out tensely upon an elegant settee of rosewood and yellow silk.

Alexandra ran her fingers along a fine old rosewood chest fitted out with brass fixtures in the Chinese style. Across the top of the gleaming wood was arranged a hodgepodge of painted miniatures set in gilt frames. She chose one at random and raised it for closer inspection.

A young boy stood with a spotted spaniel at his feet. There was no mistaking the duke's glossy black hair, piercing eyes, and erect posture, even at the age of eight or nine. It was a charming composition, and yet to Alexandra's eye there was something stiff and unnatural about the picture.

"My likeness, as you've so astutely guessed. My mother was inordinately fond of that one. Don't ask me why."

"It's a good likeness." She hesitated.

"And yet?"

"And yet there's something odd about it. The formal pose, I imagine—it seems little suited to the setting."

"We Sommertons were never much for informality. In fact, my father considered informality to be faintly disreputable—for a Sommerton, at least—and not far behind the twin evils of Whig heresy and the ranting of revolutionists." Hawke studied his empty glass thoughtfully. "No, informality was in no sense a part of my upbringing."

"I see."

Hawke's eyebrows rose in sharp slants. "And what precisely does that mean, Miss Maitland?"

Replacing the miniature and raising another, Alexandra appeared not to have heard. A pale young boy of four or five with a thin clever face looked out from the painting in her hands. He was resting against the broad trunk of an oak—the Sussex oak in Hawkeswish park, unless she was mistaken. But it was his eyes that held her attention, for they were bold and perceptive, yet touched with haunting sadness. "And this, I take it, is—"

"My son, Robbie. Poor little lad—not that she cared how it might affect him, damn her soul."

"It was recently painted?"

"Last year at his birthday. Lawrence caught his likeness rather well, I think." Hawke's voice hardened. "Right down to the sadness in his eyes."

The boy's face disturbed Alexandra more than she cared to admit, and she forced herself to remember whose son he was. "He looks very clever and more than a touch willful. But that is to be expected of your offspring, I suppose."

Hawke's eyes flashed sparks of silver fire. "Next you'll be telling me you have gypsy blood," he said mockingly. "When I need a fortune-teller, I must be sure to send for you."

Alexandra's fingers tightened on the miniature.

"Don't do it," Hawke warned. "I'm not so weak that I can't make you very sorry."

"You are as crude as ever, I see. I won't take this ceaseless bantering and sarcasm, do you hear?"

Her breath came fast and jerky as she glared back at him, the air between them electric with tension.

"Then leave my son out of it. He's had enough pain. This affair is between you and me only!"

Just then, there was a commotion outside the door, followed by a babel of voices and insistent knocking. Shadwell appeared at the door, his face white and his usually pristine livery askew.

"Well?" Hawkesworth demanded sharply.

"A footman's just come from London, Your Grace." Shadwell's voice was unsteady. "There's news—very bad news, I'm afraid." The butler held out a cream-colored envelope. "He brought this."

Hawke ripped open the envelope, and his eyes flew across the scribbled lines. For long moments he stared blindly at the page, an expression of disbelief on his face. Finally, he looked up at Shadwell, his jaw hard and set. The letter fell forgotten to the floor. "Let's have the rest of it."

"You know about—about what happened yesterday. The boy's been half out of his mind since, it seems. The footman says he slipped from the house later in the afternoon and was out in the rain for several hours before they found him. His—his lungs may be affected. He's been coughing and feverish, asking for you regular. The doctor fears he'll get worse before he gets better and begs you to return as quickly as possible."

Hawke's long fingers closed tightly around the rosewood arm of the settee. His eyes were stark with pain, reminding Alexandra of his son's. Blindly, they searched out the miniature in her hands.

A painful silence settled over the room in the wake of the butler's words. Wretchedness welled up in Hawke's face as he stared at his son's picture.

None of this mattered to her, Alexandra reminded herself. She hated this man. She would always hate him.

"Robbie," the duke whispered hoarsely, "what in God's name have we done to you?"

* * *

In the next hours pandemonium descended upon the great house. Nervous footmen darted up and down between the study and the duke's chambers, readying baggage and taking a flurry of last-minute instructions. Wide-eyed housemaids sped back and forth between the kitchens and the stables, a thousand questions trembling on their lips.

Jeffers and Pence prepared the fastest coach for the trip to London. Hawke decided to spare the aged Jeffers the rigors of the trip and take one of the younger men. But the old servant fairly sputtered with anger when Hawke told him.

"You do that, and I reckon I'll—I'll be turning in my notice, Your Grace. No matter that I've worked here for thirty-five years nor don't find myself desirous of looking for a new position."

A faint glimmer of thanks pierced the dark distraction of the duke's face. "Thank you for coming with me, Jeffers. 'Twould be hard to replace you."

"The postchaise'll be around in a half hour," Jeffers said. "Everything else is being prepared as you directed."

"Good man," Hawke said, then returned to the letter he was scribbling to his solicitor.

A knock at the door brought him up with a frown. "Oh, it's you," he said curtly to Alexandra, who had come at his summons. With a distracted air he directed her to a chair beside the desk. "You're to accompany me to London," he announced, his tone clipped and impersonal. "Be ready to leave within the hour."

Alexandra gasped at his colossal arrogance. "Not in an hour or a day or a year!" she snapped.

The duke's lip curled. "I don't recall offering you a choice, Miss Maitland."

"Of course not! It would be beneath you to make a polite request of anyone."

"Damn it, must you always argue, woman?"

"Must you always be so insolent?" she countered furiously.

Hawke put down his pen and stared at her, his expression forbidding. "You are coming with me," he said acidly. "I'll not risk Telford getting his hands on you."

"Or me getting away from you." Alexandra did not blink before his harsh gaze. "Very well," she said finally. "Since you'll be far too busy with your son to pay much attention to me. Especially if the contagion has set into his lungs." Yes, she would enjoy watching Hawke suffer, Alexandra told herself.

The man at the desk frowned, his mouth tightening into a thin line. "You are familiar with the disease?"

"Sickness is a way of life in India. I've seen pneumonia and a great deal worse," Alexandra said grimly. "If the boy truly has pneumonia, the chief danger will come in the first days. The fever builds, you see, until it saps every last bit of the victim's strength." She spoke very clearly, taking merciless pleasure in describing the course of the disease.

"Good God!" Hawke passed an unsteady hand across his face, and it came away damp with sweat. Shaken, he stared at Alexandra, but with a hint of steel about his eyes. "What else? You think to hurt me, but the more I know, the better I can prepare."

"If it is pneumonia, the boy will be in a great deal of pain. He won't want to rest or drink, but he must to survive. And if the fever is extreme, he will recognize neither you nor his surroundings."

Every word drove another spike into Hawke's heart. "I shall try to remember that."

Alexandra stood abruptly, liking herself as little as she liked the man who studied her so coldly. "Of course, if the boy is even half as thick skinned as his father, he will certainly survive." Then she was gone, leaving the faint scent of lilies drifting in the air behind her.

For long minutes the duke did not move, staring at the doorway where she had disappeared. The pallor of his face was marked, and new lines etched his brow.

Suddenly he was back at Corunna, with the clank of oxcarts and the moans of dying English soldiers ringing in his ears. The cold was fierce, and the smell of death hung over everything. . . .

Slowly, Hawke's eyes closed, and his head slanted forward onto his clenched fists.

Chapter Twenty-Six

Those first hours of travel were a nightmare. By mutual consent, the two people in the carriage did not speak. Hawke was fighting continual pain as he was bounced over rutted country roads. Sitting in the post chaise was impossible, so he stretched out along the length of one seat.

The sun had been disappearing in a blaze of crimson when they left Hawkeswish's main gate, and twilight had soon bled the landscape to gray. With the advent of darkness the journey had become even rougher. On the box Jeffers had to squint to judge the road in the meager light cast by the carriage's two lanterns. Occasionally, Alexandra heard the old man grumble that it was downright dangerous to keep such a pace in the dark, and she had to agree.

She tried without success to sleep. Finally, with a frustrated sigh, she bent forward to look out the window, where the road stretched west like a ribbon of silver in the moonlight. The moon inched gradually higher, veiled by a pale curtain of clouds. At some point the roads improved—was it after hours or minutes? Alexandra wondered—and the post chaise began to bowl along under Jeffers's expert hand, raising clouds of silver dust along the chalky road.

The was no sound from Hawke. Alexandra dozed fitfully, awoke, and then slept once more. Not long after, she was roused by the grumbling complaints of sleepy hostlers and the neighing of horses. She was rubbing her bleary eyes when Hawke moved into the moonlight, the hard planes of his face suddenly splashed with silver.

Alexandra nearly gasped. His eyes were bleak and bottomless, his ashen face deeply etched with lines of pain and fatigue. The coach door was thrown open by Hawke's rangy groom.

"Uckfield, Your Grace."

Alexandra rose awkwardly to her feet and took Jeffers's arm down the steps to the ground. Without a word Hawkesworth followed, his expression stony. At the doorway of the inn a fat publican met them, hurriedly drying stubby fingers on his greasy apron. One commanding look from Hawkesworth was enough to send the man scurrying ahead to the second floor, where a hearty repast awaited them in the inn's best private parlor.

During the meal Hawke's impatience smoldered, never far below the surface. He strode to a window that opened over the courtyard. Wordlessly, Alexandra prepared a plate for him, then forced herself to eat something.

"What, no hysterics, Miss Maitland?" Hawkesworth dropped into the opposite chair, an eyebrow quirked in surprise as she offered him a heaping plate. "No reproaches about the indifferent food or the wretched pace I've set?"

"Would it do any good?"

"Nicely reasoned. But that would not keep any number of females of my acquaintance from raking me over the coals just the same." Hawke tried to eat, only to push aside his plate almost untouched a moment later. There was a hard look on his face as he reached for the excellent Burgundy the landlord had thoughtfully provided.

"Do you join me?"

"I think not."

"By that, you mean I'd best not have any either?"

"It cannot be good for your wound," Alexandra said coolly.

With a dull crack the glass crashed down onto the table, splashing Burgundy onto the scarred wood. "And what bloody concern is that of yours?" he demanded.

"Absolutely none," she answered brusquely.

Hawke's hand shot across the table and caught her fingers. Alexandra frowned, looking down at their hands upon the wine-spattered table—one small and one large, one ivory and one bronze.

One soft and one most painfully hard.

"Forgive me," he said gruffly, his long fingers tightening.

"For which offense?" Alexandra asked bitterly. "There have been so very many, after all."

"And always you were the blameless one? Your litany of virtues grows monotonous, I warn you!" Hawke shoved her hand away roughly and pushed back from the table, his chair scraping loudly upon the wooden floor. Angrily he strode to the window and jerked the curtain to one side. "What the devil could be keeping Jeffers? He ought to have made the change by now. I told him half an hour, and not one minute more." With a graphic curse he let the curtain drop, then turned back to face Alexandra, his expression menacing. "You will, by the way, continue to call yourself Mayfield while in London."

Alexandra choked on the tiny piece of roast beef in her throat. "Are you insane? I will not conceal my identity—not now."

Hawke crossed his arms over his chest, his lip curled cynically. "Not so long ago, you were determined to conceal your identity—from me, at least. Was that only when you were set on murdering me?"

"What if it was? You deserved nothing better! I've naught to be ashamed of in the name of Maitland!"

"If you want my help in clearing your father's name, you'll do as I say, woman! I don't care a tinker's damn about your father's reputation or your prickly ego, but we've made a bargain, and I intend to see it through. If your identity became known now, it would throw all my efforts into jeopardy."

Her sea-blue eyes narrowed. "As well as give Telford new ammunition against you," she guessed shrewdly.

Hawke sketched her a mocking little bow. "That too."

Alexandra slapped her cutlery back down upon the table. "You bloody bastard!" she whispered. "*Both* of you!"

"I don't know why that should surprise you," Hawke said coldly, sweeping up his greatcoat. He tossed it awkwardly over his broad shoulders, then strode from the room.

Dawn had begun to streak the eastern sky by the time the post chaise entered the outskirts of London. Alexandra was awakened by the raucous cries of sweeps and knife grinders plying their wares against the background clatter of carriages on the crowded thoroughfares. Ignoring the duke, she smoothed her tangled hair and tidied her crumpled skirts, knowing that she must look a sight after the long hours of travel.

In Bedford Square the post chaise clattered to a halt, and Alexandra wondered what sort of scene awaited them. In spite of her determination to remain aloof, she was curious about this boy who had become an innocent victim of his parents' hatred.

In a moment Jeffers appeared, his face pale with fatigue, to let down the steps. Though recently wounded, Hawke was tense with raw, explosive energy. He bolted from the carriage, crossed the sidewalk in two strides, and stormed into his elegant townhouse.

Alexandra climbed down slowly and reached for the small case that Jeffers had just brought down from the boot. She smiled on hearing faint scuffling noises inside the tan hamper. As she walked past a pair of sleepy footmen, they started, surprise creasing their faces.

"But—but—Your Grace—" the nearer one began uncertainly.

"Miss Mayfield," Alexandra corrected him, moving calmly inside, her heels tapping across a floor of inlaid marble. It was an imposing structure, she had to admit; her eyes widened at the sight of the grand double staircase of white veined marble overhung with a magnificent chandelier. As grand as its owner, she thought bitterly, stopping beside a fluted marble column that flanked the staircase.

From the top of the stairs Hawke spun around and glared down at her. "Well? What are you doing down there, damn it?"

"I haven't the slightest idea," Alexandra snapped. "It was your idea to bring me here, remember?" His eyes flashed with deadly fury, and Alexandra knew a brief moment of fear.

Never corner a wild animal. Her father's warning from long ago while they prepared for a tiger hunt flashed into Alexandra's mind as she tried not to flinch before Hawke's menacing scowl.

"Get up here," he growled, "before I carry you up myself! I'll hurt more than your pride if you don't."

Alexandra's chin rose defiantly as she climbed the stairs, pride and anger set in every line of her back and shoulders.

Hawke was already striding along the second floor. "I want your opinion about the boy," he said tersely, crossing the landing and moving to the far end of the corridor.

A hired nurse was hovering by Robbie's door, awaiting their arrival. After a quick glance at the woman's suspiciously bright eyes and ruddy cheeks, Alexandra turned to the slim figure upon the bed. He was resting fitfully, his breathing rapid. Although thinner and paler, he was clearly the same sad-faced boy she had seen in the miniature at Hawkeswish.

Hawke's breath checked as he drew close to the thin, struggling figure who tossed restlessly upon his pillow, his little frame shaken by bouts of coughing.

"Doing ever so much better, he is," the mob-capped nurse said unctuously. "Nor so hot as he was, I fancy."

"You are dismissed," the duke said curtly. "See the butler about your wages."

The woman began to set up a racket, but Hawke silenced her with an extremely colorful oath. "One more word, and you'll see nothing but the street."

Mumbling angrily, the nurse backed from the room.

Gently, Hawke stroked his son's flushed cheeks, but the boy did not open his eyes nor give any sign of recognizing his father. Hawke's gray eyes were bleak when he turned to Alexandra. "Have you seen this before?"

Alexandra touched the boy's heated forehead and noted the spots of color that stood out against the waxy pallor of his face. "I'm afraid it is pneumonia," she said quietly. "What has been done for him?"

Hawke's teeth gnashed audibly, and he smothered a curse. "I'll tell you soon enough," he growled, already plunging toward the door. "Come along."

The dark-clad doctor was waiting in the study. Without preamble Hawke strode across the room to his desk. His features hardened when he saw the half-empty glass of brandy and his best Chinese porcelain snuff box lying open before the red-faced physician.

"Miss Mayfield, Dr. Sudbury." With that approximation of an introduction, the duke flung himself down behind his desk and faced the physician, his fingers steepled. "What have you done for the boy, Sudbury? He's burning with fever, man, so weak he can't wiggle a finger!"

"It is only to be expected in an illness of this sort," the physician said defensively. "Undoubtedly, the fever will burn itself out in several days. In the interim we are following a regimen of bleeding, of course."

"How many times?" Hawke demanded.

"Three times daily," the physician said stiffly.

"That's six bloody times in the past two days! Hell and damnation, man! Is that all you can do? I won't have it, do you hear? The boy's listless enough as it is!"

"I am sorry to correct you, Your Grace," Sudbury began, bristling with angry self-importance, "but it would be criminal not to carry out a full course of venesection. The boy is young, relatively hardy, and bleeding is, in my considered opinion, the best method of reducing his febrile condition."

"Speak English, man!" Hawke said with a snort. "Let's face it —you're in a fog and afraid to admit it."

"In my considered experience," the physician began, "and I have had a wide acquaintance with lung contagions—"

Alexandra, who had silently seated herself at the rear of the room, interrupted this oration. "Does his temperature continue to climb, doctor?"

Sudbury sputtered and looked about in surprise. "As is to be expected in cases of this sort, yes." His expression showed he was put off to be discussing a case with a mere female. With a slight bow, he dismissed her and made to turn back to Hawkesworth.

But Alexandra persisted. "When exactly did the fever commence?"

"Two days ago." This time the doctor was more abrupt. "Have you some interest in this case?"

Alexandra ignored his question. "When was he last bled?"

"Your Grace, I really must protest this interference by a female—"

"Spare me your protests and give us an answer!" Hawke's command cracked like pistol fire, and the doctor recoiled almost as sharply.

"Very well. He was bled shortly after my first visit, two days ago. The fever did not abate, so I undertook a second series and this morning began a third. Because there has been no change in the boy's condition, I must conclude that another course will be necessary."

"Have ice poultices been applied?"

"Ice poultices? Come, miss, I am not expected to adopt every passing fad expounded by—"

"Answer the question, damn it!" Hawke thundered.

"No."

"Do it." Hawke's order bore no room for questioning.

"I do not provide ice poultices, Your Grace," the now fiery-faced physician said loftily. "And if you are set on contravening my orders, I must withdraw from this case."

With a graphic curse, Hawke gave a violent tug at the bellpull. Immediately, an anxious footman appeared at the door. "Dr. Sudbury is leaving. Please show him out."

Shoulders stiff with indignation, the physician marched from the room.

"Can you help him?" Hawke stood before her, one large hand clenched in a fist against his thigh.

Alexandra did not answer; her face was pale, her thoughts whirling.

"For Robbie I'll get down on my knees before you and beg," he said with barely suppressed ferocity.

Alexandra blinked, stunned by the desperate appeal in his dark eyes. Later, she would wonder why she hadn't countered with a demand that he release her from his ungodly bargain. But at that moment her thoughts were on the welfare of the innocent, anguished boy upstairs. And on the raw pain in Hawke's gray eyes.

"I've seen the poultices used in India," she said slowly. "They're no cure in and of themselves, mind you, but they might allay your son's pain and allow him to recover faster. It would help to keep offering him liquids and broths—ices too. And of course, no more bleeding."

"Agreed. How do we begin?"

"You'll need boiled water that has been allowed to cool, and ice chips rolled into oiled cloth—a tightly woven twill would be best, I think. The cook should use boiled water in preparing everything the boy drinks, for there are those who say the water itself can be a source of added contagion."

Hawke was already moving toward the door. "If you'll go up to him, I'll see to it immediately."

Very soon, Alexandra was assembling cool water and clean cloths to wash the boy, taking the bundled ice that a maidservant brought up from the kitchen. This she placed over Robbie's left side, which the boy was gripping painfully. "This may disturb you at first, Robbie, but we'll soon have you feeling better," she said gently, moving his hands away so she could work. "Yes, I can see you're a strong lad." Carefully, she tucked the frigid poultice against his chest. "Now, you must hold this just here. Then you'll begin to feel better."

There were dark shadows of pain and weariness beneath the boy's eyes, but his lids fluttered open, and Alexandra was captured by the power of keen gray irises. *"Mama?* Is that you? Have you truly come back?" His voice became confused. "But I thought you—I saw the horses—"

From behind Alexandra came the sharp rush of an indrawn breath.

Suddenly, the little boy was racked by a cruel spasm of coughing, and he would have cast away the poultice if Alexandra had not held it against him. "It hurts *s-so,* Mama!" he rasped.

"I know it hurts, but this will make it better," she said soothingly. "We'll have you up and about very soon. But I'll need your help." She reached beneath the boy's neck to raise his head gently, and as she did, she caught a glimpse of Hawke's tense face. "Your father has something for you to drink now."

"Father? Are you here too?"

"Yes, Robbie, right here." Hawke unsteadily raised a glass of lemonade to his son's lips. "Drink this."

The boy drank a little, gagged, then turned his face away. For a moment Alexandra feared he meant to refuse the drink, but Hawke bent close and whispered something in his son's ear— something that made the boy smile weakly for an instant, then drain the last of the liquid.

Almost as soon as he finished, another fierce spasm of coughing seized him. Alexandra struggled to cradle him against her to still his paroxysms. When finally the coughs subsided, he lay back pale and wan against the pillows.

Soon he opened his eyes and fixed Alexandra with a delirious stare. "You won't go away while I sleep, will you, Mama? Promise me—not again!" His small hands groped for her.

"No, I shan't," Alexandra promised, taking his restless fingers. "I'll be here. Try to rest now. When you wake, I'll have a surprise for you."

As she spoke, the boy relaxed visibly and soon settled into a light sleep, his coughing less fitful now.

"Brave boy," Alexandra whispered as she laid him back against the pillow. She had been so determined to dislike him as much as she disliked his father, but she found it impossible.

Very gently, Hawke ran his palm over the curve of his son's flushed cheek. "Very brave," he said in a ragged voice. "I'd give anything to bear the pain for him. When I think what he's suffered here without me—I should never have left him alone in my reckless obsession with Isobel." His voice broke for a moment, and he struggled to master his emotions. "He takes you for *her*, of course —a mistake we've both made recently. Thank you for letting him believe she's—returned." Wearily, Hawke drew a hand across his brow, as if to push away an unpleasant thought. "Although when he finds out—" His voice checked abruptly.

"It was little enough to do—since the boy is innocent in all this. Go and rest," Alexandra ordered coldly. "I'll sit with Robbie until you wake." At his frown, she added "It's the only way. You know that as well as I. That nurse Sudbury hired was insufferable."

So began a period of raw torment. Hawke and Alexandra took turns at sickroom duty until the old, reliable family doctor could be summoned from Hawkeswish. Helplessly, they watched the little boy wrestle with his pain, unable to offer him more than a cool touch and comforting words.

Everything depended on Robbie now, on the strength of his young body and his will to survive.

For five days the two took turns at the boy's bedside, bathing him with cool water, soothing him when he awoke in the grip of the demons of delirium. Those fears Alexandra knew well, and her hands were especially gentle when she tried to drive away the black phantoms from the boy's tortured mind.

She had seen the symptoms before, of course. What she did not tell Robbie's brooding father was that as often as not, the debilitated victim collapsed from the strain upon his body before the fever finally abated.

Alexandra found she could not be so cruel, not to a man on the brink of collapse and still recovering from a painful wound himself. She would still have her revenge, she told herself, but there would be no honor in taking it that way.

For Hawke the sickroom vigil brought back all the bitter memories of a war he had tried hard to forget. Once again he was haunted by specters of that disastrous winter of '08, when the English army had beat a nightmare retreat through the January cold from Corunna to the sea, their sick and dying carried through the mountains on planks and oxcarts.

He could still hear the moans of the wounded. Try as he might, he had never forgotten the rank smell of fear and death. There in the dim sickroom he was once again assailed by memories that had never healed, but had only been pushed deep in a vain attempt to hide them forever.

And now, witnessing Robbie's tortured struggle, Hawke saw those other faces—wounded country boys from Sussex and Yorkshire, only boys still, far from home and too young to die in the snows of a sullen Spanish winter.

Staggering under the unbearable memories, Hawke realized the only way to survive was to retreat deep within himself and cut off all feeling and pain, to focus his entire being on his son. So it was that in the days that followed, the duke became a stern shadow. Glimpsed only at the changing intervals of care, his dark face was set in hard lines that repelled any attempt at conversation.

On the fifth evening after their arrival Robbie's fever suddenly climbed higher. With trembling fingers, the alarmed Alexandra bathed his face and chest, talking all the while—babbling, perhaps —giving courage to herself as much as to him.

"There, that's better. Now, here's some water and a fine lemon ice your father fetched from Gunthers. What a lucky boy you are! You mustn't let such a splendid treat go to waste!" She set the cool confection against Robbie's dry lips, drizzling some of the sweet slush into his mouth. After anxious minutes the boy took a weak swallow, then twisted his head away.

With growing concern at his lassitude, Alexandra set down the ice. The crisis was nearing; she could feel it. "Come, Robbie, you're not fighting! I know you've more pluck than this!"

She lifted his feverish form from the bed and settled him on her lap, trying to rouse him with gentle pressure, but he did not respond. "Come, Robbie! Havers means to give you a splendid fishing pole and net. He told me they're awaiting you even now at Hawkeswish. Just think how proud your papa will be when you pull out a fine sparkling trout."

For an instant she thought she saw the boy's eyelids flutter.

"Your father has also given his solemn word that you're to have your own pony this year," she continued desperately, "along with a fine red pony-cart to carry you all across the downs. Mrs. Barrows will prepare us a basket of food, and we'll go exploring, just you and I. Wouldn't you like that?"

Was it her imagination, or did his hand move?

"Listen to me, Robbie. I've come back for good. I'll never leave you again." May God forgive her for the lie, Alexandra prayed. "We shall have lovely times again like we used to. We'll go to Astley's circus and visit the animal specimens at the British Museum. We'll—we'll—" She swallowed a lump in her throat. "Come, Robbie, you tell me what we're to do! You must list all your favorite places, and we'll visit them one by one. Do you hear me, Robbie?"

Alexandra was crying silently now, desperate to kindle a spark of life in that small tired body. "Dash it, Robbie, talk to me! Tell me all the outlandish places where you mean to drag your father and myself. Tell me, young man! If you don't speak this instant, I shan't keep my promise!"

There was a gentle pressure against her chest, and the pale face shifted. His cheeks were waxy, and his tongue was dry and parched, but the words he whispered were quite clear. "Even to a balloon ascension, Mama? Jeffers told me they're ever so exciting. Might I go up in one?"

With unsteady fingers Alexandra smoothed the disheveled black curls away from his tired face. "Yes, my sweet child, of course you may go to a balloon ascension. If your father approves, we'll *all* go up in the outlandish thing. I'm sure he'd fly to the moon if it would make you feel better."

"No need to fly that far," the boy answered in a grave little voice, staring at her strangely.

There was moisture on Alexandra's hand when she released the boy, and his forehead was hung with beads of sweat. "Thank God," she whispered. "The fever has broken at last."

Robbie coughed hollowly, and she began to rock him in her arms. "Hush, Robbie. Everything will be fine now."

Quietly, as the pale light of dawn stole through the windows, Alexandra began to sing an old Yorkshire lullaby that she had heard long ago from her mother.

> *Doves are in their cotes.*
> *Cows are in their byre.*
> *Puppies now are sleeping,*
> *Dying doon is the fire.*
> *At the end of daytime,*
> *Sleep is only reet.*
> *So cuddle doon, my little luve,*
> *And say goodnight.*
>
> *Hullets hoot in the fir trees,*
> *Foxes still awake.*

> *Badgers under the owd oak*
> *With each other like.*
> *Like a golden bonfire,*
> *The moon is toppin' the rise.*
> *Like stars are laughin'*
> *Granny Dear, fra the skies.*

As she finished, the boy stirred slightly. "Yes," he whispered, "I think I'll sleep now, for I'm very tired. And thank you—whoever you are—for I know you're not my real mama." His voice trailed off drowsily. "You're ever so much nicer than she was, I think."

From the shadowed doorway a tall figure watched, unmoving and unseen by the woman and the tired boy. Her sweet song and the sight of his son in her arms shook the wall of bedrock that Hawke had so fiercely erected around his heart over the long and bitter years of his life. His defenses crumbling, the Duke of Hawkesworth watched Alexandra and his sleeping son, feeling helpless and vulnerable, knowing he was poised on the very brink of a new life. And that realization frightened him very much.

He soundlessly stepped back from the doorway, careful to conceal himself. Buffetted by raw emotions, he returned the way he had come, ashamed to let the two people inside witness the tears seeping onto his cheeks.

Chapter Twenty-Seven

As soon as the crisis had passed, Robbie began to mend quickly. Overnight, his temperature returned to normal, and as it did, his energy returned. It then became a challenge to keep him distracted over the days of inactivity during his recovery.

Hawke threw himself into this task with a wry good humor, amusing the boy with a vast set of tin soldiers brought down from the attic. Through the long afternoons their two dark heads were bent over the painted pieces, as father and son orchestrated vast battles that swept across the bedcovers and spilled down onto the floor. Soon the whole house was warmed by noisy laughter from the sickroom. For his part Hawke was delighted to see the boy lose some of his diffidence, although a hint of sadness still crept about Robbie's eyes when he thought his father was not looking.

With the crisis over the old nurse had resumed her care of Robbie. Soon after, the family doctor had arrived from Alfriston and was pleased to pronounce the boy well on his way to recovery.

Finally, just as a measure of calm was restored to the house, a new chaos ensued: word of Hawke's return to town had spread among the *ton*. Of course, such an event could not be long kept secret, even though Hawke continued to regard his duties seriously and did not leave the house.

Hadley, the duke's very superior London butler, spent a good deal of his energies receiving the cards of inquisitive acquaintances. Every day, by early afternoon, the lacquer table in the hall would be buried beneath dozens of engraved cards conveying regards and extending invitations to all manner of balls and fêtes.

Rain rattled sharply at the window of Hawke's study one evening a week after his return to town. As he idly sifted through the pile of correspondence on his desk, his eyes fell upon a thick waxsealed envelope half concealed by the cheerful clutter of invitations. His eyes narrowed when he recognized the precise calligraphy of his solicitor.

Hawke cursed under his breath. Impatiently, he attacked the heavy vellum envelope and spread out five sheets closely written in the elegant hand of his man of business.

Your Grace,

It has been some weeks since I am in receipt of Your Grace's last missive, but owing to my investigations' yielding no fruit, I have delayed writing until now. Only a fortnight ago, in fact, did certain information unexpectedly become known to me, which I convey now with alacrity. Your Grace will understand my reluctance to reveal the sources—they would be lost to me forever were I to divulge them.

Your Grace's letter expressed a particular concern about the present situation of the Governor-General of Madras and his immediate family. I shall not begin to describe the difficulties of this investigation; suffice it to say that there were unusual circumstances. Matters in Madras are still somewhat unsettled, and this has added to the difficulty of the thing. Furthermore, I have been mindful of your injunction to conduct my inquiries in absolute secrecy, and this has hindered my progress to no small degree.

The governor-general, Lord Percival Maitland, fourth Viscount Maitland, long resident in India, had been nine years in his post when the unrest broke out at Vellore. Lord Maitland had on numerous occasions warned that there must be sepoy dissension if the Crown pursued its policies of provisioning and protocol without consideration of Indian customs and religious beliefs. Even Lord Maitland, however, did not anticipate the ferocity of the rebellion, when it came, and he considered the loss of lives a direct result of his own error in judgment and leadership. Despite the vehement support of his friends and defenders—and there were many, among both Indians and British—Lord Maitland was left a broken man. The day he received word that his third petition for restitution to the East India Company Board of Control had been denied, he put a pistol to his head and took his life.

His body was discovered by his daughter, the Honorable Alexandra Maitland, who is his sole surviving heir. Her emotions on the occasion may well be imagined. In other circumstances the young lady's lot might have been improved by her receipt of her father's considerable fortune, as Lord Maitland was the possessor of some 20,000 pounds, even without the funds still owed him by the Crown. But Miss Maitland soon found herself in a position of considerable difficulty due to the disappearance of her father's man of business in the unhappy days following the governor-general's suicide.

Hawke's fingers tightened on the heavy vellum, and a vein began to throb at his forehead.

Some say the man was murdered; others swear he chose an opportune moment to flee with the funds Maitland had entrusted to him for his daughter's protection in the event of some calamity. In either case the results were very nearly the same, for Miss Maitland was left in virtual penury. Of relatives, I can trace none. Lord Maitland's father appears to have had some sort of falling out with his younger brother, which resulted in a total rupture between the two families. I have been able to find no further information about other relatives.

The next part of the story is curious, indeed. Impossible though it may sound, the young lady seems to have dropped from the face of the earth. She stayed for several days with friends in Calcutta prior to taking passage on an East Indiaman bound for London, but she has not been seen since the ship's arrival. The captain recalls that Miss Maitland was not met at the docks. He tried to offer her assistance, but in the chaos of disembarkation she slipped away. I can find no further trace of her. Whether she is still in England or whether she has returned to some barren outpost in India, I am unable to say.

Hawke looked up slowly. How ironic, he thought. Ever since the Vellore decision he'd felt a sense of uneasiness and a nagging suspicion that the board of control had made a mistake in its severe treatment of Lord Maitland. News from India had been slow in reaching London, and finally, Hawke had set his man of business upon the matter, for he wanted to find out what had become of the governor-general and his family in the wake of the board's decision.

And then one night Alexandra Maitland had come running out of the fog right into his hands.

Hawke's face was somber when he looked down and began once more to read.

It may be of interest, furthermore, that mine was not the sole inquiry being made about the young lady. She numbers many friends in Madras and Calcutta, at every station, and these friends are greatly concerned about her present situation. There are also those in London who show an interest in her whereabouts—whether for idle curiosity or for more calculated purpose, I was unable to ascertain. It appears, in short, that Miss Maitland's history has evoked considerable sympathy among those who know of it.

About your wife's particulars, I have only one new point of intelligence. Six weeks ago, someone answering the duchess's description was seen to board a ship in the West Indies bound for London. I have endeavored to verify this report with the ship's captain, but to no avail, for this poor man was soon after struck down with apoplexy.

Of Telford, I can learn nothing new. He guards his tracks closely.

Your Grace will not need me to reveal my suspicions. If the duchess has returned to England, can Telford be far behind? I fear that when news of the divorce bill becomes known, as it must very soon, the pair may be driven to recklessness. In the interim I am pleased that Your Grace has engaged the man I recommended. John Hardy may not perform exemplary service as a footman, but Your Grace will find nothing lacking in his protection of the household. He served bravely at Badajoz and can be counted upon in all matters.

Keep him close. Telford will shortly be a desperate man.

I remain,
With the greatest respect,
Your Grace's
Most obliged and obedient servant,
Bartholomew Dodd

Hawke's mouth tightened grimly as he read the hastily scrawled postscript at the bottom of the last sheet, dated almost a week before.

Your Grace will forgive my hasty addendum, but I have just learned of the terrible accident and your son's illness. I trust you will see the boy soon recovered.

The magistrate has been here, as you directed, and has given me what particulars are available regarding your wife's accident. The hackney driver was drunk when apprehended and is presently in custody. I have questioned him in great detail, and his story seems to be exactly as he first related it.

Perhaps of greatest import, the man has no familiarity with James Telford or anyone answering his description.

I apologize if the following details give you unnecessary pain, but they must be mentioned. Because the victim's face and body were badly disfigured by the hooves of the team, the magistrate had some question about verifying her identity. When he understood your presence was required because of your son's illness, however, he was content to accept the verification of those witnesses to the accident, which included several of the household staff, who were quite able to attest that the woman was without a doubt your wife.

Her body has been buried in accordance with your requests. Lest your son be given further pain, I shall endeavor to keep the matter from becoming public knowledge for as long as I can, but I fear it will not be very long.

Regarding Telford, I shall continue my inquiries, but I think it safe to predict that his efforts will be hampered by this new and tragic development. As I receive further information, I shall, of course, keep you informed.

Please accept my sincerest condolences. It is tragic that the whole affair should end this way. I await your direction.

B.D.

Slowly, Hawke looked up. All was quiet in his study; the only sound came from the soft whirring of the mechanics of an ormolu clock on the mantel.

For long minutes he continued to hold his solicitor's letter, twisting the heavy vellum sheet between unfeeling fingers. Outside, carriages continued to clatter by in the street, and late-roaming vendors walked on, crying their wares in the night.

Life continued in all its fierce, ceaseless rush. Only for the Duke of Hawkesworth had the world halted upon its axis.

So it was truly over, he thought, strangely numb when faced with what he had dreamed of for so long.

Isobel was dead. Telford was blocked. The old urgency was gone. No more would he feel the tortured restlessness that had always signaled her presence.

And what now? Could he start anew and leave the distractions of London behind for a quieter life in the country? He had long considered doing just that, and Robbie was growing old enough to enjoy the outdoors—hunting, riding, and fishing. The boy belonged at Hawkeswish, Hawke knew.

And what about Alexandra Maitland? a cynical voice asked. There was still the matter of their bargain. It would be difficult to reverse the decision about her father's case, Hawke knew. It would, in fact, require all of his considerable influence to persuade the other members of the board that Maitland might have been dealt with unfairly. Yes, he thought impassively, it would be very difficult—but not impossible.

Then what? the voice persisted. Would he follow through with his threat and exact his payment? She had saved his life, after all; she had probably saved his son's life as well.

How could he repay her with cruelty?

And yet how could he let her go? She stirred his blood; she goaded him to fury and excruciating awareness of her latent sensuality. She was like a glowing ember that needed only a little kindling to explode into a passionate inferno.

Even now, with his wound not yet healed, Hawke hungered for her slim legs to be wrapped around him, her body eager and frantic beneath him. His manhood swelled painfully at the thought.

With a long graphic curse the duke tossed down his solicitor's letter and stood up to pace the room restlessly. The little ormolu clock on the mantel chimed nine times.

What was she doing right now? he wondered. Was she as restless as he, haunted by memories of their fierce passion during the storm?

Hawke's mouth tightened. By God, he hoped she was! If not, he'd do everything in his power to make her remember!

Some impulse called him to the window. He drew back the brocade curtain and stared down into the street. At first he saw nothing but darkness; then, gradually, his eyes began to pick out solid forms. He thought he saw a sliver of black shift against the blurred outlines of the street, then disappear a moment later.

Hawke's eyes narrowed. Finally, satisfied it had been nothing more than his imagination, he released the heavy curtain.

His face was deeply lined as he poured himself a glass of brandy and dropped wearily into the tufted leather wing chair beside his desk. Again and again his thoughts returned to the brave woman upstairs who had been forced to endure so much tragedy in her young life.

He did not yet know what he would do about Alexandra Maitland, but one thing was certain. He could not let her go. Not now.

Perhaps not ever.

Rain rattled sharply at the sitting-room window. Alexandra shifted restlessly, trying to concentrate on Miss Austen's latest work. Finally, with an irritated sigh, she snapped the book shut and moved to the window, where she pulled back white damask curtains to study the rain-streaked street.

Only those with no choice were out this evening, she saw: a bedraggled flower seller and several liveried footmen darting about on urgent errands. Across the street a thin man hunched his back against the driving rain and drew his hat lower above his face. Watching the wind lash his muddied brown cloak against his legs, Alexandra felt a moment of pity for the man. Just then, something made him look up at her window, and his expression of cold dislike made Alexandra forget all thoughts of sympathy.

Still carrying her novel, she returned to the crimson settee, where half a dozen volumes borrowed at random from the duke's library lay untouched. Alexandra's slender fingers played restlessly with the long ribbons at the front of her emerald muslin gown. At last, with a frustrated sigh, she reopened *Emma* to the same page she had begun reading two hours earlier.

"Am I disturbing you?"

Alexandra jumped and dropped her book, then scolded herself to a semblance of calm.

Hawke stood upon the threshold, magnificent in buff-colored breeches and a bottle-green jacket perfectly molded to his broad shoulders. He filled the doorway, his powerful presence reverberating through the very depths of her being. Just the sight of him was enough to set her blood pounding in the most infuriating fashion, and his silver-gray eyes glittered as if he could read her response.

To compensate for her slip, Alexandra limited her answer to a cool nod, then retrieved the fallen volume, holding her fingers deliberately in her place.

"Can the book be so fascinating?" Hawke asked mockingly.

Alexandra drew herself up to her full height against the settee. "I take it you prefer a woman to be untutored, uneducated, and unthinking, Your Grace."

Hawke moved to the empty chair beside her and seated himself with a fluid grace that set all Alexandra's senses jangling. Irritated, she kept her eyes to the floor—and so was treated to a leisurely display of hard muscles rippling beneath his form-fitting breeches.

With a notable absence of haste Hawke stretched his booted legs comfortably before him until they just grazed her ankle. "Oh, not untutored, I think. At least, not in certain matters."

Alexandra jerked her foot back, cursing the warm flood of color that stained her face. Furious but determined not to let him see how successfully he provoked her, she raised the book from her lap and opened it, staring blindly at the blurred page.

There was a small cough as strong fingers lifted the book from her hand. Hawke turned the volume right-side-up, then raised the spine for a closer scrutiny. "Entirely fascinating, I quite agree. *A*

Practical Essay on the Scientific Repair and Preservation of Roads," he read coolly, "by John McAdam. Does macadamization hold some special attraction for you, Miss *Mayfield*?"

Alexandra could have screamed with frustration. "I was reading Miss Austen's latest work, if you must know, and mistook the books when you charged in here so rudely."

"Charged? Rudely? It is, after all, my house. But tonight I refuse to be baited. Your book," he said lazily, tendering the slim leather volume. He held it flat on his open palm with his fingers curled around the edge, so that she would have to touch him to take it back.

Alexandra hesitated, cursing herself for acting like a naive miss with jitters before her first ball. Her expression was icy as she slid her hand along his fingers and fairly jerked the volume from his grasp. In her haste she miscalculated, however, and the book dropped to the carpet with a faint slap.

"You're very jumpy today."

Alexandra did not deign to reply.

"I trust you will not make such agitation a habit. It looks poorly of one who has charge of children." The duke leaned down to lift the forgotten volume from the floor, managing to brush her thigh as he did so.

At his touch a spark leaped up Alexandra's leg, tightening muscles she had not even known she possessed. Her heart hammered, and she had a sudden memory of their savage lovemaking in the storm. She did not speak, certain that only a croak would have emerged at that moment.

Hawke's eyes narrowed, and he raised a mocking eyebrow, missing nothing of her response. "I have accepted several invitations on your behalf," he said abruptly. "We go first to Astley's, three days hence. Robbie has already begun plaguing me with plans for all the places we're to visit. Then we're engaged for Lady Rockington's ball Saturday week." It was neither an invitation nor even a suggestion but a ducal command.

Alexandra's eyes widened, flashing dangerously. "Do we indeed?" She snatched her book back from his hand.

"We do. And tomorrow night to Vauxhall."

This was too much for Alexandra. Her eyes snapped angrily,

and her fingers twitched on the slim volume. "And you can go to blazes! As I recall, our—ungodly pact extended only to—to—"

"To your compliance in my bed?" Hawke studied Alexandra's clenched hand with a meaningful glance. "I quite understand the temptation to throw the book, my dear, but you do better to restrain yourself. It does not do for a governess to be throwing books at her charges, you know."

"What the devil are you talking about?"

Hawke studied her lazily. "You said you planned to look for a position as a governess, did you not?"

"You know quite well I did. But what—"

"I am merely helping you go about it."

Alexandra's mouth settled into a thin angry line. What sort of vile plan had he hatched now? "I'll not be flaunted as one of your light-skirts, I warn you. It's bad enough I must share your company in private!"

"Just as I thought—all this talk about finding employment was a sham." Hawke looked down and brushed an invisible speck from his sleeve, hiding a smile of triumph.

"Damn you! I *do* wish to find a situation, but I won't—"

"Did you expect prospective employers to come in search of you then?"

His tone was quite calm and reasonable, which only goaded Alexandra to greater fury since she had not, in fact, considered the matter very closely. Too much had happened since that morning not quite four weeks ago when she had gone looking for employment, only to be so curtly rejected.

"The story I've set about," Hawke continued smoothly, "is that you're a relative of my wife. Your resemblance will certainly be remarked upon, so we might as well turn that to our advantage. With you but newly arrived from India, what could be more natural than that I show you about town?"

"But I am *not* related to your wife!" Miss Austen's novel dropped forgotten to Alexandra's lap.

"Isobel will not be here to contest the explanation," the duke said, suddenly grim.

"Someone will. And anyway, it's a lie."

"Is it?" Hawke countered coolly. "Do you know that for a fact?

For myself, I rather think there must be some connection between the two of you to explain the startling resemblance. Will you have some sherry?" he asked impassively.

His calm assumption of control over her life provoked Alexandra almost past enduring. She felt as if she were dangling from a string while he toyed with her unmercifully. "No, I do not care for sherry, you wretch! Nor do I wish to embark on this masquerade you propose. I won't become your plaything!"

"Such cynicism, my dear! It's quite unbecoming in one so young. Or did you acquire some miraculous potion of youth from the fakirs in India?"

"I am three and twenty," Alexandra replied frostily, "as you might have found out easily enough had you asked directly."

Hawke nodded, his lips pursed. "A very good age for a governess. You're certain that is the position you intend to seek?"

"You know perfectly well it is, knave!"

"I'm glad to hear it," he said blandly, "for if you mean to dangle after a rich husband, I fear you'll find it beyond even *my* considerable abilities to help you."

Alexandra nearly choked. *"Husband?"* she exploded when she could once again speak. "What kind of tasteless joke is this?"

"None at all, my dear. I am merely giving you a bit of practical advice, in case your sights are set too high. A position of governess should be within my capability to arrange—yes, even a very *superior* sort of governess, as long as we're careful to keep your background a secret. But if you mean to plague me to find you a husband, then I must tell you now it's out of the question."

Seething with anger, Alexandra could barely manage to answer her arrogant interrogator. "I do not consider m-matrimony, you blackguard, be the man rich or poor! I seek only a position as governess in a decent family. Can't you get that through your witless head?"

"Brava! I fancy that tone will stand you in good stead when you need to set your unruly charges in their place. But let us turn to more important matters. You'll need clothes, of course. I must send for Madame Grès. Then we must plan where to make your opening sortie."

"What," Alexandra snapped, "in God's name are you talking about?"

"I am speaking, my little fool, about finding you a position. I should have thought that was obvious by now. We shall have to bring you to the attention of those who are hiring. A word here, a nudge there, and I believe you might receive several offers."

"I am not your little anything," Alexandra muttered, frowning. She did not trust him—not in the slightest. "Does this mean our bargain is off?" she demanded, not daring to hope he would free her so soon.

Hawke's eyebrow quirked in mocking surprise. "Of course not. Unless you've decided to give up this quest to restore your father's honor."

"Never!"

"Then, Miss *Mayfield,* our bargain stands as well. Still, you must support yourself somehow after you leave my protection, and it is never too early to begin looking for a suitable position."

"How base you are! I should have known that—"

"Yes," Hawke agreed coolly, "you should have."

"Very well, since you are dead set on being a bastard," Alexandra fumed, "let's dispense with playing cat and mouse."

"A fine idea. Now, let me see. There's Cripplegate and his mixed brood. The man is notorious for his lechery, of course, but the salary would be considerable. Then there's Lady Sedgewick," he continued ruthlessly. "I understand she's looking for a companion. Faintly eccentric old thing, but nothing of harm about her. That son of hers is a different matter altogether, however." Hawke pursed his lips thoughtfully. "The fellow's been impregnating the housemaids at an amazing rate, so I hear. No wonder Lady Sedgewick is so hard put to find female domestic help."

Alexandra felt sick, but she refused to let Hawke see her dismay. "If you hope to frighten me, you may forget it. I do not scare so easily. You of all people should know that!" Despite her brave words, Alexandra's face was pale, and her fingers twisted restlessly in the ribbons at her waist.

Expressionlessly, Hawke watched her valiant struggle for optimism, knowing he had succeeded in upsetting her.

Curiously, the thought gave him no pleasure—quite the opposite, in fact.

A spark leaped from the hard flint of his gray eyes, and a moment later he jumped to his feet. "Goddamn it, Alexandra! Marry me!"

At first she did not move, unable to believe what she had heard. Her heart mocked her, pounding erratically as she studied his face, amazed at the raw hunger reflected in his silver-gray eyes.

In the stunned silence that fell between them Hawke knelt before her and grabbed her hands roughly. "Marry me, Alexandra!" he persisted urgently. "You're a creature of fire and passion. You were not meant to be a governess! Let me take care of you. Let me share your days and your nights. I'll never give you cause to regret it."

Too shocked to speak, Alexandra stared at him, her breath coming quick and jerky. "M-marry?" she stuttered.

Hawke's fingers tightened painfully. "Is it such a surprise? After all, you saved my life—Robbie's too. You must feel something for us!"

For a moment—just the barest span of one erratic heartbeat—Alexandra considered Hawke's startling proposal, which shocked her far more than his crude demand that she share his bed. Cold uncomplicated lust—that she expected of this man. But an offer of marriage? From the exalted Duke of Hawkesworth?

As the Duchess of Hawkesworth, she would be safe and protected. No more wandering. No more worry about how to pay for her next lodging.

Shuddering slightly, Alexandra fought to regain her grip on reality.

Cold hard reality! she told herself desperately. Just like the flinty gray light flashing in his eyes.

Damn the man! He was married already, Alexandra reminded herself, terrified that she had come close to blurting out her consent. "Are y-you insane?" she cried at last, when she found her voice. "Is this some sort of new and vile insult?"

Hawke's face darkened. "You consider it an insult that I ask you to become my wife?"

"Would you add bigamy to your list of crimes against me?" she demanded in terrible, unthinking fury. At that moment she hated him with every nerve and sinew of her rigid, quaking body.

Just as she hated herself for having considered his offer, even for the briefest instant.

With an explosive curse Hawke jerked her upright and slammed her roughly against his broad chest. "My wife is dead, Alexandra!" he cried hoarsely. *"Dead,* do you hear? She died trying to steal Robbie away from me ten days ago."

Alexandra gasped, shock halting her wild struggles against his iron grip. Her ivory brow furrowed. Isobel dead? She blinked, feeling the room spin around her.

With a low groan Hawke trapped her face between his hands and forced her to meet his hungry, searing gaze. "Don't you understand, woman? I love you! I think I've loved you since the first moment I saw you run out of the fog. Even then I must have known—" Whatever he meant to say was forgotten as he slanted his mouth fiercely over hers. "Marry me!" he whispered against her heated skin. "Marry me very soon!"

Alexandra shivered, inexorably drawn like a moth to an ancient, primal flame. Vainly, she struggled against this deadly attraction. Marriage to her ruthless captor? To a kidnapper and a murderer?

No! she screamed silently. It was impossible! Honor forbade even considering such a thing!

Yet consider it she did, as the heat of his body scorched her trembling frame. She hesitated, immobile within the span of his tense arms.

"Say something, Alexandra," Hawke demanded hoarsely. "Say anything—anything but no." All his insouciance and fine speech seemed to have deserted him.

It was that very loss of control and stripping away of pretense that caught Alexandra and held her spellbound long after she should have fled. And with the recognition of his weakness came the knowledge that she was in a position to take revenge on her captor at last.

"Let me go!" she cried, straining against his chest. "With your wife but a week in her grave, you would search for a new mate?"

Alexandra forced herself to laugh coldly. "You defile the very idea of matrimony!"

Hawke's face darkened with pain and fury. "This is how you reply to my offer? Can you hate me so much?" His hands fell from her face and bit into her shoulders like talons. "Very well, then, I'll make the choice simpler. It's wed me or bed me," he said in a voice raw with rage. "You'll not escape me, woman, for I mean to have you, and when I do, it will be your desire as much as mine!"

"Never, you vile bounder!" she cried, struggling against his cruel grip, feeling the hot, hard shaft of his manhood scorch her belly through the thin muslin of her gown. With strength born of desperation she wrenched free and flung herself toward the door. But her flight was cut off in its first steps as Hawke caught her gown and dragged her back against him.

"Let me go, damn you!"

With a twist of his wrist he spun her about, pinned her hands behind her back, and hauled her against his chest. "Don't ever walk away from me when I'm talking to you!" he thundered. "Not unless you want me to teach you some manners."

"Don't threaten me, you m-miserable, contemptible—"

"Oh, 'tis no threat but a promise, of a certainty! Shall I prove it to you, woman?" he taunted. "Shall I mount you here and now? On the carpet? Across the settee? Why not both places?" he continued savagely. "My wound is nearly healed, and I'm good for a night of whoring. Plowing you would be as good as plowing any other tart." Reeling with the pain of her curt refusal, Hawke spoke with deliberate cruelty, making his words as crude as possible, hoping to hurt her as she had hurt him. "A little fear only sharpens lust, as you'll learn soon enough. Maybe I should truss you when I take you."

"Stop!" Alexandra screamed, horrified at how quickly his fierce tenderness had transmuted into bestiality. She wrenched her body away from him, only to discover one of her ribbons was caught on a button at his breeches.

Hawke smiled insolently at her predicament. Slowly, his long fingers slipped along the ribbon until they just grazed her sensitized breast. His eyes were hard and knowing as he felt the dusky crest tighten at his touch.

Alexandra's breath caught in her throat, and her lovely eyes glistened with unshed tears. "Stop it, Hawke, please!" she rasped.

"Tell me why you won't marry me," he demanded harshly, his fingers teasing her taut nipple unmercifully.

Alexandra did not answer. A dark skittering emotion came and went in her haunted sea-green eyes, and then she began to twist like a wildcat in his grip.

Guilt? Hawke frowned in disbelief. What could she be ashamed of? "Hell and damnation, never tell me you're married already?" he growled.

"No!" Alexandra snapped. "And I'll never marry. I'll be a slave to no man!"

Hawke's mouth tightened into a hard line. "It seems I have lost Isobel only to find her again in you."

From the door behind them came a soft scuffling noise. "Papa?" It was Robbie's voice, sleepy and confused. "I heard noises." The boy stood uncertainly in the doorway, one hand rubbing sleepy eyes, the other clutching his favorite wooden soldier. "What are you doing to Miss Mayfield? Why is she crying?"

Hawke bit off a curse and untangled the ribbon from his breeches, releasing his angry captive in the same quick motion. "For a boy who ought to be in bed asleep, you ask a great many questions!" He strode across the room and took his son into his arms. Above Robbie's head Hawke's angry eyes searched out Alexandra's face. "Miss Mayfield and I were just talking about promises, if you must know, and about how important it is to keep one's word." Dark with warning, Hawke's eyes raked her pale face. "If you make a promise, you must expect to keep it, whether you like it or not. Remember that, Robbie. Just as I'm sure Miss Mayfield always will."

Hawkesworth's face was set in harsh lines, and his steely eyes promised limitless retribution as he carried his son from the room.

"Like bloody hell!" Alexandra spat, almost tripping over the forgotten volume at her feet.

A moment later, the book struck the door with a loud resounding crack that echoed all the way to the attic.

Chapter Twenty-Eight

Upon arising the following day, Hawke sent a hastily scrawled note around to Madame Grès, a very select London modiste. He smiled, having a very good notion of her surprise and keen curiosity upon receiving his summons. Well known to be a connoisseur of female beauty and apparel, with a long string of high fliers under his protection, the Duke of Hawkesworth was a generous and coveted client.

Not for nothing had Madame Grès—or Miss Gray, as she had been called when Hawke discovered her in a small seaside town near Brighton and took her up—scaled the heights to become the unrivaled purveyor of fashionable dress to the *ton.*

There was nothing to suggest vulgar curiosity in the coolly professional reply sent back to Bedford Square in rather less than an hour. *Madame Grès will be happy to wait upon the Duke of Hawkesworth at eleven o'clock,* the lines read.

Yes, Miss Gray had learned her lessons well, Hawke thought as he perused the neat yet fluid handwriting. A small smile played about the corners of his mouth.

At eleven o'clock precisely Hadley ushered a small slender woman with smooth skin and jet-black hair into the spacious front drawing room. Unwillingly, Alexandra went down to meet the modiste who had come at Hawke's command.

Neatly dressed in gray kerseymere with a brooch at her neck, Madame Grès was not at all what Alexandra had expected.

"So you are to be my client, *oui*?" the smiling woman said with a soft yet very light French accent. "But you have so much the look of—" She stopped in confusion, coloring.

Isobel bedamned! Alexandra thought, then remembered the woman was dead. She shivered slightly. "I am Alexandra Mayfield—an, er, cousin of the Duchess of Hawkesworth, which explains the likeness." She'd better get used to the lie, Alexandra told herself. "The duke speaks of your establishment in the highest terms," she said and invited the woman to a seat by the sunny back window.

"Monsieur le Duc is very kind. It will be a privilege to have the clothing of one so beautiful." The modiste's small head tilted, birdlike, as she scrutinized Alexandra from head to toe. "With so vivid a coloring, we must dismiss the pastels usual for young debutantes. This hair like fire calls for something rich and bold—evening gowns of lapis, perhaps, or emerald."

"I fear there has been a misunderstanding," Alexandra said with growing awkwardness. "I do not look for a wardrobe of the sort you describe. I am—"

The drawing-room door opened, and the Duke of Hawkesworth appeared at the threshold, comfortably surveying the two women. "Ah, Miss Mayfield, Madame Grès—I fear I was delayed. The Battle of Hastings took rather longer to win than I anticipated. You have met, I take it."

Hawke moved to the empty fireplace, where he leaned his shoulder against the gilt mantel and placed a booted foot upon the fender. His eyes were faintly mocking as he saw Alexandra's irritation. "Nothing too suggestive, you understand, madame. Miss Mayfield does not want to attract attention of the wrong sort. Several walking costumes, a riding habit, and two or three evening gowns, I should think—at least, to begin."

The tiny woman's eyes widened with surprise, which was as quickly concealed. "*Mais oui*, Monsieur le Duc—something becoming, but not 'crossing the line,' as you English would say.

With mademoiselle's elegant lines, she will have a great success, I think. But everything *comme il faut*, I quite understand."

"Exactly. With her hair and coloring pastels will not do, of course. Richer tones—lapis, jade. Even chestnut, I think. Have you brought samples?"

Blaze and bedamned! They spoke about her as if she were a bloody fashion doll! Alexandra seethed as Madame Grès nodded and rose to summon her two assistants, who brought in cases laden with fabric, fashion dolls, and trimmings. Soon the furniture around Alexandra was swathed in a rainbow of fabrics, white satin lying crumpled upon crimson velvet and aquamarine sarcenet.

The Duke of Hawkesworth knew a great deal about women's apparel, Alexandra discovered; quite an intimate knowledge, it became clear as he fingered lace and satin. He took an interest in the selection of every part of her wardrobe, right down to her chemisettes.

As she sat motionless in silent fury, Hawke and the modiste animatedly debated the merits of each color and fabric. Even when Madame Grès draped bolts of silk across her rigid shoulders, Alexandra remained tight-lipped and aloof.

"Not the crimson, I think," the duke said coldly.

The modiste looked up quickly and searched his face before thrusting the crimson velvet back into its case. "A bad choice—you are right. But the jade is most suitable, rich and warm with a certain something of sweetness about it."

Beneath lazy eyelids Hawke's gray eyes were sharp and quick. "Very good. You may prepare the three walking costumes and two evening gowns. We will need them in two days' time."

The dressmaker's mouth opened in dismay. *"C'est une plaisanterie, non?"* When the duke did not reply, her mouth shut tightly. *"Bien.* It will be difficult, but—" Madame Grès turned to Alexandra. "If you please, with the shortness of time, will mademoiselle permit a fitting now? It would be impossible to finish otherwise."

Two pairs of curious eyes leveled at Alexandra, who still felt like nothing so much as one of the fashion dolls clutched in the assistant's hands. "Permit?" she said icily. "Why not? Who am I to refuse two such expert advisers?"

With chin high and two bright flags of color in her cheeks, she rose from her chair and walked to the door, carefully avoiding Hawke's face.

The very next day, Madame Grès returned with two walking costumes and an evening gown. Grimly, Alexandra submitted to the attentions of the intense little modiste, who finally pronounced the dresses to be absolute perfection. Even Alexandra, staring pensively at her image in the cheval glass, had to admit that the walking dress of bottle-green merino cloth suited her to perfection. Molded close to her body and decorated at the waist with rich ribbons of ruby and green, the dress was a perfect complement to her hair and creamy complexion.

The ribbons at the hem and sleeves were more decorative than she thought appropriate for the situation she was seeking, but the modiste convinced her the dress could not be changed.

"Mais non!" the woman cried in great animation. "It is of the most suitable. *Très distinguée!* Without the ribbons the dress is— oh, of the dowd!"

Seeing the woman's sincere distress, Alexandra broke into unwilling laughter. "Very well, madame, you have convinced me. I do not think I would care to debate any issue with you."

For a moment the smaller woman did not reply. Her head was averted as she readied the York tan gloves and black kid half-boots that completed Alexandra's costume. When she looked up, her expression was oddly serious. "I say only what my eyes tell me, mademoiselle. You must not think that I say this only for flattering you."

Touched, Alexandra reached out and impulsively pressed the modiste's tiny wrist. "What a terrible ingrate I am, to be sure, when you are all that is kind. Forgive me, madame."

"As to that"—the woman tossed her shoulders philosophically —"there is nothing to forgive. If I offend you, it is I who must make the apologies." She straightened a matching pilgrim's cloak of green merino cloth around Alexandra's shoulders, then stood back to study the effect. *"Regardez!* The cloak is all of the crack this season. Can you doubt my words now?"

The effect was indeed distinguished, Alexandra had to admit, as she studied her reflection in the large cheval glass. The dress was rich but not flamboyant—a perfect complement to her vibrant hair and face. Suddenly, Alexandra understood why Madame Grès commanded such high prices.

She was presented with an occasion to wear her new attire sooner than she'd expected. Seeing that Robbie's energy was fully restored and the boy was champing at the bit to be up, Hawke announced a surprise.

"What sort of surprise, Father? A balloon ascension?"

"It would be no surprise if I told you, young jackanapes," the duke said indulgently, ruffling the boy's dark hair. "You must be very good today, and if you are well rested, you'll find out later on. Along with Miss Mayfield."

Alexandra, who had been quietly stroking Rajah in a wing chair on the opposite side of Robbie's room, stiffened as she saw Hawke's mocking smile. Resolutely she bit back the question she'd been about to ask. She would not give Hawke that pleasure, she decided. He might order her about, but he would have no source of pleasure in her curiosity.

Nor could Robbie coax any further information from his father, who remained resolute throughout the day. Soon after luncheon he bundled Robbie up and took him to the front door. There a smiling Jeffers waited, with Pence in his wake.

"Ah, Jeffers, punctual as always. You have the direction?"

"Indeed I do, Your Grace. I fancy we'll make it with time to spare."

With a nod Hawkesworth lifted Robbie up into the closed carriage, tucked a blanket about the boy, then turned to assist Alexandra. For a moment his hard gray eyes played over her face, studying her elegant form in the new walking dress. "I really must give my compliments to Madame Grès."

"You put me to the blush, Your Grace," Alexandra answered acidly.

"It would take a great deal more than a few well-turned phrases to put you to the blush, Miss Mayfield." Suddenly, Hawke's fingers circled her waist, and he pulled her against him as he lifted her up into the carriage. By the time he released her, she was indeed blushing, certain of his desire and furious at her own agitation.

For almost two hours they traveled, Robbie pressed to the window glass all the while, bombarding his father with a thousand questions. The duke showed himself remarkably agreeable, and even Alexandra found herself interested in the information he imparted about the passing countryside.

"I believe we are nearly there," Hawke said at last as the coach left the turnpike road and snailed it along a narrow track bordered by hedgerows bright with bluebells. It was nearly twilight. Alexandra peered into the gathering shadows, growing more suspicious about Hawke's promised surprise by the moment.

They were not the only travelers out this night. When they topped a rise, Alexandra saw before her a meadow dotted with stalls and colorful tents, oxcarts higgledy-piggledy with farm wagons, and everywhere a bustling press of people.

"Oh, capital, Father! A fair!" Robbie's eyes were bright as he studied the gay scene below. " 'Twill be ever so much fun! May we see the pugilists and Punch and Judy and fire eaters and—"

"If you can restrain your impatience a few moments longer, we shall, my little bagpipes."

At his father's words Robbie turned from the window, his young face trembling and hesitant. "I beg your pardon, Papa, Miss Mayfield," he said in a small voice.

Hawke reached across the carriage and took Robbie's pale face within strong fingers. "I'm the one who should apologize. Forgive me?"

Robbie smiled tremulously and nodded. "Will you buy me a monkey that runs up a stick?"

"Now it's blackmail, is it?" Hawke pinched Robbie's chin lightly, and though the boy flushed, he did not pull away. He was learning that his imposing father was not always to be taken seriously. "Very well, scamp!"

Slowly, the carriage crawled through the throng of fair-goers, heavy now that the stalls were before them. Lanterns began to wink brightly against the darkening landscape. Finally, Hawke tapped the roof with his cane, and the carriage halted.

"Ready son?"

"Oh, yes, Father!"

The duke took Robbie's hand, suddenly serious. "There may be some rather unsavory types here tonight, so you must stay close by and not wander off."

"Yes, Father," the boy said obediently, his thoughts flying to the marvels outside.

Over Robbie's head Hawke studied Alexandra. "The same holds for you, Miss Mayfield."

A cool wind ruffled Alexandra's hair, and she felt a faint prickling of the hairs at the back of her neck. But she shrugged and reached down to lift Rajah from her lap. "With Rajah along why should I be afraid?"

Hawke handed Robbie and Alexandra out of the coach, then turned for a final word with his groom. "You know where to find us, Jeffers," the duke said cryptically.

Just then, a pair of large and very intoxicated men wove their way unsteadily before the coach. Robbie pressed close to his father. Without speaking, Hawke slid an arm around the boy's shoulders, then fixed Alexandra with a warning glance. "Don't lag behind," he said sharply.

"Pray forgive me, sahib," she answered through tight lips. Ignoring Hawke's frown, Alexandra moved next to Robbie, whose round eyes were scanning the fair's entertainments.

They stopped before a stall with a painted backdrop, where a rope walker balanced precariously above the applauding crowd. At the neighboring stall, a ruddy, thick-set man prodded a small brown monkey into putting on a tiny vest and velvet pantaloons. Once dressed, the animal bowed to the audience and hopped forward to pass a hat for coins. Rajah squeaked with interest and trotted off for a closer look at this curious simian.

There were jugglers, conjurers, and a company of country players presenting Shakespeare's *Taming of the Shrew*. Overwhelmed by the noise, the smells, and the close press of bodies, Alexandra felt she had stepped into an old canvas by the Dutchman Bosch.

Then someone grabbed her arm roughly and clamped a greasy hand across her mouth. A thin pockmarked individual hissed into her ear, "No need for vapors, Miss. Just give us a guinea, and we'll be on our way, and no one the wiser." The man's leering mouth hovered in a gap-toothed smile before her. "Lady like you with such a fine dress won't mind sharin' a little with those what be more needy."

His dirty fingers squeezed her waist suggestively, and maneuvered her away from the crowd into the shelter of an empty ox-cart.

"Let her go!" Hawke's voice cracked like a whip, causing Alexandra's captor to lose his sullen arrogance. She gasped as the dirty hand left her mouth, and she watched paralyzed while Hawke tossed the man sprawling to the ground. "Unless you wish for more potent medicine, you'll find a new lay and a greener cove, cribbage face! I'm no Johnny Raw."

On the ground the dirty man rubbed his swollen jaw and studied Hawke's broad shoulders with a mixture of fear and fury. Fear won out, and he scrambled to his feet, only to turn when well out of reach and heave a great mouthful of saliva in the duke's direction.

Hawke cursed fluently under his breath and made to go after the insolent fellow, but Alexandra held him back with a hand at his wrist.

"Let him go, please. I should hate to spoil Robbie's pleasure. He's so enjoying himself."

Hawke's eyes flashed and his scowl deepened as he watched the man disappear behind a line of wagons. "Keep up then, damn it!"

This time Alexandra did as he ordered and took Robbie's hand, warmed by the gentle pressure of the boy's fingers.

"Only look over there, Father! It's Mr. Punch!"

Alexandra followed the boy's pointing finger toward a farm wagon. A length of thin white cotton was stretched from front to back to form a stage, and from behind the cloth a lantern cast colorful moving images of racing horses and flying dragons against the white curtain. A leather-faced old musician who might have been Turkish or a mixture of many things leaned against one side of the wagon, eyeing the audience expressionlessly.

"Not Mr. Punch, Robbie. Those figures come from farther afield—all the way from China. *Ombres chinoises,* they're called— 'Chinese Shadows.' "

As the duke spoke, a mounted warrior with long pheasant

feathers atop his headdress charged violently and unseated his enemy, while the audience clapped in delight. With swords drawn the warriors shot back and forth across the shimmering back-lit stage, accompanied by the clang of drums and clappers.

Heavy smoke drifted from the oil lanterns backstage. Alexandra watched, entranced, thinking she had never seen anything so lifelike. All too soon, the enemy was overcome and the performance concluded in a crescendo of odd discordant noise.

The flickering lanterns cast grotesque shadows over the surrounding faces of the audience. Suddenly, Alexandra felt the ground spin and she swayed, dizzy with the press of unwashed bodies, the suffocating smell of soot, and the strange pounding music. She shivered, feeling someone's gaze upon her. At the back of the wagon a tall man half in shadow melted back into the crowd.

He'd been watching her—she was certain of it!

"Is this the surprise, Father?" Robbie asked. "May we go backstage, Father? May we? Please?"

Hawke smiled down at his son's animated face. "Yes, this is my surprise. And yes, I shall force myself to ask that rather venomous-looking individual leaning against the wagon if you may have a look backstage."

As he spoke, another black wave of vertigo crashed over Alexandra, and she stiffened, unable to take a single step.

"What's the matter with you?" Grim faced, Hawke frowned at her. "I think my son has more wit about him than you do." When Alexandra still did not move, he caught her arm in a rough grip. "Very well. Since you persist in ignoring my warnings, you'll remain in the carriage with Jeffers."

Assailed with pounding waves of vertigo, Alexandra could only protest weakly, flinching as the duke pulled her in the direction of the carriage.

"Must we leave so soon, Father?" Robbie's face was ashen.

"Miss Mayfield is unwell and must return to the carriage," Hawke said shortly, pulling the two unwilling figures along on each side of him.

Alexandra gave up her token resistance. She wanted nothing

more than to escape from the assault of drifting soot, raucous laughter, and crowding, unwashed bodies.

Jeffers arose in surprise from the front of the team, where he had been inspecting the leader's fetlock, with Pence crouched at his side.

"Miss Mayfield will remain with you, Jeffers," the duke said peremptorily. "Keep a close eye on her. Robbie and I are going to take a look at the shadow stage." The duke looked down at the groom's young assistant. "Care to join us?"

Confused, Pence glanced back to see whom the duke might be addressing. When the truth hit him, a ragged smile broke from cheek to cheek, and he leaped to his feet, nearly sending the high-spirited team plunging. He moved quickly to calm the nearby leader, and by the time he turned back, his face was controlled, stiff with resolution. "Thank ye, Yer Grace, but I best stay and help Mr. Jeffers with the horses."

"Be gone with you, young rascal!" the groom said gruffly. "Don't keep His Grace waitin'. I reck'n I know how to mind a team for a quarter hour without your help!"

Pence's happy cry was answer enough. Without a further glance at Alexandra Hawke strode off, the two boys trotting at his heels, leaving her to climb inside the coach and lean her head wearily against the tufted morocco seat. After a few minutes she began to recover somewhat, although a queer ringing persisted in her head.

She heard a faint scratching at the carriage door and glanced down just in time to see Rajah dart over the crest of the hill.

Blaze and bother! Where was the rascally creature gone to now? If Hawke came back before the mongoose returned, he'd no doubt order him left behind.

Alexandra sighed and pulled her pilgrim's cloak tightly about her shoulders. If she was careful, she could be gone and back without Jeffers ever the wiser.

One thing, at least, she could be thankful for: in the last week, during Robbie's illness, she had done so little walking that her ankle had almost recovered its strength.

Occupied with inspecting the leaders' traces, Jeffers was paying little attention to the passenger in the coach. When he knelt between the two horses for a closer look, Alexandra slipped open the door and crept down the steps.

There was not a great deal of light, and she had to move carefully over the rutted ground. The moon was no more than a faint sliver passing in and out of the clouds, casting shifting shadows through the ancient grove of yews at the top of the rise.

"Rajah!" Her soft call went unanswered. From the wagons ahead came the smell of strong cider and frying sausage. Alexandra's stomach twisted in protest at the sharp odors.

She moved in silence through the long grass, her steps only a rushing whisper on the spring wind. Just at the edge of the yew wood, a bearded man in a smocked coat squatted beside his wagon, cooking a late meal by the dancing light of the fire. Somewhere to her left, at the edge of the grove, a nightingale launched into its sad refrain. Something about the song made Alexandra quicken her pace.

In her haste she overlooked the gnarled yew root at her feet.

A cry of pain tore from her throat as something hard caught at her ankle. By reflex, she threw her hands before her face.

The last thing she remembered was the cold black earth rushing up to meet her.

Chapter Twenty-Nine

By the time Hawkesworth returned to the shadow stage with his charges, the crowd had thinned considerably. The leather-faced man, Hawke discovered, was the troupe manager. At first he shook his head emphatically, dismissing Hawke's request for the boys to look at the intricately carved leather silhouettes. But a few coins from Hawkesworth soon brightened his expression.

As the boys happily watched the man demonstrate how to control the colorful figures, Hawke's thoughts returned to his infuriating, intriguing captive.

Damn the woman, anyway! And damn him for losing his control so totally two nights before! His offer of marriage had come quite unconsciously, as much a surprise to him as it was to her. Yes, Alexandra had a very fair notion of his character, Hawke thought grimly. She knew that marriage had not figured in his plans for her.

Then why had he made the rash offer? Was he falling under her spell, just as he had fallen under Isobel's?

"Goddamn her!"

"What, Father?"

Hawke realized he had cursed aloud. He sent his son back to his amusements then, wondering if Alexandra Maitland had already succeeded in driving him crazy.

By God, tomorrow he'd seek out his last mistress and relieve this ache in his groin! Come to think of it, Françoise was still his mistress, Hawke thought wryly. He'd never stopped paying the rent on that luxurious house off Oxford Street.

Hawke scowled. For some reason the thought of a night spent with the voluptuous Frenchwoman was totally unappealing. No, what he wanted was a taller woman, with long slender legs and burnished hair. A woman with haunted eyes the color of the Channel in spring.

This time Hawke's curse was long and very lurid.

Shouts of laughter recalled Hawke to his whereabouts, and he smiled to see Pence and Robbie neatly twirling leather silhouettes against the white curtain.

"Look, Papa! See how I can do it all by myself!"

A sudden pressure tightened Hawke's throat when he heard his son's happy cry. "Papa," the boy had said—for the first time he had called Hawke something other than "Father."

"Yes, lad," the duke said quietly. "I'm very proud of you."

Stunned by what his son had said, Hawke did not hear the bark of laughter behind him, nor see the tall elegant figure slip away from the crowd that was gathered before a sweating pair of pugilists.

"Be damned if it isn't the Black Duke himself! Almost didn't recognize you without your horse."

Hawke turned and was immediately enveloped in a solid embrace. His eyes widened as he scanned the lean dark face with snapping eyes the color of a robin's egg. "Never tell me it's you, Morland! By God, so it is, and damned fine you look too!" The duke fingered his friend's stiffly embroidered waistcoat of silver and crimson. "You'd make one hell of a target for Boney's men in this thing, old friend."

"Wouldn't I just?" the man said amiably. For once Anthony Langford, the fifth Earl of Morland, dropped his air of weary boredom. "But I dress for different campaigns these days, don't you know?" he added with a lazy smile.

"What brings you to this desolate hamlet?" Hawke asked curiously, stepping back to get a better look at his friend. Lord Morland's tall frame was elegantly turned out in form-fitting breeches above gleaming hessians, and his cravat was perfection itself. Hawke shook his head in amusement as Morland made him an elegant leg. "You haven't changed a whit, Tony. If you've come looking for more of your precious antiquities, you'll find yourself sadly out. Nothing here but mountebanks and conjurers."

Morland threw back his head and laughed. "Treasures of a different sort, my dear duke." Behind him a shapely maid dressed in thin muslin and a prodigious quantity of crimson ribbons called out impatiently, tossing her guinea curls.

"I might have guessed," Hawke said. "But you're hunting rather far afield, are you not?"

"As to that, a little variety is the best recipe for a jaded palate. Didn't your sire ever tell you that?"

Hawke smiled thinly. It was just the sort of advice his debauched father would have given him, had the man ever bestirred himself to speak to his son. "I hardly recall," Hawke said lazily.

"Well then, now you've heard it from me, and I can vouch for it being amazingly true."

"If you keep the little temptress waiting much longer, you'll be sleeping alone tonight. Didn't your father tell you that?"

Morland shrugged indifferently. "Daphne is a woman of amazing talents, I own, but she begins to grow tiresome."

Hawke shook his head. "You are a sad scamp, Tony," he said fondly.

"You've the right of that at least," his friend said, but the seriousness of his tone was belied by the twinkle of his piercing blue eyes. "Which, if my lamentable memory serves, was exactly what you told me that night in Lisbon, just before we both passed out at the feet of the charming Magdalena." His blue eyes narrowed, his face suddenly sober. "By God, it's good to see you again, Hawke!"

"So it is to see you, Tony," the duke said quietly. This time his eyes offered his friend a silent apology. "Someday I shall explain—"

Morland waved his hand dismissively. "No need. Only glad we crossed tracks again this way. But what brings you to this place?"

The deep lines of Hawke's tanned face relaxed somewhat. "The reason stands right over there, my friend, mauling those poor leather figures. My son—Robbie. The other lad works in my stables."

Morland's eyebrow rose to a precarious slant. "But you intrigue me, my dearest duke."

Hawke smiled faintly. "It's a long story, Tony, one I don't mean to launch into now. But come, I must introduce you to my son. Let him plague *you* with questions about the war. You were always a great one for tall tales, as I recall."

For long moments all was darkness and pain. Then hard fingers bit into Alexandra's arm and dragged her up from the ground where she had fallen.

She flinched, shaking off her confusion. "Hel—"

Her cry for help was ruthlessly cut off before it left her mouth. Alexandra's heart pounded as she struggled against her silent enemy—a tall man, she saw, dressed in some sort of hooded farm cloak.

He dragged her behind him into the shadows of the yew grove, careful to keep his hand over her mouth all the while. His hard fingers stabbed her throat until she choked, fighting for air, feeling a deadly numbness steal across her limbs. Wild with terror, she struggled against that ruthless, clawing grip.

"Unpleasant, eh? What I'll do next will be a good deal more unpleasant still, my girl."

The dry laugh at her back raised the fine hairs along her neck.

Using the last of her energy, Alexandra lashed out with her foot, striking blindly, and on the second attempt her heel met bone and muscle. With a curse the man released her throat, jerking her around to face him.

"I'll make you very sorry for that, you bitch!" He twisted her head roughly, so that the shifting moonlight played across her face. "By God, it's hard to believe, even now!"

Alexandra's strength returned as air filled her lungs. Suddenly, she wrenched one hand free and tried to pry his fingers from her mouth so that she could scream, but he caught her hand like a pesky insect.

"If you scream, you're dead. Remember that." His colorless

eyes narrowed. His fingers loosened slightly and slid to her chin, where they rested menacingly.

"What do you think you're—"

"I'll ask the questions, bitch, and you'd best give me answers if you value your life." He reached into the pocket of his jacket and withdrew a metal blade that glistened coldly in the thin light of the moon. "What's the lay with Hawkesworth? Talk!"

"It's no business of yours!" Alexandra choked out but almost immediately regretted her words when his silver blade came up to trace the line of her cheek.

"Oh, but it is," the man breathed, his voice low and ragged with tension, which Alexandra recognized as a man's desire. "Shall I force you to answer?" His blade pressed into her cheek, cutting deep and searing her with pain. "It would be such a pity to leave you disfigured. . . ." His voice trailed off meaningfully.

Alexandra's mind raced. "I'm Alexandra Mayfield, may the Devil take you! I am governess to the Duke of Hawkesworth's son."

"Such spirit for a governess!" the man said mockingly. "But I've no doubt you provide services for both father and son. The Black Duke could never resist a temptation such as you warming his bed."

Alexandra recoiled at the hate in his voice, but the cloaked man gripped her tightly. His blade followed the line of her throat down to her neck and then to the swelling curve below. The honed point slid to a halt at the tip of her breast, where it rose and fell with the rhythm of her ragged breath.

Alexandra tasted fear then, raw, acrid fear such as she had never known. Please God, let Hawke come and look for her!

"What, no scandalized denials? No outrage? I thought as much. 'Tis a good position for a servant, after all." He laughed harshly. "A good position, by God, to have the duke between your legs!"

"You're wrong!" Alexandra cried, her voice unsteady with fear and anger. "He's nothing to me, nor I to him. But it's a good job, and one I want to keep, so let me go before he discovers me missing."

"Nothing to you, is he?" The colorless eyes measured her skeptically. "Perhaps I have a use for you then. Nothing demanding. It would come very easy to one of your talents."

"What sort of use?" Alexandra rasped, feigning a note of sly cunning.

"So you are interested?" His laugh was explosive with triumph. "This grows better and better, by God!"

His fingers closed roughly around the swell of her breast, and Alexandra could barely keep from shuddering. Through clenched teeth she answered, "It all depends upon the type of service. And upon the rewards, of course." She tittered, twisting away coyly when the man's fingers dipped lower. "Not so fast, dearie." She laughed, slapping his hands away.

His eyes glittered, as pale as the moonlight. "I can see why he keeps you, my dear. You'd be a pleasant diversion on a cold night. Unfortunately, I have other plans. Plans that render you infinitely *de trop.*" His eyes flicked over her, blank and impersonal, like the death gaze of a coiling snake.

"Let me go!" Alexandra screamed. Dimly, she felt his hands loosen as a shrill squeak exploded in the darkness.

Cursing, her attacker stabbed the empty air with his dagger, but the weight that had fallen on his shoulders would not be dislodged. Rajah's eyes were bloodred with fury as he sank his teeth into her assailant's neck.

Alexandra turned and stumbled down the hill, knowing Rajah had given her precious minutes to escape. Overhead, the moon slipped from the clouds, lighting her path, and she sobbed in relief to see a pair of lanterns swinging up from the meadow.

"Where have you been?" the duke growled as she came hurtling down the slope.

But Alexandra, blind with panic, only threw herself into his arms, clutching his jacket with rigid fingers.

"What is it, Alexandra?" Unconsciously, Hawke circled her waist and drew her closer against his chest. With a frown he looked up to the high ground from where she'd come.

"A m-man," she rasped. "T-Telford, I think. Rajah's with him now. P-please!"

"Up there?" His face darkening, he pulled out of her grip and hurtled up the hill, where he disappeared into the yew grove.

Long minutes passed with no sign of movement from the dark grove. Finally, Hawke appeared at the top of the hill. His expression was unreadable in the moonlight as he strode back down. Following behind him at a brisk trot came Rajah, his tail arched in triumph.

"There was no one there," Hawke said flatly, disbelief written on every inch of his face. Suddenly, he raised his lantern and pulled Alexandra beneath its light. "What have you done to your cheek?"

"Cheek?" she repeated woodenly.

"Yes, damn it! There's blood on your cheek."

"Blood?" Her hand crept up to the mark left by Telford's blade. Her fingers traced the sticky line of half-dried blood, and she winced with pain. "He—he had a knife."

Hawke dropped the lantern abruptly, his face a frozen mask. Behind him Alexandra saw Jeffers, tense with worry, shepherding the two boys back to the carriage.

"So," Hawke whispered, "the game is not over after all."

Back at the George and Dragon, Anthony Morland pulled himself away from a lazy contemplation of his bed partner's ripe charms. His nostrils wrinkled in distaste as the tousle-haired beauty began to snore, and he leaned back against the headboard, hands clasped behind his head.

By God, Hawkesworth had changed! Morland thought in amazement. There was a warmth about him now, an ease that had never been there before, not even in their most drunken moments of leave during the Peninsular Campaign.

Bad business about his wife, Tony thought. He'd caught only bits and pieces of the affair, for the dust had already begun to settle by the time he got back to London. But the scandal was still talked of in many quarters, and Tony had learned enough to feel a sharp stab of sympathy for his friend.

His blue eyes narrowed as he stared up at the ceiling. Lord, those had been bad days. Their men had died from cold and hunger as often as from the enemy's grapeshot. Yes, very bad days, he thought grimly.

At one time he'd believed that the Black Duke had come

through it all unscathed, with his cool, unruffled superiority intact. But later, when Morland had chanced upon his friend in London, Hawkesworth had been entirely closed and remote. Damn if Hawke hadn't looked right through him, like a complete stranger! Tony frowned as he recalled how he'd slapped the duke on the back, certain it must be some sort of joke; but Hawkesworth had cut him off coldly, clearly anxious to be on his way.

Well, a man didn't have to be told some things twice, Tony thought. He'd dropped the association after that. But now, after seeing Hawke again, the earl began to think his friend a new man.

Lord Morland's blue eyes widened appreciatively as he recalled the woman who'd half run, half stumbled down the hill. Not the duchess, Tony realized, despite the close resemblance. No, this woman was softer—all fire, just waiting to burst into flame.

Damn it, Hawke was a lucky man! Tony thought, a lazy grin on his face. This one was a regular stunner alright. Leave it to his friend to have all the luck. But then Hawke had always had a way with women—maybe it was his air of brooding indifference. Positively defied a female to break through his shell, Tony thought with a cynical smile.

He frowned thoughtfully, wondering how far the affair had progressed. A tension about Hawke had suggested things were far from settled between the two.

Just then Morland's companion snored sharply and rolled to her side. Her hands reached sleepily to Tony and stroked his thigh with long nails. She arched her back, murmuring something under her breath, and he leaned closer.

James, was it! the earl thought angrily. That damned caper merchant! She planned to play them off one against the other, did she?

The fair Daphne had become a dead bore, the earl decided. Yes, it was time for him to shake this dust of the country from his boots and find out what was going on in the metropolis.

Careful to make no noise, the tall man with piercing blue eyes uncurled his long legs and slipped from the bed.

He only wished he might see Daphne's face when she awoke and found her pigeon had flown.

Chapter Thirty

Alexandra's nausea did not go away; nor did the nightmare vision
of a lean face with glittering, colorless eyes. After the night at the
fair something seemed to leach her energy, and even asleep she
could not escape the memories of that shadowy face, nor the cold
sense of evil that had hung about the man.

In an effort to discourage such grim memories she threw herself
into Robbie's company over the next days, filling his eager ears
with tales of India and the heroic men and women who had
shaped a new life on a strange continent. To all of this Robbie
listened spellbound, with an almost pathetic attention that caught
at Alexandra's heart.

She was careful to time her visits with Robbie during the early
morning or late afternoon, when she knew Hawke was likely to be
occupied elsewhere. Her other hours she spent in her room or in
the quiet upper saloon, where she tried to read.

It was not that she was avoiding the duke; it was rather that she
did not go out of her way to find him. When the news of his return
to London blazed among the *ton,* invitations had rained down
upon the townhouse in earnest, and the door knocker clanged
from morning to night.

And Hawke at last was accepting some of them. In the afternoon he sparred with Gentleman Jim at his boxing establishment, and as often as not, he joined an acquaintance or two for dinner and an evening of cards.

At least, that was what he told Robbie his evenings were given to. Alexandra guessed that he had also found companionship of a more intimate sort. Toward her Hawke's attitude was curt and impersonal. Yet she was always conscious of him, of his quiet step in the hall, of his deep, rumbling laugh while he played with Robbie. Through the long hours she waited, tense and smoldering, for the dread moment when he would come to collect his payment.

In spite of her care to avoid him they occasionally met at breakfast or in passing. Whenever they were close, the air around them grew electric with tension. Even Robbie noticed.

Soon, Hawke's steely eyes promised.

My body, and nothing more, Alexandra's stormy eyes countered.

Like an Indian monsoon their hostility grew, feeding on itself and the frenzied energy of life in the capital, building to a violent strength that neither could have imagined.

The air was unseasonably cool on the evening Alexandra joined the duke for their trip to Vauxhall. In spite of herself she'd been looking forward to the event, for she had long heard of this celebrated place where the low born and the noble, the rich and the poor alike, could mingle freely for a night's pleasure.

She wore a gown of jade-green velvet caught high at the waist in a stomacher of deep rose trimmed with white silk. Above the rich velvet her shoulders rose in cool splendor, although in deference to the night air she draped a mantelet of rich burgundy tissue silk loosely across her upper arms. Her burnished tresses were caught up behind and fell in artless ringlets against her neck. As the final touch she'd threaded a ribbon of velvet and mock pearls through her hair and across her forehead.

It was not the costume of a governess, of course, but Alexandra did not dwell upon that thought. Tonight she meant to ignore the arrogant duke and enjoy herself for once.

In the foyer Hawke turned from his guest as Alexandra slowly descended the curving staircase, and his dark eyes narrowed. By God, she was magnificent! he thought. Desire as sharp as a blade plunged through his groin when he glimpsed the pale curve of her shoulder and the creamy expanse of her chest that was revealed by the low-necked gown. Unconsciously, his hands tightened on his buff kid gloves. She was not dressed as a governess tonight, he thought, admiration dissolving into irritation. And where had she gotten those damned pearls decorating her forehead?

Blue-green eyes flashing, Alexandra crossed the foyer and waited for a scowling Hawke to make the introductions.

The duke merely raised an eyebrow and studied the ribbon inset with pearls. "Another curious Indian custom, Miss Mayfield?"

Her laugh was like tinkling bells on the wind. "I cannot claim the idea as my own, Your Grace. It had been the style for quite six months before I left Madras."

Hawke's companion cleared his throat pointedly, recalling Hawke to his duty. "Miss Mayfield, may I present Lord Morland?" the duke said coolly. "He is something of an old friend, but I caution you to accept whatever he says with a callous ear, for he is a notorious flirt." The duke turned to his tall companion. "Tony, may I make known Miss Mayfield, a relative of the duchess, recently arrived from Madras."

The tall man bowed gracefully over Alexandra's gloved hand. "An unexpected honor, indeed. What superior good fortune that you eschew a mask." His twinkling blue eyes lingered upon her face. "One had no idea the eastern colonies held such jewels as these."

"Are masks customary then? You did not tell me, Your Grace." Alexandra shot Hawke a reproachful look before turning back to Lord Morland. "As for the pearls, I'm sorry to disappoint you, my lord, but they are entirely sham."

"Oh, the jewel is quite real, my dear, I can assure you." His eyes lingered appreciatively on her face. "And your hairstyle will be all the rage by the morrow, mark my words. Soon *La Belle Assemblée* will be speaking of nothing but hair dressed *à l'Indienne.*"

Alexandra laughed and shook her head. "You are very kind, but I recognize when I'm being flattered shamelessly."

"Oh, surely not *shamelessly*, Miss Mayfield."

Hawke had begun to slap his gloves in irritation during this exchange and now abruptly interrupted their pleasantries. "As you recall, Tony, the concert begins at eight o'clock. If you mean to detain Miss Mayfield much longer, we shall never arrive in time for the fireworks."

Unflappable, Lord Morland merely bowed to his scowling friend. "I am entirely at your disposal, my dear boy. Lead on, and I shall follow."

Alexandra stifled a laugh as Hawkesworth's scowl grew more pronounced.

Hawke began to feel a decided distaste for this outing. Something about Tony's warm glance forced him to acknowledge Alexandra's wit, charm, and striking beauty.

She would capture many eyes tonight, he knew suddenly.

And what if some bloody fellow captured *her* eye in return? Morland, even? His eyes hardened into flint chips. No, by God, she was his! No one else would ever touch her!

Busy drawing on her long kid gloves, Alexandra did not at first notice the expression on Hawke's face. She knew his eyes were upon her though, and when she looked up, his mouth was thin with distaste.

She flinched as if he had slapped her. Her cheeks burned crimson as she lifted her chin proudly. "Changing your mind again, Your Grace? Must I remind you that this excursion was your idea?"

Hawke smothered a curse, feeling Morland's curious gaze upon them. He caught her arm in a viselike grip, and his dark eyes snapped a warning. "You give me no leave to forget it, Miss Mayfield. Nor *your* feelings upon the occasion."

In stiff silence Hawke escorted her outside to the carriage, ignoring Morland's wicked smile, and each was soon caught up in a different train of thought.

Perhaps that was why none of them noticed a thin man scuttle out of the darkness to hail a hackney as soon as Jeffers rounded the corner.

* * *

A thousand dancing lanterns greeted their arrival at Vauxhall. It was as close to a fairyland as she would ever come, Alexandra decided, mesmerized by the swaying pools of color beneath the tinted lanterns. Narrow gravel walks meandered through secluded groves guarded by white marble statuary, while darkened gazebos guaranteed privacy for those who desired it.

Judging by the slurred speech and leering laughter from behind the thick hedges, a great many people were in search of privacy this night. Indeed, the gardens were already thronged with revelers as a lilting waltz drifted over the laughter and gay conversation.

Ignoring Hawke, Alexandra turned to Lord Morland for a description of the pleasures to be found.

"It's been a while, I'm afraid," he told her, "but I recall a hall of mirrors, a Swiss cottage, and some sort of Turkish chamber, along with the usual assortment of musical spectacles. Then there's the Dark Walk, of course—not a place to go without escort, you understand." He looked thoughtfully toward Hawke's shadowed face. "Perfectly safe if you're with one of us, though."

There was a short explosive snort from the far corner of the carriage. "Don't let us clip your wings, Tony. Feel free to forage as usual. Miss Mayfield will be *perfectly safe* in my company."

The duke had reserved a private box within view of the orchestra, but Alexandra begged to look about a little before they were seated. Falling under the influence of the gay revelers, the drifting music, and the swaying lanterns, she felt herself relax.

Everything would have been perfect, in fact, could she have escaped the raw tension of Hawke's company and the frequent contact with his hard, muscled body as they walked down the narrow lanes before the performance. When it became clear there was room for only two to walk side by side, Lord Morland silently fell behind.

In the darkness even the smallest action took on a sense of intimacy. Their feet scraped quietly over the graveled path, while strains of the waltz drifted from an unseen orchestra. Colored lanterns shaped like stars and crescent moons cast a mysterious beauty over the grottoes and shadowed walks.

Dreamily, Alexandra wondered what it would be like to explore the darkened alcoves with a responsive companion. Someone with strong hands and ardent lips. Someone tall, with broad shoulders and speaking silver eyes—

She snapped out of her reverie and found Hawke's hand lying rigid upon her arm. There was no warmth, no consideration in his touch, and that harsh realization struck her like a blow, so that she stumbled slightly upon an overturned flagstone.

Immediately, Hawke pulled her flush to his body with an iron hand around her waist. "We've done enough walking for one night," he announced stonily. "It's time to find our box."

He was not so graceless as to mention her limp directly, but he had come as close as possible, Alexandra thought.

Damn you! she cried silently. Damn you for ruining this evening, which I was set on enjoying! Damn you for manipulating me, for goading me, for destroying my future!

Most of all, damn you for fascinating me as no man ever has!

Her hand froze upon the fragile mantelet at her throat, her eyes emerald pools in the half-light of a green lantern. Horrified, she studied Hawke's lean face and the angry frown that lined his forehead.

It was true, Alexandra thought, sick with comprehension. He *did* fascinate her—at the same time that he repelled her. He had set his mark upon her that day by the high stream at Hawkeswish, just as he'd made her blood race with savage passion during the storm upon the cliffs. He had taught her ecstasy, and in so doing he had accomplished his threat.

He had made her his woman.

She could deny it to him, but to herself she could not.

Choking back a sob, Alexandra curled her hands into fists and flailed blindly at his powerful fingers. "Go away!" she cried. "Haven't you hurt me enough already?"

"Get a hold of yourself!" Hawke hissed. "I shall be delighted to release you once I'm sure you can walk." His fingers bit cruelly into her white shoulders.

"You're hurting me, you brute! Let me go!"

"Then stop fighting me. You can never win this game."

"But neither can you," she sobbed. "Because I'll always fight you, don't you see? It matters not that you're stronger, richer, and more powerful. I'll always hate you, and I'll never give in!"

Abruptly, Hawke's hands fell to his sides. He frowned to see the dusky shadows of his fingers on her shoulders. There would be bruises there tomorrow, he realized.

A single tear glistened upon the pale curve of Alexandra's cheek. With rigid fingers Hawke brushed away the perfect silver drop. "I had no idea you hated me so much," he said, his eyes like smoke. He took a step away from her. "Since you find my company so distasteful, I shall ask Morland to attend you. No doubt you'll find him a more amiable companion." He made a slight mocking bow and then slipped off in search of his friend, haunted by the beauty of her pale, tormented face.

Anger and pain warred in Alexandra's eyes as she watched Hawkesworth stride away. Suddenly, she'd had enough—enough of this manipulation, enough of being taunted, enough of being a pawn in this cruel game between two ruthless men.

A gust of wind sent the lanterns swaying wildly, making shadows dance upon the path. But Alexandra barely noticed, her hand frozen at her throat as she watched Hawke's broad-shouldered form disappear down the walk. A cold trail of tears slipped down her cheeks, and she probed her tiny reticule for the scrap of cambric she carried there.

A light step at her back told her Lord Morland had come. Embarrassed, Alexandra turned from the light and wiped her cheeks surreptitiously with the back of her hand.

As if by magic, a folded square of white linen appeared before her blind eyes. "Thank you," she mumbled, keeping her back turned as she scrubbed her wet cheeks.

"Have you ever noticed that handkerchiefs are never to be had when one needs them most?" Morland asked conversationally.

Angry at her momentary weakness, Alexandra applied the cloth ruthlessly to her eyes, then sniffed defiantly and turned to face Lord Morland. "Invariably—which must make me grateful that you were on hand." She held out the cloth, a somewhat watery smile upon her face.

"Keep it, keep it. The cloth acquits itself more nobly in your use than in mine." Morland turned to study the quiet path where

Hawkesworth had vanished; his blue eyes narrowed thoughtfully. "He can be the worst sort of brute. I think the war did that to us. No excuse, of course, but there it is. The things we saw—the things we did to survive." He shook his head and turned back to Alexandra. "I'd go after the bloody fool and call him out if—if I didn't think that was the very last thing you'd wish me to do." His tone became gently inquisitive. "Am I correct, Miss Mayfield?"

"I think, my lord, you see far more than most people see, and a great deal more than is comfortable."

Morland smiled, but his eyes were deadly serious. "I'm afraid that the duchess is also to blame. You know about all that, of course."

Alexandra carefully folded and refolded the scrap of white linen. "I know most of it—at least what Hawke has told me. I'm not really a relative of hers, you see," she confided. "He only set that story about to explain our resemblance."

Morland whistled silently. "Good God, what's the Black Duke gone and done now? I've a feeling I won't like it by half!"

Alexandra said nothing, her eyes bleak with sadness for a moment.

"Tell me," Morland urged quietly.

"What good would it do?" Alexandra's laugh was sharp with bitterness. "He's ruined me. There's nothing you or anyone else can do to change that."

"By God, I'll see that the b—"

"Don't get involved. He's—he's a man possessed." She put her hand on his sleeve in entreaty. "I wouldn't want *your* death on my conscience too." My father's death is enough, she thought.

A shrill titter made her stiffen, and she turned to see a large party bearing down upon them, Hawkesworth at its head. The duke's silver eyes flickered across Alexandra's tear-stained face, hardening at the sight of her hand upon Morland's sleeve. Then the small woman walking beside Hawke said something that made him turn and smile down at her.

After a tiny squeeze Morland took Alexandra's hand, set it within the crook of his arm, and pulled her briskly toward the advancing party. "Ah, Hawke, we were beginning to despair of finding you. I'd forgotten just how sprawling this place is."

"Yes, a place easy to get lost in, but easy to be found in as well. Lord Liverpool, Lady Wallingford, Miss Wallingford, let me introduce Miss Alexandra Mayfield, a relative of my wife. This, of course, is Lord Morland, whom you must certainly know already."

There was a small, awkward silence during which three pairs of shocked eyes studied Alexandra's face.

Lord Liverpool was the first to speak. "Well, well. Should never have thought to see another so beautiful as the duchess. Deuced remarkable, in fact. But where have you been keeping yourself, Miss Mayfield?" The prime minister smiled conspiratorially at Hawke. "Duties keep me busy, but not so busy as that, I daresay!"

"Miss Mayfield is only recently arrived from India, which is why you have not seen her about, Liverpool."

The prime minister, an unprepossessing man with thinning white hair, studied Alexandra thoughtfully for a moment. "India, is it? Must seem frightfully strange to you here then. But never mind, I'm sure Hawke will take you in hand." Liverpool's keen eyes settled upon Hawke's shuttered face. "We've missed you these last months, Hawke. Glad to see you back and about. Have a few matters I'd like to discuss with you, in fact. Must get together again—soon."

Hawke bowed formally.

The short, rather plump woman beside Lord Liverpool pushed closer to stare at Alexandra nearsightedly. "Are you one of the Tunbridge Mayfields, my dear? Went to school with a Georgina Mayfield. Ages ago, of course—dear girl, never knew where she disappeared to." The peacock plume adorning Lady Wallingford's turban fluttered perilously.

"Of course she is not, Mama," Hawkesworth's small dark-haired companion answered, chiding her parent brightly. "And she must think it the *oddest* question." The younger Wallingford extended her hand to Alexandra. "You must count me as your friend in London, Miss Mayfield. If there is any service I can render, pray do not hesitate to ask. I'm sure everything here must seem quite—overwhelming after India."

The younger woman's eyes sharpened for an instant, and Alexandra had the keen impression of being scrutinized like a specimen at the Botanical Gardens.

"There are some differences, but not as many as I expected," Alexandra said coolly. "Everything is very elegant, of course, but we all must breathe the same air, as my father used to say."

"Air?" Lady Wallingford repeated owlishly. "Surely it must be prodigiously warm over there in India. Why, dear Marjorie"—here she paused to nod energetically at that lady's husband—"was telling me just last night that humid night winds, especially the warm ones, destroy the complexion. She had it from no less than Prinny himself, who had it from the royal physician—Sudbury, I believe the man's name is."

Alexandra could not resist a quick glance at Hawkesworth, whose lips tightened at the mention of the doctor's name.

"When the night wind carries stinging insects, as it often did in India, then I must agree with you. As for the air itself, there are those who argue for its healthfulness."

Lady Wallingford threw up a plump hand and nervously fanned her face with a peacock feather fan. "What a frightful thought! I hope you will not mention it to the dear prince. It would give him the most dreadful upset."

Alexandra thought it very unlikely she would be conversing with so august a person as the prince regent, so she was quite willing to nod her assent.

The party regrouped and moved forward toward a broader avenue leading to the supper rooms. Alexandra and Lord Morland fell into conversation with Lord Liverpool, while Hawkesworth and his partner moved slightly ahead. Morland's steady hand upon Alexandra's arm offered her sorely needed support.

Just as they drew abreast of the large colonnaded pavilion where the orchestra was playing, Hawkesworth heard his name called loudly.

"Hawkesworth! Glad to see you back, by Jove! Haven't met you this age! Now I've seen you, I mean to press you into service again, I warn you!" The tall speaker stopped, spying Lord Liverpool behind the duke. "So that wretch Liverpool's found you already, has he?"

"Indeed I have, Canning. You'll have to rise early to beat me out, my good man." The white-haired prime minister smiled at this long-established but good-natured rivalry with George Canning, president of the Board of Control of the East India Company. "What does Hawkesworth want dabbling in Indian affairs, anyway? Boring bunch of nonsense—especially now that the cursed Vellore business is behind us. The real problems face us from the continent, man, even though Boney's routed at last." Here the prime minister stopped to pat the plump hand of his sister-in-law, Lady Wallingford, reassuringly. "But no more of this talk. Don't want to bore the ladies, you know."

At the mention of Vellore, Alexandra had stiffened. Unconsciously, she dug her fingers into Morland's sleeve. A tiny choking sound emerged from her throat, and she took an unsteady step backward. Fortunately, the rest of the group were oblivious to her response, since George Canning had turned to introduce another man into their circle.

"By God, you'll find someone here to dispute that, Liverpool. Sir Stanford Raffles has just been telling me all about Java, and how England's future lies in exactly that direction. Paints a powerful picture of the riches in the East—aye, just waiting for the first country farsighted enough to step in and take them."

Lord Liverpool only laughed. "Sounds grand enough. But the actual doing of the thing may not be so easy. Have to discuss it over dinner sometime, Canning."

Alexandra pulled away from Lord Morland's grip, her heart hammering in her chest. Well she knew Sir Thomas Stanford Raffles's grave intelligent face, for he had been a frequent visitor at Government House during his sojourns in Madras.

He had been a simple Mr. Thomas Raffles then. It had been four years since he'd last seen Alexandra, but he would certainly recognize her.

Oblivious to Morland's anxious look, Alexandra slipped farther away from the group. She stumbled blindly toward a stream of gay couples bound for the supper rooms and soon was lost in a sea of laughing, milling humanity.

Somewhere in the darkened bowers a clock chimed the twelve strokes of midnight.

Thick hedges along the walk muffled the sound of her flying

feet. She slipped farther into the darkened heart of the gardens, her nervous fingers clutched the fragile mantelet tighter about her shoulders. For the first time she noticed that the statues were only cheap plaster and that thick layers of slime overlaid the stagnant pools.

Muffled laughter from a nearby pavilion told her she was not alone, but she saw no one as she passed. Gradually, the walk curved, coming to an abrupt halt before a gazebo guarded by a haughty naked Adonis.

Suddenly, she was overwhelmed by wrenching nausea so fierce it drove the breath from her lungs. In great black waves it crashed over her, sweeping away reason itself. Shuddering, Alexandra reached a weak hand to circle the base of the unsmiling Adonis.

There, in the lee of a boxwood hedge, her forehead braced by the cold white plaster, she slid to the ground and was violently ill.

Chapter Thirty-One

"Foxed, eh?" A heavy figure lurched from the shadows before the gazebo. "Damned unpleasant to cast up one's accounts. Nothing else for it sometimes though." The hearty, slightly slurred voice echoed jarringly in Alexandra's ears as she fought down swelling waves of nausea. "What you need's a man's steady hand, m'dear."

"Leave me, please. I—I need no help," she gasped unsteadily.

She was still kneeling when his heated breath, reeking of spirits, played across her ear. "Nonsense. Wouldn't dream of leavin' you in such a state. 'Specially now as I see you're a damned prime article!" Hot, beefy fingers slid across her shrinking flesh. "Night air'll soon clear your head, m'love."

Dimly, Alexandra felt a cool draft on her shoulders and realized he had dragged off her mantelet. "Let me go!" she cried desperately, twisting against his hot fingers.

"Come, m'dear. Like a bit o' fight myself, but no need to carry it to excess." He leaned over her kneeling form and groped for her shoulders. "Here's a gold sovereign that says your body's willing and mine's damned able. Let's have a go in the dark then, eh? You'll see how generous I can be." Abruptly, his fingers yanked the velvet fabric from her shoulders and pinned her arms behind her, revealing the full upper curves of her breasts.

Raw anger ripped through Alexandra, and she struggled to rise from her knees. For the first time the lantern light fell full on her features and those of her pursuer.

She saw a man's face, fat and beefy, punctuated by two hard little eyes. Pig's eyes, Alexandra thought, sickened by the way they devoured her nakedness.

"Stap me! Didn't recognize you, Isobel, m'love! Bloody good fortune, seein' you here like this. Damned glad that brother of yours ain't around though. Man's not good *ton,* if you don't mind me sayin' so, m'dear. A very bad sort. But forget about him, for we've better fish to fry." The hard little eyes tightened. "Don't try to tell me you've forgotten the last time we were here!"

His beefy face swam before Alexandra's eyes, and his upper lip was hung with beads of sweat. With a groan, she twisted her shoulders, trying to wrest free, but her movements only inflamed her drunken swain.

Laughing hoarsely, the man dropped to his knees and hooked his fingers in the fabric at her shoulders, then jerked her hard against his bloated stomach. "Come, filly, it's not like I don't know that teasin' body of yours already. Just thinkin' o' the last time makes me stiff as a damned pike, by God!"

Alexandra shivered, feeling the obscene tumescence shove against her thighs. "Then you also know my husband is a very jealous man. He's close behind me even now," she lied desperately. "He'll carve you into a thousand tiny pieces if he catches you at this game."

But her pursuer was too far gone to listen. "Rubbish! Time enough for a quick thrust or two. Besides, Hawke'll never find us here." His eager fingers probed her chest, and he caught his breath sharply. "By God, but you've got a damned fine pair o' tits. Never saw any to compare."

Alexandra recoiled, fighting his stubby, jabbing fingers, but her bout of sickness had left her very weak. Bile pressed against her throat, and she began to sway dizzily.

The man beside her laughed and pinched her sensitive nipples, rolling them between rough greedy fingers. With a grunt he dropped his hand to force up her skirts.

Sobbing, Alexandra lashed out with her sandal-shod foot and

caught him soundly on the side of his knee as he squatted before her.

"You little slut!" His open palm cracked against her cheek, sending her reeling against the plaster statue. "By God, if it's rough you want, it's rough you'll get!" Before she could regain her balance, the man lurched forward, his narrow pig's eyes hard and brittle. His fingers clawed her shoulder and wrenched the fabric of gown and shift brutally, leaving a jagged hole above her pale breasts.

Panting breath thick with whiskey fumes bathed her face as he pried at the remaining strap of her shift. "Come, Isobel. You've the heart of a whore, or so you once bragged to me. Let's see you prove it." He was thrusting against her wildly now, inflamed with desire. "Should have been rougher with you last time, by God! Would have made even better sport."

Caught up in his lust, he did not hear the quiet powerful footsteps upon the walk. Out of the night Hawke strode, an unrelenting sweep of black—sable hair, shadowed face, and darker garments. The only points of light came from his silver eyes and the shining folds of his neckcloth.

Without warning Hawke's hard muscled arm shot beneath the man's fat chin and jerked him high into the air, lifting his bulk until his feet dangled helplessly above the ground and he choked.

The sound of harsh, desperate gagging made Hawke remember other men who had choked as they died—men who had pounded across the dry Portuguese plains as if nothing or no one on earth could halt their forward rush.

He had seen brutality there. It was expected on the fields of war. But to see it unleashed joyously against a terrified peasant woman had been more than he could take. There in Portugal he had heard the sound a man's skull makes when it cracks against naked stone.

It had been gut-wrenching and totally satisfying.

At that moment murderous rage surged through Hawkesworth once again. His fat captive thrashed in his grip, but Hawke did not notice for he was swept back to that hot dusty day in Vimeiro, to the acrid stench of fear and the fury for the kill. The memories blazed in his head until he forgot all else.

The French soldier had been young and cocky, nearly Hawke's size, and he had been backed up by three compatriots. They'd been too much entertained with bayoneting a young village girl to hear his approach, and Hawke had cut down the other three almost before they'd noticed him.

Which left only one. But he was a man cornered and armed, while Hawke was weaponless.

They'd circled for long restless minutes, his enemy fast and clever. Hawke had let the cocky Frenchman draw blood twice, just to fuel his arrogance; then he'd feinted and ripped the bayonet from his adversary's hands.

What had followed was sickening and totally unforgettable— the dull crack of a human skull splitting against naked stone.

Now Hawke yearned to hear that sound again. His blood was screaming, and all he could think of was Alexandra's terrified eyes. The fat man in his hands kicked vainly, fighting for breath.

"No, Hawke! You'll kill him!"

Surprised, Hawke looked down at Alexandra's strained white face, wondering at the fear in her voice. She should be glad, by God! Didn't she understand this was for her?

The gazebo and its iron-sided benches were only a step away. Hawke's face was a grim mask as he carried his struggling captive closer.

"Oh God, Hawke, please stop! Listen to me, before it's too late!"

The blood was roaring in his ears, and he had to fight to hear. He scowled down at the ground where she was sprawled in the shadow of the grotesque Adonis. She was clutching her torn dress together, a trickle of blood beneath her cheekbone. Naked terror in her eyes. Why terror now, he wondered?

"No more, Hawke! You must stop. This is madness!"

Finally her words penetrated the blinding haze of his fury. His fat captive sagged, a dead weight in his arms.

Madness, she had called it. Slowly, Hawke lowered his motionless burden to the ground.

Madness.

She was right, of course. She had been right about everything. And that thought only goaded him to savage anger at her.

"You bloody little fool!" he roared. "Why in hell did you bolt that way?" Glowering, he knelt beside her, irritated that her fingers clutched the rich green velvet.

"I was s-sick," she said, shuddering.

"Bloody stupid thing to do! You might have known you'd run into someone like that." He nodded toward the dark figure on the ground. "What would you have done if I hadn't come when I did?"

"Gotten raped, probably." Her laugh was brittle, at the edge of hysteria. "Not for the first time." In the taut silence her fingers grated against the heavy velvet.

Hawke cursed savagely. "Have you no idea what a prize you are?" he growled. His eyes were silver-flecked slate, his anger almost palpable. He ached to hold her, to shake her, to wipe the terror from her haunted face, but he was afraid that once he touched her, he wouldn't be able to let her go.

"But it wasn't me he was after," Alexandra rasped. "It was Isobel, you see. He—he thought I was your wife." She laughed unsteadily.

"Just be glad it wasn't Telford who found you," Hawke snarled.

Suddenly, he frowned and dragged her fingers away from the ripped fabric at her chest. The cloth fell open, revealing her silvered curves and the perfect dusky crests at their center. Dark bruises marred the pale sweep of skin, dirty footprints against virgin snow.

"Stop!" Alexandra cried, her chest heaving as she sought to cover her shame.

But Hawke could not tear his eyes from the vicious marks, terrible reminders of how close she'd come to real harm.

And then desire exploded through his loins. His breath caught and he fought the savage hunger that gripped him at the sight of her nakedness. His hands trembling, he released her, then forced his eyes away, concentrating on removing the diamond pin from his neckcloth. "So Orde did this?"

Alexandra's eyes were bright with unshed tears, and yet the set of her chin was proud. "It appears he knew your wife quite intimately. Naturally, he assumed he could pick up where they'd left off." She was angry enough to want to wound him now, just as he had wounded her by refusing to leave her any scrap of dignity.

Hawke's movements at his neckcloth ceased for only a fraction of a second. "Oh yes, our friend Orde knew Isobel very well," he said stonily. "But he did not know her well enough, it seems. My wife would be quick to discover when a man was not as flush as he pretended to be. No, she never countenanced the attentions of a man who could not reward her handsomely. My wife did not really enjoy physical intimacy, you see," he added harshly. "It was all a cold-blooded game with her, purely a means to an end—for all that she was a consummate performer."

"Hawke!" Alexandra choked at his cold words. "You mean—"

"No," he cut her off ruthlessly, "no more about it—not now. Perhaps not ever." Grim-faced, Hawke pulled together the jagged edges of her dress and secured them with his diamond pin. Though his touch was gentle, he felt her flinch and pull away.

From the far side of the hedge came a shout of drunken laughter. A moment later came Lady Wallingford's grating titter, then a booming rejoinder from Lord Liverpool.

"I can't be seen like—like this," Alexandra whispered, her fingers tightening convulsively on the lapels of his jacket. Her huge haunted eyes pleaded with him desperately.

"I'll send a message to Morland that you were unwell and I took you home," Hawke said. Unconsciously, his strong fingers cupped her back, smoothing the corded muscles at her spine.

A harsh muffled sound escaped from her throat, half sigh and half sob. "Please, let's go! Anywhere, as long as it's away from here."

Hawke felt a shudder shake her body as he rose and caught her slim form against him.

The ground rocked abruptly, and Alexandra feared she would be sick again.

Silver eyes scoured her face. "Are you all right?"

Mutely, she nodded, unaware how sharply her white lips belied her answer. Unbidden, the vision of a fat face with narrow beady eyes returned to torment her, and she choked back a sob. Hawke pulled her tighter, her breasts crushed against the hard ridge of his ribs as his lips caressed her forehead.

"Close your eyes," he ordered, urging her head down against his chest. "I'll have you away from here in a few minutes."

Alexandra shivered and gave in to the warm comfort of his arms. Beneath his crisp linens she heard the heavy rapid thump of his heart, echoed an instant later by her own.

It was some moments before the motionless Orde began to recover from unconsciousness. First he broke into ragged coughing, and when that abated, he lurched unsteadily to his feet and shook himself like some great shaggy canine.

How like Orde! thought an unsmiling figure who watched in the shadows at the far end of the walk. As always, the drunken sot was boringly predictable.

Damn it, if he'd been only seconds earlier. . . .

But James Telford did not task himself with regrets. There would always be a next time—and he would be waiting.

In the meantime this was one more bit of information to add to his store. He knew, for example, about the disastrous turn Orde's fortunes had taken at Watier's two nights before. As a matter of fact, he knew precisely to the pound how much the drunken gambler had dropped at play.

It was his business to be informed, the man with colorless eyes thought, a thin smile on his sallow face. There was always a use for such facts. One found them and stored them away—even the most trivial details—because one day they would bear interest in the most unexpected fashion.

Like the information he'd gained tonight. Yes, maybe it was a godsend he'd been too late just now, for he had gained a precious clue. He'd seen Hawkesworth crumple Orde and lift the frightened beauty into his arms. The duke's expression as he pulled her head down against his chest had not escaped the motionless figure who watched from the shadows.

So that was the way of things. But how delicious! And how exquisitely vulnerable it made the cursed Black Duke!

Not that the duke was an easy man to deceive. For six months he'd been Telford's unwitting source of information about key details of the English campaign on the Peninsula, details that had been worth a great deal to the right people. But not even Hawke's infatuation with Isobel had blinded him to the leak within his own household.

And when the Black Duke had discovered its source, he'd meted punishment swiftly and mercilessly. There had been no public mention of the incident, of course, for Hawkesworth would never have permitted such a scandal. But in private he had shown no restraint.

In the darkness the man fingered his cheekbones, tracing the faint ridges that remained even now. His lips curled with hatred as he remembered the savage beating he'd taken at the Duke of Hawkesworth's hands. It had been six months before the wounds had healed—six months of agony during which Telford had done nothing but lie in bed and plan how to exact his retribution.

And now, from a totally unexpected source, the means had been handed to him.

The woman, of course! She was the key to the whole affair. He should have seen it sooner. She could never deliberately mislead Hawkesworth, for her face was too transparent for such deception. Unlike his beloved sister's, Telford thought, his eyes hardening. But she would serve her purpose well.

In the last quarter hour he'd learned everything he needed to know, and all that remained now was to put his plan into action. For Telford was a master of ferreting out secrets and putting them to good use. Yes, this time his old enemy would pay dearly. With what he had learned tonight he could at last bring the arrogant Duke of Hawkesworth to his knees.

And then he would repay broken bone for broken bone, wound for bloody wound. In truth, those were only the first of the torments Telford had in store for his hated victim.

Soundlessly Hawke slipped through the darkened groves, past the drunken lovers, hard-eyed Cyprians, and prowling bloods in search of an evening's pleasure. His eyes were grim as he pulled Alexandra's silk mantelet up about her head and shoulders, veiling her face against a chance encounter with one of his acquaintances.

Better to let them think she was an unknown impure, the duke thought bitterly, and that he was engaged in nothing more than an errand of simple lust. This, society would always understand. That he should feel something more was what would damn him.

Not that lust was lacking, Hawke thought with harsh self-mockery. The painful truth was that the ache in his groin left him barely able to walk. And yet his lust was compounded by a thousand other emotions—tenderness, possessiveness, and respect—even now when he yearned to lay her down in one of the secluded bowers for which Vauxhall was famous and brand her with the marks of his passion.

But he did not.

He forced himself instead to ignore the low laughter of trysting lovers and the tangled bodies half hidden in the shadows. Each instant, his chest burned with the exquisite agony of Alexandra's touch, the liquid heat of her breath against his shirt. Every step drove her thigh against his groin, tormenting him with soft, agonizing friction.

No—not yet, he told himself.

She was not heavy, but a faint haze of sweat soon covered Hawke's brow, and it seemed an eternity before he finally found the carriage.

Jeffers darted a quick look at Hawke's face, then hastened to lower the steps. "Home, Your Grace?"

For a moment Hawke did not answer. Then, in the silence, a new voice rang out.

"Where are you taking her?" It was Morland's voice, cold and precise.

Hawke spun about and frowned to see his friend stalking out of the gardens behind him.

"I repeat, Hawke, where the devil are you taking her?"

Alexandra struggled to raise her head from Hawke's chest, but he curved his palm around her forehead to hold her where she was. Without another word he turned, carried her into the carriage, and deposited her on the leather seat.

His body was rigid with tension as he climbed down the steps to face Morland. "Let me have the use of your apartments tonight, Tony. I can't take her back to Bedford Square—not yet. She's had a bad night. It was Orde, damn him! Bloody fool took her for Isobel and nearly—"

"Far less than what you did to her, as I understand it," the earl said acidly.

Hawke's jaw froze into a hard line, and his whole body bristled with an air of barely restrained ferocity. "Don't press me, Tony, I warn you! Not tonight."

"Is that a threat, my dear Richard?" Morland's voice was as deadly as a honed blade.

Hawke's eyes blazed. His fist was halfway to Morland's face before he caught himself, drew a long ragged breath, and shook his head.

Dear God, was it happening to him all over again? Had he exchanged one nightmare obsession for another? "I just need some time with her, don't you see?"

Morland's blue eyes were frankly skeptical. "Why? So that you can hurt her more?"

"For a stranger you're bloody interested in this woman all of a sudden!"

"She's not one of your damned opera dancers, Hawke. You can't just—"

"I can do anything I please with her. She's mine, by God!" The duke's fists clenched and unclenched at his sides. "She'll always be mine."

"Are you mad?"

Hawke shrugged, then hunched his broad shoulders and thrust his balled fists into his pockets. "Perhaps so. But there are things we must settle between us. Alone. I can't take her back until that's done."

"Settled to whose satisfaction?" his friend demanded. "Hers, or yours?"

"To our *mutual* satisfaction, I trust," Hawke answered grimly. "If not, I give my word I'll let her go, free and clear. I don't much like what I've become either, you see." His voice grew very tired. "Somehow, I feel this is the last chance I'll ever have."

Morland studied his friend warily, skepticism darkening his tense features. "Very well," he said at last. "Give Whitby the night off—or what's left of it. The rest of the staff will be asleep already.

But I'll be around to see you tomorrow, by God, and I'd better have the whole story then, do you hear?"

After a moment's hesitation Hawke nodded. "Time enough," he said flatly. "Time enough to discover where her heart lies. Men's futures have been decided in far less time."

Chapter Thirty-Two

Alexandra's eyes were wide and searching when Hawke entered the carriage. With a lurch the horses began to move.

"What did you—where are we going?"

"Tonight I call for payment, Alexandra. But before I do, I'll give you one last chance." His eyes flickered over her torn bodice and her tear-stained face, her lips swollen and moist where she had bitten them during Orde's assault. "Would you do me the signal honor of becoming my wife?" He bit off the sounds harshly, in sharp contrast to the elegant politeness of the words themselves.

Alexandra's eyes widened. Mutely, she shook her head.

"Very well. I shall have you *my* way then. I'll take you again and again until you beg me to stop." Tonight she would be his, by God, body and soul, with no more barriers between them! And then maybe . . .

She fought down a sob. "It is good that your mother cannot see what her son has become," she rasped. "You're nothing but a contemptible savage!"

"Yes, I'm a savage," he growled. "You make me so. You make me hate you, adore you, and desire you mindlessly, beyond reason. One look, and I burn to hold you, shake you, and love you. It was bad with Isobel, by God, but this is a hundred times worse, witch, for you give me hope one minute, only to rip it away the next."

Alexandra shrank back against the leather seat, frightened by the slashing steel of his eyes. Her head began to pound, and she closed her eyes against the insistent throbbing pain at her temple. Her white fingers slipped to her mouth as she fought her way through waves of nausea.

"Never tell me you're going to be sick again?"

White faced, she leaned toward the door. Her hand was upon the handle when she tensed. . . .

Hawke jerked her back just as she was about to hurl herself from the swift-moving carriage. With a savage curse he dragged her into his arms and pulled her head back to glare into her face. "You gave your word, remember? Or have you no honor in that as well?"

Alexandra went limp in his arms until his grip relaxed. Then, sea-green eyes flashing, she swung her open palm against his cheek with all her strength. The sound echoed and ricocheted in the closed space with all the explosive force of a pistol shot.

Hawke's face was dark with fury as he captured her clawing fingers. "Maybe we'll have a storm tonight, Alexandra," he taunted. "Then at least you'd have an excuse when you purr for me and arch like a cat in heat."

"Damn you!" she cried. "If I were a man, I'd call you out for that, you bastard!"

"Ah, my dear—if you were a man, you wouldn't be here."

He did not release her until the carriage halted some minutes later on a quiet side street. He jerked her, stiff with fury, to her feet and forced her down the steps before him. At Hawke's tapping, a servant appeared at the door of the townhouse.

"Whitby, is it? The earl has given us the use of his apartments tonight. He said you might take yourself off until morning."

The man's eyes flickered over Alexandra's tear-stained face. Whitby knew the Black Duke by reputation, of course. He began to think Hawke's nickname well earned. "Very well, Your Grace," he said with complete impassivity. "Will Your Grace be needing anything before I leave?"

"Nothing."

The saloon was in near darkness, lit only by glowing embers in the grate. Hawke pushed Alexandra inside and kicked the door shut with his boot, the sound cracking ominously through the silent rooms. Morland was obviously a lover of art, for paintings and oriental curiosities flooded every corner. The fire's red glow bounced back from the walls, every inch of which was hung with an eclectic mix of travel scenes, architectural drawings, and botanical prints.

Wordlessly, Hawke strode across the room to stir up the coals, for the night had turned cold. Under his probing the flames jumped to life, bathing his face in red light and giving his eyes a coppery glow. When he turned around Alexandra was jerking off her mantelet. Hawke studied her coolly, his eyebrows raised to mocking points.

"Let's get this over with, shall we? You've toyed with me long enough." Angrily, she flung her mantelet onto the floor and dragged off her gloves.

Hawke's brow furrowed as she threw her gloves onto a nearby leather wing chair, then sat down to rip at her sandals. His eyes flashed crimson in the firelight as he shrugged off his own black coat and untied his neckcloth. His lips curled slightly when Alexandra's dainty sandals went flying past him, followed by her reticule.

A moment later, she ripped his diamond pin from her bodice and threw it blindly at him, her fingers trembling with anger. "Don't forget your damned jewel!" she said shrilly. "I wouldn't want you to think I was trying to rob you."

Her eyes were huge and stormy as she jumped to her feet and furiously began to strip off her gown. The jagged hole ripped farther, exposing ivory skin from her neck to her navel, but in her fury she did not notice. "Maybe you want the dress back as well!" She suited her actions to her words, yanking the dress down and kicking it toward a grim-faced Hawke. "And I mustn't forget the chemise. You can always use it for your next mistress."

"Stop it, Alexandra!" he growled, low and threatening.

"Stop now? Just when we're getting started?" she said mockingly. "Isn't that how you phrased it once before? Well, what's stopping *you* now? Or have you changed your mind again?" Her voice rose in brittle laughter. "And they call women fickle!"

His iron fingers snaked across her wrists as she struggled to pull her chemise from her shoulders. "Stop it!" he ordered.

Alexandra only threw back her head and laughed wildly. "I believe that was supposed to be *my* line, Your Grace! Well, you won't hear it from my lips, do you hear? Because I'm sick of this game. Let's just get the whole filthy business over with, shall we?"

With a fierce snarl, Hawke grabbed her shoulders and held her motionless. "You don't call the shots here, witch! Tonight it's *my* game, and I'll give the orders." His lips pulled back to reveal clenched white teeth. "Unless you mean to turn your back on your father."

A tiny shiver fled down Alexandra's body. Then she set her mouth in a mocking smile and looked up to study him beneath lazy, half-closed eyelids. "No, our bargain still holds."

When he did not move, she launched her sharpest arrow. "Come, Hawke, you can do it. You're a fine specimen of a man," she hissed. "You must remember how. Or is it that you're unable? Yes, maybe you need a woman's pain and fear to stir your blood. In that case, of course—"

His eyes snapping with deadly fury, Hawke hauled her against his chest until their faces were only inches apart. "Oh, I'm bloody well able, Alexandra. If Isobel couldn't emasculate me, did you think you could? Yes, you can feel how able I am right there against your belly." He forced her thighs against his rampant manhood, smiling cruelly when she flinched. "The question," he continued viciously, "is whether *you're* worth the effort. And whether I want you after another man's had his hands all over you."

Alexandra's breath came and went in explosive little bursts. "You vile, detestable *scorpion*!"

"And you so eager to know my sting," he jeered.

"You're poison!" she rasped. "Everything you touch turns to poison! Your wife, your son—"

"Leave Robbie out of it, damn you! I warned you once before not to drag the boy between us. Isobel couldn't do it. Neither can you!" Without warning his hands loosened, and he flung her away from him.

Alexandra stumbled and barely managed to catch her balance before she struck the carved rosewood arms of a settee. With a ragged sob she sank to her knees, feeling the room spin crazily.

Behind her she heard his angry footsteps as he stalked toward the door. For a wild moment she thought he was leaving, but the sharp clink of crystal sent her heart plummeting again: he'd merely gone to fortify himself with Morland's liquor. Tears pressed behind her eyelids, but she blinked them away, refusing to declare defeat before this loathsome creature.

"Don't worry, witch, I'll limit myself to one glass," he snarled. "It would be unforgivable if I disappointed you after you've gone to such trouble to arouse me." The glass in his hand crashed back onto the lacquered cabinet.

Alexandra sank down onto the floor. Her mouth flattened into a stony line as she forced herself to look at her captor. "Everything about you is already unforgivable. From the very beginning all you've done to me has been unforgivable. Why make this night any exception?" she demanded bitterly.

Flames flickered across Hawke's face, transforming his hard features into a gleaming red mask. He suddenly remembered how she'd fought him during the storm until he'd turned her frenzy into passion.

With a low curse he pushed away regret. One woman was much like another, after all. Why this obsession with an intractable, inexperienced, and damnably provoking female from the wilds of India?

But Hawke knew the answer even before he asked. From the first she had stirred his blood with her pride and her spirit, arousing a host of discordant emotions. Nothing would ever be simple between him and this woman, he realized.

With the fire at his back Hawke's eyes were fathomless and unreadable. "It doesn't have to be this way, you know." He was halfway across the room before Alexandra quite realized it, and he mesmerized her with the strange hunger in his voice. "You saved my life, Alexandra, when I was on the point of dying at the hands

of Telford's hired thugs. Can't you save me again? Just one night
—that's all I ask. We'll let the future take care of itself."

Alexandra's hand slipped to her throat, which was suddenly
cold. Her skin stood in goose bumps all over her motionless body.
Her mouth was dry. She tried to swallow the lump in her throat,
unable to speak.

"I won't force you. After all, our bargain was that you come to
me willingly."

He was standing over her now, and his fingers dipped to trace
the faint shadows at her cheek bones. How beautiful she was!
Hawke thought. His fingers trembled as he touched the curve of
her cheek, blushing in the fire's glow. Gently, he traced her swollen mouth, ignoring the wild drumming of his heart. "It's up to
you. I don't want to hurt you. I never wanted that. And whatever
happens, I owe you my thanks, for you've taught me a great deal
about myself." His fingers settled at her chin. "Even though not
all of it was good."

She did not move, studying him, paralyzed, from the floor. A
stricken look in his eyes, Hawke slowly turned toward the fire.

He was whipped and beaten, Alexandra realized dimly. All his
wildness was gone. So why wasn't she gloating?

Pride had been her father's sin. Would it be hers too?

Without a sound she slipped to her feet, driven by a force she
did not herself understand. Her fingers twisted and untwisted at
her waist as she studied the weary slant of Hawke's shoulders. She
lifted one hand—and the room started to swim wildly.

"Hawke—"

He caught her as she began to fall, lifting her fiercely and
searching her white face with ruthless intensity. A vein throbbed
at his temple as he strode with her into the adjoining room, where
a single silver candelabrum cast its pale light over a bed hung with
a crimson velvet canopy and curtains.

She hardly noticed that he went out and returned; then he
raised her shoulders and lifted her against the corded muscles of
his arms and the hard line of his thighs. A cold ridge of glass met
her lips. "Drink this. A little only. My God, you're as white as a
ghost!"

Maybe it *was* a ghost Alexandra saw then. All too clearly she knew what pride could drive a person to do. She remembered her last angry argument with her father, just hours before he shot himself. As usual, they had quarreled about her future. Why didn't she marry that nice energetic fellow just out from England? her father had asked. He was head over heels in love with her, after all. She could start a family, leave something to be remembered by.

And as usual, Alexandra had merely snorted and flatly refused. Only that time there had been an odd look on her father's face, a special plea that she had been too naive—or too selfish—to recognize.

Yes, looking at Hawke's face and the weary set to his shoulders was almost like seeing her father's ghost.

"I'll never forget the way you looked when I first saw you," Hawke said softly, interrupting her painful reverie. "An apparition in the fog—

> *. . . a Phantom of delight*
> *When first she gleamed upon my sight,*
> *A lovely Apparition, sent*
> *To be a moment's ornament . . .*

I think even then I knew you weren't Isobel. You turned out to be far more than a moment's ornament. So much more."

Hawke's fingers tightened, and somewhere deep in his being, in a part of him he had thought long dead, a strange, raw sensitivity leaped into being. In Spain he had heard of men who lost a leg in battle yet continued to feel sensation where the limb had been cut away.

That was what he felt now, in that still, quiet part of him that he had cast away so long ago. Perhaps it was his soul that gathered itself so, or maybe the dreams of his youth. But this feeling of burning awareness, of restless seeking, quickened and grew until it surpassed any emotion he had ever known.

Hungrily, Hawke's silver eyes swept Alexandra's face, devouring her etched beauty so that he could keep the memory with him always. The stormy blue-green eyes flashed, more lustrous than jewels, and desire gnawed at his groin.

He did not trust himself to bring her closer, for her body was already intoxicating him. The scent of jasmine rose on a cloud from her warm skin, while a tendril of red-gold hair stirred in the gentle currents from the window. Unaware that he moved, Hawke reached out and captured the long strand.

His eyes grazed her face and fixed themselves upon her lips with a desperate hunger.

Helplessly, Alexandra felt the force of his desire break over her, carrying her before it. She closed her eyes, arching her neck and shivering slightly as her own longing welled up in answer.

She wanted the mark of his hands upon her skin, the taste of his tongue on hers. She longed to sweep the weariness and pain from his eyes.

As if in a dream, Hawkesworth watched bright color stain her face, and his heart tightened with a wild reckless hope. "Is it yes then, my love?" he breathed, taking her chin in his hand and tilting her face up to him. He memorized her features, missing neither the graceful stain across her cheeks nor the dazed look in her haunted aquamarine eyes. With unsteady fingers he stroked her cheeks, and his large hands were very deliberate, as if he feared hurting her. "Tell me, Alexandra," he muttered, his voice harsh with emotion.

But Alexandra could not speak—not, at least, with her mouth. It was her body that answered, speaking a language older and more primitive than words. A wild tension gripped her and snaked down to her stomach and thighs as she leaned closer against his chest.

Suddenly, she understood this man very well. Fate had made them enemies, and yet they were much alike, right down to the disastrous mistakes they had made in the name of honor and self-respect.

Silence enveloped them as Hawke cupped her face, and his breath caught when her tongue came out to moisten suddenly dry lips.

"Alexandra!" he groaned, her name torn from his throat. "Sweet swan, I must have you. Once more—let me love you tonight! Give me your fire one last time. I shall know how to make it last forever."

Hawke's voice washed over her like rich sweet wine, and she heard the slight tremor, wondering that he made no effort at concealment. Perhaps it was her discovery of his vulnerability that made her heart twist and disappear into the depths of those bottomless silver eyes.

She swayed before the desolation she saw there, finding suddenly that she could deny him nothing. Not tonight. Her mouth began to shape an answer, but Hawke could wait no longer to taste her sweetness.

The curtains at the window fluttered gently as he brought his lips down, demanding her flavor and giving his own in return. An instant later, her breath checked as a moan escaped their joined mouths.

Whether it came from her or from him, Hawke could not say. Desire knifed through him, twisting in his groin. He found it hard to breathe when her tongue slid gently between his lips to trace the soft contours of his mouth.

Pleasure swept over him in dizzying waves. With rigid control he held himself back and allowed Alexandra to continue her exploration in her own way, reveling in the tentative strokes that became bolder as she touched his tongue. When he heard her half-sob, he drew her tongue deep in his mouth and closed his lips fiercely about her.

I am drowning, Alexandra thought. Drowning in this man, in this sea of molten silver he flings me into. Her body was languid and inflamed, bathed in liquid fire. She felt herself flower, opening to his driving need.

"Yes, my sweet love, give me all!" His silver eyes never left her face as he lowered the straps of her chemise. "Alexandra, I learned to live only when I met you that night in the fog. Everything before was a dream."

A muscle flashed at Hawke's jaw as his fingers pushed the thin chemise from her shoulders. With a gentle whisper, the fine batiste dropped away, and a cool wind touched her sensitized skin. Hawke's lips followed, searing a path over her neck and shoulders.

"Perfection itself," he whispered against her heated skin, feasting upon the iridescent curve of her shoulders and the proud swell of her breasts. "Fuller. More beautiful even than I remembered. Ripe. Impudent—here," he rasped, his lips grazing the dusky buds already swollen with desire. With a groan he cupped her fullness and drew one perfect taut peak into his mouth. His lips tightened around her, suddenly demanding. "Open your eyes!" he said urgently. "Let me see your passion. It gives me unimaginable pleasure."

Alexandra's eyes fluttered open and she moaned, sliding her fingers deep within his dark hair. "My fierce and stubborn hawk. Ask and I must give you anything tonight."

"Where were you so long, my heart?" he whispered. "Why could I not have met you six years ago?" His voice was ragged with desire. "Yes," he growled against her skin as he slowly lowered himself along her body, tracing a moist path across her ribs and lingering over the taut concave of her belly.

Alexandra sighed and took his head within her fingers, giving herself up to the fierce singing in her blood, dizzy with this raw pleasure that was exquisite pain.

His eyes were bottomless. "Stop me now, Alexandra, if stop me you would! For soon there'll be no turning back."

She watched him, paralyzed, unable at first to speak, so that his fingers bit into the tender silk of her belly.

"Do you understand?" Hawke demanded, his voice thick with the passion he fought to hold in check.

Alexandra could only nod mutely. Their eyes locked, blue-green sparks kindling silver flames. A moment later, the starched length of his linen neckcloth went flying onto the carpet. What he said next was muffled in the tangle of white fabric pulled over his head.

And then the wide muscled beauty of his chest drove the breath from Alexandra's lungs. She had forgotten how powerful he was, how perfect his body. With trembling fingers she touched the mat of wiry sable hair. Fascinated, she kissed his flat male nipples.

Hawke tensed abruptly, and Alexandra drew back, unsure of herself.

Deep within Hawke's eyes, some emotion flashed and disappeared. "Oh God, don't stop now!" he said hoarsely. His fingers dipped into her hair and tightened.

With a tiny smile Alexandra slid closer and touched the dark sensitive circles, delighting in the salty taste of his skin.

Suddenly, Hawke's hands tightened in her hair and pulled her head away. "No more," he growled threateningly, "or I throw aside all my good intentions and take you here and now!"

Sweet wantonness curved her lips. "Would that be so terrible, Your Grace?"

Hawke groaned and pushed her back against the bed. "This time, yes. For I mean to drive you wild before I take you, little hellcat. I only hope I can," he muttered darkly, catching Alexandra's hand and nipping the sensitive skin at the base of her thumb. Abruptly, he surged to his feet, worked his breeches free, and kicked them away.

The lean bronze sweep of his thighs made Alexandra gasp. She had a dizzy impression of taut skin covered with a mat of mahogany hair before her startled eyes returned to his amused face.

The quirk of Hawke's lips told her he had missed none of her discomfiture. "Come, love," he whispered softly, "it's far too late for missishness. You were made for love—made for *my* loving," he corrected. "Let me prove it to you now."

With tantalizing slowness he slanted his hard body over her. Nowhere did he touch her, and yet it was as if she were everywhere branded by his fire—frozen and aflame at the same time.

"Hawke?" she asked in a strangled voice, twisting restlessly.

But his only answer was the harsh rasp of his breath and the play of muscles held agonizing inches away from her.

Suddenly, she felt the stirrings begin, as woman's emptiness sought hard male, and liquid softness reached for a rigid mate.

Her breath echoed harshly, and her hips shifted beneath him.

"Yes, love, it will be heaven between us, I promise you."

Just when she thought she could wait no longer, his open mouth found her straining breast, and she cried out with the savage pleasure of his touch. He suckled her fiercely, hard teeth against yearning flesh. And then his powerful body engulfed her, scorching her from neck to ankle.

Moaning, Alexandra turned her burning cheeks into his neck, drowning in the exquisite pleasure of his hard weight crushing her, searing her with the heat of his passion.

Abruptly, he rolled over, pulled her on top of him, and ran his hands along her back and down over her pouting bottom. Gently, he urged her legs apart until he found her buried sweetness, smiling when she gasped at this intimate invasion. But the smile fled when he felt her stiffen. "No, Alexandra," he pleaded roughly. "Don't stop! Flower for me, love. Open yourself, body and soul. I must have you tonight—*all of you*—just as I give all of myself to you."

"Hawke, I—"

"No, no more words," he muttered hoarsely. "Only this fierce hunger, this shared aching which ends in oneness. Only *this . . .*"

And then, as he ordered, there were no more words, only the dark rustle of skin against heated skin, legs tangling, hands searching, as their bodies learned the thousand small delights that only lovers share.

When she was swollen and damp, aching for him to bury himself inside her, he lifted her and rolled them over as one, capturing her beneath his hard thighs. His hands never left her, stroking her, claiming her, as if he feared she might suddenly disappear. Yet all the time he demanded more, provoking her with urgent hands and expert lips while he whispered harsh pagan praise against the sweet hills of her breasts and belly.

With glazed eyes, beyond thought or understanding, Alexandra watched him love her. His magnificent body tensed and strained against her, teasing, coaxing, demanding. Pressing but never joining. Hungry and insistent. Loving her in a thousand different ways until she could wait no longer for his final claiming.

Her small hands clutched his shoulders, desperately urging him closer, seeking his rigid length in an instinct as old as man and woman.

And then with a hoarse groan Hawke finally shifted over her and plunged deep within her velvet sweetness. His touch was fire itself. She moaned wildly as she received his swollen shaft.

"Yes, my love, take me," he whispered roughly. "Take all of me, just as I've imagined in a thousand reckless dreams. I could never forget how you hold me!"

His body was pleasure beyond imagining. Inch by powerful inch, he surged into her softness, and inch by white-hot inch, he withdrew, again and again, until she was mindless and panting with need. Relentlessly, he coaxed her, shaping and driving her until she became pure liquid sensation beneath him, trembling and spilling around him like wild waters in a spring flood.

She cried his name in a frenzy, kneading the corded muscles at his neck as with each powerful stroke he swept her closer to the whirling vortex, toward the dark mystery at passion's heart.

"Not yet!" he cried against the vein that pounded in the hollow of her neck. "So, oh God . . . sweet."

Alexandra's blood sang. A net of silver shimmered around her, coiling around their heated, yearning bodies. Suddenly she was caught and thrown upon a far shore, where time and space dissolved in an explosion of joyous molten sensation.

She tensed, crying out his name.

"Yes, love, feel it," Hawke grated against her lips, sensing her tremors begin and drinking her wild, breathless cries with his lips.

But even then he did not find his release, though it cost him dear when she rippled around him with such sweet abandon. Still he waited, determined to see her passion spent and then rekindled. With rigid control he held himself back until her tremors passed, anchoring her in his iron grip. Only when she smiled tremulously and opened shining, love-dazed eyes did he begin to move inside her again.

The first thrust drove the breath from Alexandra's throat. The second made her moan and throw back her head. Without warning, her muscles tensed around him once more.

Hawke could wait no longer. With a raging fury he let himself go, plunging deep within her trembling velvet, at last releasing the iron restraint he had imposed upon himself for so long. "Yes," he gasped, "take me!"

His hands lifted her, anchoring her hips as he exploded against her; he pulled her legs around his waist so that stroke followed unimpeded stroke.

Just when Alexandra thought she must die of the exquisite sensations, the dissolution began again, and this time her pleasure was blinding, unimaginable, untellable.

For this time she shared it with him, catching him close and savoring his fierce shuddering release until finally they fell together, tired and languid, back to the quiet earth.

Chapter Thirty-Three

In the darkest hour of night the dream came to Alexandra again. She was in India once more, the gleaming white marble steps of Government House before her. All was strangely quiet, just as it had been that night ten years before.

No dogs barked, no laughter floated on the wind. All was heat and oppressive silence.

"Hawke!" she cried from her sleep, throwing her arms out to him but meeting only emptiness where her ardent lover had lain. She jerked upright in bed, her eyes stark with fear, and awoke to find herself alone, the sheets cold and rumpled. Not even his faint scent remained in that chill hour before dawn.

From the window there came a faint rustling. Alexandra pulled the covers around her protectively, grimacing at the unaccustomed soreness of her thighs. "Rajah?" she whispered sleepily.

It was a few moments before she recognized the strange surroundings. Unfamiliar velvet curtains at the window fluttered in a chill breeze.

Lord Morland's rooms, she realized at last. The candles had gone out, she saw, shivering. All was darkness save for a faint glow from the doorway. With a ragged moan Alexandra stumbled from the bed, heedless of her nakedness.

Hawke was bent over the fire with one arm braced on the mantel as he studied the fierce glow of the flames. The wound at his side was angry red, she saw, and his frowning face was set in hard lines, which the red firelight only seemed to make harsher.

Her bare feet made no sound on the thick Persian carpet, and her fingers were upon her lover's bronze torso before he knew it.

He jumped back from her like a cat from a flame. "When did you plan to tell me?" he growled, his copper-tinged eyes surveying her with cold feral dislike.

She who had awakened with love on her lips and hope in her heart saw her brightest dreams shattered in that very instant.

"When?" he repeated savagely. "After the baby began to show? When you were certain of your control over me?" He shook his head, a mirthless smile twisting his lips. "Ironic, isn't it? It came to me only a few minutes ago, as I pondered your extraordinary beauty. Your body has changed, you see, since that night four weeks ago when I first glimpsed your nakedness. The changes have already begun—your breasts are fuller, your nipples dusky now. My God, did you think you could hide it from me in bed? I've seen it before, don't forget, when my late and wholly unlamented wife was carrying our son!"

At the mention of Isobel Hawke seemed to lose his last vestige of control, and his teeth bared in a snarl as he wrenched a trembling Alexandra against his chest. Like a man unhinged, he bent her back in his arms and forced her toward the fire.

The flame at Alexandra's back scorched her naked unprotected skin, but even then she did not speak, mute with shock.

"Do you know what it does to me? Do you know how I burn when I think of that part of me lodged deep inside you, innocently growing while you laugh in triumph at how well you've tricked me!"

"Hawke! S-Stop. You're hurting me!"

His laugh was dark and demonic. "Woman, you haven't learned the meaning of the word. Not yet—but I mean to teach you full well." In the firelight his face was a pure sheet of molten fury. With cruel force he grabbed her fiery curls and jerked her head back, snarling into her pale face. "Now tell me," he demanded savagely, "what were you plotting next in that sick little mind of yours?"

"S-sick?" Alexandra's blood was churning, and she had to fight for every ragged breath. *"Sick?"* Suddenly, she was choking with hysterical laughter. "Y-You dare to call *me* sick!"

The muscle at Hawke's jaw jutted out, rigid against his skin. "Did you plan to go away when the pregnancy began to show?" he shouted, his eyes all smoke and slate. "Or did you have a different plan in mind? Was the child to be your final instrument of revenge against me?" His hands tightened savagely in Alexandra's hair, making her wince with pain. "But I've seen through your schemes. I've seen them all before, remember, in my years with Isobel. And you won't succeed, mark me well! No child of mine will be used in such a foul mercenary game! *I* was a pawn in a loveless marriage, and I know too well the scars that are left on the innocent victims."

"Yes! T-true! All true!" Alexandra cried, desperate to conceal the searing agony of his wild accusations. Even more than that, she was desperate to deny the truth he had uncovered, that new life was growing in her womb: *life from his seed*.

Dear God, the pain was too great. She couldn't face it!

"T-too bad you saw so soon. But you're hardly innocent. Whatever cruelty I might have planned was no more than you deserved!"

For Hawke all hope died at that moment when her flashing eyes and sneering lips confirmed his worst suspicions. Up until then he had dared hope that she was guiltless, incapable of such cunning.

He dropped his eyes, unable to bear the cruel pain of her triumph. With a brutally crude curse he pushed her away and stalked to the settee for his shirt, blindly jerking on the crumpled white cambric.

When he turned back to study Alexandra's heaving form, his face was devoid of emotion. She flinched, he saw scornfully, and she brought her hand to ward off a blow. The sight made him laugh hollowly. "Don't worry," he growled, "I won't touch you again. But you'll take my name, by God! For the child's sake you'll do it, even if I have to drag you to the altar with a pistol at your back. Yes, Alexandra, you'll have my child, and then you'll disappear without a trace—back to India, I should imagine, leaving the innocent creature for me to raise without your corrupting influence. I'm only sorry that I can't do anything worse to hurt you."

His eyes shone bloodred in the firelight—just like Rajah's, Alexandra thought hysterically, when the fierce bloodlust was upon the mongoose.

Even then she did not speak or try to deny Hawke's accusations; her pride and blinding anger held her aloof.

Scornfully, he threw her ragged gown into her face. "Now get dressed. It will soon be light." His lips curled up in contempt. "I don't care to become a further laughingstock when someone sees us returning together from a furtive tryst at dawn."

"It is very beautiful, madame." Alexandra's voice was strangely wooden as she studied the perfect beauty of the silver tissue-silk gown reflected in her cheval glass. From low squared neck and fitted sleeve to beaded hem, the gown fell with exquisite elegance. The pale silk set off the rich depths of her eyes and the flame of her hair, vying for purity with the alabaster of her skin.

Yet to her, it meant nothing at all.

"You are a true artist." Alexandra's numb fingers smoothed the silver folds, oblivious to their exquisite crispness, which was so much like her own skin.

Since the night at Vauxhall a week before, she had seen very little of Hawkesworth. He had begun, it appeared, to pick up the threads of his previous life in earnest, meeting politicians like the prime minister, George Canning, and a host of others who sought him out as soon as they learned he was about in society once more. He had even brought Sir Stanford Raffles home for lunch one day, as Alexandra discovered when she returned with Robbie from a tour of the Botanical Gardens. That was how she'd discovered where her old friend was lodging in London.

She would look him up soon, she told herself. But she found she had no spark for any task, and her joy, even her pride, was gone. She moved through each empty day like a sleepwalker.

On the very morning after their visit to Vauxhall, an elderly aunt of Hawke's had appeared on the doorstep. A sweet, tiny thing, Lady Babbington was hopelessly boring as well as stone deaf, but Hawke had flatly informed Alexandra that she was to go nowhere without his aunt and the tall, brawny footman Hardy, who had recently arrived from Hawkeswish.

Telford again? Alexandra had wondered.

What could he do that was worse than what Hawke had already done? she thought hollowly.

As for the baby growing inside her, she simply pushed that thought out of her mind along with everything else, unable to bear the pain of it.

They were to have nine for dinner, Hawke had told her flatly one morning—had it been two or three days ago?

It really did not matter. Nothing mattered, in fact.

"Au contraire, you do me the honor, mademoiselle." The modiste's words recalled Alexandra to the matter at hand—completing the final touches on her dress for the dinner party. *"Dieu,* but it is fine to clothe one who ornaments my creations, rather than the opposite." Her quick eyes flickered over Alexandra's pale features, turning shrewd for a moment. "You will catch many eyes at your dinner party tonight, I think."

Alexandra frowned slightly. She did not want to catch many eyes tonight.

"And what woman would not wish to capture such attention?"

Suddenly, Alexandra felt a spasm of nausea grip her stomach, and she reached for a high-backed chair of aqua brocade. Her fingers dug into the rich fabric, her knuckles white with tension.

"But mademoiselle is unwell!" Madame Grès cried. "Come, you must sit! Some wine will restore you."

Alexandra shuddered at the thought of wine—of food or drink of any sort, in fact. Wearily, she slid into the brocade chair and rested the back of her head against the thick cushions. "It is just that I am very tired."

Madame Grès's eyes were measuring. "You have lost weight, *non?* The dress is somewhat large, although it was fitted but last week. You must take care of yourself, mademoiselle. Not only for your sake—"

Alexandra stiffened.

"If you will not talk to Madame Grès, perhaps you will consider speaking with a Miss Gray from Brighton." The rolling French cadences suddenly dropped away, and the modiste's voice became thoroughly different—thoroughly English, Alexandra realized.

She frowned. "But—"

"I'm no more French than you are, Miss Mayfield. But it is necessary for the sort of business I am in—something the Duke of Hawkesworth understood immediately. The name was his idea," she said thoughtfully, sitting down beside her surprised client. "I was working in a second-rate milliner's shop near Brighton, half starving, when he found me. Believing that I showed talent, he set me up and introduced me to a few close acquaintances. Oh, it was entirely a question of business," the small woman said quickly, seeing wariness darken Alexandra's eyes. "Though for my part—" She shrugged suddenly and her voice hardened, almost as if she expected an argument. "He is a fair man, Miss Mayfield, and I can speak only good of him. That is why I reveal my masquerade to you now." Her head tilted to the side, birdlike. "For I think you have need of someone to talk to, someone who understands how you feel. Am I right, or have I dreadfully overstepped my place?"

Alexandra reached out to touch the modiste's slim fingers. "No, of course you have not."

Her companion's eyes were warm and faintly chiding. "My dear girl, it is not something long hidden. You and he have been lovers, have you not? No, don't answer," she said quickly, holding up a small hand. "Just listen. You've been sick lately, tired perhaps. It is merely a passing illness, you tell yourself. And your monthly flux—?" Miss Gray paused delicately.

Alexandra's face turned white. The modiste had discovered her secret too! Her heart pounded as the knowledge she had tried to deny burst fiercely into her consciousness, traveling along every path of blood and nerve, sweeping up to her constricted heart.

Yes, God help her, she was pregnant. With the bloody Duke of Hawkesworth's child!

"Have you told him?"

Alexandra did not move. It was all a horrible dream, she told herself. If she concentrated hard enough, it would go away and she would wake up. Her long slim fingers dug into the pale aqua armrests.

"It is your decision, of course, but I think it would make him very happy. The Duke of Hawkesworth is a generous man. He would take care of you and the child. His response, in fact, might surprise you very much."

Alexandra's nails raked the stiff brocade, and her face was a mask of pain. "Surprise?" she said bitterly. "Yes, his response surprised me very much."

Miss Gray frowned sadly. "I am sorry that all is not well between you. Perhaps . . ." Realizing that she was treading on dangerous ground, the modiste stood up and clasped her hands together briskly. "*Eh bien,* mademoiselle," she began, the French cadences restored, "you have a party to go to, *n'est-ce pas?* And I have a score of commissions awaiting me at my atelier."

In a trance Alexandra stood up, submitting as the woman carefully refitted the beaded sash at Alexandra's bodice. This part of the gown, too, required restitching, for the fabric now strained uncomfortably across her full breasts.

Hawke had seen. Madame Grès had seen. How long before the world saw? Alexandra only wondered why she had not seen it sooner herself. As the seamstress hovered over her, she recalled her conversation with Hawke on this very subject, when they had argued about what was owed to a child and whether love could replace the material benefits the duke could offer.

The question, it seemed, was no longer academic.

At last Madame Grès completed her delicate labor and stood back to admire her handiwork. "*Bien,*" she said, "finished—and with ten minutes to spare. It is good," she added thoughtfully. "Monsieur le Duc will be *épris.* There are few men, I think, who would not grant you anything you asked tonight, mademoiselle." The modiste smiled slightly. "Think well on what you request. What you want and what you need may be closer than you know."

Then, with a quick curtsey, she was gone.

Alexandra was still standing before the cheval glass, the modiste's words echoing in her ears, when a gentle tapping came at her door.

"Come in," she called out woodenly.

Robbie entered, looking very grown-up in a dark blue velvet jacket and lace-trimmed jabot. For the first time he was to accompany his father downstairs to welcome their guests, and he was very conscious of this special privilege. "How very grand you look, Miss Mayfield!" he blurted out with youthful enthusiasm, before lapsing into painful embarrassment.

"May I return the compliment, My Lord Marquess. The duke will be very proud of you."

"The duke *is* very proud of him," Hawke corrected from the doorway. His broad shoulders filled his impeccably tailored blue jacket, which he wore over a waistcoat of silver brocade. Elegantly severe black pants molded his powerful legs and disappeared into burnished boots.

The shimmering silver garment matched his eyes, Alexandra thought numbly, as her own gown did.

Hawke's face was dark and shuttered as he crossed the room to her and pulled from his pocket a leather box. "For you," he said coldly.

Alexandra's fingers were stiff as she opened the long burgundy rectangle embossed with the Hawkesworth coat of arms—a rampant lion beneath a soaring hawk. How appropriate, she thought bitterly. Inside the box a necklace of diamonds and shimmering square-cut emeralds winked against black velvet. "It is beautiful, Your Grace," she said tonelessly. "But of course I could not wear it." She made to return the precious necklace, but Hawke's fingers tightened on her wrist.

"Hadn't you better go and ask Hadley about those ices, Robbie?" Hawke reminded his son. A moment later, he and Alexandra were alone.

Hawke's eyes scrutinized Alexandra's pale face. Soundlessly, he walked behind her and lifted the necklace to her skin. "Ah, but it is entirely unexceptionable—for the woman who is to become my wife."

Alexandra watched frozen as their reflections merged in the mirror, silver fusing with silver, fathomless gray eyes probing luminous aquamarine. Hawkesworth's fingers brushed her collarbone, and she flinched at their cold strength.

His eyes mocked her. "Yes, we'll make our happy announcement soon," he said in a voice harsh with sarcasm. "And then we return to Sussex. Robbie's been plaguing me for the pony I promised him, and several other matters in the country require my attention." He studied her reflection in the cheval glass, waiting for a protest that never came.

She was achingly beautiful tonight, Hawke thought. There was a strange fragile radiance about her, almost like perfect crystal that could be shattered with one careless gesture. No, that was a rare joke, he thought. She was a diamond, rather, that would leave its hard mark on any other substance. "What, no protest?" he taunted.

The cold weight of the necklace fell against Alexandra's skin, and she shuddered. His eyes scrutinized her face, and she forced herself to respond with the careless cruelty he expected of her. "Yes, by all means—let us be away from London. I should not like to be seen with my figure spoiled."

His eyes flashed, and she knew she had angered him. With a mocking smile Alexandra held out her hand.

With arms touching but hearts far apart they walked together down the corridor to the wide spiral staircase.

Below, the knocker echoed loudly in the entrance foyer. Their dinner guests had begun to arrive.

The evening commenced with all the success that was due a duke. Robbie acquitted himself well, and even the prime minister pronounced himself impressed with the lad's aplomb. At the last stroke of nine Hadley showed the guests into the formal dining room, lit with winking candles. They sat down surrounded by tulips in white porcelain bowls, and soon their careless laughter swelled up to the high, vaulted ceiling.

The first course began with turtle soup and a savory cream of almond soup, followed by salmon, crimped cod, and matelote of carp. In keeping with the increasingly popular French style of service, there were two removes—a saddle of mutton and turkey in a curried sauce (at which the excitable French chef had nearly balked)—followed by entrées of lobster patties, turban of fillets of rabbit, dressed quails, and roast pigeons.

Lady Liverpool and Lady Wallingford made discreet but steady inroads upon the lobster patties and washed them down with liberal drafts of champagne. Hawke's deaf aunt, Lady Babbington, ate little and spoke less. The almond soup was well received, the curry sauce was pronounced a novelty, and the roast pigeons accounted perfectly succulent.

All in all, the evening looked as if it would be a great success. Alexandra let herself slip into numbness. The liveried footmen had just arrived with the second course—pheasant, apple *suédois,* and lemon soufflé—when Hadley announced a late arrival.

"Sir Stanford Raffles," the butler intoned gravely, with just a trace of censure for this example of tardiness.

Alexandra started and half rose from her chair. Hawke had not told her that her father's friend was to be among their guests!

But no one noticed her reaction, their attention focused on the handsome intelligent face of the recently knighted Raffles, who could be expected to delight them with tales of his ten years in the Orient. His stories of the peculiar native customs, the strange flora and fauna, and the mysterious statues hidden in the jungles of Jokyakarta were the stuff of which great dinner parties were made.

Unnoticed, Alexandra slid back into her chair, her heart drumming painfully, as Sir Stanford apologized gracefully·for his tardiness. He had been detained at Carlton House in an interview with the prince regent. Nothing less could have kept him so long, he vowed warmly. He only hoped the Duke of Hawkesworth and his guests would forgive him.

No matter, Hawke said carelessly. He was only happy that his distinguished guest could accept on such short notice. They had just begun the second course and the evening was still before them. Was Sir Stanford acquainted with the other guests?

In a blur Alexandra heard the polite words spoken. White faced, she waited for the moment when her friend would recognize her.

"Lord and Lady Liverpool you know, of course. Lady Wallingford and her charming daughter. The Wallingford lands march next to mine in Sussex. My friend Morland you must remember as well—his reputation makes him difficult to forget." Everyone laughed, well entertained by Hawke's lazy charm. Everyone but Alexandra. "I fancy you haven't forgotten George Canning, either. He is very taken with your ideas on the course we ought to steer in the East, particularly now that Java is to be returned to the Dutch. But I think you have not met—"

"No, you do not know me, Sir Stanford," Alexandra interrupted, laughing brightly—too brightly, "but I must avow myself thrilled to meet you at last. I am delighted for the chance to hear your descriptions of Java. In fact, I hope I might engage you in discussion about several points of interest of my own."

Sir Stanford's eyebrows rose sharply and he bowed, carefully concealing his surprise at seeing the daughter of an old friend profess to be a stranger. "With the very greatest pleasure. But I'm afraid I did not grasp your name."

"Miss Mayfield," Hawke interrupted coolly.

"Miss Mayfield," Sir Stanford repeated, his eyebrow raised fractionally. "I look forward to answering any questions you might have. Perhaps later you might even answer a few of my own."

"Is it true you sent Princess Charlotte those charming ponies for her phaeton, Sir Stanford?" Lady Wallingford began breathlessly. "And that you've brought a Malay servant with you, along with all manner of Javanese treasures? Some two hundred cases?"

"Quite true, Lady Wallingford. It would be criminal to deny to the English public the beauty that I discovered far across that vast waste of seas, where English sovereignty yet burns so brightly."

Lord Liverpool nodded and his wife smiled complacently over her laden plate. It appeared that the prime minister had forgotten his disagreement about Raffles's assessment of the Crown's proper policy in the Orient.

"Well, Sir Stanford," George Canning said briskly, "your labors in Java alone would entitle you to a knighthood, even had you not enhanced them with this monumental two-volume *History of Java*. The prince regent seems delighted with the work—so much so that he actually appears to have exerted himself to read some of it."

"It is a small enough contribution on my part," the diplomat said with quiet dignity. "We have yet a great deal to learn about the East, but if we gain such knowledge we will be greatly re-warded in future decades."

"Is it true you barely escaped slaughter at the hands of a hea-then sultan?" Lady Wallingford demanded, in one of her grating shifts of subject.

Raffles laughed dryly. "The Sultan of Jokyakarta and I had a—shall we say—minor disagreement about protocol, Lady Walling-ford. Fortunately, we were able to resolve the problem amicably."

"That's not the story I heard," Canning interrupted with a booming laugh. "One false step, and his soldiers would have cut your head off and fed it to the wild pigs, or so the dispatches to the board of control read. No need to disparage your contributions, Sir Stanford. God knows, we do quite enough of that back here in London."

Raffles's face became thoughtful. "In the East life is very differ-ent, you know—different almost beyond belief unless one has lived there. In the Orient such a thing as the placement of a chair or the degree of one's bow may make the difference between courtesy and the grossest disrespect. Sometimes it is difficult for those ac-customed to the rational and enlightened behavior of London to understand those idiosyncrasies."

Hawkesworth's eyes were drawn to Alexandra's face. She was very pale, he noticed, her pallor sharpened by the emeralds flash-ing around her neck.

"With all due respect, Sir Stanford," the prime minister coun-tered, "you must recognize that we hold the larger picture back here in London, and we are unswayed by local prejudices. Yes, we're the ones best equipped to make decisions that affect more than one region or even one country. Just take this wretched busi-ness in Vellore, for example."

Raffles's eyes darted toward Alexandra, who had meticulously replaced her silver upon her plate. Hawkesworth felt a sudden prickling along his spine, a sort of primitive intuition of danger.

"On July 10, 1806," the prime minister began dramatically, "the sepoys—that's the name for the native troops in India," he explained, with a condescending smile for the ladies at the table—"took it into their heads to revolt. In the early hours of the morn-ing they captured the weapons stores at Vellore and attacked our forces, who were outnumbered five to one. Over 250 Europeans were slaughtered that night, slaughtered in cold blood before a detachment of cavalry could be summoned from Arcot to put down the revolt."

An uncomfortable hush fell upon the table.

"At the time there was considerable disagreement about the cause of that revolt, Liverpool," Hawke said, a sudden tension in his voice. "Some felt that the orders upon the commander-in-chief and the governor-general were too strict. After all, the country is barely emerging from the Middle Ages."

"Nonsense!" the prime minister announced dismissively. "You assented in the final decision, Hawkesworth. Your name was on the board's letter of recall, right alongside Canning's. Our instructions to Lord Maitland had been quite clear. He chose to ignore them, to his misfortune, and he was recalled in disgrace for that refusal—and the slaughter that attended it. We *must* have conformity among our troops, and they must be brought up to the high standards we set back home. If they don't care to shave their beards or remove their marks of caste," the white-haired official announced angrily, crashing a fist down upon the table for emphasis, "why then, they must be stripped of their rank and drummed out of our regiments, by God!"

An uncomfortable silence blanketed the room in the wake of Lord Liverpool's outburst. Alexandra sat up very straight in her chair, ignoring the wild drumming in her head.

"Did you know," she said quietly, "that the sepoys in India are paid only one-sixth the wage of our British troops there?"

"They probably don't deserve even that," Lady Wallingford said with a disapproving sniff.

"Did you also know," Alexandra continued, ignoring the laughter Lady Wallingford's comment had provoked, "the sepoys spit in the dust when a British officer passes? That they salute with their left hands—a mark of gravest insult? Perhaps you want to know what they say at night when they camp around their fires. *Kabhi sukh aur kabhi dukh; Angrez ka naukar.* 'Sometimes pleasure,'" she translated slowly and clearly, "'sometimes pain—to be in the service of the English.' How could it not be so, when our officials ignore the fact that the sepoys are as different from each other as they are from any European?"

Hawke was gripped by a frozen sense of inevitability, watching that perfect crystal facade shatter into a thousand pieces.

"Jats and Sikhs may drink from a water vessel of skin," Alexandra continued, her eyes dark and shimmering, "while Rajputs and Dogras require water vessels of brass. Brahman soldiers require food prepared by a Brahman cook, lest they be profaned by the meal. The Muslim may eat beef but not pork. The Hindu may eat pork (if it is not the meat of a female pig), but not the flesh of the cow. This made even the Duke of Wellington despair of ever organizing a system of supply in India. Yet Lord Maitland was expected to enforce a system of English rules in complete disregard for the ancient customs and religious practices of the country."

"Are you saying that the Vellore decision was unjust, Miss Mayfield?" the prime minister asked stiffly.

"I am saying that the decision was both unjust and uninformed —nay, unpardonable!"

Alexandra looked at her hated enemy and she saw him as if through a tunnel, everything to right and left a blur. His face was expressionless—only his glittering eyes hinted at his fight to control his anger.

"It was a policy," she continued, ignoring the silver sparks flashing from Hawke's eyes, "made by men who were lamentably ignorant of the real situation in India, men who seemed almost proud to preserve their ignorance. I am saying," she said, rising white faced from her chair, a fierce fire in her eyes, "that Lord Maitland was ordered to do the impossible, and that innocent men died because of the intransigence and carelessness of well-fed bureaucrats back here in London!" Her heart was pounding as she saw Hawke's lips twist in fury. She turned to the prime minister. "I am also telling you, Lord Liverpool, that this was not the first time a sepoy regiment has mutinied—nor will it be the last! And now I'm sure you will excuse me."

Raising a trembling hand to her mouth, Alexandra slipped from her chair and ran from the room. Her limp was pronounced as her kid slippers clicked loudly in the tense silence that gripped the room in her wake.

Chapter Thirty-Four

"By God—" the prime minister announced angrily, but his wife's hand upon his arm silenced him in midsentence.

"I beg Your Grace's indulgence," Sir Stanford said gravely, studying Hawkesworth's hard face. "Miss Mayfield, so I understand, has particular ties to India, where she was long resident. This must explain her emotion in this matter. I am sure the prime minister, too, being a man of broad experience and tolerance"— Raffles nodded gravely toward the mottled face of Lord Liverpool —"will be indulgent enough to overlook her outburst. For my part, I would beg a word with Miss Mayfield. I fancy, as a fellow resident of the Orient, I might be of assistance to her in her distress."

The duke looked at Raffles's troubled face, seeing the grave features move but hearing nothing. Hawke's blood was pounding too fiercely, and savage anger coursed through him with each surge of his heart.

She had dared to do such a thing! By God, if he weren't so furious, he might almost laugh at her boldness. As it was, Hawke burned to run her down like a small animal, crushing her fragile frame within his hands.

But he did not, because the very ferocity of his feelings frightened him. And he had guests to mollify, powerful guests. So Hawke sat immobile in his chair, the vein pounding at his temple the only sign of his rage.

For thirty-eight years the Duke of Hawkesworth had been trained by the most exacting of masters to conceal his feelings. Parents, tutors, and peers had conspired to teach him this hard lesson, and he had learned it so well that he sometimes wondered if he had lost his emotions altogether. Sometimes, clasped rigid in passion against an anonymous female form, he felt as if he had lost the better part of his soul somewhere along that long, treacherous journey to manhood.

And now one slip of a green girl—one fragile, stubborn, exquisite creature with a frail ankle—had managed to strip away his hard-won facade and probe the raw, wounded heart beneath.

Rage consumed him for a moment, and his fingers trembled against the fragile crystal anchored in his hands.

But Hawke was still the man his past had made him. Because of that past he did none of the things he was burning to do. Instead, he reached slowly for the champagne bottle that a startled footman had left on the table during Alexandra's outburst. Very carefully, he tipped the sparkling liquid into his goblet.

The uneasy silence around him finally jerked Hawke from his fierce interior landscape, and he realized that Sir Stanford had spoken to him.

About what, Hawke had not the faintest idea, for he'd heard nothing that his guest had said. Since he couldn't very well ask the man to repeat his question, Hawkesworth merely nodded curtly. The duke admired Raffles's sangfroid at such a time as this. The man was a born diplomat, Hawkesworth thought. He would go very far indeed.

Silently, Raffles rose and walked from the room. His departure rekindled the spellbound group around the table.

"Whatever can have gotten into the girl?" Lady Wallingford demanded of no one in particular. "Perhaps the unwholesome air of that heathen country. Dr. Sudbury told me—"

"Not now, Mama," her daughter cut her off sharply.

"Well, really," the older Wallingford began pettishly, but one look at her daughter's face silenced her.

Miss Wallingford, meanwhile, was watching the Duke of Hawkesworth refill his champagne glass for the third time. Smoothly, he tipped the crystal goblet and emptied it, only to reach out and pour himself another. In the candlelight the angular lines of his face were very harsh.

Miss Wallingford's eyes narrowed fractionally. "It is a shame to spoil a wonderful evening, Your Grace," she said. "Shall you not proceed? I am persuaded that Miss Mayfield would want you to."

"Quite right," Hawke drawled. His face was carefully expressionless as he nodded to the liveried servant who stood nearby. "The dinner must go on—you are entirely correct. And now, Canning," Hawke said, turning indolently to the man seated beside Miss Wallingford, "tell me, can this news that Byron's wife is seeking a medical statement concerning his sanity possibly be true?" His voice was lazy with amusement as he wove a spell over them all, leading them to forget the scene that had just transpired. "What can the woman's aunt, Lady Melbourne, be about to countenance such a thing? No doctor's report can be more damning than Caro Lamb's, at any rate. One hears she is even now readying a literary account of their affair. For his part, poor Byron places little store upon the success of her characterization. 'The picture can't be good,' so he told me only several weeks past, 'for I did not sit for it long enough.'"

In disbelief Lord Morland watched his friend lazily recount Byron's latest witticism at Caro Lamb's expense. Hawke's eyes glittered, and laughter sprang easily to his lips. For all the world he looked unconcerned, the urbane host conscious only of diverting his guests with the latest scandalous *on-dit*.

They had come through many things together, the earl thought grimly, both in war and in peace, but never had he known dislike for another human being so fierce as he did now for this callous stranger he had once reckoned his closest friend.

It's useless, Alexandra thought, angrily pulling the gossamer gown over her head. Useless and pointless, the whole thing. Her father was dead. What words could ever bring him back?

With a frown she cradled the silver fabric and laid it across the bed. The gown was badly creased, she saw—extra work for some poor housemaid.

She smoothed the soft folds for a moment, her face blazing with defiance. She had had her say, at least, damn them all, even if . . .

Alexandra shuddered and shook her head, trying to force down the old doubts. She stepped out of her chemise and into the fine lawn nightgown that Daisy, the upper housemaid, had left out on the bed for her.

Sir Stanford, of course, had been all that was kind. He had listened quietly while she poured out her story—carefully omitting her abduction by Hawkesworth—and offered her whatever assistance lay within his power. He was preparing to return to Java in several months' time, and she was warmly welcomed to join their party. His wife would be glad of Alexandra's companionship at Bencoolen, Sir Stanford assured her.

Numbly, Alexandra sat down on the bed. The sheer fabric of her nightdress rustled quietly as she stared down at a white shape upon the carpet. She realized she had dropped the embossed card that her friend had pressed upon her before he left.

Tomorrow morning he would be at home; he begged her to come around then. She was not friendless, he assured her, nor had her father been. Even now, in fact, there was a movement afoot to demand that Lord Maitland's case be reopened.

Still Alexandra did not reach for the card. Something held her from commitment to the course Sir Stanford offered. Her thoughts sluggish and confused, she picked up an ivory fan from the bed. Frowning, she opened and closed the fragile sticks, thinking about the scene at dinner and the narrow lazy minds her father had fought all his life. Unconsciously, her fingers stole to the gentle concave of her stomach. How much longer until her condition became apparent? she wondered. What would Sir Stanford say if he knew she was carrying the Duke of Hawkesworth's bastard?

No, not bastard, she told herself fiercely. *Her* child—a gentle creature to be loved and nurtured far from the taint of Hawkesworth's influence.

"Going to bed already?"

Alexandra froze as the object of her hatred swirled into solid, heart-stopping reality before her eyes. He said nothing at first, merely surveyed her with cold arrogant eyes. When he saw the card on the rug, he bent to pick it up and study the elegant letters.

"So, my dear, you waste no time in securing a new protector. I wonder what Sir Stanford's new wife will have to say about this *ménage à trois*. Such arrangements must be common in the East, however."

Hawke wanted to hurt her, to make her bleed as he had bled when he heard her outburst, as he was bleeding now. His large fingers crumpled Sir Raffles's card into a shapeless wad of pulp and dropped it into his pocket. "But our dinner is not over," he said, his voice frozen with rage. "You will dress and go downstairs, where you will apologize to Lord Liverpool and the rest of my guests. Your behavior was inexcusable."

"I will not!" Alexandra snapped, white hot with anger just as fierce. "Everything I said was true, and I'll take nothing back—not for you or anyone else!"

"On the contrary, your outburst was unforgivable, the shrill histrionics of a Drury Lane harpy."

Alexandra's fingers tightened upon the delicate ivory spokes of the fan.

"So I wanted to hurt you! Why should I not make you feel the pain my father felt?" Alexandra cried. "Had you been a man of principle or reason—a gentleman rather than a *nobleman*, in short —none of this wretched business would have come to pass. I did not devise the degrading little melodrama you began at Seaford!"

"But the plan to find me was your own," Hawke countered implacably.

Suddenly, the ivory fan in Alexandra's fingers snapped. The anger that flared between them was almost a palpable thing.

Alexandra closed her lips in a hard line. "You did not believe my father, either. He warned you what must be the outcome of such ill-judged policies in India. Everything was wrong, don't you see? The policy was wrong, and the punishment was wrong. *Someone* has got to speak for those who cannot!"

Hawke studied her, his legs braced, his hands curled into fists. "I see only that you have disgraced yourself, insulted my guests, and exposed us both to ridicule. *You* may care to have your name bruited about by every gossip and self-proclaimed wit in town. *I* do not. You have also, I might point out, destroyed any chance of reversing the judgment made in your father's case."

Alexandra clutched the broken fan sticks, her face a mask of fury, for he told her only what she knew herself. Her voice, when she was finally able to speak, was raw and unsteady. "How contemptible you are—all of you! All that matters to you is that you be well fed and amused, never mind at whose expense. Manners, or the brittle facade that passes for manners among your set, are all that is important to you, because morals might get in the way of your pleasure. You are like the rest of the *ton*—you drink and laugh and eat and philander, while others sweat in the merciless Indian sun, all so that you might have the leisure for such idleness. You disgust me!"

A thin white line appeared around Hawke's tightened lips. Her words hurt him more than he dared admit, even to himself. He had known his share of toil in the sun and the taste of death on the field of battle. He'd had his fill of that on the Peninsula, by God, but he'd be damned if he'd justify himself to her or anyone else!

"If what you say were true," he said coldly, "I would not be doing what I am about to do, what I have planned to do for some time. Not even your execrable conduct will make me change my mind. So now you will put on that gown and accompany me downstairs, where you will apologize for the monstrous scene you just enacted. You will plead the strain of the dinner preparations, and when you speak, you will be contrite and entirely sincere." His eyes were harsh as he rapped out his orders with the flat precision of an officer accustomed to command. "You will remain below, looking pale and remorseful, for a quarter hour, after which time you will beg to be excused on the grounds of a headache. Then you will retire for the rest of the evening."

Alexandra gasped, speechless with fury. "I will do no such thing!" she exploded finally.

"You *will* do it!" Hawke announced furiously, his fingers shooting out to grip her arm. "You will do it because I tell you to, and because it is the only way you'll ever have your father's case reopened. Liverpool is a very powerful man, and Canning is almost his equal. With them in opposition, you haven't a chance in hell of success. Or is all this concern about your father just a sham?"

Her fingers itched to slap his shuttered face, to wipe that frozen hauteur from his taut countenance. But Alexandra did not, for she knew Hawke was right. Without Liverpool and Canning's support —without Hawke's support, as well—her father's case would remain a closed book.

Stiffly, she pulled her arm from his grasp. "Very well," she said through clenched teeth. "I shall meet you downstairs as soon as I have dressed."

"On the contrary, my dear, you will dress here and now." A thin sneer curled Hawke's lips as he lifted the gown from the bed. "By the time a maid can be summoned, our guests would be gone."

Alexandra did not move, only stared mutinously at the silver float of fabric Hawke held out to her. Her color fluctuated wildly, roses amid melting snow, and her eyes were dark with anger.

"Shall I help you put it on?" Hawke growled, stalking closer.

"You think to gloat, do you not?" she cried angrily. "To mock me for my naive idealism. But you cannot gloat, for it's not idealism that drives me, but guilt!"

Hawke's eyes narrowed as he studied her wild haunted face.

"*I* killed him, don't you see? With my pride and my stubborn refusal to marry. That night he came to me, pleading with me to marry Lord Wexford's son. But I just laughed, as I always laughed at his requests. Not for me, marriage with a foolish young fop just out from England. Oh, God!" she cried, angry tears slipping from her flashing eyes. "Why couldn't I hear the desperation in his voice? He wanted a grandchild to dandle on his knee. He wanted to know the Maitland line would not disappear. If only I had given that to him, then—"

"Then he might not have killed himself?" Hawke demanded. "You can't really believe that, can you?" His fingers dug into her trembling shoulders. "He did it for himself, Alexandra, not because of anything you or anyone else did or did not do. He was probably a great man, your father, but a very selfish man as well, as great men often are."

Alexandra stood frozen, her hands clenching and unclenching

at her sides as she tried to fathom this explanation. "I only wish I could believe it," she said at last.

"Of course you can believe it—unless you wish to go on torturing yourself," Hawke said ruthlessly. "Rubbish! It's all rubbish. The decision to marry was yours, Alexandra, not your father's. Just as the decision to end his life was his alone."

Outside in the street a carriage clattered noisily past and left a hollow silence in its wake. Hawke glared down at Alexandra, his eyes glittering like cold stars in the dark night of his face. With fierce concentration he jerked the fine lawn nightgown over her head. His eyes grazed her body as she stood unflinching before him, knowing that this hurt him most of all.

"Put on the damned dress!" he growled, jerking the silver silk over her head. Angrily, he pushed her around and began to force the tiny covered buttons through their closures. "The necklace, too."

Alexandra's back was rigid, her muscles entirely unyielding beneath his expert fingers. Very well, my bloody duke, she thought, I'll play out my part. I'll crawl along Bond Street on my hands and knees if it will get my father's case reopened. Maybe then, at least, she would know some relief from this horrible nagging guilt.

And after that, there was always Sir Stanford's offer, she thought. The natives in Java could be no more savage than the people she had met so far in London.

Thirty minutes later it was done. Alexandra had humbled herself and begged forgiveness in a performance worthy of Mrs. Siddons. She had endured Lady Wallingford's disapproving sneers and her daughter's mock sympathy. By the time it was over, her plea of being unwell was no longer feigned.

She was standing by the bed clutching one of the carved wooden bed posts when she heard a faint scratching at the door.

Surely Hawke could not have followed her so soon. With a frown Alexandra cracked the door slightly ajar. Strangely, the hall was empty. A moment later a draft at her feet drew her attention lower, and she smiled tremulously as Rajah shot through the narrow space between door and frame.

"Ah, love, how I've been neglecting you!" She stooped and

gathered the little creature into her hands, stroking his brown fur gently. "But all that is at end," she said softly, her eyes bright with unshed tears. With a little sob she laid her cheek against the mongoose's sleek pelt. For a long time she did not speak.

Rajah sniffed and stared up at her intently. His pink nose twitched as he registered the currents around him.

"I hate him!" she said angrily.

But she did not.

"I'll run away."

But she could not.

Tears pressed against her eyelids. "Oh, Rajah, whatever am I going to do?" Finally, the silent tears spilled down her face in a silver rush. Rajah squeaked in puzzlement, arched his long tail, and fluffed up his fur. With narrowed eyes he angled his head at the unhappy face of his mistress. He did not move, only chattered gently as if to coax her from her distress.

When the first salty drop struck his fur, the little mongoose squeaked. A moment later, Alexandra felt his gentle paw upon her shoulder.

Downstairs, the dinner party finally drew to a close. Canning had been the first to leave. Now Lady Wallingford and her daughter were waiting for the escort of Lord and Lady Liverpool before departing.

"Delightful evening, Hawke," the prime minister announced. "Damn if that ornamental confection of Vauxhall wasn't perfect to the last detail. Have to get the name of your chef."

"It was Miss Mayfield's idea, as a matter of fact. Perhaps she's been doing too much. I'm afraid the strain is beginning to show."

"Ah, Miss Mayfield." Lord Liverpool's voice dropped slightly. "Unpleasant business. Still, Raffles had the right of it, I think. Put it down to all the strain of traveling and her understandable concern with India. Yes," he continued more loudly, congratulating himself as if the idea were his own, "nothing more than female irritability. Mustn't be too harsh on the ladies, you know." He reached down and squeezed Lady Liverpool's hand fondly. "Lady Liverpool would be happy to guide her in such matters, I'm sure. Must send her around for a chat some time."

And so the matter was to be overlooked, nicely relegated to female distemper, forgiven and forgotten at the same time. This was exactly what Hawke had hoped for. Yet Liverpool's condescension irritated him.

"You're too kind, Liverpool," Hawke murmured, "and I will give Miss Mayfield the message when she's more herself. I'm sure she could use a little guidance."

"And as for the other matter," the prime minister said conspiratorially, "let's just say that you may be surprised at how fast we can act when it suits us."

Five minutes later, everyone was gone but Hawke and Morland.

"And now, Tony, I think I'm entitled to something a bit stronger than champagne. Fortunately, I've been holding some excellent brandy for just such an occasion." He turned and looked at his friend, his eyebrow arched questioningly. "Do you join me?"

"I'm afraid I cannot see the slightest reason for celebration," Morland answered stiffly.

Hawke's eyes narrowed. "Best say what you have to say in a quieter place, I see."

Morland followed the duke to his study. Neither spoke while Hawke filled a glass with brandy and then tossed it down. "Now then, Tony, let's have it. Why are you bristling like a damned cat?"

Morland eyed his friend angrily. "You need to ask? Because of your bloody behavior, that's why! You must know Miss Mayfield's real identity as well as I do. She had a right to speak as she did, in view of the circumstances."

Hawkesworth's fingers froze upon the glass. "Did she tell you who she was?"

"No, she didn't," Morland said impatiently, "but it didn't take a great intellect to figure it out from what she said tonight. You led me to believe you had her best interests at heart, man! And yet you deliberately subjected her to the worst sort of humiliation. Oh, yes, I could tell that she was apologizing under duress."

"Come, Tony, we've never tangled over our women before, and I see no reason to begin now. Let's cry friends."

But Morland was not to be placated so easily. "I wonder if I know you at all, Richard," he said coldly, "if I *ever* knew you."

"Oh, blows the wind from that quarter?" Hawke asked, his voice dangerously quiet. "I warn you, she's not your type, Tony. Too willful and stubborn by half." Hawke's voice hardened. "And even if she were your type, you'd steer clear of her. Because she's mine, do you hear? She'll *always* be mine, no matter what I decide to do about her. If you value your skin, you'll remember that, by God!"

"You had no intention of letting her go, did you? You're a fool, Richard," Morland said acidly. "That's why you'll lose her in the end. And when you do, I'll be there to catch her." His blue eyes snapped angrily. "Don't bother to see me out. It will be a pleasure to find my own way."

Chapter Thirty-Five

It was some minutes before Hawke moved, and then it was only to pour himself another glass of fine aged brandy. A crash of the door and his friend's angry footsteps rang hollowly in his ears as he swirled the last dark spirits at the bottom of his glass.

Damn Morland, anyway! He and Hawke had known each other since they were in leading strings. Who'd have thought Tony would cut up stiff over a woman—particularly another man's woman?

But Alexandra Maitland, Hawke thought bitterly, was something entirely out of the common way. The woman seemed to have a knack for setting people at sixes and sevens. Only look what she had done to his own life since that night she'd come running out of the fog!

Hawke's face was deeply lined as he slid wearily into a tufted leather arm chair, glass in hand. With a sigh he propped his elbows on the desk, staring blindly at the polished rosewood surface, seeing neither it nor the little ormolu clock nor the Sèvres figurine of a shepherdess he'd always detested.

Suddenly, he reached down to release a latch at the front of his desk. With a quiet click a secret compartment sprang open. A muscle leaped at Hawke's jaw as he pulled a lock of curling red-gold hair from the hidden drawer and laid it gently in his palm, his eyes dark with pain.

Alexandra Maitland had almost as many demons as he did, Hawke thought, remembering how he'd come upon her screaming in terror on the wind-blown cliffs. And now he knew she carried the guilt of her father's suicide along with everything else.

Damn, why couldn't things ever be black and white? Why was nothing ever easy?

With a weary sigh Hawke leaned back in his chair and studied the lock of Alexandra's hair, soft and rich against his fingers. Soon he'd be waxing sentimental, Hawke thought, smiling grimly. He was half foxed already, and in a few hours he'd have a devil of an aching head.

Just as the ormolu clock chimed the quarter hour, the Duke of Hawkesworth rose tiredly to his feet and made his way slowly off to bed, the burnished lock of hair still gripped tightly in his hand.

Not even fierce loyalty can override the curiosity of a mongoose for long, and so it was with Rajah. Gradually, Alexandra grew aware of his slight movements as he slanted his head to sniff some new and perplexing scent. London was new terrain to him, after all, she recalled ruefully, terrain he was hungry to explore. She felt a pang of guilt that she had kept the mongoose from his adventures so long.

"Very well, my little friend, I shall open the window for you. But mind you don't wake the household, or we'll have Hadley clambering in here looking for a thief."

The little mongoose issued a sharp, high-pitched squeak as Alexandra bent to open the window. Situated at the rear of the house, her bedroom looked out over a narrow backyard that opened onto the mews. In the small garden a May hawthorn had just come into bloom, spilling its rich fragrance into the night air. A gentle spring wind ruffled the curtains as Rajah jumped lightly to the sill and perched there for a moment, sniffing briskly. His pink nose twitched and he arched his tail gracefully, then turned to give Alexandra a last lingering look.

"Oh, be off with you!" she said with mock severity, then smiled when he disappeared. Almost immediately, she missed his company. For some minutes she stood at the window watching his sleek form jump deftly from sill to sill until he found a drainpipe and slipped down to the garden.

The cool wind played across her shoulders, and Alexandra shivered. She was still wearing her silver gown and the necklace of diamonds and emeralds. The large square-cut gems hugged her skin, heavy and cold against her bare neck and shoulders. She wondered suddenly if Isobel had worn them, and the thought made her feel sick. Very carefully, she unhooked the metal clasp and returned the precious necklace to its case. But she wondered as she did so why an odd, cold sensation hung about her skin.

Just then, the curtains fluttered open to reveal a boy's grimy face. "Ye be Pence's friend?" a small shadowed figure demanded. "Said as 'ow ye was a flamer." He must have seen her eyes widen in fear, for he added quickly, "Gone and got 'isself in a bit o' trouble, and needin' yer 'elp, is our Pence." His thin legs slipped across the window sill and he stood up to assess the room by moonlight. "Said ye was a rum 'un what wouldn't run shy, so 'e did."

"Pence? In trouble?" Alexandra repeated in confusion. "But how—"

"Best stow the whids." Seeing her incomprehension, the boy added impatiently, "No time for questions now. Digger'll be givin' me a bastin' as it is fer comin' 'ere."

Digger. Alexandra shivered, remembering that Pence had refused to speak of the man who represented a past the boy was desperate to forget.

"Reck'n I'll shab off the way I come then, and wait fer ye in the mews." Silently, the boy moved back to the window. One leg over the sill he turned, his eyes narrowed as he studied her. "Best make it fast. There ain't much time 'til Digger finds me out. Give ye three minutes, then I pikes off, 'ear? And don't blow the gaff to nobody, or it'll go bleedin' 'ard with Pence."

"Wait!" Alexandra called desperately, but the boy had already slipped noiselessly into the night.

Her head spinning, Alexandra ran to the door. Hawke! She must find Hawke.

He would know what to do.

* * *

Hawke's head had already begun to ache as he paused outside his bedroom door. Curiously reluctant to enter, he turned and looked down the corridor to the closed door behind which Alexandra slept.

No good, old boy, he thought grimly. Get yourself to bed before you do anything else you'll regret in the morning.

His candle guttered in a sudden draft as he opened his door. Across the room a slim figure slipped from the darkness, but Hawke did not notice, engaged in lighting an oil lamp by the door.

"Hawke." The low soft whisper made his whole body freeze.

" 'Tis I, truly, and no dream."

Slowly, the duke raised his head and studied the beautiful woman sitting before him on his bed. He blinked and shook his head, afraid to believe his eyes, afraid the brandy was fogging his brain.

"Love me, Hawke. Let me love you." Long arms reached out to him, white in the candlelight.

With a ragged groan Hawke stumbled across the room to the bed, kneeling before the woman. She studied his face intently, a soft smile curving her red lips.

"At least you haven't forgotten me."

"I could never forget," he mumbled hoarsely, struggling free of his jacket and waistcoat, anxious to feel her warm skin against his. Her hands soon came up to help him, freeing his shirt, then moving to the buttons at his breeches.

A moment later, he stood naked before her, burning and urgent in the semidarkness. When her cool fingers reached out to stroke his stiff manhood, Hawke nearly gasped. Fire shot through him as her white hands circled him possessively.

His muscles tightened in immediate response, hungry for more. Slowly, her fingers began to move.

From outside in the hall he heard a whisper of feet approaching his door, and somewhere in the back of his mind he felt a sharp prickle of uneasiness.

He frowned, trying to fight the fire snaking through his fevered body. Behind him the footfalls ceased. His doorknob clicked.

"Hawke?" It was the merest whisper, soft and uncertain. "Are you there?"

Frozen with shock, he stared down at the glittering eyes of the woman before him. "My God!" he rasped in disbelief. "It's impossible!"

And that was how Alexandra found Hawke and his singularly undead wife. When she stepped into the room, the pair was caught in that most intimate of contacts, Isobel's silken talons wrapped around her husband's jutting manhood.

Alexandra choked in horror, too stunned by Hawke's betrayal to wonder how his wife had come back to life. With a strangled sob she flung herself back toward the door, desperate to escape the nightmare vision before her.

"Stop!" Hawke cried hoarsely, but the woman he loved was already at the threshold.

"B-bloody, cheating snake!" she sobbed. "I wish you both joy of each other!"

Isobel's jeering laughter followed Alexandra down the hall.

"Away from me, succubus!" Hawke thundered, but his wife only gripped him more tightly, her fingers cruelly efficient.

With a curse Hawke pinned her wrist in a deadly grip that threatened to crush her very bones. Isobel released him then, falling back against the bed and laughing demonically.

Savagely, Hawke yanked on his breeches, ran for the door, and dashed past two startled footmen on the staircase. The entrance door was still open as he pounded out into the street.

A carriage rounded the corner, moving fast; it nearly ran Hawke over as it hurtled down the empty street.

"Alexandra!" he screamed. "Wait!" His bare feet hammering across the sharp cobblestones, Hawke raced in pursuit, but the horses were already at a gallop. His mouth twisted in pain and frustration as the carriage disappeared around a corner, leaving him ashen-faced and disbelieving, crushed as he watched all his dreams vanish into the night.

Thirty minutes later, he was banging at Morland's door. Whitby's thin eyebrows rose in surprise as the duke hurtled past him into the foyer.

"Damn it, Tony, where are you? This is urgent!" Hawke bellowed.

Morland strode angrily out of his bedroom, silk dressing gown swirling at his ankles. "What in the name of God do you want now?" he demanded.

Hawke's tense fingers gripped his friend's sleeve. "Has she come here to you?" he asked hoarsely.

Lord Morland did not pretend to misunderstand. Dragging his arm from Hawke's grip, he spun about and stalked toward his study. When they were safely inside, he turned to Hawkesworth with an angry look. "Miss Maitland is not here, you fool! Why do you persist in imagining enemies wherever you look?" Then his eyes narrowed, seeing the raw despair that darkened Hawke's face. "She's left you then?"

Wearily, Hawke dropped into a trim leather chair by the window and accepted the glass that Morland pressed upon him. He took a small sip, then rolled his head tiredly against the back of the chair. "Yes, she's flown, Tony, just as you said she would. I still cannot believe it. My God, Isobel was there, and Alexandra—" His voice ended in a sound of inchoate pain. "I'd hoped that she came to you."

Slowly, Morland sank into the chair opposite. "I've seen nothing of Miss Maitland since dinner. Maybe she went to a friend."

"She knows no one in London." Suddenly, Hawke sat up straight in his chair. "No one except Sir Stanford Raffles, that is." His face tightened in fury. "If she's gone to that silver-tongued orator, I swear, I'll see him stuffed and hung alongside the rest of his museum specimens!" Hawke jumped up and made for the door.

"I'd better go with you," Morland said quietly. "In such a mood there's no telling what sort of scrape you'll get yourself into."

But Sir Stanford, when they found him, declared himself as ignorant as they of Alexandra's whereabouts, and his obvious concern convinced Hawkesworth that he was telling the truth.

"Where can she be?" the duke ranted as he and Tony walked back down the steps in front of Raffles's townhouse.

"Is there no one else she might have gone to?"

"No, no one," Hawke muttered, drawing an unsteady hand across his face. "But when I get my hands on her, I'm going to thrash her within an inch of her life!" He turned tortured eyes upon his friend. "If I find her. Dear God, Tony, where can she be?"

"Buck up, man!" Morland ordered. "She can't have gone far, not in such a short space of time. Did she have no relatives, no old friends of her father's—old military men put out to pasture? A nanny, perhaps, or an old retainer living nearby?"

Hawke's eyes flashed to life with fierce intensity. "That's it, Tony! by God, you're a bloody genius! She *must* be there." Suddenly, he sprinted down Berners Street.

He found Madame Grès in her shop working late on a trousseau. She received him with quiet composure and ushered him into the privacy of her sumptuous office. There she offered him a glass of sherry while he caught his breath.

It had to be Miss Mayfield, the modiste thought, a tiny smile playing around her lips. No other person or thing could make the duke appear on her doorstep at such an hour.

But Hawke's hoarse question soon wiped the smile from her face.

"No, Miss Mayfield has not come here," she said in surprise, frightened by the blackness that settled over Hawke's features at her words. "Oh, God, Hawke, never tell me she's left you? She's alone, with no money!"

"Don't you think I haven't told myself that a thousand times?" he cried in a tortured voice. "Don't you think I haven't pictured what might have happened to her? Where she might be lying right now?"

The woman's small fingers gripped his shoulder reassuringly. "Now, don't be plaguing yourself with dark fancies. Miss Mayfield is a sensible female and well able to take care of herself. She'll turn up shortly, either here or somewhere else. Take heart, for this brooding does no good—either to her or to yourself."

"You're right, of course, Olivia. I'm making no sense." His hand, cold but strong, found hers and squeezed it briefly.

Before he could say more, the modiste stepped gently away from him. A faint note of regret entered her voice. "You must go now, Hawke, go and find her. Find her soon," the woman said tensely, "for she carries your child."

The Duke of Hawkesworth groaned and ran an unsteady hand through his dark, disordered hair. The last vestiges of color drained from his face, and his glass of sherry fell unnoticed to the carpet, bleeding in a crimson pool across a chorus of smiling cupids.

"*Alexandra!*" Hawke cried, his voice hoarse with shock and pain. "Where are you?"

Alexandra.

It was no more than a dry whisper of wind through long grass or the wild beating of birds' wings. But the sound inched its way into her consciousness, into the dark, throbbing tunnel of pain where she slept.

Numbly, Alexandra opened her eyes, and blackness opened into blackness. Tentatively, she raised cold fingers to her forehead, where the first blow had caught her. Gingerly, she explored the swelling. Her teeth clenched in pain, only to begin chattering from the cold a moment later.

The boy had been waiting all right—along with a scowling coachman, who'd swept her inside his carriage and away before she could do more than deliver one hoarse scream.

Where she was now, Alexandra did not know. Around her all was unrelieved darkness, no glimmer of light to be seen anywhere. If only she could make out where she was, discover a means of escape! From the muffled silence, she thought she must be in an enclosed space, and an echoing drip of water confirmed that guess.

Then her head swam, and she gave up trying to plan or reason. Every ounce of energy was given to fighting the black waves of pain and nausea that swept over her. But she failed.

Alexandra.

Again it came, a sudden trembling in the silence of her mind. The word gave her hope. He would come for her, Alexandra told herself.

She had to believe that he would come.

Chapter Thirty-Six

The Duke of Hawkesworth's face was dark and shuttered when he left Madame Grès's establishment, ignoring the curious glances of a strutting trollop as he dashed past.

His mind raced back and forth like a cornered animal's, pondering the same question, always the same question: Where could she be, damn it? No one had seen her. She'd left not the slightest trace. How, in a city with as many curious eyes as London had, was such a thing possible?

He'd returned to his room to discover his cursed wife vanished as well, just when he'd been yearning to wring some answers out of her. And Hardy, that damned footman Bartholomew Dodd had recommended to protect the duke's household, had taken himself off as well.

With a scowl that sent two drunken dandies scurrying out of his path, Hawke jumped over a half-collapsed section of gutter and dashed across the street. Maybe hard exercise would clear his head, he told himself and decided against hiring a hackney coach to carry him home.

There had to be an answer, if only he could think clearly!

Hawke's long strides carried him along quickly while he fixed his mind on the problem before him. Frowning and preoccupied, he did not notice the greeting called by an officer he had known in Spain, and the man sniffed and remarked to his companion how damnably broodish the Black Duke had become of late.

Ah well, the officer's companion remarked philosophically, a wife like the Duchess of Hawkesworth might drive any man to brooding.

Unaware of the slight he had just delivered, unaware of anything at all except finding Alexandra, Hawke stalked along the midnight streets. In a matter of minutes he reached a less populous part of town.

A horse neighed suddenly, and the duke halted his long strides to allow a carriage to cross the narrow side street before him. Impatiently, he waited for the coachman to move, signaling the fellow with a hard jerk of the hand to make haste. But the man's eyes tightened, and he showed no inclination to set his horses in motion.

"Are you blind as well as stupid, man?" Hawke called angrily to the man upon the box. "Or merely desperate for a fare?"

Then the duke had his answer, for a slim white wrist swung open the carriage door. The interior was in shadow, and Hawke could make out no more than a dim female form. But then she drew closer and slid the hood of her cloak away from her face.

His blood hammered as he gazed upon creamy cheeks, bright red tresses, and flashing aquamarine eyes.

A cool laugh drifted from the carriage, freezing him where he stood.

"You pick your moment well, madame," Hawke growled, "but not well enough, I think. Canning is all set to introduce the divorce bill in Parliament. He plans to dispense with a judgment in the courts and anticipates no difficulty in the bill's swift passage—particularly not in view of your well-documented infidelities. Which means, my dear, that you and your brother will soon be adrift once more among the dregs of society, precisely where you belong."

"How dreary of you, Richard—but how precisely what James predicted! You do understand that it cannot be permitted, of course. I've become dreadfully attached to the quarterly allowance you made me, pitiful though it is."

Hawke's hand snaked out to crush her crimson-tipped fingers. "Five hundred pounds? Pitiful? What a mercenary bitch you are!"

The duchess's eyes narrowed in fury and pain and then she regained control of herself, ignoring his brutal grip. "And how crudely vigorous you are, Richard! Which puts me in mind of something else. How have you fared during my absence from your bed, dear husband? Have I interrupted your interlude with the little cripple? James will be terribly amused when I tell him of the scene in your bedchamber. I suppose the creature's deformity adds a certain novelty to your bed play."

Hawke's fingers dug into his wife's shoulders and shook her so sharply that her head snapped with an audible click. *"What have you done with her?"*

"Take your clumsy fingers off me, Richard, or you'll never find out," the duchess hissed, her eyes glittering with unmasked hatred. "She's beyond your reach by now, beyond anyone's reach— unless you choose to cooperate, that is."

Hawke swallowed the fear that threatened to choke him and let the old dispassionate cunning take its place, just as he had done on the battlefields of the Peninsula. When he finally spoke, his voice was cool and slightly ironic. "I might have known your brother was involved. The scheme carries all his earmarks."

"Yes, James was very clever to arrange my death, was he not? It put you off the scent wonderfully."

Hawke's expression didn't change. "And what's your price *this* time?"

"Oh, you'll find out soon enough, my dear husband, if you'll just step in and let the driver go about his business. I vow we've been following you about for the better part of two hours. Such an ardent lover!" she mocked, laughing coldly.

But Hawke was prepared now and refused to be baited. Lazily, he settled his broad shoulders back against the opposite side of the carriage and folded his arms across his chest. He looked for all the world as if he were engaged in a routine social call with his wife rather than the most important errand of his life.

He found one source of satisfaction in the encounter, however, for he discovered that he had not a jot of feeling left for his wife; he was released once and for all from her deadly coils.

But Hawke could not enjoy the knowledge, for he knew that the woman who had rescued him from Isobel lay right now in the hands of his ruthless enemy.

"Wake up, wench! This ain't no gentry ken, nor me no upper 'ousemaid neither!" A surly female voice penetrated the haze of Alexandra's nightmare.

First pain, then darkness. Abruptly, Alexandra woke to a harsher nightmare. "What—what place is this?" she whispered, her tongue awkward with sleep and cold.

"La-la! The fine lady wants to know where she been brought!" A slatternly old woman, lank tresses drooping beneath a grimy mobcap, angled into view beneath the circle of light from her upraised lantern. " 'Tain't Bedford Square, I can tell ye that!" The woman threw back her head and laughed riotously, revealing a row of brown, uneven teeth.

Alexandra shuddered and huddled against a wall covered with grime from years of mildew and dripping water.

With a muttered curse the old crone sent her heel flashing against Alexandra's shin. "Get up, doxy! The gentleman wants ye, though fer the life o' me I can't see why. Nothing but a scrawny little chicken, that's all ye be!"

"Is the boy here?" Alexandra asked urgently. "Is Pence here?"

"Boy? Plenty o' boys 'ereabouts, as ye'll see soon enough. Now, 'urry up!"

"What has Digger done—"

"Digger!" the old woman spat back. "That's one name ye best use careful, my 'igh an' mighty miss." The woman darted a nervous glance into the darkness behind her. "Now get up, an' no more talk."

Alexandra tried to stand, uncurling her legs slowly, for the cold and damp had set her old wound throbbing. Irritated by the delay, the woman jabbed Alexandra sharply in the ribs so that she fell back against the grimy wall.

"Move it, wench! Be rest enough fer ye tomorrow!" Her mouth curled into a secret smile as she pulled a length of fabric from beneath her arm. With surprisingly gentle fingers the crone shook open the cloth to reveal a gown of crimson satin trimmed with insets of black lace at the neck and hem. For a moment she ran her fingers jealously over the rich fabric, then cursed and threw the dress at Alexandra. "Put it on, damn ye!"

Slowly, Alexandra raised the gown, appalled by the deep, plunging neckline. It was the costume of a Cyprian! "I most certainly will not!"

The harpy grinned and leered at Alexandra. "Reck'n ye'll enjoy 'avin' Digger put it on fer ye then!" Her raucous laughter echoed in the darkness, making Alexandra's skin crawl.

Faced with that appalling alternative, Alexandra reluctantly unbuttoned her sedate gray gown. When the crimson satin was in place, she caught her breath in embarrassment, tugging vainly to cover the brazen expanse of flesh now revealed. Then she set her teeth and forgot about modesty. She had her survival to worry about.

"That way." The older woman pointed into the darkness, holding up the lantern to cast a pale circle of light upon the straw-covered floor.

Slowly, Alexandra moved along the damp wall in the direction the woman pointed. She grimaced as pain shot through her ankle, then resolutely thrust that from her mind too.

Think! she told herself. She might have only one chance to escape. She had to be ready when it appeared.

The lantern flickered across a greasy flight of stone steps that led up from what appeared to be some sort of subterranean chamber. Stiffly, Alexandra negotiated the slippery stairs, and as she climbed higher, the air changed. Now she smelled the pungent scents of fermented tea, tobacco, and horse dung, along with the salty tang of the ocean. In the distance she heard the steady slap of water upon a stone barrier and the rhythmic creak of timber.

They must be at the docks, Alexandra realized. She'd smelled these scents before, outside the East India Company godowns in Calcutta. If there were ships, there were sailors. She had to believe they would help her.

"Step lively, else ye find that limp gettin' worse," the woman behind her ordered, punctuating the command with a cruel jab to Alexandra's back.

At the top of the stairs the lantern revealed a rough planked door. The woman brushed by Alexandra and tapped lightly. "Tell 'im the gentry mort's ready!" she called to the face that appeared briefly. Then the door yawned open with a squeal of rusty hinges.

From inside the room drifted a cloud of tobacco smoke and the stench of cheap spirits. Alexandra coughed as her companion thrust her forward into the large, dimly lit space. It was a warehouse of some sort, Alexandra decided, frowning at the wooden crates arranged in a rough circle. Two lanterns at opposite ends of the room cast overlapping circles of light onto a dozen or so men, who stared at her as they leaned against the crates or squatted on the dusty floor.

Alexandra had seen men like these before, skulking on the Calcutta docks in the shadows of the great East Indiamen. These were not sailors, for they lacked the bronzed strength and squinting eye of men years before the mast.

No, these were men who lived off the sailors and off the sailors' cargo. Their skin was pallid and soft, like that of scuttling creatures who teemed in dark places. Not one of them moved nor spoke, but their eyes probed her, missing no detail of her face and form, and their cold-blooded assessment of her body in the satin dress made her shudder.

At the opposite end of the room a squat, stooped figure emerged from the gloom. "Well, Mazie," he said coldly, "what 'ave we 'ere? A fine pigeon to be plucked, for all she's got so little down. But enough where it counts, I figure, an' mebbe even all the same red color," he added, laughing shrilly.

As the man came closer, Alexandra saw that his face was almost gray, in sharp contrast to the reddish-brown scar running from his forehead to the corner of his thin mouth.

Behind her, the woman snorted and spat on the floor close to Alexandra's feet. "Skinny little 'en, she be. Beats me why ye'd want to—"

The squat man rounded on her, his face twisting into a scowl. "Mean to tell me my business, woman?" he snarled.

"Nay, nay!" the woman cried, recoiling in fear. "None o' my affair."

"Aye, an' ye'd best remember that," he hissed, "else the morrow find ye workin' the roughest flesh marts in Whitechapel!"

Abruptly, he turned and signaled to one of the men. "Fetch the boy!"

Pence! If Pence was here, this man must be Digger. Suddenly, Alexandra shivered with cold and embarrassment at the brazen scarlet dress she wore—the only spot of color in that great grim room of black and gray. She did not speak but furiously fought to absorb any information that could help her escape. All the while, she felt the eyes of Digger's men watch her like snarling, fearful dogs waiting for the scraps their cruel master might toss from the table.

The next moment, Pence was dragged in.

"An' now we're all right and tight, fer our Pence's come back to us, an' 'is gentry mort too."

"Leave her alone, Digger, ye—" the boy cried, but his words were cut off by a well-aimed kick to the ribs. Pence sagged slightly, grinding his teeth, but he did not flinch or cry out.

"Ah, Pence," Digger said mournfully, "ye could o' been the best, the very best. But ye couldn't see the way o' things, could ye now? Not that Digger's king o' these streets an' all 'ere do my biddin'. Now ye'll die fer it, my boy, an' suffer a bit first. 'Ere's my army to witness it, right, fellows?" The men scattered around the room hooted and stamped on the floor in approval.

Alexandra watched in growing panic, but she dared not move nor show any sign of weakness before this pack of ravening dogs.

"Mr. Stubbs!" Digger commanded. A thin man with one arm cut off at the elbow jumped up to proffer a length of coiled leather. The boy was forced forward and stretched over a crate, his arms fully extended, his back bared.

"Now let's see what it takes to make ye cry, boy!" Digger's voice was soft with menace. The next moment, his whip snaked through the gloom and cracked down against Pence's back, while the men crouched in silence, eager to see the boy's misery. But Pence denied them that pleasure, and their eyes grew sullen and angry. Alexandra caught back a little sob as she saw the slash of red that oozed from the welt across the boy's back.

"Oh, lad, I've plenty o' time, never ye fear." Again the leather snapped, this time in the opposite direction, making a perfect X on Pence's back.

Alexandra twisted her hands tightly as the boy turned rigid, struggling against his pain. "How much to let him go?" she demanded abruptly.

A score of hostile eyes turned upon her.

"Ye offerin' to pay fer the boy?" Digger asked with mock civility. "But ye've nothin' to pay with!" Behind her the harpy lifted Alexandra's reticule and turned it inside out, to the resounding laughter of the men. "Or mebbe ye mean to pay in some other way," he snarled.

"I've funds at my disposal," Alexandra said coolly, summoning up all the haughty disdain she could muster. "Gold enough to secure the boy's services for the rest of his life. Why not spare yourself this trouble? He's an irritating pest, as anyone can see, and answers to no master but himself."

"True enough," Digger said with sudden interest. " 'Ow much ye offerin'?"

"One hundred pounds," Alexandra said firmly, and the onlookers set up a flurry of jeers and laughter.

"Quiet!" Digger roared, and the noise immediately ceased. "Why, the lad could make that much in one night, 'e could! No, we'll jest 'ave to see the thing through my way. But never ye mind, dearie—ye'll 'ave yer uses yet."

For a third time the whip arched high in the darkness, then snaked down across Pence's back. This time the boy slumped over and did not move again.

"Enough!" A new voice broke into the silence caused by Pence's collapse. "Leave the boy!" A tall man moved slowly into the circle of the crates. Something about him was vaguely familiar to Alexandra. "Ah, the governess!" he said languidly as he walked toward her. "I doubt not that this costume suits you better than the last."

Telford, Alexandra thought, fighting the icy tendrils of fear that gripped her at his approach. His face was lean, his eyes as flat and colorless as that night when he'd attacked her at the yew grove. He was dressed in the style of a gentleman, Alexandra saw, although his cravat was not entirely white and its folds were slightly askew.

"You interest yourself in the boy?" His voice was toneless and slightly bored.

"Yes, and shall pay well to see him released."

"It may not come to money at all, my dear," the man said. "A simple matter of cooperation may suffice." At her sudden stiffening he shook his head in amusement. "No, not that sort of cooperation, at least not if you prove useful in other ways. I need your assistance at persuasion, my dear. You are very good at persuasion, I think—almost as good as I." He was very close now, and his colorless eyes assessed the harsh rise and fall of her chest in the abbreviated gown. He held out his arm in an elaborate gesture of courtesy. "Shall we discuss the matter further?"

"And the boy?"

His thin lips curled. "Such concern for one sniveling brat! The boy will be unharmed, provided you are successful."

In a daze Alexandra placed her hand on his arm and allowed him to lead her out of the circle of lights. They passed through a door and came to a flight of wooden steps, where he waited politely for her to precede him.

Climbing the narrow steps was hard going. When she reached the top, Alexandra found herself facing a small room fitted out as office and sleeping quarters. An oil lantern, a bottle, and several empty glasses rested upon a large wooden crate next to a desk littered with papers. Her eyes flashed to the room's sole window, but she could make out nothing in the grime that covered the pane.

Without a word her companion moved to the crate and filled two chipped glasses with wine. "The Duke of Hawkesworth has forced my hand, you see." He turned and offered her a glass, shrugging indifferently when she refused it. "The divorce, you understand—or perhaps you do not understand at all. Hawkesworth finally intends to make good on his threat to divorce my sister. It is you, my dear, who have brought him to that point after all this time. You should be very pleased with yourself, for there are few women who could have done it. But such a rupture would leave my sister and I—how shall I say?—sadly circumstanced. So Isobel had to die. Or at least *appear* to die."

Alexandra shivered at such cold calculating evil. How much

money had the pair wrested from Hawke over the years? she wondered grimly.

Isobel's brother seated himself carefully in the room's only chair and offered Alexandra a seat on the bed, which she stiffly refused.

"Which brings us to you, my dear."

"How can I possibly be of interest to you?"

"Do not let us play at cat and mouse, Miss Mayfield. Or should I say Miss Maitland? You see, I know everything about you. Hawke has had his man looking into your whereabouts for a considerable time, and it was through his unwitting lapse that I discovered your identity. Yes, we may even count ourselves cousins, which explains your striking resemblance to my sister. The connection was severed in our grandfather's time, I believe. A charming irony, is it not? And yet so nice to keep things within the family."

"You do not answer my question," Alexandra said flatly, her head spinning with this new intelligence.

"Then I shall do so now. I need the Duke of Hawkesworth's signature on a document that will tender a certain sum of money to me upon my demand, with no questions asked. Upon his signing you will be rid of me and my sister forever. It is as simple as that."

Somehow, Alexandra knew, studying those flat, colorless eyes, that the matter could not be nearly so simple. "How much?" she asked finally.

"One hundred thousand pounds."

Her gasp was loud in the small room. "He could not give you half that amount."

"Such an innocent!" Telford said chidingly. "He can offer that much and more besides, but I am not a greedy man. Enough to settle Isobel and myself for life with the comforts we have come to enjoy—we ask no more than this."

"One hundred thousand pounds would buy you a kingdom and a crown," she said flatly, "and break Hawke in the bargain. But perhaps that is your intention."

"It had entered my mind, yes," Telford drawled. "But you have very little choice, Miss Maitland, for if you refuse to help us, your young friend will find his just deserts at Digger's hands, and your beloved duke will find his at mine. So come, give me your answer, that we may be easy."

"Very well," Alexandra said finally, for she could see no other way out of the trap he had set so cleverly, using her as bait.

"Excellent! Now, would you care to seal the bargain with this quite tolerable port before the duke arrives? No? A pity to waste it." He drained both glasses, then poured himself another and turned to survey her with cold leering eyes. "I fancy Hawke will be especially pleased by your attire. It leads a man to all sorts of speculation, I can assure you."

"You'll never succeed!" Alexandra said fiercely. "One way or another, he'll see you punished for this."

"Ever the optimist! But you are quite wrong, my dear. If your dear duke does not do precisely as I say, you will never see his face again, I assure you." Telford straightened suddenly, alerted by a slight sound from the warehouse below. "Ah! Here, unless I am sadly mistaken, is your hero come to you now."

Chapter Thirty-Seven

A pair of pistols were trained on Hawke's back as he lunged into the small room, half staggering, half pushed by two of Digger's brawniest men. Although a ragged wound oozed blood from his temple, Hawke would have been more than a match for either man—maybe for both—had they been weaponless. His eyes flickered across the room to Alexandra, seated motionless on the bed with Telford close beside her.

At the sight of the blood on Hawke's forehead she had stiffened, and only the severest willpower kept her from crying out. But she did nothing and said nothing, for Telford had warned her precisely what would happen if she did not do what he told her.

"So, my dear brother-in-law, you are arrived at last. How long has it been? Two years? Three? You'll pardon me if I don't ask you to sit down." Telford's cold fingers slid up Alexandra's arm and played suggestively across the creamy expanse of skin bared at her chest. "Just look who is here, my dear! It is your lusty employer, come to rescue you."

"Let her go." Hawke's voice crackled with menace, and his two guards stiffened warily.

"I think not, my dear brother-in-law. She is worth so much more to me here. You always had excellent taste in women, and I am happy to see you still do. She is remarkably like Isobel, is she not? But not nearly as inventive in bed, I should imagine." Telford's pale eyes glittered maliciously. "I shall let you know. If you are still alive, of course. Yes, the little governess—or should I say Miss Maitland?—stays."

A muscle flashed at Hawke's jaw, and he looked down at a piece of straw dangling from his sleeve. "Mayfield, Maitland—one woman is much the same as another."

"Ah, so you've received Bartholomew Dodd's report. It's only fair, of course. I learned of it myself through the men he set upon the inquiry. How do you fancy bedding the daughter of a man you drove to suicide?"

Hawke's eyebrows rose, and his nostrils widened in faint distaste. "Really, Telford, one despairs of ever shaking the mud from you. You must constantly betray your father's vulgar origins."

Eyes darkened in fury, Telford jerked his head at one of Digger's henchmen, who rammed the butt of his pistol into the wound on Hawke's forehead.

Her hand raised to her mouth, Alexandra watched in horror as Hawkesworth staggered and then drew a finger across his forehead, grimacing as he wiped a fresh streak of blood from his brow.

Hawke's head dropped to his chest as he choked down the fury that threatened to strangle him. Face lowered, he studied the room, quickly assessing the numbers and the odds, calculating a defense and a possible escape route.

Right now, the odds looked very poor indeed.

When Hawke straightened, the fire in his blood was carefully banked, and his voice was neutral. "The girl means nothing to me, Telford. She was a passing novelty, no more, and now that the novelty has gone . . ." The duke shrugged indifferently. "You know how these things run their course."

"Bravo! A fine performance—I applaud you. But not good enough. You see, your eyes betray you. Isobel was right; you really are devilishly transparent."

"Cut line, Telford. This thing is between the two of us." A low note of menace entered Hawke's voice. "Let her go," he taunted. "Or is your bravery found only among a woman's petticoats?"

"That remark," Telford growled through thin white lips, "will cost you dearly. One hundred thousand pounds, to be exact. If you fail to pay, the boy and the fair Miss Maitland will be turned over to the tender mercies of Digger and his men, who have been looking forward to a bit of rough sport. After I've taken my pleasure with the wench first, of course."

As Telford spoke, his thin fingers slid lower and slipped beneath the neck of Alexandra's dress to move cruelly upon her sensitive skin. She flinched but clenched her lips against the pain he inflicted.

Her captor continued in a tone of exaggerated patience. "Come, my dear duke, all I require is your signature. Then we may draw our little drama to a close."

"You filthy blood-sucking maggot!" Hawke growled in a deadly voice that promised vengeance.

Immediately Telford's fingers tightened, and this time Alexandra could not hold back the sob that escaped from her lips. She forced her eyes away from Hawke's face, not wanting him to see her misery or take it as a plea to accept Telford's offer.

The silence stretched out, and the two men studied each other like skirmishing dogs. "Very well," Hawke said finally, his voice faintly bored. "How do I transfer the funds?"

Telford's hand stilled against Alexandra's skin. From the corner of her eye she saw his lips quirk into a thin smile, but there was no warmth in his eyes. *"You* do nothing. The funds will be disbursed directly to me upon my presentation of this document." Abruptly, Telford pushed Alexandra away and strode to the desk. He pulled a long sheet of vellum from the clutter and raised it for the duke's scrutiny.

Hawke moved closer, and to Alexandra's anguish, he looked very weary. Without expression he accepted the document and scanned it cursorily as a look of distaste curled his lips. "I see you have prepared for every eventuality, Telford. My congratulations."

His enemy bowed in mock politeness.

"You were always a careful man," Hawke said thoughtfully. "It was only by a stroke of luck, after all, that I discovered you were the source of the information that was leaking to the French."

"My wits have yet to fail me, brother-in-law. I am sorry I cannot say as much for you." He held out a pen to Hawke. "Now, perhaps you will dispense with these pleasantries and oblige me with your signature."

Alexandra's tortured eyes sought Hawke's face at last. *Is there no other way?* she asked. His dark eyes flashed once in answer, and he gave a tiny, almost imperceptible shake of his head.

I will spend the rest of my life repaying you for this, my love! Alexandra promised silently, tormented by the knowledge that she had been the duke's weakness, the lure that had drawn him into this trap. As she watched the line of blood seeping down his forehead beneath the matted hair, she vowed that somehow she would replace what he had just given away for her.

Without a word Hawke stepped to the table and lifted pen to vellum. He signed his name very slowly, and every scratch of the nib was excruciating torment to Alexandra.

Straightening, Hawke held out the document to Telford, who grasped it quickly. His eyes shone with greed as he scanned Hawke's signature. Flush with triumph, he did not notice the duke lunge at him. An instant later, two pistols thundered in the confines of the small room.

Rigid with horror, Alexandra saw Hawke stagger. Then Telford wrenched free of his large adversary and jumped to snatch the document that had fallen to the floor.

"Hawke!" Alexandra screamed, running to catch the duke as he wavered. She threw her arms around his waist and fought to hold him as he slowly sank before her.

"My—only love," he whispered hoarsely, a mere stirring of the air. His eyes were warm on her face for a moment; then, with a groan, he collapsed against her, pulling her to the floor along with him.

"No," Alexandra whispered. *"No!"* When she pulled her fingers from his back, they were covered with blood.

"So very predictable," the cold voice behind her sneered. "Ah well, it makes the rest of my work that much easier."

"I'll do anything," Alexandra said brokenly, her dazed eyes never leaving Hawke's face. *"Anything* you ask, do you hear me? Only help him! He'll die if he's not quickly tended."

"But that is precisely my wish, Miss Maitland."

Alexandra looked up then, her eyes flashing in anger and raw grief. "You never intended to release him!"

"Of course not," Telford said coolly, pocketing the document with Hawke's signature and strolling to the table to pick up his half-filled glass. "You could not really expect me to, could you? Honor, my dear, is a luxury reserved for youthful idealists and men born to wealth and power, of which I am neither. Hawkesworth was as great a fool as you to expect it of me."

"Murderer!" Alexandra sobbed, her tears mingling with the crimson pool on Hawke's forehead. In a daze, she heard Telford's cold, sneering laughter.

"Yes, when those two incompetents bungled the affair at the coast, I realized that sterner measures were in order. We considered several plans, Isobel and I, chief among them blackmail and kidnapping the boy. All of them soon paled, however, for as long as Hawkesworth lived, we would know no pleasure in our wealth."

On and on the cool voice droned, echoing hollowly in Alexandra's ears. "So we decided that he could not live." Telford paused to refill his glass. "The question then became how to accomplish the thing. First it was necessary to throw the duke off guard. Our staged accident did that nicely, did it not? Yes, I rather pride myself on that. As for the rest, you know that well enough."

Suddenly, coarse fingers pried Alexandra's numb hands from Hawke's motionless body. A wild fury overcame her, and she clawed the hands that sought to pull him from her, but in the end they overpowered her and threw her roughly back onto the bed.

"Take him away," Telford said with a negligent flick of his hand. "His usefulness has ended."

As she sank into a haze of pain, Alexandra saw Digger's men drag the heavy body from the room, and every muffled thump was a dagger plunged into her heart. At the door the men halted, sweating, while they maneuvered the large body over the steps.

Wild with grief, Alexandra knew a desperate urge to fling herself after Hawke over the stairs and into the emptiness below. But Telford saw her intention and ran to hold her immobile, her arms behind her back.

"Not so fast, my dear. I still have uses for you." His eyes narrowed speculatively. "It might be amusing to bed a woman who could almost be my sister. And after I've had my fill of you, Digger and his men will want their turn. If you pleasure me well, however, I might exert myself to spare you that."

With all her strength Alexandra spat into the sallow face that bent over to kiss her.

Flat fury descended into the colorless eyes. "That was most unwise of you," Telford said, roughly plunging the neck of her gown lower so that the full swell of her breasts was exposed to his cold gaze. "I think you will indeed make delectable entertainment, my dear. I shall enjoy your pain. Too bad Hawke won't be here to witness it."

With what remained of her will Alexandra wrenched one arm free and dug her nails into his cool cunning face, glorying in the bellow of fury and pain that followed. She stumbled from the bed and pushed herself unsteadily to her feet, just as the door burst open behind her.

The Duke of Hawkesworth stood framed in the doorway, thighs braced, a cocked pistol in each hand. Around his forehead stretched a white strip of cloth that already showed red stains seeping from the wound beneath. "Come here to me, Alexandra," he ordered, keeping both pistols trained on the snarling Telford.

Frozen in shock and disbelief, she hesitated for a moment—and that moment was her undoing. Telford's hands caught her and tightened around her throat.

"Move back, Hawke! Unless you mean to shoot her too."

Slowly, the pistols fell.

Telford's laughter echoed across the narrow space between the two men as he forced Alexandra backward, careful always to keep her between himself and the duke.

"Hawke—" she cried, her heart beating a wild crescendo, but Telford's fingers cut her off.

"Shut up!" he growled.

He thrust her toward the window and dropped to the floor for an instant to grasp a wooden stave lying nearby. With a crash he shattered the glass, and Alexandra had a quick impression of moonlight on black slates. She heard the raucous cry of sea birds as wind gusted through the jagged opening. And then Telford stepped into the night, jerking her through with him. A point of glass slashed her elbow but he did not stop, always careful to keep a firm hold on the wooden stave.

The wind whipped Alexandra's skirts as she looked down to find herself upon a narrow railed porch. In the distance a forest of masts rocked in the harbor, where the Thames glistened silver in the moonlight. To her right a slate roof adjoined the warehouse, running across to another deserted storage building of some sort.

In the moonlight Alexandra saw that the old structure was gutted with great black holes, where sections of its roof had caved in. The narrow planks that ran in a bridge from the balcony over the courtyard to the dark roof beyond looked equally unstable.

Telford's fingers bit into Alexandra's wrists. "After you, my dear." Before she could gain a breath, he pushed her out onto the half rotting walkway, which creaked ominously beneath her weight.

Her heart pounding, she watched the wooden planks sway. A moment later, Telford smashed his heel into the rotting wood so that the whole structure crumbled, and she plunged down into emptiness.

Desperately she threw out her arms as she fell, clutching for anything of substance. Her fingers tightened upon the one wooden rail that still hung suspended in midair.

Above, satisfied that he needed do no more, Telford shouldered his wooden stave and jumped across to the neighboring rooftop. His boots clattered hollowly against the slates as he ran up the steep incline, using the length of wood to brace himself.

Alexandra saw his black figure clamber to the crest of the building, where he was silhouetted against the rising moon for a moment before disappearing down the opposite side. Then she closed her eyes in mute terror as the wood splintered beneath her fingers.

"Damn his bloody soul to hell!" A curse erupted from the porch—Hawke's curse.

But there was no time for questions. The raw edge to his voice told Alexandra all she needed to know about the precariousness of her position. "Up here, Jeffers!" he roared.

Boots thundered across the narrow porch, and suddenly the taut faces of Lord Morland, Jeffers, and Hawke's burly footman swam before Alexandra's eyes. With the odd clarity of a drowning swimmer she wondered how they had all come to be there.

"Brace me, Tony! I'm going across!" Carefully, Hawke inched his way, stomach down, across the single swaying plank, while Morland anchored his legs from the balcony. The wood strained beneath his weight, and Alexandra caught her breath, feeling her heart constrict as Hawke inched closer.

Beads of perspiration began to form on Hawke's brow beneath the makeshift white bandage. Once more the wood groaned, and a corner of the rail ripped away from the roof.

"Go back!" Alexandra whispered to Hawke, her heart in her eyes.

He ignored her, moving as slowly as possible to avoid jarring the unstable structure. And then his strong hand closed upon her wrist just as the plank gave away with a crack and plunged in one thunderous stroke to the cobblestones below, sweeping the pair with sickening force against the wall of the warehouse.

The savage impact slammed the breath from her lungs. The whole side of her body screaming in agony, Alexandra fought for breath, concentrating on Hawke's face above her. He grunted, straining, then dragged her closer so that both hands circled her wrists. "Now, Tony!" he rasped through clenched teeth.

Slowly, inch by terrifying inch, they were dragged back over the edge of the roof. Alexandra knew that the pain where the ragged slates cut into Hawke's stomach must be terrible.

Then she was in his arms, his breath warm on her face, his lips drinking the salt tears from her cheeks.

"I'm here, my heart. Don't cry," he whispered against her skin as he shrugged out of his coat and caught it around her shoulders to cover her ragged dress.

"Oh, Hawke, I thought—"

"Hush," he said hoarsely, murmuring dark inaudible words against her skin and bathing her face in kisses. Then he found her mouth and convinced her they were joyously, vibrantly alive still.

Heedless of the others on the balcony, Hawke molded her trembling body against his hard frame, grinding his lips fiercely against her mouth. His tongue plunged within, and everything but the velvet fury of his touch was swept from Alexandra's mind.

The clatter of slates on cobblestone roused them. Alexandra felt his body stiffen. She knew what he would say even before he caught the ragged breath to say it.

"I must go after him."

Her heart and mind screamed to restrain him, but Alexandra nodded mutely and released him, knowing that if Hawke did not return, her own life was over as well.

One last time he kissed her, hard and quick, then turned to surge across the roof in the direction Telford had gone. A moment later, Hawke, too, disappeared down the opposite incline.

A cough pulled Alexandra's eyes to Jeffers's anxious face. "Someone to see you, miss."

A brown ball of fur erupted into her arms, and she caught the little mongoose in a desperate hug. "Oh, God, Rajah! He's wounded," Alexandra whispered, for she had to share her fear with someone or something.

The thin intelligent face looked up at her, his pink nose quivering as his long tail arched and fluffed. He squeaked then, a long, staccato rush of notes, and wriggled from her arms.

"Rajah!" she called desperately.

But the creature had already darted off across the roof where Hawke had disappeared, his eyes gleaming red in the moonlight, for the ancient bloodlust of the hunter was upon him.

"Help him!" Alexandra whispered, and the sighing wind carried her words across the rooftops.

When Morland's arm came around her shoulders to comfort her, Alexandra turned tortured eyes upon him. Neither spoke, and the silence seemed to go on forever, hinting at a thousand horrible possibilities.

Suddenly, a bellow erupted from the abandoned bungalow across the way. Two figures appeared on the jagged roofline, arms locked as they fought for balance, their straining bodies black against the rising moon. A line of slates came free and rained down upon the cobblestones below. An instant later, the larger figure swayed and lost his balance.

Rigid with terror, Alexandra watched Telford press home his advantage with a cruel blow of his stave to Hawke's face. When the duke reeled, Telford wrenched free and jumped back to safety.

In all the paralysis of a nightmare the silent group on the narrow porch watched Hawke stagger. Slowly, Telford began to advance for the kill.

And then, just as a cloud swept before the moon, a third figure appeared, a small arched shape that rocked and swayed on the crest of the roof. Alexandra could almost make out the sharp eyes like bloodred coals, calculating the precise instant to strike.

Once again Hawke staggered, tossing a hand across his eyes, and Telford hoisted his wooden stave for the final killing blow.

In that same instant Rajah leaped from the roof with a shrill cry of fury and exploded against Alexandra's enemy with savage force. Sharp teeth sank into human skin, muscle, and pounding blood.

Alexandra did not see what happened next; later, she would remember only a blur of noise and movement, a muffled struggle, and then Telford's howl of pain echoing across the rooftops.

Slates rained down noisily as he grappled with the mongoose, but Rajah was not to be cheated of his prey. For long moments the two lurched desperately on the jagged roof as the great masts of the East Indiamen rocked behind them in the harbor. Then Telford plunged with a terrified scream to the cobblestones below.

They made a strange-looking group gathered beneath the shadowed vault of the warehouse: a giant of a man in a blood-soaked headband, a flame-haired beauty in tattered black lace and crimson silk, and an urchin with a young-old face and dark twinkling eyes. Perhaps strangest of all was the sleek, regal creature perched upon an upturned barrel with all the majesty of a sovereign reviewing his subjects.

"You took your bloody time about getting here," Hawkesworth said tautly to Morland. "'Twas a damned near thing!"

"Nor would we have found you at all, had we not come upon your footman lying bloody in Bedford Square. He'd been following you when you so injudiciously accepted Isobel's hospitality. Unfortunately, one of Digger's men was also in pursuit and took him from behind. Poor Hardy barely managed to drag himself back before collapsing on your doorstep, where Jeffers and I found him. But never mind. All's well that ends well, and you both seem to have managed quite well without us," Morland said with a rakish smile that held only a trace of sadness. "You've dispatched your friend Telford once and for all. And it appears," Morland added with a bittersweet smile for Alexandra, "that you've won the fair maiden as well."

"Yes, I have, haven't I?" Hawke said grimly, turning to the woman he held loosely in his arms. "Whether she likes it or not!" Fierce gray eyes plumbed bottomless aquamarine. "For I mean to have you, Alexandra—will you, nill you. I give you fair warning here and now. What happened with your father is over and done with. It has nothing to do with us."

There were two spots of feverish color on Alexandra's cheeks as she glared up at the arrogant stranger before her. "Is that your notion of a marriage proposal?" she asked icily.

"No, by God, it is not!" the Duke of Hawkesworth thundered. "It's a bloody order! As soon as Liverpool hands me the bill of divorcement, you *will* become my wife—even if I have to carry you drugged to Scotland to accomplish it!"

Alexandra's fragile shoulders were unbearably stiff. "Over my dead body!" she snapped.

Hawke's quicksilver eyes flashed dangerously, as if he were considering that possibility as well. "You'll marry me, my girl, or I'll tell everyone who'll listen that the Honorable Alexandra Maitland is the most wretched, calculating sort of fortune-hunter! I'll tell anyone who'll listen that this woman insinuated herself into her cousin's household with the express intention of seducing her cousin's husband. That in short, she is a determined, heartless little baggage"—the duke's voice dropped to a hoarse growl— "and that I adore every conniving, stubborn bone in her treacherous body and couldn't live another day without her!"

Then Hawke was on his knees before her, his eyes hungrily searching her face. "Marry me, Alexandra," he entreated, ignoring the ring of fascinated spectators. "Promise me all your nights. You'll never regret it, my heart, I swear this to you."

The object of this disjointed diatribe blinked suddenly. Then a glow of such radiance swept across her face that more than one of the male onlookers felt a lump tighten his throat.

Like a seasoned campaigner Hawke pressed home his advantage. "We'll have six children, and each one will be more stubborn than the last. I'll open a charitable school in the Whitechapel slums." His long fingers bit into the fine bones of her hand. "I'll live one year out of five in India. I'll release all the swans at Hawkeswish."

Alexandra's smile, which had been growing wider, suddenly halted in a look of dismay. "Oh, no, Hawke! Never that! The swans belong on the high stream, just as they have been for eight generations. God willing, they may grace your lands for another eight." Unconsciously, her hand slipped to the hollow of her abdomen in a gesture that made Hawke's eyes smoke.

"Then you must come to keep an eye on me," he growled. "See that I don't shirk my duties."

"Very well, my love," his radiant wife-to-be answered, running a gentle finger across the bruised skin beneath his bloody bandage. "I accept your offer, sahib. Indeed, I quake at the thought of denying you anything."

"Little liar," Hawke said lovingly, rising from bended knee to sweep her into a fierce embrace. Then he stiffened, and his eyes were hard upon her face. "What of the man in India?" he demanded. "You swore I would never be his equal."

"My father," Alexandra said softly. "And I find you are in every way his match. But no matter," she added in a voice of calm certainty, "like Isobel, he shall haunt us no more."

With a groan Hawke swept her against his hard frame and covered her face with hungry kisses, oblivious to the circle of interested onlookers.

A roar of approval went up from the men around them, echoing to the rafters of the cavernous room, but the two lovers did not appear to notice.

For they were far away from the tumbledown warehouse by the bank of the Thames, far from the tangled webs of revenge and betrayal, already halfway to heaven.

Epilogue

A summer breeze swept across the grassy slope, tossing the long blades like waves upon a vast sea of green. Right up the crest of the hill the wind hurried, then fled down the other side, scattering the broad leaves of a towering linden whose magnificent branches trailed nearly to the ground. From the dappled shade beneath the green canopy came the sounds of gentle laughter.

"But she is always ravenous! I cannot think how you keep her satisfied."

The Duke and Duchess of Hawkesworth were lying beneath the luxurious foliage while their three-month-old daughter rested from her luncheon beside them. Hawke's criticism was belied by the besotted look of fatherly pride on his handsome face.

"Come, admit it, Richard. Julietta is perfect, as well you know." Alexandra hesitated for an instant. "You do not regret that our firstborn is a girl, do you?"

Hawke's eyes were dark and chiding. "Little fool," he whispered gruffly, "I am delighted with our firstborn. She is perfect in every way, from her glossy curls the color of sun-drenched honey to that stubborn little chin, which I rather fancy she inherited from me."

"Oh, quite, you may take all the credit for her stubbornness!"

"Wretch! She might just as well claim that heritage from you, for you have been fighting me with unflinching obstinacy from the first moment of our meeting!"

A shadow crossed Alexandra's eyes, and Hawke read her thoughts at the same moment.

His gentle finger brushed her lips. "I would have it no other way, my heart. I fear I should grow most lamentably bored were you different in any detail." The warm light flooding his smoky eyes convinced her of his sincerity. "Now," he continued, after clearing his throat, "it appears that the *ton* is to accept us, in spite of the furor over the divorce. Davies tells me that a carriage full of gifts has arrived from London, where they've been gathering dust since we so precipitously fled. Everyone is claiming a part in the affair, in fact. Canning and Liverpool led the way, while Morland has been offering violence to anyone rash enough to breathe a word of opposition. Poor fellow—he's more than half in love with you himself, I think."

Alexandra touched Hawke's sleeve. "I grieve to think I gave him pain, for he was a friend when I needed one badly."

"Nevertheless, Morland will have to find his own heart's desire —which I have no doubt he will soon do, for he's always had a knowing way with the ladies. So no more worrying over Morland, if you please. It reminds me of my own pigheadedness," Hawke said darkly, his eyes tense upon her face. "Soon I would wonder that you ever forgave me."

"It was not easy," his wife said enigmatically, "but fortunately, I discovered that you have certain redeeming traits."

"Indeed," Hawke said. "Would you care to enlighten me?"

Alexandra's laugh tinkled across the shimmering summer air. "Very well, Richard. You see, I've found you out."

A crease worked its way across Hawke's forehead.

"Oh yes, I've discovered the Black Duke's secret at last." To Alexandra's very great delight, he looked worried. "Why, Richard! You are squirming! Have you been hiding a mistress or two somewhere about the countryside while I've been occupied with Julietta?" She managed to make herself sound affronted.

"God help me if I have. There are quite enough females about my estate already." His fingers skimmed her lips, which were threatening to curve into a smile at any moment. "Now, out with it, sphinx! What is this terrible secret you've discovered?"

"Why, I've discovered," Alexandra said softly, "that the Duke of Hawkesworth is a good man, caring and fine, but he would die before he let anyone see that."

A muscle flashed at Hawke's jaw as he stared into Alexandra's luminous face. "Thank God I found you, sweet changeling. Otherwise, I might have haunted the high stream forever in search of one perfect white swan."

"And here she is," Alexandra whispered, "with your swan mark upon her to prove it."

"Are you, my love?" Hawke asked, rough uncertainty in his voice. From behind him he pulled one perfect dusky rose and gently traced her cheek with it. "Almost as soft as your skin. Take it, my love, and know that with it goes my heart."

Alexandra's eyes were huge and radiant as she accepted his gift. "No more than I give myself."

"No regrets for the past?" he persisted. "For the country you left behind? You might go back, you know, now that your father has been cleared of culpability in the uprising. Say the word, and I will take you."

"How like you to offer, Richard," his wife said, deeply moved. But Alexandra knew she would never go back to India. Her life was here in England now, beside her husband and child.

Not that she would ever forget the country of her birth.

On still nights when the moon was the color of saffron floating in an ebony sky, she would always see the faint line of snow upon the distant Himalaya.

When a hot summer wind fanned the noonday heat, she would always imagine she caught the elusive hint of cardamom and ginger.

But of regrets, she had none. "I am here until the next swan-hooking ceremony—and the next and the next, as long as you will have me, Richard."

"Forever," Hawke vowed darkly, sealing his lips against her neck. Deeply, he drank from the shadowed well beneath her jaw, but it did not nearly quench the fire that exploded through his veins. Indeed, his desire threatened to rage out of control, after he had so carefully held himself in check these last months.

With a muffled curse Hawke set her from him and leaned back stiffly, brushing a white linden petal from his navy coat. "I do not mean to be sidetracked, however. Now, where was I? Oh yes, Lady Jersey is wild to meet you, and Prinny has even rumbled something about showing you his plans for the new pavilion at Brighton. A signal honor, I assure you."

Alexandra shook her head. "How strange it all seems! And yet only one year ago—"

"No," Hawke said sternly. "That time is behind us. Telford is dead, and Isobel is . . . nothing but a shell since his death. She will never harm us again. I suspect there was a great deal more to that relationship than I knew. No," he continued, seeing the question in Alexandra's eyes, "ask me nothing more. Suffice it to say she lives in a dream world now, but in tolerable comfort—which is much more than she deserves. And now," he said resolutely, with a dangerous look that warned her that the subject was closed, "you will find that Madame Grès has sent us an exquisite set of christening clothes for Julietta, along with the express order that you present yourself to her before you set foot in London society again. It would damage her reputation beyond repair if you came back looking like a country dowd, she vows." His eyes narrowed suddenly. "By the way, what did you say to Robbie? The boy's been floating on air the last several days."

"I only told him the truth about why I married you."

"Indeed? Don't stop now," Hawke growled.

"Yes, I confessed 'twas him I fell in love with first. Unfortunately, the only way I could have *him* was if I married you." The shining blue-green fire of Alexandra's eyes belied her laughing words.

"I shall have to punish you for that. Now, what else had I to tell you?" Hawke pretended to be lost in thought, while Alexandra waited impatiently for him to continue. "Oh yes, I've received news that Pence's brother Tom has been located at last. He was desperate with worry about his brother and was only too happy to accept employment here at Hawkeswish. He wishes to be a gamekeeper, it seems. Which reminds me—just as I came from the stables, Havers presented me with a sturdy miniature fishing rod of whittled oak. At the very same moment, however, Jeffers appeared carrying a painted horse of his own design. The two of them were positively scowling at each other, waiting to see whose gift would receive precedence. It was a dangerous moment, I can tell you."

"Dear friends, one and all," Alexandra said quietly, her eyes glistening with sudden moisture.

For a moment the two were silent, pondering the strange fate that had brought them together, the friends who had stood firm, and how close they had come to losing each other forever. Their fingers met and clasped tightly.

"I am glad that Rajah will have company," Alexandra said after a little while. "It was very kind of Sir Stanford to make us a present of the little female mongoose he had been meaning to take back with him."

"Raffles is a stubborn man, but I think history may well account him a genius. I only wish I could persuade him to delay his return to Java."

"He is very like my father," Alexandra said, "with a strict code of honor."

"His mongoose is certainly giving Rajah a run for his money, which is only what the little potentate deserves. In fact, I rather fancy him living under the cat's paw, for it is no more than I shall do."

"Indeed, Your Grace?" Alexandra asked, a martial light in her eyes.

"Most assuredly." Hawke's free hand slipped to the curve of her cheek. "But I mean to take a page from Shakespeare and tame my shrew. And although I have been most admirably denying in the last months, my abstinence is nearly at an end." His long fingers traced her graceful throat.

Beside them the infant cooed contentedly and popped a fat thumb into her mouth.

Alexandra's eyes widened. "But Richard, what if one of the staff should come upon us? I still flame with embarrassment when I think of Havers—"

"Nonsense! Havers long ago willed himself to forget everything about that day. As for the rest of the staff, they've been warned under penalty of death to come nowhere near this corner of the estate."

Alexandra's hand flew to her cheek. "Richard, you have not!"

"I most certainly have," her husband said gruffly. "And they are blessing you for it, for I've become devilishly short-tempered of late. You can well imagine why." His eyes softened for a moment. "Unless you truly find you need more time . . ." His strong fingers stilled upon the dark hollow beneath her collarbone.

His heart leaped then, for he read the ardent answer in her eyes. But the crunch of brisk footsteps startled them.

"There you are, my lady." It was a female voice, low and foreign and frankly scolding. "What are you about to lie here in the cool winds with no blanket?" The dark-skinned woman who appeared amid the linden branches lifted a fine shawl of paisley cashmere and unfurled it about Alexandra's feet.

"I should have known you'd be above listening to any orders I might give," Hawke said to the intruder in irritation. "You may be certain that I will not allow the duchess to grow cold."

"Humph," the old Indian woman said, dismissing this assurance. "I trust my little one will not, now that I've brought a blanket for her. And as to this talk of duchesses, I say nonsense! She has always been my little one, my Sadis. Nothing will change that."

"What does it mean—Sadis?" Alexandra asked curiously, glad to distract the pair from their hostility. "You've called me that as long as I can remember."

The old Indian woman frowned for a moment, puzzling over the proper words in English. "She is the goddess of wisdom and music, she who rides a swan." She gave Alexandra a mysterious, enigmatic smile before she turned briskly to the drowsy infant. "And now, *minakshi,* come back to the house with Ayah, and I will tell you a story of Krishna." As she spoke, the Indian woman deftly scooped up the contented infant and tucked her into the crook of her arm.

"Thank you, Ayah," Alexandra said.

"I do not require thanks, mistress," the old woman answered over her shoulder, for she was already climbing the slope to return to the great house. "And it is good that I do not. For what thanks is there for me in this barbarian country, with its disagreeable climate, with no heat, no spice, and no punkahs? By the Lord Shiva, I will remain six months and not a single day more. I tell you that, *minakshi,* and not even your liquid eyes will persuade me to stay an instant longer." Her voice was fading as she passed over the brow of the hill. "No bazaars to trade gossip in! No food worth eating! Bah! A barbarian country."

Alexandra looked up at Hawke's irritated face and laughed guiltily. "Bless you for sending for her, my love, and please find it in your heart to forgive her. She is an old woman far from home."

"Old retainers must be the same everywhere," Hawke said dryly. "My nurse was just the same. And your ayah *is* the only one you'd trust with our child, is she not?"

"Absolutely."

"Then I must learn to bear her presence." An odd light crossed his face, and his slate-gray eyes became measuring. "Only you must give me some incentive so that I don't backslide."

"Incentive?"

"Yes," the duke growled, "solace. Relief from this gnawing ache I bear for you." His fingers gripped her shoulders. "It is too late to be coy, changeling. You've swum into my net, and this time I shall not let you go." He caught her and rolled them over as one until he lay beneath her. His eyes burned across the white lace chemisette still open above the loose bodice of her pale pink muslin gown. "Ah, love, more beautiful than ever you've become! I never dreamed it possible." There was a trace of awe in his voice as his fingers grazed the proud peach crests where his child had rested.

His touch was feather-light, but it sent a wild tremor through Alexandra, teaching her how much she had missed him in the months since their daughter's birth.

"Hawke?" she said faintly, her voice uneven with a passion of her own.

"I warn you, my heart's delight: When you say my name just *so,* I can deny you nothing."

"Nothing at all?" Alexandra asked, a tiny smile playing about her lips.

"Nothing—'tis a lost man you see before you."

Laughter tumbled from her lips then, and she moved to nip his lobe playfully and whisper something in his ear.

Hawke groaned. "With the greatest of pleasure," he said unevenly. And then he saw to it there was no more talking between them.

The sun was high and the bees were busy in the hyacinths as a small brown figure parted the grass a few minutes later. His tail twitched lazily as he halted before the sweeping linden tree. Satisfied with what he saw there, the little mongoose turned silently and jumped to a flat boulder warmed by the afternoon sun.

He fluffed out his fur and settled back upon the rock, contentedly surveying the green valley and the great stone house beyond.

It was a strange world he had come to. The trees were too tall and green, the ground too cool. He tucked his head for a moment and nursed the painful bruise on his leg where the last viper had lashed him. Still, it had been the evil creature's final act on earth.

Rajah thought of the five balls of fur hidden even now in the hollow trunk of a gnarled tree on the other side of the valley. Not even the mistress knew of them yet, for the young ones were too tiny to be brought out for her cossetting. She had her own small honey-haired creature to worry about, anyway. Later, he would present his young to her.

Yes, there was much for him to do in this valley, Rajah thought contentedly. All humans needed guarding, of course, and guarding them was no more than a mongoose's duty. Especially this pair, he decided, his long tail twitching, for they were the most unpredictable humans he had ever encountered.

Not that a mongoose could ever predict what a human would do next.

Still, it was fine to hear his mistress laugh again. The tall man was good for her, just as Rajah had foreseen. Her masterful mate would soothe the pain from her eyes, while Rajah kept them and their young one safe from the dark death that coiled among the grasses.

Yes, Rajah thought, it was a challenge that suited him very well, and one that his children would also accept in their time.

After a final glance at the shadowed figures below the canopied linden, the little mongoose turned and jumped down from his comfortable perch. Curiosity was upon him once more.

In truth, how could he rest?

There were vipers to be conquered, after all, and a new world just waiting to be explored.

FREE FROM DELL

with purchase plus postage and handling

Congratulations! You have just purchased one or more titles featured in Dell's Romance 1990 Promotion. Our goal is to provide you with quality reading and entertainment, so we are pleased to extend to you a limited offer to receive a selected Dell romance title(s) *free* (plus $1.00 postage and handling per title) for each romance title purchased. Please read and follow all instructions carefully to avoid delays in your order.

1) Fill in your name and address on the coupon printed below. No facsimiles or copies of the coupon allowed.

2) The Dell Romance books are the only books featured in Dell's Romance 1990 Promotion. Any other Dell titles are not eligible for this offer.

3) Enclose your original cash register receipt with the price of the book(s) circled plus $1.00 per book for postage and handling, payable in check or money order to: Dell Romance 1990 Offer. Please do not send cash in the mail.
Canadian customers: Enclose your original cash register receipt with the price of the book(s) circled plus $1.00 per book for postage and handling in U.S. funds.

4) This offer is only in effect until March 29, 1991. Free Dell Romance requests postmarked after March 22, 1991 will not be honored, but your check for postage and handling will be returned.

5) Please allow 6-8 weeks for processing. Void where taxed or prohibited.

Mail to: Dell Romance 1990 Offer
           P.O. Box 2088
           Young America, MN 55399-2088

NAME_____

ADDRESS_____

CITY_____STATE_____ZIP_____

BOOKS PURCHASED AT_____

AGE_____

(Continued)

Book(s) purchased:_____

_____

_____

I understand I may choose one free book for each Dell Romance book purchased (plus applicable postage and handling). Please send me the following:

(Write the number of copies of each title selected next to that title.)

☐ **MY ENEMY, MY LOVE**
Elaine Coffman
From an award-winning author comes this compelling historical novel that pits a spirited beauty against a hard-nosed gunslinger hired to forcibly bring her home to her father. But the gunslinger finds himself unable to resist his captive.

☐ **AVENGING ANGEL**
Lori Copeland
Jilted by her thieving fiancée, a woman rides west seeking revenge, only to wind up in the arms of her enemy's brother.

☐ **A WOMAN'S ESTATE**
Roberta Gellis
An American woman in the early 1800s finds herself ensnared in a web of family intrigue and dangerous passions when her English nobleman husband passes away.

☐ **THE RAVEN AND THE ROSE**
Virginia Henley
A fast-paced, sexy novel of the 15th century that tells a tale of royal intrigue, spirited love, and reckless abandon.

☐ **THE WINDFLOWER**
Laura London
She longed for a pirate's kisses. . . even though she was kidnapped in error and forced to sail the seas on his pirate ship, forever a prisoner of her own reckless desire.

☐ **TO LOVE AN EAGLE**
Joanne Redd
Winner of the 1987 *Romantic Times* Reviewer's Choice Award for Best Western Romance by a New Author.

☐ **SAVAGE HEAT**
Nan Ryan
The spoiled young daughter of a U.S. Army General is kidnapped by a Sioux chieftain out of revenge and is at first terrified, then infuriated, and finally hopelessly aroused by him.

☐ **BLIND CHANCE**
Meryl Sawyer
Every woman wants to be a star, but what happens when the one nude scene she'd performed in front of the cameras haunts her, turning her into an underground sex symbol?

☐ **DIAMOND FIRE**
Helen Mittermeyer
A gorgeous and stubborn young woman must choose between protecting the dangerous secrets of her past or trusting and loving a mysterious millionaire who has secrets of his own.

☐ **LOVERS AND LIARS**
Brenda Joyce
She loved him for love's sake, he seduced her for the sake of sweet revenge. This is a story set in Hollywood, where there are two types of people—lovers and liars.

☐ **MY WICKED ENCHANTRESS**
Meagan McKinney
Set in 18th-century Louisiana, this is the tempestous and sensuous story of an impoverished Scottish heiress and the handsome American plantation owner who saves her life, then uses her in a dangerous game of revenge.

☐ **EVERY TIME I LOVE YOU**
Heather Graham
A bestselling romance of a rebel Colonist and a beautiful Tory loyalist who reincarnate their fiery affair 200 years later through the lives of two lovers.

TOTAL NUMBER OF FREE BOOKS SELECTED _____ X $1.00
= $_____ (Amount Enclosed)

Dell has other great books in print by these authors. If you enjoy them, check your local book outlets for other titles.